Confluence

A Novel of Post Pandemic Survival

By Lisa Harnish

Confluence

Author's Note

I started writing this novel during the summer of 2019, immediately after finishing the *Consolidation* trilogy. I finished the first draft of this book on January 20th, 2020. At that time, information about a new disease emerging in China was just starting to appear in the general news media. During the editing cycle for this book, the novel Corona virus, Covid-19, errupted into a worldwide pandemic. While I endeavor to craft a plausible tale, this story is fiction. It is not based on current events happening at the time of publication of this book. Partly, I am following the timeline established in the previously published books. Partly, my goal is to show what comes after a worst-case pandemic scenario plays out.

The events of *Confluence* run parallel to the events in the *Consolidation* trilogy. It is not necessary to have read the other books, in order to enjoy this one.

Available on Amazon, Kindle Unlimited, and in paperpack through major online book retail websites.

Chapter 1

"Turn me out, so I can see!" Paige's tinny voice came from Rochelle's phone.

Rochelle turned the phone around, to face the door she was pulling open. As soon as she stepped into the boutique's main room, she spotted her mother, sitting on the fancy circular bench in the middle of the elegant room.

"There she is," Rochelle said to Paige in the phone. In a softer voice, she added, "Holding court, just like always." She heard Paige snicker.

Rochelle approached her mother and said, "Okay, we're here. Sorry we're late. Traffic. Parking. Where's the glowing bride-to-be?"

Catherine Tylin Daniels turned to greet her newly arrived daughter. "You know traffic is always terrible on holiday weekends. You should have left earlier," she said.

Rochelle's shoulders slumped. "I did," she drawled out, but then quickly tried to divert the subject. "What'd I miss? Where is she? Has she picked out the dress yet?" She looked around for her youngest sister, Nerissa, who was nowhere in sight.

The room was fairly spacious, with surprisingly few racks of dresses to flick through. A few mannequins were posed in the sunny windows facing the street, dressed in the latest bridal fashions. A short hallway led away to the back of the building where the changing rooms were located. A few store personnel hovered nearby. A well-dressed mature woman stood at a nearby table, pouring a few small glasses of champagne.

"She's in back with Hollan, trying on the first one. She'll be out in a minute. Is that Paige?" her mother asked, gesturing at the phone in Rochelle's hand. She was still panning slowly about the room so that Paige could take in the environment. She and Paige were Facetiming the experience, since Paige was actually on the opposite side of the country at the moment.

"Yep, got her right here. Say hello, Paige." Rochelle said, turning back to face her mother.

"Hello, Paige!" Paige said in a parrot voice.

Their mother frowned. "Paige, can't you take anything seriously?"

Rochelle held the phone out at arm's length to the side, so they could both see Paige's eye roll. Paige said, "Oh, for heaven's sake, if we can't have a little fun while helping our baby sister shop for her wedding dress, when can we?"

Catherine just raised her eyebrows and said, "Well, it would be even more fun if you could actually be in here in person. It is a long holiday weekend. Surely you could have gotten the time off to come home? And isn't all that bandwidth costing you a fortune?" She waved at the phone.

Paige answered, "Mom. Don't worry about it. We got it covered. And it's not a question of time off, it's a question of flight availability. I found out about this too late to get any. If you really wanted me to be there, you should have let me know weeks ago, not days ago."

Rochelle mentally scoffed at that. *Not likely.* Paige avoided coming back East as much as possible. She'd left home for college on the West coast and had settled in Oakland, with as few visits back home as she could get away with. But that didn't stop her from maintaining a close relationship with her sisters via cell phone.

Due to the time difference between their locations, Paige was still in pajamas, sitting at her kitchen table, drinking coffee. While talking and looking at the phone, she was also scanning stuff on her nearby laptop computer as well.

Catherine squinted at Paige. "Aren't you even dressed yet? You may not be here in person, but people can still see you, the way Rochelle is waving that phone all over."

Paige's eyes rolled again. She glanced down at her chest. She had a robe on over an old over sized sleeping t-shirt. "It's only 8 a.m. here. I'm fine. No nips showing. I don't really care what others see." She shrugged to demonstrate her nonchalance.

This time Catherine's eyes rolled. Before she could get a full head of steam going on the importance of being properly dressed when out in public, Nerissa stepped out into the main salon area, dressed in a flowing white gown. Rochelle's eldest sister, Hollan followed, examining the short train of the dress and bending over to twitch at it, arranging it to swirl around Nerissa.

Rochelle stared in astonishment. Most of the time when she thought of her youngest sister, she visualized a skinny short tomboy in ripped jeans, playing softball in the street with the neighborhood boys at dusk on summer nights. This version did not correlate. The dress was sleeveless, with a tight bodice and nipped-in waist. The skirt hugged her legs and then flared out in a mermaid ruffle below her knees. She looked like a grownup.

"Wow, sis! That looks amazing!" Rochelle exclaimed.

Nerissa wrinkled her nose at them, but was mostly focused on the mirror behind her, trying to see her complete profile. "Yeah, I'm not too sure about this one. Chris said he wanted a mermaid, but I don't think this is going to work. I can barely walk in this thing. Is that Paige?" She turned to squint at the phone Rochelle was still holding. "Hi Paige! Glad you could make it!"

Their mother spoke up again. "I agree. This one is not going to work. That ivory color is the wrong shade for you. You're a winter. You can wear bright clear tones. I think a snow white will work better on you." She gestured at one of the shop attendants, who turned back down the hall, to prep the next dress for try-on. Meanwhile, the store manager served them the small glasses of champagne. Rochelle took one to be polite, but silently reminded herself she needed to drive back to D.C. in a few hours.

Hollan took a seat next Catherine, to wait while Nerissa changed dresses. The four of them chattered for a bit. As usual, the conversation devolved into a competition for Catherine's approval. Hollan almost always won these.

Hollan told them about her brilliant toddler's latest accomplishments. Paige countered with a summary of a hot new project she was involved with at the tech company where she worked. Rochelle could only respond with a quick listing of her next round of classes. She was just starting the last year of her three-year

MBA program. It was a prestigious program, at a prestigious school, but all Catherine could say was, "And are you still working at that place? That *bar*?" She exaggerated the last word like it might give her cooties.

Rochelle took a breath and answered calmly, "Mom, Paulbicki's is one of the longest-running, most respected establishments in the city. It's an historic landmark. All kinds of important people go there to do their drinking and deal-making. It's not like I'm working at Jugaloo's anymore."

Her mother just rolled her eyes at that. The short skirts and tight tops required at her previous employer had absolutely mortified Catherine. She had agitated and pestered Rochelle relentlessly, until Rochelle had acquired enough experience to upgrade to a better class of bar-tending and waitressing. The fact that Rochelle had to work for pocket money at all, was an even more sore subject that they all politely ignored, for the sake of keeping the peace.

Rochelle's father, Catherine's first husband, Mitchell Tylin, was paying for most of Rochelle's education. To be fair, he had or would be paying for the majority of all the girls' educations. But thanks to the divorce, there wasn't a lot of spare cash to go around to cover living expenses. Catherine and Mitchell still spent most of their infrequent communication with each other arguing over money.

Rochelle wondered who was footing the bill for the wedding. It was clear that this boutique was definitely in the high rent zone. And her mother certainly had champagne tastes. But she knew better than to directly dig for info on whose beer budgets were funding this. Catherine had quickly remarried, but her new husband had made it clear from the outset that he would not be financially supporting mostly grown children.

Nerissa tried on several more dresses. During the process, Rochelle discovered the shop had several more rooms filled with more styles and choices. They kept the main front room sparse and focused on providing personal assistance to locate the perfect dress. After about half a dozen different tries, Nerissa finally settled on a simple halter style dress. It was an elegant concoction of beaded lace and embroidery, covering her chest modestly, but leaving her back exposed. It also had a mermaid style skirt, but was more loosely constructed and easier to move in. Their mother nattered at her about making sure she didn't develop any odd tan lines on her back that would show. Thankfully, Hollan managed to distract her with questions about how long a train to get and what heel height the shoes should be.

About halfway through the dress selection process, Paige disconnected from the Facetime call, saying she had things to do, but she could rejoin them at any time if needed. Rochelle was annoyed with her, for leaving them one daughter short of the quorum needed to deal with their mother. So she blasted out a steady stream of pictures and texts, just to make Paige's phone blow up.

Once the dress shopping was finished, they walked down the street to a nearby restaurant. The casual chic eatery was the public facing operation for a catering business. Catherine wanted to hire them for the wedding, since they had just been top ranked by one of the regional lifestyle magazine she subscribed to. Catherine insisted they all try the tasting menu, which presented hors d'oeuvre sized bites of their most popular dishes available for weddings. Rochelle would have rather had something else, but once Catherine made a declaration, fighting it was an exercise in frustration resulting in hurt feelings. And she was really making an effort to not be the problem child today. Today was Nerissa's day, not hers, so she deliberately kept her mouth shut.

Over lunch, the girls discussed more wedding ideas. Rochelle, never having been married, didn't have much to say on the topic. Hollan had been married six years ago, straight out of college. Paige didn't appear to have any intention of ever getting married. If she even had any boyfriends, she never told any of her sisters about it. Rochelle had wondered if maybe she had girlfriends, but hadn't found a good way to ask yet.

Rochelle sat back and listened to her mother and sisters talk, mentally checking out. However, her attention snapped back when the subconscious part of her brain noticed the slightly whiny, rising tone in her mother's voice.

"But don't you *want* your wedding to be perfect? It needs a unified theme. If you have a theme, then all the service providers will know exactly how to respond and won't waste our time on irrelevant ideas."

"Mom, the theme is that we're in love and getting married. It doesn't need to be any more thematic than that." Nerissa was rolling her vowels, dragging out the words. They could all put on the Southern Virginia Belle accent whenever they needed to express their annoyance subtly.

"Did you look at those web pages I sent you? I thought those enchanted fairytale ones were just darling."

Rochelle looked around the table. Hollan was looking a little exhausted. There were dark circles under her eyes, underneath the makeup. Her mother was looking a little flushed, too, like she was building up a head of steam. Nerissa was just getting pinched around the mouth, which meant she was digging her heels in. Hollan nudged Rochelle's ankle under the table. The cue to intervene.

"Mom, did you try the beef wellingtons? They're pretty scrumptious. So is the salmon. Nerissa, do you plan to offer a veggie option at the dinner?" Rochelle asked.

Catherine fell for the bait. "You don't need a vegetarian option. If anyone doesn't want to eat meat, there will be plenty of salad and side dishes. They can just leave what they don't want. Too many entree options just disrupts the catering operation."

Rochelle could sense Hollan's mental sigh of relief. She let the conversation continue to meander around her again. She had mentally phased out again, when Nerissa inflicted her own deflection.

"Mom, this is *my* wedding. If you want what you want, maybe you can get that when you plan Rochelle's."

Catherine responded, "Well, heaven knows when *that's* going to be. I'll probably be old and dead before that happens."

Rochelle frowned. "Hey!" she spluttered.

Catherine frowned back. "Rochelle, I'm sorry, but it's true. The older you get, the less likely it is you'll ever get married. And that frustrates me to no end. I just worry about you. I worry about who's going to take care of you when I'm gone. Life is so much easier when you have a partner with you. You need to get serious about finding a man. Is there any chance of you and Aaron getting back together?"

Aaron was the college sweetheart that she had broken up with two years ago. He'd decided to stay in Chicago, when she had made the decision to come back to D.C. for grad school.

Rochelle sighed and looked her mother straight in the eye. Inside, her stomach clenched. She hated disagreeing with her mother. In a calm voice, she replied, "No, Mom. That's ancient history. I've tried to explain this to you before, but Aaron was not the perfect man for me after all. He's a great guy, but he's not my version of 'Mr. Right.' I'm over him. You need to get over him, too." Rochelle was a little astonished at herself. She couldn't recall the last time she'd ever contradicted her mother.

Catherine looked over the rim of her reading glasses at Rochelle. "Hmmph. Well, you are in that bar all the time. Don't you meet any eligible men there?" Catherine paused and coughed delicately into her napkin. Her train of thought continued, "You keep saying it's such a nice, sophisticated place."

Technically, that was true. There were lots of people coming and going there. And plenty of guys hit on her. Sometimes she even accepted their offers and enjoyed a short fling with them. But somehow, the more she got to know them, they more they ended up disappointing her.

"Mom, being single is not the end of the world. I'm fine. I have plenty of time yet. You don't need to worry about me."

They stared at each other for a few moments. Rochelle nudged Hollan back, under the table, ready to turn over the talking stick to someone else. Hollan spoke up. "So, Nerissa, have you and Chris picked a honeymoon spot yet?"

And once again, the conversation flowed into another channel.

When they finished eating, they met with the manager in her office to review catering menus and prices. After that, Rochelle thought they were going to go back to Catherine's house, to look at more things online, like photographers and musicians. But Catherine suddenly announced she was not really feeling very well. She looked pale and held her hand to her temple.

Hollan said, "Okay, then. Why don't you go home and get some rest. We can do the rest of the planning online in a conference call. Maybe next weekend. We don't have to do it all today."

Catherine nodded at that and took advantage of the offer. She walked to her car, which was parallel parked a few spaces up the street.

The sisters looked around at each other, startled at the early end to the outing.

Nerissa spoke up. "Maybe I should follow her home, make sure she gets there okay?" Nerissa still technically lived at home with Catherine and their step-dad, but she spent about half of her time at her fiance's apartment. She had driven her own car to downtown Manassas that morning, meeting everyone at the dress shop.

Rochelle and Hollan nodded their agreement. Hollan shuffled her purse and bag of take-home leftovers and then made an excuse about wanting to get back to relieve the babysitter. She hugged Rochelle and headed off to her own car. That left Rochelle free to head back into D.C. earlier than planned.

***

Rochelle was happy to have the chance to drive home, change her clothes and then ride her bike into work. Car parking near the bar was hideously expensive. It was just far enough away from her apartment to be too far to walk safely, but not close enough to be worth taking the bus. George encouraged his employees to use their bikes and provided a small storage room in the back to lock them in while on shift.

Rochelle arrived half an hour before her 6-to-2 shift started. Sometimes she waitressed, but tonight she was bar-tending. George waved two fingers at her when he saw her wander into the break room, adjacent to his office.

George Paulbicki was the owner and proprietor of the self-named Paulbicki's, a traditional, old-school Georgetown eating and drinking place. Located near the waterfront, at the confluence of two major streets in the historic neighborhood, it attracted a broad range of patrons. Middle and upper management types commuting from their jobs at the alphabet agencies in the business district wandered through regularly. Professors and doctors from the nearby university and hospital also came in for a quality meal away from their workplace. They even got occasional politicians and military brass stopping in for serious huddled conversations.

Two stories tall, the old Georgian brick building had a beautiful view of the Potomac River. Or it would have, if not for the elevated steel highway that had been built right in front of their second story. That project had ended up blocking most of the natural light coming in through the front windows, so George had had skylights installed. On sunny days, the light filtered down the central open stair case. The second floor was the main dining area and the ground floor was mostly drinking area. The place was decorated in old dark wood paneling, beer logo mirrors and plenty of brass fixtures. A long, "L" shaped bar with tall stools lined one side of the room. Free standing tables were arranged on the opposite side. A vestibule welcomed people coming in the front. Behind the short arm of the bar, a window and a door was cut through the wall separating the kitchen from the bar area. Behind the kitchen, there were storage areas, including pantry and walk-in fridge and freezer. Across the center hallway was the usual assortment of rest rooms. Stairs also led to a small storage basement. An electric dumbwaiter had been installed to move inventory to the storage basement or upstairs. George's office was on the second floor, along with the break room, where Rochelle prepared for the evening shift.

"Hey George. How's it going?" Rochelle greeted her boss.

"Hey Rochelle," he returned. "Okay, so far."

Rochelle paused, leaning into the office. George was shuffling through some papers. "Should we expect anything unusual tonight?" she asked. It was a common discussion between them. Most weekend evenings were ordinary busy. If there was a festival or major event like a march or a protest going on, they might get crazy busy.

"Hard to say. It's a holiday weekend, so a lot of people are out of town. But then, some out-of-towners might be visiting for the long weekend. So, probably not the usual crowd. Could get a little weird." George shrugged.

Rochelle nodded and ducked into the tiny locker room to change. Paulbicki's was a classy joint. The standard uniform for men and women alike was black pants and a white shirt. Rochelle usually selected a button-down version, closely fitted and open just enough to show a hint of her modest cleavage. On really hot nights, she had some tank top versions she was allowed to substitute in. George was flexible about letting the girls vary the uniforms enough to show off their assets, so long as they didn't cross the line into slutty. Nicely fitted, attractive clothes helped them earn better tips, which George was all in favor of.

Downstairs, Rochelle clocked in and set to work. Since Paulbicki's was both a restaurant and bar targeted at working professionals and local residents, there was a distinct rhythm to the business. Early evening, drinks were for people waiting for a table or already seated. Middle evening, the dining crowd mostly filtered out and only the drinkers were left. That lasted through the late evening. Music and TV were kept at low to moderate volumes, so that people could hear their own conversations. Customers either talked in small groups at the tables, or sat at the tall bar, alone or maybe in pairs. If it was a good night with a good vibe, the drinkers were a happy crowd, laughing and joking around. If it was a bad night, someone would get too drunk and would sour the vibe. That didn't happen very often. If someone was getting out of control, they started watering down his drinks and slowed down the service. Or worst case, they just told the guy to leave.

During the dinner service, the pace was busy enough to keep everyone hopping. There was little time for gossip or chatter. But after 10 or 11 p.m., the remaining staff could relax a little and goof around with each other. Rochelle had made several good friends among the other waitresses and bar staff and enjoyed her time with them.

This Saturday evening of Labor Day weekend was only a little bit weird, as George had prediction. As he had suspected, there were quite a few unfamiliar faces in the crowd. But there were a few regulars, too. Neighbors and patrons bringing visitors to their favorite watering hole. After the kitchen closed, the customers were drinking harder than usual but were not getting unruly or boisterous.

One of the many things that Rochelle liked about working at Paulbicki's was eavesdropping on other people's conversations. While tending bar, it was a perfectly acceptable thing to do. Just standing at a counter, cutting up more limes or unloading a tray of clean glasses, she could listen in on fascinating tidbits of conversations.

A young couple were sitting about midway down the long arm of the bar, twirling martini glasses around on the counter in the small puddles formed by the condensation.

The woman asked, "Do you believe in soul mates?"

The man asked, "Like, we're destined to be with one and only one person?"

"Yeah, like that."

"Nah. There's too many people in the world to think that there's one and only one person who's just right. What if that one person is too old or too young? What if that person is totally different than you, a complete opposite? Destiny is too erratic. The world is too big - what if you never meet that one person you're destined to be with?"

"Hmm. Maybe. I think if someone is the right person, they balance you out. They help you become a better person. They become your soul mate over time."

Rochelle had no idea if soul mates were a real thing or not. In spite of her protests, her mother had made it clear she thought Rochelle's ex, Aaron, should not be an ex. Rochelle suspected her mother would scoff at the idea of waiting for a soul mate to appear. Before should could follow that line of thinking any further, an order for a large round of drinks for a group upstairs claimed all of her attention.

A little later on, she noticed a man in a military uniform, sitting next to another man in a three piece suit, at the far end near the window. They were leaning into each other, talking softly. Rochelle didn't know which service the military guy was in, or what his rank was, but from his age, he was probably pretty high up, she thought. The other man looked equally mature. He had that silver fox thing going on.

The suit said, "It's not looking good. Early reports suggest this thing may have mutated from several different strains."

The military man said, "Is there any information on transmissibility yet? How far and how fast?"

The suit replied, "Don't know yet. My guy's team is still running tests on it. They're having issues culturing it. Says they need to replicate it consistently, over successive generations, to be sure they develop the right kind of vaccine."

Rochelle moved a little closer to them and silently waived a bourbon bottle, asking if they wanted another. They shook their heads, smiled politely and waited for her to move out of range, before continuing their conversation.

At midnight, George would let the remaining staff still on shift have one drink per hour, to finish out the night. He wouldn't tolerate outright drunkenness while on the job, but a little bit of lubrication at the end of a long shift was permitted, so long as the employee was able to keep control. Rochelle liked margaritas, so she mixed a weak one for herself. After these long shifts, a drink or two helped her get to sleep later on at night. Without it, her brain tended to keep functioning in work mode, hyper-alert and surveying her surroundings, looking for the next customer to attend to.

At 2 a.m., George locked up the bar and dismissed the staff with his thanks and their redistributed tips for the evening. Rochelle rode her bike home.

Rochelle shared a ridiculously expensive, two bedroom apartment in the Glover Park area with one of her best friends from school. Apurva had gone straight on to medical school after her undergraduate work. She was currently doing her residency at the nearby hospital. Apurva's parents wanted her focused exclusively on her education, so they covered the lion's share of the rent. Daughter of immigrant Indian parents, Apurva was smart and driven to succeed. She wasn't always very good at dealing with people, though. Rochelle figured the social skills would improve with time, once she had a moment to recover from the intense regimen of medical training.

Apurva was actually home and awake, when Rochelle arrived. That was kind of unusual. Apurva's hectic residency schedule didn't leave her much free time and when she did have it, she was usually sleeping. At the moment though, she was seated on the small sofa in the main room, her legs curled under her.

"Hey, what are you doing…" Rochelle started, but shut up when she realized that Apurva was on her phone. Rochelle could hear tinny noise, but couldn't make out the words. Apurva waved at her and whispered "Nanna," while pointing at her phone. Rochelle nodded and went to her room. She stripped off her work clothes and took a quick shower. Paulbicki's might be a classy joint, but it could still get hot and sweaty on steamy summer nights and it had been a long shift. A nice shower usually helped her unwind in preparation for sleep, too.

Once cleaned up, she rejoined Apurva on the couch, who was finishing up her phone call. She cheerfully repeated her goodbyes in her grandmother's native tongue several times. She pushed the 'off' button and dropped the phone in her lap.

"Aieeee, but Nanna can just go on and on and on…"

Rochelle grinned. "What are you still doing up? Kinda late for you."

Apurva shrugged and tilted her head back against the top of the sofa. "Haven't talked to her in a while. Thought it would be a good idea to just check in. It's the middle of the day over there. How was the bar?"

Rochelle shrugged. "Eh, busy. Mostly. Holiday weekend normal, I guess. How was the hospital?"

This was their normal routine, after not seeing each other for a few days, due to crazy schedules. Apurva's eyes were closed. She frowned and answered, "Not normal, actually. There's something weird going on. My boss said there's some kind of viral outbreak happening in Asia and they're worried about it spreading."

"Huh. That is weird. What kind of virus?" Rochelle asked.

"Influenza, I think."

"Huh." Rochelle said again. "Are they going to make a vaccine for it?"

"Of course. It'll take about 6 months or so for that to be distributed. One of the few things where we can say the egg does not come first. The virus does."

Rochelle squinted at her. It was too late and she was too tired to follow her friend's loopy silly logic. But she asked anyways, "Whaddya mean?" and instantly regretted the onslaught of too much information.

"Influenza vaccines are mostly grown in chicken eggs. But first they have to identify and neutralize the virus." She sat up and opened her eyes. She had that gleam she got whenever she had a chance to get technical about any medical topic. Her hands came up in excited gestures, for emphasis.

"This is really fascinating! First, they have to figure out that the virus is new, different from other strains. And there's always other strains floating around and they go through antigenic shifts and drifts, always changing. Then once they've identified a new one as unique, they mix it with some known laboratory strains, to create a hybrid. That gets tested and if it's all working, they can prepare the reagents. Those get sent out to all the pharmas who will be making the vaccine. The pharmas test the growth of the new hybrid and then set up bulk manufacturing. They have to inject the hybrid version into eggs, let it grow for a bit and then extract it back out. They kill the virus and purify it to create an antigen. That gets diluted, packaged and shipped out as the vaccine. There's a bunch of testing and checking along the way, too. That's why it takes six months or more to get them made and distributed."

Rochelle had thought about asking her what a reagent was. Or an antigen. But held her tongue. Apurva would just answer the question with another long gibberish monologue that she couldn't follow. Rochelle was an educated, intelligent person, but it was late and the mellow margaritas had softened her brain. She was having a hard time tracking Apurva's explanations.

"Fascinating. Will you be involved in the testing? I thought you were just doing a general medicine residency at the moment."

"I am. I'm not involved in any vaccine development. I just think it's really interesting how the process works."

Of course she did. That was how Apurva's brain worked.

Rochelle shifted gears. "When do you have to be back at work? If you've got any free time tomorrow, maybe we could go out, get brunch or something?"

"Oh, sorry. I've got to be back at hospital by 10 a.m." She winced apologetically.

"Okay. Off to bed with you then. I'm done too. I had a couple of margaritas. I think I can get to sleep now." She yawned to prove it.

Chapter 2

Rochelle awoke to her phone's buzzing on the side table next to her bed. She reached out and knocked it to the floor, which required her to heave up and fumble for it. She was shocked to see it was only about 8:30 a.m. Much too early to be up. She had another shift at the bar that day, but didn't need to be there until about 1 p.m. Plenty of time for more sleep.

Her phone was buzzing because of incoming text messages. The Gang of Four message thread was lit up.

Nerissa: *Hey, Mom is legitimately sick. We think she's got the flu. Just letting you know.*

Hollan: *Make sure she gets plenty of water, juice or soup.*

Paige: *Do you people really have to bombard my phone at 5 in the freakin' am?*

Nerissa: *You could just turn your phone off until you're up, you know.*

Paige: *Can't. Mom has a hissy fit, if she can't reach any of us, at any moment.*

Rochelle pushed the button to turn the phone's screen off and flung it back down on the table. She rolled over and rearranged herself, trying to settle back into sleep. But her bladder decided it was time to get up.

After peeing, she stumbled around her room, wondering if she could still get back to sleep for a little bit longer. The windows were open in the living room and bright morning sun was streaming in, setting off her circadian rhythms. Ten minutes after laying back down, her body knew it was time to be up, even if her brain wanted just a little more sleep. With a huff, she flung off the covers.

She had just returned from starting a load of laundry, when she found Apurva standing over the kitchen sink, shoveling some cereal into her face.

"Hey, I gotta get back to hospital," she said. "My boss texted me, said to come in early."

"Yeah, I got a bunch of early morning texts, too. Just my sisters, though," Rochelle responded. "What's going on?"

"Not sure. But he said they got a bunch of new cases coming into the ER last night and we need do some follow-up work." She stood up and quickly rinsed out her bowl, grabbed her bag and hustled out the door. Rochelle visualized the little cartoon whirlwind left behind when the Roadrunner took off.

Rochelle took the scenic route to her own job. During the day, she liked to bicycle down the trail through the park. The green trees and lush foliage made it easy to forget, for a few minutes, that she was in the middle of a major urban metropolis. She avoided it at night, though, for safety's sake.

Rochelle was scheduled to work almost every day for the next week, by request. Classes would be starting the following week, so she wanted to get in as many shifts as possible before then, when she'd have to scale back her hours. Sundays at the bar were pretty tame. Paulbicki's was not specifically a sports bar, but they did have several TVs mounted in the corners and would tune them to whatever the customers wanted. Today, one was tuned to a baseball game. Rochelle was not much of a sports fan, so she didn't pay much attention to the game. But during a quiet moment, she overheard the sportscasters talking about the crowd.

They told us this is a sold out game, but that doesn't look like a sell-out crowd to me. Dick, what do you think?

Joe, you're right, that's not full occupancy at all. Can we get a closeup of some of those sections?

Rochelle glanced up at the monitor. A camera zoomed in on request, panning over the crowd. About a quarter of the seats appeared to be empty. A few people were wearing surgical masks over their faces.

Rochelle was called away by one of the waiters to pour a new round of drinks, before she could hear what the sportscasters said about that.

A moderate dinner rush occupied all of Rochelle's attention for most of the the evening. The next time she had a moment to pay attention to the TV, it had been switched to a news channel showing stock footage of a dense urban metropolis, with the sun rising over it. She thought it looked like Hong Kong, but she couldn't be sure. The camera cut to scenes of streams of Asian people strolling through subway tunnels on their way to work. About a quarter of them were wearing masks. She knew it was pretty typical for Asians to do that, ever since the SARS outbreak years ago. She thought maybe some of the behavior was also protection from dust and pollution.

A crawl strip at the bottom of the broadcast read, *Asian flu virus circulating widely. WHO racing to identify, develop a vaccine.*

Rochelle frowned. There was that word again, "flu." Her sister and Apurva had both mentioned it in the last 24 hours. She pulled her phone out of her pocket and checked her messages. A little more chatter from her sisters off and on throughout the day, but nothing major. She typed into the Gang of Four thread:

Hey, how's Mom doin? Still sure it's flu?

Within a few minutes, Nerissa replied, *Yeah, its def flu. Came on sudden, fever, chills. I'm feeding her ibuprofen and chicken soup. She's being her usual self.* That was followed by a frowny emoji.

Rochelle thought about telling her to give her a Mom a hug for her, but Nerissa probably wouldn't appreciate the direction to get within germ range. So she just replied, *Tell her I said to get well soon.*

***

It was several days before Rochelle saw her roommate again. That was not unusual. They often went days at a time without seeing each other, due to their mismatched schedules. During that time, she saw several people walking the Georgetown streets wearing surgical masks. One of them walked right past the front windows of the bar.

She got home from an early shift to find Apurva slurping down some microwaved dinner from a frozen food container. "Hey, what's up!" Rochelle greeted her. She sat down at the tiny kitchenette table with her.

"Ugh. I'm so exhausted. We've been absolutely swamped. Swamped, I tell you!" It was an old joke between them, to repeat themselves.

Rochelle pounced. "Are you getting flu cases? I've seen some newscasts at the bar, about the flu outbreak in Asia. Is that the same thing that's happening here? Did I tell you my Mom has been sick?"

Apurva looked alarmed. "When did your Mom get it? Why didn't you tell me? Is she at home? Who's taking care of her?"

Rochelle answered, "Nerissa is taking care of her. She says it's just a typical case, as far as she can tell. She's got her on bed rest." As she spoke, she pulled out her phone and tapped open the conversation thread. She scrolled back in time a little ways to show the recent updates. She expanded a picture of her mother sound asleep, looking pale, haggard, hair messed. The sisters had joked about using that image for future blackmail. Their mother never appeared in public in anything less than perfect grooming.

Apurva frowned. "Oh, she does not look good. She should get her to the hospital. I'm calling her." Apurva tapped to Nerissa's number and pushed the call button.

Rochelle grabbed the phone out of Apurva's hand. "Hey, don't do that! You might wake Mom. Let me text Nessy first." She knew that Nerissa had custom rings and vibrations for different incoming contact. She tapped out a quick message. Nerissa dialed her back immediately. Rochelle opened the call on speaker and held the phone up in the air between them.

Nerissa greeted them, "Hey, what's up?" Her tone was clipped and short.

Apurva blurted out first, before Rochelle could, "How's your Mom doing? Is she getting enough fluids? Has she had any hallucinations or seizures?"

Nerissa was a little taken aback. "Uh, I don't think so. I've been running things to her, but I haven't been there the whole time. Isn't rest supposed to be the most important thing? She's been sleeping for days."

Apurva asked, "Are you sure it's flu? Fever, chills, sudden onset, total body aches?"

Nerissa said, "Yep, yep and yep. Why?"

Apurva continued to rapid fire diagnostic questions at her. "Did she get a flu shot in the last year? She might have last year's version of the flu, if she didn't get a shot."

Nerissa answered, "I don't know."

"Is she showing any signs of dehydration? Thirst? Dizziness? Rapid heartbeat? Not enough pee, or very dark pee?"

"I don't know," Nerissa said again. She was starting to draw out her words, a sign of frustration.

Apurva sighed. "Okay, you should really take her to your local hospital. How long ago did you say she got sick?" The last question was aimed at Rochelle.

Rochelle answered, "On Saturday."

Apurva said, "Yeah, you definitely need to take her to hospital. They can run tests, see which version she has. There's still some of the old virus floating around, but there's been some cases of the new one in the States already, too."

Nerissa didn't answer right away. Rochelle pictured her staring around in bewilderment, trying to figure out how to accomplish that. She was probably going to call Hollan and make her do it for her. Nerissa was the baby of the family. When it came to crises, they all turned to Hollan to fix things.

Rochelle spoke to the phone, "Nerissa, it's going to be okay. Get her to a doctor. It's okay to call Hollan. If you need me to come down there too, just call me back. I can bail on work, if I have to. They'll understand."

"Uh huh," Nerissa mumbled. It sounded like she was climbing up the stairs of the house in Manassas, to their mom's room. "Okay, I gotta go. I'll get back to you."

With a ding, the call terminated. Rochelle looked at Apurva. "What's really going on? Why all the stress?" Apurva's voice had been rough and she had bags under her eyes. It looked like she hadn't showered in a couple of days, either.

Apurva shook her head. "I dunno. Everyone is freaked. My professor, my boss and all the other doctors have been in and out of hush-hush meetings, running around. There's this really weird vibe going around. They sent all the interns home to get some food and sleep. I'm supposed to go back in at midnight."

"What's the rumor mill cranking on?" Rochelle asked her.

Apurva stared back, wide eyed. After a moment, she said, "The rumor mill says it's bad. Real bad. That its already spread really wide. And its really intense."

Rochelle continued to stare back at her friend. "So, the people wearing the masks around town are not crazy?"

Apurva shook her head slowly. She turned around and reached for a plastic bag sitting on the kitchen counter behind her. She pulled out several masks and handed them to Rochelle. "I brought a few of these home for you. They're rated for eight hours of use in an actual surgery environment. But you can get away with a lot more than that, just walking around on the street."

Rochelle examined the masks. "You really think this will help?"

Apurva shrugged. "Might. If you're in densely crowded areas for long periods of time. Like a bar."

"You don't expect me to wear this at work, do you? George is pretty easy going, but this will not meet his dress code standards."

"In a few more days, you'll look like the odd woman out, if you don't have one on. Pretty soon, there's going to be a big scramble just to get these. If you've got time, you might even stop in at the drug store and stock up on some extras. There's going to be rush on them."

Rochelle and Apurva stared at each other for awhile. "Crap. Bad. Real bad." Rochelle repeated Apurva's earlier words. Apurva nodded back solemnly.

***

Apurva's words proved to be prophetic by the very next day. Two bar patrons came in wearing similar surgical masks. They moved them carefully out of the way to sip at beverages through straws, but otherwise conducted their discussion while fully masked. They were seated at a corner table, so Rochelle couldn't overhear them. A few masked people wandered past the front windows, as well.

The TV mounted in the corner behind the bar was tuned to a news station again. The pleasant conversation around her died out, as everyone's attention turned to it. One of the customers gestured for her to turn up the volume. A news anchor gave a brief summary of the current situation. Then the screen split, moving the anchor to one block and a second head appeared in another block. The anchor was interviewing the second person.

The CDC confirmed today that the recent Asian influenza outbreak contains elements of both avian and swine flu. This is an unusual and unprecedented mutation in the virus family. We go now to Doctor Maddox, of the CDC. Dr. Maddox, what does the CDC know so far about this virus?

Well, because it contains genetic markers of two different strains of flu, it seems to be much hardier than previously studied viruses.

Has it been conclusively confirmed that it originated in China?

We're not completely sure about that. It's hard to say, because China is not very forthcoming with statistical information. It appears to be circulating widely throughout China, but there are suggestions that it may have originated elsewhere in Asia.

Can you tell us where that might be?

I really can't say at this point. We do not have sufficient information yet to pinpoint the origin.

I see. We've had reports of cases here in the United States and in Europe. Is there any hope of limiting the spread of this virus?

At this point, it's going to be very difficult. There's been enough cases emerging nearly simultaneously all over the world, in Europe, Australia, the Middle East and the United States, to suggest that containment by quarantine may not be very effective at this point. Many of the known cases have not traveled abroad, recently, either. That suggests they have contracted the disease from other vectors.

Doctor, you may have heard this elsewhere. There are rumors going about that this version was engineered and released from a lab, either accidentally or on purpose. Do you think there's any credence to that idea?

No, I don't. Look, it really doesn't matter where this originated.

Confluence

The pattern of outbreak is that cases are being reported all over the world, in direct proportion to the the local or regional population. It's breaking out in a fairly even distribution pattern, not radiating outward from a central origin point. That means it has already been spread globally, incubating until it sickens the carrier.

So you don't think border closures and quarantine is going to help, then?

No, not on a city or national scale, its not. That would just be closing the barn door, after the horse got out.

So Doctor, what is the prognosis for this virus, then?

Well, we expect this to be a very severe form of influenza. Anyone who thinks they have it, should stay at home, rest, drink plenty of fluids and take anti-inflammatories, such as aspirin or ibuprofen. They should also contact their family physician by phone, first, to see if they should be tested or not. Young children and elderly may need hospitalization for re-hydration or pain relief, as well.

What can we do to prevent it?

Well, the usual recommendations still apply. Wash your hands frequently and thoroughly in hot soapy water. Get plenty of rest, eat a healthy diet. If you need to cough or sneeze, direct that into your arm, not out into the open. If you expect to be in large crowds for long periods of time, you might want to consider wearing a mask, to prevent transmission of the virus.

I thought the CDC said masks were not necessary?

Well, there's some conflicting information about that... Naturally, we don't want anyone to panic and cause a rush on limited supplies. But if you happen to have a dust mask or painters mask lying around the house, it might be good to keep that handy. It can't hurt.

I see. Dr. Maddox, what about a vaccine for this strain?

The pharmaceutical companies are working on a vaccine just a quickly as possible. It normally takes six month or more, to develop and distribute a new vaccine.

Thank you, doctor. We're out of time, but we do appreciate your contributions.

The broadcast switched back to full screen display of the anchor, who moved onto another story. The people around the bar looked silently at one another. Several glanced at the masked pair in the corner, who did nothing. Rochelle wondered if it would be just too weird to pull out her own mask right now. She had one in her purse, upstairs in the employee break room. No one else reached for a mask, so she decided it would be silly for her to do so.

Chatter slowly resumed. Rochelle eavesdropped on a few conversations.

A pair of old men at the end of the bar sipped their whiskey sours.

"I heard it was the North Koreans."

"That's crazy. Thye don't have the native technology to bio-engineer a tomato, let alone a virus. Nah, it had to be the Iranians."

"No, now that's crazy talk. This other other guy I know, he said it was the Illuminati."

The two men looked at each other, grinned and roared out laughing at themselves.

At the other end of the bar two younger guys, middle management types, were drinking beer.

"You think maybe we should get out of town for a couple of weeks? Wait for this thing to run its course?"

"How the hell are we supposed to finish that proposal, if we take off? You know it's due in two weeks and it's going to take three weeks of work to finish it."

The first guy grumbled for a bit.

Rochelle carried glasses of ice tea to a table of middle-aged ladies on their lunch break. One of them gently grasped her arm and asked, "Dear, can you tell me where the nearest pharmacy is?"

Rochelle answered, "Just up the street, about a block, on the opposite site. Can't miss it." She smiled reassuringly at the woman, who nodded her thanks.

Chapter 3

Two days later, Rochelle was again rolled out of sleep by her phone buzzing. This time it was a direct call, not just texts. She thumbed open the call from Hollan.

"'Lo?" she mumbled.

Hollan's voice was frantic. "Chelle? Are you there? Mom's gone. The hospital just called."

Rochelle frowned. "Whaddya mean, gone? Where'd she go? I thought she was sick?"

"I mean gone, gone. She died. She's dead." Hollan's voice cracked on that last part.

Rochelle felt an icy chill wash over her. She sat up in bed.

"What do you mean, dead? She can't be dead."

"She is. They just called me. I tried to call Nerissa, but she's not answering her phone. It's too early to call Paige yet."

"No, that's not possible. She's too young. She's, what, 58 or something?" Rochelle was shaking her head in denial. Their mother had always been pretty cagey about her age, so Rochelle actually had a hard time keeping track of it.

"She was 60. But you're right, that's much too young." Hollan gasped a little bit, her voice was getting a slightly hysterical pitch to it. "Chelle, my little Blaise has it too."

Rochelle was confused all over. Blaise was Holland's two and half year old toddler. "How did he get it? You didn't take him to see Grammy when she was sick, did you?"

"Of course not!" Hollan nearly yelled in denial. "I wouldn't do that! But he's been feverish and throwing up since yesterday morning. Benjamin and I were getting ready to take him to the hospital right now, when they called us. We're still going to do that, but I had to call you. Can you please keep trying to call Paige and Nerissa? We need to make plans."

Rochelle heard some mumbling in the background. Probably

Hollan's husband, hustling her and the baby out the door to the car.

"Yeah, I'll call them," she said. She let Hollan's call drop and leaned back for a moment, the shock washing over her in chill waves. Then she wondered if Apurva was home. She leaped out of bed to check on her roomie, but she was nowhere around. She checked the schedule on the fridge and saw that her roomie was scheduled to be at work two hours ago. She hated to interrupt her friend during work, but this seemed like it might be worth it. She tried dialing direct. Apurva didn't answer, so she left a voice mail, saying that her Mom had just died. It sent a new round of chills down her spine, saying it out loud like that. Then she fired off a text message, telling Apurva to check the voice mail when she had a private moment. They both tended to ignore voice mail until they had a convenient moment. But texts got almost immediate attention.

Next Rochelle tried calling Nerissa again. Still no answer. Then she message bombed Paige, hoping to wake her with the buzzing, just as she had been, minutes before.

Rochelle took a quick shower, trying to warm up her icy skin. She wondered if it was too early to call George. She was going to need the day off, maybe several. She didn't have the slightest idea what it would take to put together a funeral, but she knew she couldn't leave it all to Hollan. Not while Hollan's child was sick too.

She also realized she'd better call her Dad. Mitchell Tylin, her real dad, would at least be gracious enough to not crow about the old bat being finally gone. He'd offer his daughters his sympathy, a shoulder to cry on, if they wanted it. But he wouldn't mourn directly.

But where was Craig Daniels, her mother's second husband? She hadn't seen or talked to him in weeks. Which was not unusual. They weren't particularly close. He'd been kind and friendly with all of Catherine's daughters, but Rochelle had never fully warmed up to him. Out of all of the girls, he was closest to Nerissa, having spent the most time around her. And Nerissa was a naturally open, outgoing personality. Easy to get to know.

Rochelle vaguely recalled her mother saying something about Craig being out of town on a business trip, during lunch last weekend. Had it only been a week since the wedding dress shopping? Only a week for her mother to get sick with the flu and die? How could this possibly be happening?

She tried calling Craig's number and also got voice mail. She left a vague message there, asking him to call her. She was sure her voice sounded odd, quavering. It would set off anyone's alarm bells and that would be enough to get him to call. She wondered if Hollan had tried him yet. Maybe he was home from the trip and had been to the hospital to visit her? Had they already notified him first?

Rochelle piled into her car to head to the family home in Manassas. She still hadn't reached George yet, so she decided to stop by the bar, to see if he was in early. She found him in the stock room at the back, unloading supplies from his little pickup truck. Most of their food and drink was delivered, but there were a few things George liked to pick up personally.

"George! You're here!" Her throat felt funny, tight. It was a wonder she could even talk. He turned and smiled at her, raising his hand and two fingers in greeting.

George was a plump, round man, with a basketball for a stomach. He kept his thinning gray hair cut close to the scalp. He usually wore the same uniform as his employees, black pants and a white shirt. During the dinner service, he would add a tie to make it clear to the customers that he was management.

"Rochelle! What brings you by so early? You're not on until later."

"Its… Its my Mom." Rochelle's voice cracked. "She died this morning. Or last night. Oh god, I'm not even sure when, exactly…"

"Oh my goodness! Are you okay? What happened?" He set the box he was holding down on the floor, in preparation to hug her, if she signaled it would be okay.

"Uh.. I don't know. But I need to go down to Manassas and do stuff. Oh gawd, I don't even know what to do!" Rochelle's face crumpled, so he reached out and wrapped her in bear hug, squeezing just tight enough to keep her from slumping to the ground.

After a few moments, he walked her over to the first table in the bar room and pulled out a chair for her. He grabbed a couple of the clean linen napkins from a tray on the bar counter and handed them to her.

"Take it easy, honey. Its going to be okay. What happened? Was it an accident?"

Rochelle shook her head. "No, she had the flu, that bug that's going around."

George's eyes went wide. "Oh, I'm so sorry. I didn't know. I've heard of a few people getting it."

"It doesn't make any sense! People don't die of the flu. They get sick, take a few days off and get better. Only the elderly, the ones with the compromised immune systems, die from it. Mom was always healthy as a horse."

George just patted her knee, listening intently as she rambled.

Rochelle nodded. "So, I guess I need the day off and maybe tomorrow, too."

"Of course. You can have as much time as you need. Do you know where she is? Was she at the hospital, or at home?"

"Hospital." Rochelle's throat closed up before she could say anything else. She dabbed the napkin at a few tears that were leaking out.

George nodded and started waving his two fingers around. "Okay, here's what happens next. You and your sisters pick a funeral home and let the hospital know which one. They'll have her body transferred there. You go to the funeral home and decided if you want her buried or cremated. Unless she already made other arrangements. You don't happen to know if that's the case, do you?" George raised his eyebrows in question.

"Uh, I have no idea. Probably not. She never talked about it. Nobody ever thought she'd die. She was a freakin' force of nature. We called her Hurricane Cat, behind her back." Rochelle giggled through her tears at that memory.

George smiled with her. "Okay. So, you and your sisters get to decide how you want to proceed. Wait, didn't you say you had a step-dad?" Rochelle nodded.

George continued his gentle lecture. "Well, check with him, too. He might know what she wanted or have his own preferences. Did they go to church? There might be a particular cemetery they want to be buried in." Rochelle shook her head. Her mother had stopped dragging them to church when they went through their rebellious adolescent phases. And without having her daughters to show off to her peers, she hadn't found much reason to go on her own.

George waved that away. "Okay then. So, from there, how much ceremony you want to have is really up to you. A funeral is a way for you honor your mother's memory. Sometimes they're calling it a 'Celebration of Life' now and making it much less formal, more like a party. It's really about how you want to say goodbye. It's not something to be afraid of. Don't be afraid to let the grief out. It can be wonderfully liberating to hear what other people thought of the deceased. That's part of what the funeral rituals are for."

Rochelle considered him. She'd heard from her coworkers that he was a widower. And at his age, he'd probably outlived his own parents, too. So, yeah, he had some experience with funerals.

Before he let her leave the bar, George quickly whipped together a few ham sandwiches and packed them with some cold side dishes for her to take to Manassas. Another common part of the mourning process he said, was to shower the bereaved with food. Rochelle wondered why that would be, given that her throat was nearly choked closed. The thought of swallowing anything at all nearly made her retch.

*****

In the car, Rochelle tried calling Nerissa again. This time she got through.

"Yeah, I'm here. I know. Are you coming down?" Nerissa greeted her sharply.

"Yeah, I'm in the car. Is Hollan there or at the hospital?"

"She's at the hospital with Blaise." Nerissa's voice was harried, short and clipped.

"Okay, I'm on my way. Have you heard from Craig yet? Where is he?"

"He's in California. Some big project he's working on. He's been there for two weeks. I can't reach him. Listen, I couldn't say anything last weekend because we didn't have any time alone, but I don't think Craig and Mom were doing too well. I'm not sure he's going to make much effort to come home."

Rochelle frowned. "Huh."

"Listen, just get here as fast as you can. I'm kinda freaking out." Nerissa was the baby of the family and rarely had to deal with much pressure, so this was probably unfamiliar territory for her. Not that Rochelle wasn't having her own freak out.

"Okay, I'm heading out now. But it's Friday morning traffic."

"Yeah, but you're going out-bound, not in-bound. Traffic shouldn't be that much of a problem for you."

"Traffic is *always* a problem in this town," Rochelle groaned.

Rochelle headed out. Shortly after clearing the Beltway, her sister Paige finally returned her call. Rochelle had her phone plugged into the car charger and the ear bud in her ear, ready and waiting for hands-free communication. "Hey, what's up? Why the early morning blitz?" Paige asked.

"Have you talked to anyone else yet? Do you know?"

"Know what? What are you talking about?" Paige was clearly confused.

"Mom died this morning. At the hospital, I think. Of the flu. Well, of complications from the flu, is how they say it," Rochelle said. Her own shock had been wearing off. She'd been chanting it inside her head for the past thirty minutes, *Mom is dead, Mom is dead,* just to get used to the feel of the words.

"What?" Paige nearly screeched. "That's impossible!"

"Hollan called me and I just talked to Nerissa. It's true." Rochelle clenched her teeth.

She let Paige splutter in denial for a few minutes and then interrupted her. "Listen, I think you need to get back here as soon as possible. Can you take some time off of work?"

"Have you guys already made arrangements?" Paige was shocked all over again. "Dang time zones!"

"No, I haven't even gotten to Manassas yet. I'm on the road right now. But Blaise is in the hospital with the flu, too. I think Hollan is going to be pretty freaked out. You, Nerissa and I need to step up and help take care of things."

"Uh, okay. Yeah. Right. Okay." Paige was mumbling and fumbling, clearly trying to do multiple things while also talking on her cell.

Rochelle waited a few moments. Paige finally came back clear voiced. "Okay, I'm going to work on getting a flight back there. I'll call Scott and tell him I'm out for a few days. Tell Hollan I'm praying for Blaise, too. Talk to you in a bit." Paige tapped off the call and left Rochelle alone with her thoughts.

At the family house in Manassas, Rochelle picked up Nerissa and they both went to the local hospital, where they connected with Hollan. Her toddler, Blaise, had been admitted into pediatric care and was on an IV fluid drip. He was groggy and mostly asleep, thanks to the pain meds flowing in with the fluid. Hollan's husband, Benjamin, was sprawled on the armchair next to the bed, looking exhausted.

Hollan motioned them out of the room to talk. They walked down the hallway to a small conversation and waiting area filled with comfortable sofas and chairs.

Hollan said, "I had Mom taken to the Manassas Mortuary. It was the first name on the list they gave me that I recognized. I used to drive past that place all the time, before we moved out to Gainesville. I hope you don't mind, but they needed to process the paperwork."

Nerissa and Rochelle nodded in agreement. "That's fine. I don't think it much matters which funeral home we use," Rochelle said. Nerissa nodded in agreement.

The three sisters settled down to discuss arrangements. They concluded that their Mom would have preferred burial to cremation and that she would have wanted a big, well-attended funeral. Hollan was torn between going with Nerissa and Rochelle to the funeral home to handle the rest of the arrangements and staying with her son. In the end, she elected to let her husband stay, while she made the trip, clearly feeling guilty the whole time. Rochelle resolved to try to step up and do more. After their initial meeting at the funeral home, Rochelle sent Hollan back to the hospital, while she and

Confluence

Nerissa went back to their mother's house.

The rest of the day was spent in a rushing haze of errands and paperwork. They needed to dig into Catherine's personal paperwork, find her bank accounts and see if they could get Catherine to pay for her own funeral. Realizing that none of them were co-signers on Catherine's accounts, they traipsed back to the hospital, collected the official death certificate, took that to the bank and waited for more paperwork to be signed and processed, to release the accounts. The bank added the two sisters to their mother's private checking account. But several more accounts were held jointly with Craig, so the bank refused to add them, until and unless he also consented. The girls did not protest this.

Rochelle and Nerissa went back to the funeral home to pay the deposit on the casket. Then at home, they pulled out their mother's address book and started calling her friends. Nerissa drafted an obituary to send to the local newspaper. Rochelle posted an announcement on Facebook. Sometime after dark, Rochelle pulled the sandwiches that George had made out of the fridge. She realized that she had not eaten all day and was actually very hungry. They even cracked open a couple of Craig's fancy beers and swigged them down.

Hollan joined them at the house just as they were starting to feel the buzz. She was too tired to drive the rest of the way to Gainesville, only another thirty minutes and planned to crash at the house. Catherine's home was a huge five bedroom colonial in a very nice neighborhood. She and Mitchell had bought the house when Hollan and Paige were still toddlers and Rochelle was just a baby. The Tylins had raised their family there until their marriage fell apart and Mitchell had moved out. Catherine had kept the house in the divorce. Later on, Craig had moved in with her.

The sisters sat on the screened-in back porch, watching the last of the fireflies wink and blink in the dark. They had Paige on a Facetime call again. Paige was sitting in a gate waiting area at the San Francisco airport. She was booked on a red eye flight back to Dulles and would be with them in person in the morning. She was only half watching her cell phone, though. Her attention was partly distracted by a TV hanging from the ceiling in the waiting area.

Paige asked, "Hey, have you guys been watching the news lately?"

Rochelle answered, "Some. It's been on at the bar."

"They're running a lot of coverage about this flu thing. They're calling it a super flu bug. They say it could be worse than the Spanish flu almost a century ago." Paige summarized the coverage she was watching.

Hollan grimaced. She was looking pale and freaked out herself, worried for her son. She'd left her husband on night duty with the baby, while she was supposed to get some sleep. She was wolfing down a sandwich in very un-lady like haste. Rochelle imagined her mother's disapproval face, if she could see Hollan now.

Nerissa asked Paige, "If it's really that bad, aren't they supposed to quarantine everything? The hospital is really busy, but I didn't see anyone in hazmat suits."

Paige shook her head. "There's some talk of canceling stuff. I'm just hoping they don't close the airports in the next hour. About half the people around here are wearing face masks. I'm splashing on Purel every fifteen minutes, but I still can't help feeling like I'm swimming in a petri dish."

Rochelle thought about turning on a TV in the house, to get a clearer picture of what was going on. But the beer buzz was finally mellowing her out. She didn't feel like she could even lift her arms at the moment.

Nerissa said, "I can't help thinking about how Mom would have a fit over the inconvenience of it, if they start closing things. Can you imagine her not being able to go to the mall?"

The girls snickered.

"She's probably having fits over just being dead. So inconvenient," Rochelle added.

Hollan said, "And she's probably trying to tell the mortuary guy exactly how to do her makeup and hair."

"Crap, we gotta pick out a suit for her, too, don't we?" Rochelle asked.

Everyone rolled their eyes at that. After that, the conversation devolved into the usual bitch session where they vented their frustrations over their mother's exacting standards and the pressure she had put on her daughters to be socially perfect.

When the giggling finally petered out, Hollan was the one who pointed out the stark truth. "You know, we're actually free now. She's gone and we don't ever have to do things her way again. We can dress the way we want, say what we want and do what we want. Nerissa, you can run your wedding anyway you want, now. Rochelle, you can date whoever you want. Paige, you can... well, you can whatever you want." She waved a hand at the phone. Hollan was tired and having a hard time stringing words together coherently.

They contemplated that freedom silently. It sounded good. But Rochelle had been hearing her mother's disapproving voice inside her head for too long, to believe it would just go away now.

***

The next several days were a blur of activity, as they notified family, friends and acquaintances. Catherine didn't work professionally, but she had been active with several large charitable organizations in the region. She'd always kept a busy and full calendar of board meetings, volunteer time and parties. Those organizations had been suitably shocked to hear of Catherine's passing.

Hollan spent most of her time at the hospital with her own son, who was not improving, in spite of the broad spectrum antivirals and steady drip of hydration fluids. She developed bags under her eyes and her skin seems to grow permanently pale. Benjamin, her husband, looked even worse.

Nerissa, Paige and Rochelle stopped in to visit their nephew at least once a day. The hospital was a hectic place, with staff hurrying about, wheeling mobile beds filled with patients. Outside, they could hear ambulance sirens pulling into the emergency entrance almost every hour. They saw several medical helicopters coming in and taking off as well.

Confluence

The sisters planned the funeral for the Monday afternoon following their mother's death on Friday. They had finally managed to raise Craig on his cell phone. He swore that he was as shocked as they were and promised to try to catch a flight home as soon as possible.

Rochelle stayed overnight in Manassas on Friday and Saturday, but elected to go back to her apartment in D.C. on Sunday for a fresh change of clothes. She stopped into the bar to update George on the plans. He hugged her again and told her to take all the time she needed. He even insisted on feeding her more food before she left again. She was sitting at the bar, watching the corner TV, as she ate a chicken sandwich. The talking heads were getting belligerent. A news anchor was interviewing some specialist. Rochelle missed the introduction that explained what the guy was an expert in.

The CDC has confirmed several thousand cases of the Asian super flu virus in the U.S. Doctor, don't you think it's time we closed our borders to international travel?

Actually, Dan, at this point, that's not likely to help any. The fact that it's already here means its too late to quarantine the country from outsiders. Outbreaks are developing simultaneously in major cities all over the world.

Well, shouldn't we lock down those cities where outbreaks have occured? We need to stop this thing in it's tracks.

Internal lockdowns aren't going to prevent people who've already got the virus, from getting sick. We'd probably be doing more harm than good, if we restricted freedom of movement. Hundreds of thousands of Americans are traveling or working abroad. Millions of people inside the country need freedom of movement for their jobs: delivery people, first responders, educators, healthcare workers, transportation, construction, food processing and distribution. If you lock down the cities, the economy is going to take an enormous amount of damage. And I really don't think it will work to stop this specific bug. Early indications are that this virus has a very long tranmissibility period. That's the amount of time that someone can have the virus and pass it along to others, before they even know they are sick. Shutting down a couple dozen cities isn't going to help the other towns around it, if someone has already passed the virus along. But it will harm their economy needlessly.

"Well then, what can we do to stop it? When will vaccines be ready for distribution?"

"It usually takes five to six months for vaccines to be ready for wide distribution. The laboratories are still in the identification and testing stage. It will be a few more months before it's ready for wide distribution."

"And what do you recommend doing in the meantime?"

"At this point, if anyone has the option of self-quarantine at home, they may be able to avoid contact with infected people. If you can telecommute for your job, or don't need to go out, we recommend staying home as much as possible."

"As you pointed out already, that's not really practical for most people. They need to be able to move about their communities to go to school, work, church, shopping."

The guest expert looked frustrated.

I realize its difficult, but minimizing contact with other people for the short term is the best way to avoid infection. Wearing a face mask will help somewhat. It keeps you from accidentally introducing the virus into your system by touching your nose or mouth. That and we can't emphasize this enough: Wash your hands frequently in hot, soapy water.

The anchor thanked his guest for the interview and switched back to another newscaster, who was narrating images of a burning car. In the background, Rochelle could see ambulances and a large building that looked like a hospital. The captions said "Brooklyn, New York City." The gist of the story was that someone got angry when their loved one died of the flu and crashed his car into another parked one, setting them both on fire.

Inside the bar, there were only a couple of customers enjoying food or a beer. For a Sunday afternoon, it was extremely quiet. Outside the bar, a few people strolled past the windows. Most of them were wearing masks now. Juan, Rochelle's fellow bartender and sometime cook was wiping down the counter and stocking up.

Rochelle nodded in the direction of the window. "Anyone wearing masks while working yet?" she asked Juan.

"Not yet. I asked George if he thought we should start doing that. He's not crazy about the idea. Thinks it might scare the customers," he answered.

Rochelle nodded in acknowledgment. On the one hand, if a customer saw staff with surgical masks, they might be afraid their food or drink was contaminated. That would drive away even more business. On the other, they might think it was a protective gesture for their benefit. Hard to say which way the customers would go.

***

Catherine's funeral flowed by in a numb blur for Rochelle. She'd been dealing with so many practical mundane details that she'd been able to shove the grief aside. On the day of the event, it felt like she was sitting in the back seat of a car, leaning and bracing while the car gently flowed around curves in the road. Meet the sisters at the house, convoy to the funeral home. Greet the guests. Talk with guests. Sit in the front row. Listen to the eulogies by her mother's charity colleagues. Thank the guests. Convoy to the cemetery. Sit in the front row again. Watch the coffin lower into the ground. Drop the ceremonial flower. Convoy back the house. Put out the food. Greet the guests again. Listen to the guests. Thank the guests.

Rochelle's numb haze evaporated when the final guest left the house. It must have disappeared for her sisters as well, because Paige burst out, "Where the hell is Craig? Why isn't he here?"

Nerissa answered, "He tried to get a flight, but couldn't. He was booked on, like, three different ones and they kept getting canceled."

Paige frowned. "Seriously? I didn't have any trouble getting one."

Nerissa said, "You left a day earlier than he did. I heard this morning that they're thinking of closing all the airports. When's your flight back out there? You should check on it."

Paige grimaced and pulled out her phone to start checking.

Hollan announced, "Listen, I need to get back to Blaise at the hospital. Can you girls take care of cleanup?" The sisters nodded. Hollan was paler than ever, looking like walking death herself. They'd tried to get her to leave earlier, but she couldn't bring herself to leave when there were still funeral guests in the house. They hugged her goodbye and promised to call in the morning.

Paige mumbled crap at her phone a few times, stabbing at the screen. She finally resorted to calling the airline's customer service. Nerissa and Rochelle idly listened while they tidied up the kitchen. From what they could hear of Paige's conversation, her own flight the next day was getting canceled, but the airline could get her on one that evening. Leaving in about three hours. Paige rushed off to pack up her things. Rochelle offered to drive her to the aiport. They hugged Nerissa goodbye and rushed out the door. Rochelle felt guilty for abandoning Nessy in the huge empty house. She resolved to text her youngest sister later, to check in on her.

Rochelle was disappointed she would not have more time to spend with Paige in person but understood the desire to get back home. She was itching to get back to her own bed. She hadn't talked to Apurva in days, either, aside from a brief condolence call. Apurva had not been able to get off from work to come to the funeral.

Rochelle hugged Paige goodbye at the airport and headed for her own tiny home in the city.

Chapter 4

Rochelle woke the day after her mother's funeral realizing she had completely missed the first day of classes at school. She scrambled out of bed in a panic, rushed about to locate her schedule and pedaled off to school.

She spent the day finding her classes and apologizing to professors for missing the previous day. She felt like she was a freshman, panicked and confused. After several hours of running around, she forced her self to sit down on a bench on the quad and take some deep breaths. She gave herself a little pep talk. She reminded herself that she was a third year MBA grad student, not a freshman. One day of missed classes was not the end of the world. Her professors, several of whom knew her quite well by now, were very understanding about her loss.

The quad was a wide open grassy space, with large leafy trees scattered about. Rochelle noticed a small cluster of students gathering in the center, carrying signs stapled to wooden stakes. The signs read, "Online classes now!" and "Prevent Flu/Close School." Rochelle rolled her eyes when they started chanting. Time to go, she decided. She had already told George she'd cover a few hours at the bar during the dinner rush, to make up for all the time off.

At work, it was surprisingly easy to slip back into normal mode. Once the apron went on, she could turn her focus to the customers, to the drinks, to mentally tracking the tips. It pushed all the other things, like classes, sisters and dead mothers, out of her brain.

After her shift, she was pleased to find Apurva at home and still awake.

"Hey girl, what's up?" She greeted Apurva, flumping down on the couch next to her. The TV news was on. It had been on at the bar too, but Rochelle had been too busy to pay attention to it.

Apurva shrugged. "I'm so exhausted. Exhausted, I tell you." She said this softly, slowly, not in the exaggeration rhythm they normally used. Rochelle looked more closely at her. Underneath Apurva's deep coffee colored skin, she seemed washed out. There were stress lines around her eyes, which were somewhat bloodshot. Her hair was lank, as if it had not been washed in several days. It was coming loose from a pony tail.

"Are you hungry? I brought some food home. Mac'n'cheese." Rochelle pulled the bag to her and opened up the clamshell container filled with leftovers from the restaurant.

Apurva perked up slightly at the smell of the food and grabbed the extra fork that Rochelle held out to her. The girls ate companionably from the same carton for a bit, as they watched the news.

The State Department today said there is no evidence that the super flu virus was deliberately released by North Korea. However, they are opening an investigation and are requesting assistance from the UN.

Meanwhile, the White House is requesting cooperation in combating the spread of the virus. It is recommending closure or cancellation of all non-essential buildings and events, such sports games and concerts. Public transportation is to be restricted to only the most essential routes. The government is authorizing all federal offices to invoke telecommuting policies where possible. They are encouraging private businesses to do the same. The public is encouraged to stay at home as much as possible to avoid spreading the disease.

The broadcast shifted gears to a profile of the disease vector.

The Asian influenza virus appears to be a super virus, classified as such because of its severity. It is hitting the elderly and small children particularly hard. Officials are working to build a map of vector transmissions to trace how far the disease has spread. However, the project has grown beyond their databases' capabilities of mapping the connections. Further data collection has been hampered by staff shortages and premature deaths of victims.

Apurva turned to Rochelle and said softly, "They're sugar coating it. It's much, much worse than that."

Rochelle widened her eyes. "How? What's really going on?" The words were out before she had a moment to wonder if she really wanted to know.

Apurva sighed and said, "Story around hospital is that the virus has been spreading for weeks already. They think it has a much, much longer incubation period than they've ever seen before in flu viruses. Like, eight to twelve weeks. They also think it has a really high transmissibility rating. They think the virus is viable outside the human host for days at time, instead of hours."

"What does that mean?" Rochelle asked.

"That means it has already spread around all over the world and prevention is way beyond the point now. It means, it's been getting on planes and products since July probably and then incubating inside of everyone. The time line makes some of the doctors think its a tropical variant and North Korea is too far north to be the source. It's been circulating too long for that, they say."

Rochelle sat in silence, staring at the TV commercials for soda, teeth whiteners and insurance, without actually seeing them.

Apurva added, "And there's something else. This virus is much, much more lethal. You've heard of the Spanish Flu?" Rochelle nodded.

"That one had a mortality rate between two and twenty percent, depending on which regional demographic you're looking at. My bosses think this one might go 65 or 75%."

Rochelle was shocked. "Are you kidding me? Is that even possible?"

Apurva just nodded tiredly. She set down her fork in the clamshell container Rochelle was still holding up between them.

"Viruses are not sentient. They don't have a brain. But if they did, this one would probably think it's doing a pretty good job. It's been very successful at reproducing itself and finding new hosts. It's able to reproduce and move on well before it kills its host. By virus standards, that's the definition of success. By human standards, this is going to be a disaster. A disaster, I tell you."

Rochelle stared at best friend. "What are we going to do?"

Apurva stared back. "I have absolutely no idea."

Confluence

***

The next day, Rochelle received an early morning text from one of her professors, stating that class was canceled until further notice. He assigned them several chapters of reading and requested a summary essay from the students. A lecture would be setup via an online web interface for later in the week.

That was followed by even more shocking news. Nerissa called. In a flat, exhausted, monotone, she reported. "Blaise died last night. Hollan and Ben are at home. They called me and I'm calling you."

The icy feeling flashed over her again. "Oh my god. This can't be happening," Rochelle responded.

"It is happening," Nerissa snapped. "Can you come back out here? She really needs us now. I think she's about to fall apart, have a mental breakdown or something."

Rochelle glanced about her tiny bedroom. "Uh, yeah, I guess. My morning class just got canceled. But I've got a shift at 4 p.m."

"That's fine. Just come." Nerissa snapped off the call abruptly.

Once again, Rochelle scrambled to make the drive out to the Manassas area. She met Nerissa at home and then they drove over to their sister's home in Gainesville. They found Ben curled up on the sofa in the den, sound asleep. He was probably exhausted after so many long days and nights at the hospital with their baby boy. Hollan was asleep in their bedroom, but woke up when they came in.

Hollan was inconsolable, sobbing. They hugged and cried together for awhile, grieving the second loss so soon after the first. None of them had cried much over their mother, given how conflicted they felt. But the death of an innocent child overwhelmed all of them. When she could talk again, Hollan announced they weren't doing a formal funeral. They had already sent Blaise's body for cremation. Maybe in a few days they'd have a private ceremony but for now, she and Ben both just wanted to sleep.

Rochelle was completely out of ideas on how to help Hollan. Hollan had always been the strong, mature one. The one who had her life together, knew what she wanted and how to do things. So if she said she didn't need anything but rest, Rochelle accepted that at face value. She and Nerissa let Hollan curl back up in the bed and close her eyes. They went back downstairs, confirmed that Ben was still sound asleep on the sofa. There was nothing else for them to do, so they left.

At their mother's house, Rochelle dropped off Nerissa. "Hey, how's Chris doing? He didn't look too good the other day," she asked.

Nerissa crossed her arms over her chest. "He texted me this morning. He thinks he's got the flu too. He's at home in bed."

"Oh crap, I'm sorry," Rochelle said, wincing. She hadn't meant to poke at the open wound.

Nerissa shook her head. "Nothing you can do about it." She paused. "You been watching the news?"

Rochelle nodded. "And talking to Apurva. Listen, Purv says this epidemic is bad. She says it's going to be a disaster. A real bad one."

Nerissa nodded. She looked gray and pinched, far far away from the happy-go-lucky girl she'd always been.

***

Rochelle arrived for her work shift to find her co-workers wearing surgical masks.

"I thought George didn't want to scare the customers," she asked Juan. She glanced around. The few customers who were around were wearing masks too, sipping their drinks through straws.

"D.C. health department announced all food and beverage workers have to wear them for the duration. So, here we go." Juan handed her one.

Rochelle tied it around her face and set to work. When the afternoon drinkers were sufficiently sloshed to face their home lives, the bar cleared out. Juan was on kitchen duty that evening, but there was only one couple who came in for dinner, so he had little to do. With so few customers around, Rochelle took it upon herself to do some deep cleaning of the bar area, pulling out older bottles from the back shelves, dusting them off, wiping everything down with the disinfectant cleansers. In between chores, she and Juan stood about, watching the news on TV.

International coverage in Asia showed footage of a riot breaking out in Hong Kong, where masked protesters were demanding a vaccine. Turkey, South Africa, Peru and several other nations around the world had closed their borders to all international travel. The public school districts in Los Angeles, Chicago and New York City announced they were canceling classes until further notice. The FAA said it was grounding all flights. The World Series was canceled, as were several major music festivals scheduled in the next few weeks around the country. Malls and large shopping centers were asked to restrict access to only let in people who were wearing medical masks.

Rochelle had that sinking sick feeling in her stomach again. George had joined them, sitting on one of stools, facing the TV.

"What are we supposed to do? How are we going to survive this?" she asked him.

George squinted at her. He propped his head on his hand, two fingers splayed over the mask awkwardly strapped to his face, elbow on the bar.

"Well, you might think about getting stuff," he answered slowly.

"Stuff? Whaddya mean?" she asked.

"Stuff," he repeated. "Food. Toilet paper. Soap. Bottled water." He sighed. Rochelle frowned at him, still not getting it.

"Things are going to fall apart, right quick now. There's not a lot of grocery stores inside the D.C. city border. So, their inventory turns over very quickly. If people get sick, or refuse to leave their homes, transportation of stuff is going to nose dive. Container ships in Baltimore. Trains. Trucks. Delivery people, all those people who move the stuff around. That could come grinding to a halt very soon. It's hard to tell which is going to last longer, the stuff sitting on shelves or the people healthy enough to gobble up the stuff."

Rochelle thought about that. She didn't usually keep big stock piles of supplies on hand. The apartment was too small. If she ran out of something, she just grabbed it on the way to or from home. George was right, there were not many big grocery stores inside the city limits. But there were plenty of small delis, pharmacies and convenience stores around. She shopped at them frequently. Her philosophy was that the store was a good place to store her stuff until she needed it.

She glanced at the tip jar, which was disappointingly empty for the evening. Rochelle was a typical broke college student. Her bank account didn't have much rainy day cushioning, either. At least she'd kept the debt level on her credit cards pretty low, compared to most of her peers. She wondered where the balance was between getting enough stuff and managing her debt effectively.

George was watching the mental gears turn in her brain. "Go make a supply run in the morning. Get the stuff you need and use all the time. Do that every day, until… well, I don't know know until when. Until we know what happens next."

In the back of Rochelle's mind, a thought waved it's tiny hand: *What if I get it next? What do I need stuff for, if I'm going to get sick too?*

A few seats down the bar, the lone customer who was nursing a beer through a straw poked under his mask spoke up. "You might think about bugging out, if you can."

George turned to face him. "What's that, now?" he asked.

"Bug out. Head for the hills. Hide out until its all over."

George nodded sagely at that advice. But he said, "And is that what you plan to do, sir?"

The customer frowned back at George and Rochelle. Well, his eyebrows furrowed. They couldn't tell what expression his mouth formed.

George continued in his pleasant Socratic tone, "Do you have a place in the hills, all stocked with MREs and ammo? Are you heading there as soon as you finish your beer? Or are you perhaps just waiting to see if this really is the end? Maybe it's not, maybe it's just a scare. Maybe things will get better. Maybe they won't. Maybe we just want to wait a little bit longer for the really big show to get started."

George looked back at Rochelle. She could see that gleam in his eye, that one that meant he was messing with the customer.

Confluence

The customer stood up abruptly and said, "I'm waiting for my wife to either die or get better. She's in the hospital. I can't move until that's decided, one way or the other." The man pulled a $10 bill out of wallet and left it on the counter. He stormed out in a huff.

George's face fell. It was unheard of for him to piss off a customer so much that they stormed out. But he didn't do anything. He just sat at his own bar, looking morose. Rochelle picked up the money, rang up the sale and dropped the change into the tip jar.

Chapter 5

Things continued to get worse at a steadily increasing pace.

Rochelle accepted George's advice and made a supply run, driving out to a nearby Costco in the suburbs. She put the tab on her credit card, the one her Dad had given her for emergencies. If this didn't count as an emergency, she didn't know what did. She grabbed as much stuff as she could fit into her little Honda Accord and hauled it back to the third floor apartment, load after load. While the apartment was small, just barely over a thousand square feet, it was actually the largest floor plan available in the complex. It included a small den, in addition to the two bedrooms. She and Apurva had made the den into their study room, with desks, computers and bookcases filled with text books. Rochelle shoved books around to make the maximum amount of space available and stashed her newly acquired hoard into the small amount of space available. Once unpacked and organized, it didn't seem like much.

The rest of Rochelle's classes were reduced to de facto online classes. She read her textbooks and dialed into the web conference calls to listen to lectures. She emailed in her assignments. She talked to her sisters frequently on the phone. She hung out at the bar, even when not on shift. She liked hanging out there. She'd taken to studying there, since the place had grown so quiet. Few customers were coming in and the ones who did were all masked.

Ironically, just down the street from them and a few blocks south, a lot of noise was being made. Protesters had started gathering at the White House, demanding a vaccine. The news reported, many times over, that the pharmaceutical companies were rushing to develop one, but it took time for this to happen. Rochelle could only shake her head at the irony of thousands of protesters gathering in close proximity to complain about the spread of a lethal virus.

Days after Paige had returned home to California, she reported that she too had come down with the Superflu, as the news was now labeling the virus. She was holed up in her apartment in Oakland, huddled under blankets with half a dozen doses of Theraflu ready to be mixed into hot water and sipped. She sent text messages to her sisters, but refused to answer calls. The sisters pestered her to go to a hospital, but she refused. One of her final messages was, *The local hospitals are completely overrun with patients and out of supplies. The medical staff is getting sick and dying as fast as the civilians. Going there is complete waste of time. I'd rather be comfortable in my own bed.*

Meanwhile, Hollan and Ben also developed symptoms. They took to their respective bed, postponing the private ceremony to scatter their son's ashes indefinitely. Rochelle was nearly paralyzed with fear. The anxiety gripped her brain, while her body kept going through motions. She eagerly seized on any activity that would distract her from thinking about what was happening in the world around her: studying, working, shopping for supplies.

In spite of the fear, though, Rochelle continued to go into Paulbicki's. She wore her own mask most of the time, even though she was fairly certain that it was too late to do any good. Although customer traffic had dwindled, a few regulars continued to come in for their evening libations. One slow evening, in between serving the few customers who were hanging out, Rochelle sat at the bar, pretending to read a textbook. She was also eavesdropping on two older gentleman who sat a few stools away from her. They were dressed in suits and looked vaguely familiar to her.

The first guy asked, "So, are they going to evacuate Congress, or not?"

The second one answered, "This is off the record, right?"

He nodded his head. "Is it going to be Greenbriar or Raven Rock?" he asked.

"Actually, I think it's going to be Cheyenne Mountain. Lower population density out there, less chance of exposure."

"But what if someone is already infected with the virus when they go in?"

The second gentleman just stared back. After a moment he said, "Well, I guess we're all fucked, then." He downed the last of his scotch, got up and walked out.

In spite of the fear and anxiety, Rochelle and George couldn't keep themselves from turning on the news reports. It was like watching a horror movie play out. They couldn't look away, no matter how terrible it was. Keeping the TV on mute, reading the crawl strips and watching the video footage, she saw riot footage in far away places like Jakarta, Mumbai, Cairo, Los Angeles, Paris and Baltimore. The National Guard was mobilized to provide policing and guard duty around major hospitals. Dusk to dawn curfews were announced in many major metropolitan areas. Prices for gas and consumer goods were starting to spiral up. Trucks were going around major cities, picking up dead homeless people off the streets.

One particular story caught her attention, making her turn up the volume. A news anchor was getting blunt with an expert.

Dr. Maddox, what's the latest projections of mortality rates?

Well, at this point, the CDC has preliminary evidence to suggest that the mortality rate is about 65% for healthy adults. It will be somewhat higher for infants, children and patients over age 75.

And what about the infection rate? How many will be able to avoid infection?

Well, at this point, we suspect a very high rate of infection.

Yes, but what rate?

I can't really put a number on it.

Why is that?

Well, we think the incubation period is exceptionally long for this virus. We have reason to believe it can survive in a host for six to twelve weeks before growing to a load large enough to sicken the host. During that incubation period, the virus is easily passed about, because the patient is not symptomatic. Thus, they would not have taken very many preventative measures. There's also evidence that the virus can remain viable outside the host for days at a time.

So, what are you saying, Dr. Maddox?

The expert sighed and glared into the camera, clearly intended for the anchor.

I'm saying this virus has been circulating around the entire globe since July. If you have had any kind of contact with any human beings in the last two months, there's a good chance you've already picked up the virus. Masks are a waste of time. And vaccines are completely useless if you're already infected. Unless you've been living at the South Pole for the last two months, you probably already have it. It's just…

The news broadcast snapped off abruptly, leaving the news channel's logo displayed in the center. Within ten minutes, the other news channels on the other TV's started running a crawl strip saying, *CDC reports everyone already infected and there is no cure. Masks are a waste of time.*

That ratcheted up the panic, nationwide. More broadcasts showed crowds of people protesting in front of hospitals, calling out the officials, claiming they were lying and demanding a cure.

One particularly chilling video clip showed a mini riot breaking out in a Sam's Club store in Illinois. The grainy security video came from a ceiling-mounted camera. The scene showed the front half of a large crowded store. Highlighting in the image directed the viewer's attention to a woman emerging from the restrooms, with no mask on. Most other shoppers and employees in the store were wearing assorted types of face masks. A moment later, a second woman, masked, followed the first, pointing at her. Poor audio sound was dubbed over the video. They could hear the woman shouting, "She didn't wash her hands! Hey! Grab her! She has to wash her hands!" At that point, a few people nearest the pair of women turned and approached the first. The people gestured and waved their arms. Then a man grabbed the first women, who struggled to escape. More people approached, trapping the woman in a loose circle. A scuffle erupted, as the woman was knocked to the ground. More people piled on like linebackers on a fumbled football. Meanwhile, the long lines of people waiting to pay for their purchases dissolved, as people pushed past the cash registers, wheeling their carts out the doors. The video cut off abruptly at that point. The news announcer followed up, "The fight spread to most of the people in the store. It took the combined force of over 45 police officers and National Guardsmen, before order could be restored. Twelve people were taken to the local hospital with minor injuries. The primary victim, the first woman seen leaving the bathroom, died at the scene of injuries sustained during the event."

Rochelle was thankful for the supply runs she had already made, but wondered if it was worth risking similar riot scenes to try to get more. Her little den was packed to overflowing with toilet paper.

While she had barely seen Apurva in days, Rochelle discovered that her roomie approved of the project. She let Rochelle know by leaving a bag of supplies on their tiny kitchen table with an note: *R, good work on the stocking up. I grabbed a few things from the hospital pharmacy. Its an open free-for-all now. The oxy drugs are all gone, but I got you these.* The note was signed with a big 'A.' Below that, there was a simple sketch drawing of a dick with a smiley face on the tip. The bag contained a dozen boxes of Rochelle's variety of birth control pills and a big handful of assorted styles of condoms. Rochelle laughed for the first time in weeks. Then she realized it might be the last time she had a reason to laugh for many more weeks, if ever.

***

Day by day, Rochelle's world of personal connections slowly grew smaller. Paige stopped responding to phone calls and texts. So did her Dad. Nerissa called her, just a week after their little nephew, Blaise, had passed away. She was monotone, exhausted, nearly incoherent in shock. Nerissa's fiance, Chris, had also just died at the same hospital as their mother and nephew, she announced. And their brother-in-law, Ben, had had a severe fever-induced seizure the night before. Hollan had rushed him to the hospital, but he was not expected to last much longer. Worse, Hollan was with him. Not just sitting by his bedside, but actually admitted, with an IV hook-up and placed in the same room. Hollan was too sick with the Superflu to return home alone, Nerissa reported.

"Oh, Nessy, I'm so sorry about Chris. Do you need me to come out there again?" Rochelle asked her sister. They were talking on Facetime on their phones. Nerissa's eyes and nose were red rimmed and puffy from crying.

Confluence

Nerissa answered, "There's really no point. You should stay at home. There's no point in exposing yourself even more to our germs No one will go to any more funerals, everyone is too scared of gathering in a crowded place. Chris's parents had him sent for cremation. Hollan told me to do the same for her and Ben."

Rochelle just nodded at her phone. She couldn't think of what to say.

Nerissa started crying again. "Why is this happening? What did we do to deserve this?" she wailed. Rochelle still couldn't find anything to say. She started crying too.

After some extremely unsatisfying mutual tear sharing, they closed the call.

Ben died two days after being admitted to the hospital. Hollan became delirious with fever and stopped answering her calls or texts on her phone. Two days after her husband, Hollan followed suit. One by one, the people in Rochelle's life were flowing down the peaceful river of death, disappearing from existence.

Meanwhile, the price of gas shot up to $15 a gallon. Rochelle contemplated going back out to Manassas, in spite of the skyrocketing fuel prices. But Nerissa insisted that Rochelle stay put. She was still hoping against hope that if Rochelle would just stay home, she might avoid catching the virus. Rochelle didn't have the heart to tell her she was still working evening shifts at the bar. But then Nerissa took to her own bed, running a fever of 105, she reported via text. Several more delirium fueled nonsensical texts followed that, which sparked fresh new crying jags for Rochelle. Then the texts stopped coming.

Rochelle's mind was nearly frozen in fear. She was helpless, useless, to do anything for the people closest to her. She compensated by keeping her body in motion. She cleaned the apartment. She rearranged supplies, collecting as much stuff as she could from the local pharmacies and convenience stores, which were rapidly emptying out. She cycled to and from the bar.

At the bar, several waitresses failed to show for their shifts and did not respond to phone calls. Not that it mattered, much. There were so few customers or cooks, that Paul stopped serving full meals. Two of Rochelle's professors announced in their online class discussion forums, that they were unable to continue their online classes because they were also sick. Apurva texted her from the hospital, saying she'd finally presented with symptoms and was staying there, where she had access to a stash of morphine. Rochelle's social media feeds were also drying up. People she wasn't as close to, but kept in touch with on Facebook, stopped posting and went dark.

Rochelle was pretty sure there was no hope. If she had it, she had it and it was just a matter of waiting for it to start. She regretted not having her own morphine stash. She looked at the bottles of booze on the shelves of the bar, but couldn't bring herself to actually make a drink for herself. The bottles gleamed in subtle shades of brown, black and green. There were a few splashes of gaudy color mixed in. Some of them even smelled enticing. But she was rarely tempted to actually consume. The occasional margarita or beer was mostly to help her get to sleep at night. Too many of those just made her sick the next day.

So she sat on the stools, or stood behind the bar, watching fewer and fewer cars drive by on the street outside. Instead of cars, she saw military trucks cruise by. Probably National Guard, moving units to the hospitals, she assumed. Sometimes groups of masked people streamed by on foot, heading towards the White House or the National Mall. But those dwindled and got smaller each day.

Rochelle had been riding her bike to work, until the night she rode past a neighborhood convenience store with it's windows smashed in. Most of the food and beverages inside it were missing, or smashed and destroyed on the floor. After that, she drove her car to the bar and parked in the alley behind. No one gave her any flak for blocking the garbage dumpster.

Some days it got cloudy and rained. Some days the sun shined. The temperatures started dropping, reminding her that it was time to start pulling out sweaters. The trees were turning colors, mostly brown.

One by one, Rochelle's circle of family and friends fell silent. No more calls, no more texts pinging back. All her social media channels went silent too. Rochelle gave up on wearing the surgical mask.

***

About a week after she last heard from Nerissa, on a rainy midweek morning, Rochelle was camped out at the bar, sitting on one of the stools, with a steaming cup of tea beside her. The TV was on, as always, but the sound was low enough to not bombard her. She'd actually managed read a whole paragraph in her text book and comprehend it. Out of five pages. She wondered why she was even bothering.

George came in through the back entrance. One glance at him and she was surprised he'd even bothered to come in. He looked pale, except for the bright spots on his cheeks. His eyes were glassy too. She couldn't imagine where he got the energy.

The TV squawked a bulletin alarm, calling their attention before she could even ask George how he was feeling. Within moments, an anchor person appeared on air.

We have a very special announcement. We have just learned that the President of the United States has died of complications of the SuperFlu this morning. The President was at Camp David, along with his immediate Cabinet. Unfortunately, the Vice President of the United States also died last night, also of the Superflu. According to the Constitution, the Speaker of the House is next in line. However, we have not been able to contact his office or anyone else in Congress, to determine what happens next. Stay tuned to this channel, for further developments in this rapidly evolving story.

George shook his head at that. He held up a ring of keys. Each key had a twist tie with a tab on it. Rochelle took the offered set. The tab identified what each key went to: front door, back door, office, safe, his pickup truck.

"What's this?" she asked him.

"They're yours. You need them more than I do, now."

Rochelle felt her stomach clench up again. It was becoming a very familiar feeling now.

"Did you stock up on supplies, like I told you to?" George asked her.

She nodded solemnly. Before gas prices got out of control, she had been stopping at the grocery stores and big box stores between Manassas and DC. She had taken to putting the extra stuff in Apurva's room, at the apartment.

George went on. "Good. I've tried to stock up on everything here too, much as I could. There's lots of food in the freezer. As long as the power stays on, that stuff will be fine for a long time to come."

He paused for a moment and seemed to wobble a bit on his feet. He grabbed the back of the barstool next to Rochelle and eased himself onto it. He stared blankly at the wall of bottles behind the bar.

After a moment, he continued. "In a few more weeks, if you start running out of beer or liquor, try raiding the BevMo's or Total Wines out in the 'burbs. Stay away from the local distributors. Those will get picked over real quick. But if you keep this place stocked, you'll get customers back, soon as they figure out the place is open."

Rochelle couldn't speak. Her throat was closing up again.

"Stay here as long as you like. Or pack up and bug out. Not sure where you'd go, but if you have to, then go. It's okay."

George's thoughts were wandering. He rambled on. "There's a shot gun in the closet in my office. You might want to bring that down and stash it under the bar."

He nodded at his own continuity plan. His face grew red for a moment, as a flush of fever visibly spread over him.

"Okay, I can't think of anything else you need to know. You know how everything in here works, right?" Instead of waving his two fingers at the equipment around the bar, though, he was tapping his chest. Rochelle didn't, really, but she nodded anyway. Her eyes overflowed. George reached out and grasped her in a hug, a long one. Then without looking at her again, he slid off the stool and slowly walked out the front door. He closed it gently behind him and did not look back. He turned right and walked up the street. His home was a few blocks away.

Rochelle had stood up when George did. Now she slowly

crumpled to her knees, right there in the middle of the room. She wiggled around to sit on her butt and pulled her legs up to her chest. She pressed her eyes into her knees and sobbed. She rocked back and forth, sobbing until she was nearly choking, sniveling out a constant stream of snot and tears. Her nose was so blocked up that she grew short of breath. She let herself collapse over on her side, her face pressed to the slightly sticky hardwood floor. Incongruously, she wished she had some of those linen napkins to wipe her face. It was minutes or hours or days before she gathered enough resolve to push herself back up to standing again.

Rochelle found one of the clean napkins in the hostess podium, wiped her face dry, blew her nose and dumped the now dirty napkin in the laundry bin. She took a few more steps to the front table. She sat facing the windows, where she had a nice view of the park and the quiet river beyond. She waited for the next wave of sobbing to come. Nothing happened. She replayed the scene with George in her mind. Nothing happened. An ambulance screamed past on the street outside. She thought about her sisters. She checked her phone, no new messages or calls. Nothing happened.

Rochelle sat and stared out the window while the day slowly darkened into dusk. A man walked past, carrying a poster on a stick over his shoulder, slumped and hunched against the mist that was almost a drizzle. Her stomach poked a little hunger probe at her, but she couldn't find the energy to stand up and go to the kitchen. The sky outside went completely dark. Orange sodium street lights came on. Tall office buildings across the river gleamed reflected light, but did not glow from within.

When she realized that she was hunched so far over the table that her back was curved in a painful arch, she levered herself up to standing. She locked the front and back doors and turned off the lights. She dragged herself upstairs and unlocked George's office. A big leather sofa lined one wall, with an old wool tartan blanket draped over it. She laid down on the sofa, drew the blanket over her shoulders and fell unconscious.

Meanwhile, at a hospital in Arizona...

Kevin Wilson was pissed. Angry. His rages burned with the fire of a thousand Arizona suns streaming down their clear bright light.

They didn't know where his Dad was.

Kevin had just left the main entrance of the hospital. The place was swarming with people, most of them wearing masks. Tents were set up in front of the building. Doctors and nurses were rushing about, wheeling patients on gurneys and wheel chairs in and out of the building. Long lines of people stood in front of the biggest tent, the one with big red cross on the roof.

Kevin had stood in that line for more than an hour, with both his brother and his roommate in wheel chairs, sagging with pain, exhaustion and fever. When he finally got to the front, they had checked in his companions. Then he asked where his Dad was. They had just told him to go inside and ask at the front desk.

The inside line had been another half-hour wait. All they had been able to tell him was that his father had died six days ago. They did not have any information in their computer that said where they sent his body. They even printed out a piece of paper with a summary of his father's hospital stay. Kevin scanned down the piece of paper: admitted, gave fluids, no response to anti-virals, idiopathic seizure, patient deceased. That was the last thing the paper said: "deceased." It didn't say what funeral home he'd been transferred to.

When he asked the person, they had just said, "I'm sorry," and motioned to the next person in line. Kevin asked louder, but the person behind the desk ignored him. The man behind him in line said, "Fuck off dude, I'm next."

Kevin shouted, "Where's my Dad? What did you do with him?"

The guy behind him shouldered Kevin out of line. He was about to shove back, when a pair of meaty hands gripped his arms from behind and spun him about, pulling him away from the desk. An overweight security guard had grabbed him and hauled him away.

Confluence

"You need to calm down right now!" the guard hissed at him.

"But I need to find my Dad!" Kevin wailed.

The guard still gripped one of his arms, bent behind his back, shove-walking him out the entrance. "Son, there's nothing more you can do. He's gone," the guard said.

The guard ejected him out the doors of the main entrance, nearly sending him sprawling on his ass.

Kevin recovered his footing and looked around. The parking lot was almost full with cars. Most of them were parked crookedly. Some of the tents around the entrances were standing on bent poles. Rips in the fabric had been patched up with duct tape. People sat in plastic chairs, IV bags hanging from the scaffolding above them. Some wore face masks. They were hollow eyed, leaning on whatever support they could find. A few held bloody wads of tissue to their mouths and noses. No one paid him much attention. Maybe if he went back in to see his brother or his roomie, he could find a doctor or someone else who could tell him what he needed to know?

Kevin circled around the outside of the building to the Emergency entrance, where he'd dropped off his brother and roommate. They weren't in the waiting area anymore. Once again, he waited in a long line, only to be told they had been admitted and were being triaged. Once they were transferred to rooms, he could go visit them. But, due to the crisis, that might be a few hours. The nurse at the desk suggested it might be better to try tomorrow. Her look said that hanging around a busy hospital full of Superflu patients probably wasn't very good for his own health.

Kevin figured that at this point, he was already infected, or he wasn't. It would come for him, or it wouldn't. Any more exposure wasn't going to change that outcome.

Kevin showed the girl the paper the other clerk had given him. He asked if she could tell him where his Dad was. She tapped at her keyboard for a few moments, glanced at the paper and said she only had the same information that was already there.

Kevin walked slowly to his little pickup truck. It was parked at the far edge of the lot. Technically, it was parked illegally, as he'd jumped the curb to span a motorcycle spot and a patch of gravel. He didn't care. The pickup was just an old beater, a city-limit-special for getting around town. He sat behind the wheel, poking at the rips in the upholstery under his legs. He wondered how he could get the information he wanted. Needed. The main entrance was a no go. Maybe the other doors?

He started his truck and pulled out of his makeshift parking slot. He navigated around the crowds of tents, people and cars, to cruise past the other entrances, including the Emergency one he had just left. Farther around the back side of the hospital, there were entrances labeled "Diagnostic Services," "Neurology" and "Orthopedic." Smaller doors with electronic proximity sensors said "Employees only." A fenced off area sheltered the maintenance equipment. Next to that there was a loading dock with several bays. A big semi-trailer was backed into one of the slots. Several workers at the back were loading things onto the truck.

It quickly became clear that a back entrance wasn't going to help him find his father's body. Even if he could get inside, they'd just send him back to the front desk, with the same computers and the same information.

His circuit around the building had brought him to the exit to the street, but he wasn't ready to leave yet. He veered off to the side, circling around the outside perimeter of the lot. This side of the complex had fewer cars than the front side. Maybe it was employee parking? He stopped, staring ahead, thinking.

It had been days since his Dad had replied to his texts and calls. The last message he'd sent to Kevin, was that his brother, Kaden, was taking him to the hospital to be admitted.

Kevin had rushed to finish his truck route, aiming to get home as quickly as possible. He made the normally four day drive from Seattle to Phoenix in three days, thanks to minimal traffic and by ignoring speed limits and regulations about the number of hours per day he was permitted behind the wheel. When he had arrived home, both his brother, Kaden, and their roommate, Bruno, were in bed, sick, moaning and sweating with fever. He had hustled them into his little pickup truck and driven straight to the hospital. As he drove, Kaden managed to tell him he'd woken with the Superflu the day after checking their Dad in. Kaden had been too sick to even get out of bed on his own, let alone go back to the hospital to visit Dad, or even call him to check on his status.

Now Kevin knew that Dad was dead. That meant he had to make funeral arrangements. As the eldest son, that was his responsibility. He had to take care of things. He wasn't sure what came next, but he figured tracking down the body and making sure it got to the funeral home was the obvious next step. Once he did that, the people at the funeral home could tell him what to do next.

But nobody to could tell him where his Dad was. How was he supposed to take care of things, if he didn't know where his Dad's body was?

Kevin pounded the steering wheel with his fists. It jiggled slightly. He gripped it and tried shaking it back and forth. He sucked in a deep breath and let it back out in a roar of frustration. His mouth opened so wide, his eyes were forced shut. His foot slipped off the brake and the car started rolling forward slowly. When his scream ran out of breath, he opened his eyes, looked forward and moved his foot to the gas pedal. Time to go somewhere. He didn't know where.

Ahead of him, a light pole stood in the graveled end cap bracketing a row of parking spaces. The bottom three feet of the pole was encased in thick concrete. A tiny prickly pear cactus was planted a few feet away from it.

Kevin pushed his foot down on the accelerator pedal. His mind slipped outside of his head. He watched his pickup truck truck gather speed. It made minor course corrections to take direct aim at the pole. It was like the truck was guided by someone far away.

An image of himself and Kaden playing *Grand Theft Auto* flitted thorough his mind. His own truck rolling forward played on the game's screen cast. The steering wheel in his hands was replaced by a game controller.

The pole approached, slowly at first and then faster, dopplering. The front wheels of the truck hit the curb and bounced up and over, first the left, then the right wheel. The pole hit the truck's engine block dead center, but the wheels hitting the curb unevenly tilted the vehicle up to one side. The pole impacted diagonally to the truck's frame. The hood buckled. The doors popped out sideways. Glass fragmented and rained down.

Kevin's mind slipped back into his head a few minutes later. He blinked away the darkness and glassy grit coating his eyelashes.

"Hey! Hey, are you all right?" A voice was shouting at him from outside the truck. Hands grabbed his arms.

Kevin looked around, focusing on the stranger. A man in scrubs. He was still talking.

"Are you crazy? What the fuck do you think you're doing?"

Kevin shook his head. Shattered glass fell out of his hair and sprinkled over his arms. He raised an arm to the roof above him, preparing to lever himself to get out. But the roof was not in the right spot. He squinted up and saw that the roof was several inches higher than it should have been. Then he realized the steering wheel was pushing into his stomach. He never sat that close to the wheel.

The guy in scrubs was still talking to him.

"Hey, can you hear me? Do you know what day it is? Are you injured?"

Kevin shook his head some more. He flailed his arms about and finally pressed them against the crumpled roof above him, higher than normal. He twisted himself sideways to step out. His right leg was pinned between the steering wheel and center console. Bracing his left leg, he managed to squeeze the meaty part of his right thigh down enough to slide under the wheel, which was canted at a funny angle. He had to push down on the seat cushion to make room. The guy in scrubs finally gripped him by the left arm and shoulder and helped drag him clear of the crushed cabin of his truck.

Once free of the cabin, his knees wobbled a little. He turned to face the truck, gripping the side of the truck bed to steady himself. He felt the other's guy's hands running over him, like he was being patted down for weapons.

"Hey! Watch it!" he snarled at the guy.

"I'm just checking for injuries. You're bleeding from your arm. I think you got sliced by some glass."

Kevin glanced down. His left arm was dripping blood from a long ragged gash in his upper bicep. He wondered why it didn't hurt.

64

He looked up at his pickup. Hisses and pings were coming from the engine. He moved a few steps forward, to inspect it. The light pole had crumpled the front of the vehicle, leaving a half circle indentation about eighteen inches deep. The guy behind him muttered, "Hey, hold on a sec, I'm not done yet." Kevin leaned down to see coolant and oil dripping from the engine into the gravel, coating the pebbles in shiny goo.

"Dude, we need to get you inside, get that stitched up, maybe get a head scan, too."

Kevin said, "Huh?"

The guy said, "You're hurt. You need medical attention. Luckily, you just happen to be right at a hospital."

"They can't help me," Kevin mumbled.

"Yeah they can. Come on, you think you can walk?" The guy put his arm around his right shoulder and gently turned him toward the main building.

"Are you a doctor?" Kevin asked.

"Nah, I'm just an orderly. But I know where to take you. Come on, let's go."

The guy swiped a plastic card in front of the sensor of the nearest door. It clicked and opened automatically a few inches. The guy pulled it open farther and maneuvered them both inside. He walked Kevin down corridors and around corners. After several turns, Kevin lost track of where he was in relation to the outside. He was distracted by the people. Beds lined hallways outside of the Radiology and Outpatient Surgery departments. More people in scrubs and masks hurried about carrying clipboards. Moans and groans sounded from behind closed doors. One more turn and they entered the Emergency area, only from the back end, not the front, where he'd been just a short while ago.

The orderly walked along a row of bays, small areas with beds and machines. Almost every bay was filled with one or several patients. The bays were separated from each other with curtains hanging from tracks in the ceiling. The orderly miraculously found an empty bay, with a narrow bed with rumpled sheets. He whirled Kevin around to get him to lean his butt against the bed. "Can you get up?" he asked.

Kevin wiggled his hips and managed to lever himself onto the bed, with the help of his right arm. He realized his left arm was now hurting, so he had instinctively clutched it to his chest. The blood had flowed down to coat most of his hand. It was getting on his shirt, too.

"I'll send someone in to look at you right away," the orderly told him and stepped out of the bay.

Kevin looked around. His curtains were only partially pulled. He couldn't see the people in the bays next to him, but he could hear them. Groans, soft conversations and occasional wails. In addition to the people noise, machines beeped. Overhead announcements squawked out of speakers mounted in the ceiling. The smell of disinfectant mingled with the odor of vomit, piss and shit.

A woman in scrubs turned a corner into his space, noticed him and said, "Oh, for crying… Where did you come from? You're not supposed to be in here." She looked around. She was carrying an armload of laundry. She dumped that on the floor in the corner formed by the curtain.

"Have you been triaged?" she asked, looking at his bloody arm.

"Huh?" Kevin asked. "That guy just put me here."

"What guy?" the woman asked.

"I dunno. He said he was an orderly."

The woman pursed her lips. To herself, she mumbled, "Can't anybody follow proper procedure? How the hell are we supposed…" she trailed off. She stepped closer, examining Kevin's arm.

"What happened here?" she asked him in a normal volume, waving at his arm.

"My truck crashed. Got my arm cut."

The woman raised her eyebrows at him, but didn't say anything else for a moment. She peeled the torn t-shirt sleeve away from the wound on his left arm, to expose the the cut, which was steadily oozing a small trickle of blood. After a moment she asked, "Are you hurt anywhere else?"

"No, I don't think so."

A different woman, also in scrubs, poked her head around the curtain. She asked, "Hey, Rusty just told me to come take care of this guy. You got this?"

"Yeah, I got this. But he didn't come through the front. You need to start a file on him."

"Okay," the other woman said and disappeared again.

"Are you a nurse?" Kevin asked the first woman, who was pulling things out of a toolbox set of drawers near by and setting them on a tray.

"Yeah. I'm going to clean that and put some stitches in."

"Oh," Kevin said. He wondered if she could tell him where his Dad was.

Kevin watched as the nurse worked. She rolled up the remains of the torn sleeve, to move it out of the way. She used a clean wipe to carefully pat away the blood around the outside of the cut. Farther away from it, she was less gentle as she efficiently cleaned the blood off the rest of his arm and hand. Kevin winced and hissed when movement stretched the cut.

"Okay, I'm going to put a topical on that to numb the pain. This is going to take a few minutes to take effect." She carefully applied the numbing agent.

"I'm going to go get your paperwork started, while we wait for that," she finished.

Kevin spoke up, "Can you find out what happened to my Dad?"

The nurse looked at him in confusion.

Kevin explained, "He died a few days ago. The front desk couldn't tell me what they did with his body."

She asked, "Did you tell them what funeral home to transfer him to?" She looked doubtful even as she asked.

"No, I wasn't here. I was out of town. I'm a trucker. I was on a run, so I wasn't even here."

The nurse shook her head. "I'm sorry, kid. Unclaimed bodies are getting sent for general cremation."

Kevin wondered what that meant, but didn't have a chance to ask, because she turned on her heel and walked out. He looked down at his arm. The bleeding seemed to have stopped. He could feel the anesthetic taking effect. He lifted his right hand to poke at his left arm, but then noticed his hand was trembling. The trembling seemed to be spreading to his head too, as he felt a little dizzy. He dropped his right hand on the side of the bed. He shifted his legs around and up onto the bed. He laid his head and torso back. His left arm was still facing out, where the nurse could work on it when she came back. He deliberately took a few deep breaths and tried not to think at all.

After a few minutes, the nurse returned, wheeling a computer on a rolling cart.

"Okay, what was your Dad's name?" she asked.

"Korey Wilson. With a 'K'," he answered.

She typed into the computer for a few moments. Then she said, "Yep, he died six days ago. No information on body transfer to a funeral home."

Kevin already knew that. "What does that mean, 'general cremation'?" he asked.

"We've had thousands and thousands of people die of the Superflu this week. The bodies are stacking up. Literally. The morgue and the funeral homes are overrun. The government said we have to start mass cremation, to dispose of the bodies."

Kevin's face fell. His skin suddenly felt clammy cold. If he hadn't already been laying down on the bed, he thought he might faint.

The nurse worked on his arm. She cleaned the wound with disinfectant. He could feel the pull and push of the needle and thread, but it didn't hurt. He kept his eyes closed while she worked. After a time, she said, "Okay, all done. Eighteen."

Kevin frowned. "Eighteen what?" he asked.

"Eighteen stitches. That was a long gash." She was wrapping a long strip of bandage around his bicep. She added, "I'm sorry, but you're probably going to have a scar. I'm not a plastic surgeon. I can't do as neat a job of it as they can. And it's pretty ragged. Hard to get all the edges perfectly lined up."

Kevin nodded. He didn't really care. At least it had not messed up his tats. He had a swirling design of a tribal tattoo on his right bicep. He'd always wanted to get the left done to match, but hadn't gotten around to it yet.

The nurse pulled out some sheets of paper from the cart with the computer on it. "This is about wound care. Keep it clean, keep it dry, change the bandage around it. Normally, we'd insist you come back in a week to have the stitches out. But that, well...." Her voice trailed off. Her faced crumpled for a moment. Then she gave a tiny shake of her head and continued.

"Here's some antibiotics." She handed him a pill bottle that rattled. "When the wound is completely closed over, you can cut out the stitches. They're plastic thread, so they should work loose. Once they're moving freely, just snip them and pull out."

Kevin nodded. It was not the first time he'd ever had stitches. He knew the drill. "Okay. So, where do I..." he wondered how he was going to pay for this. He started digging in the back pocket of his jeans for his wallet. His insurance card was in there. He had no idea what the co-pay would be.

"Hang on, I gotta get you in the system."

At that moment an alarm sounded a few spaces down the row of bays. A voice rang out down the hall, "Loren! Need you in here!"

"Oh crap!" his nurse said. "I gotta go help them. Stay here! I'll be right back!" She scurried out of the room.

Kevin waited. After a minute, the alarm down the hall shut off, but he could hear raised voices calling out medical words in alarmed tones. After awhile, the noise died down, but the nurse did not come back. The anesthetic was starting to wear off and his arm began to ache. He wondered if they were going to give him any pain pills to go with the antibiotics.

Kevin swung himself off the bed and poked his head out of his curtain cubicle. The place was still as crazy as before. People in scrubs were hustling about. Some talked in small groups in hushed voices. Others shouted across hallways, asking for supplies. Patients wailed in pain. He could hear the sounds of vomiting, too. Rhythmic thumping in a bay a few spaces down seemed to indicate a seizure was happening, as several employees rushed in to brace the patient.

A pair of wide double doors at the end of the hallway burst open. An orderly wheeled in a woman in a chair. Through the open doors,

Kevin could see the crowded waiting room beyond. Could he just walk out?

"Hey, we're not done with you yet!" The nurse, Loren, had found him. He had only taken a few steps toward the doors.

Kevin turned to her. "Let's go up to the front desk," she said, gently taking his good right arm. He allowed her to move him along. He was still feeling a little bit lightheaded.

At the desk, the administrator glanced at them. It was a different person, than the one he'd spoken with earlier. She looked exhausted. There were dark smudges under her eyes. Her hair was coming loose from a clip at the back of her head. A dribble of coffee stained the front of her shirt.

The nurse next to him explained the procedure she'd just performed. The administrator pulled a fresh form from a stack and asked wearily, "What's your name?"

Before Kevin could hand over his insurance card, the nurse asked, "Hey, is anybody keeping track of which bodies end up on the trucks going to the pits? He lost his Dad. I wondered if maybe his Dad's body is on the truck out back."

"Could be. It's been collecting bodies for a few days. But I don't think anyone is keeping track of who's going on it. It's the second load, the first one left a couple days ago," she answered.

"Crap..." the nurse said.

"And it's stuck here until we find a driver for it. The guy who drove it in collapsed as soon as he got down from the cab."

They gave each other a knowing look. Then Loren's face lit up. She turned to Kevin. "Didn't you say you're a trucker? Do you think you could drive it out, take it over to the landfill?"

"Uh..." Kevin said, his eyes going wide.

"Look, we really need the help. It's nearly full and those bodies need to be moved. There's people over at the landfill who know what to do when it gets there." She looked at him pleadingly.

Kevin looked between them. He rubbed his right hand over his forehead and the top of his head. He felt more grit that had not shaken out. That reminded him that he didn't have any other form of transportation at the moment.

"Okay, yeah, I can do that. How do I get to the truck from here?" he looked around. Loren smiled gratefully at him, the first time she'd done that. She grabbed the arm of a passing orderly who did not have anything in his hands. It was not the same guy who had walked him in from the parking lot. Loren said, "Orlando, take this guy down to the dock. He's going to drive the truck over to the landfill."

Orlando shrugged and motioned at Kevin to follow him. Kevin looked back at the nurse. "You're not coming?" he asked.

"Are you kidding? I'm busier than a one-legged man at a butt kicking contest, here." A shout from down the hall called to her. She waved at Kevin, but moved away from him.

Kevin looked back at the administrator. She stared at him for a moment, then crumpled up the form in her hand and tossed it into an overflowing waste basket beside her desk. She turned to the cluster of people waiting patiently behind Kevin.

Orlando said, "Come on, I got things to do, too." Kevin nodded and followed him down some hallways, around more corners and down a set of stairs. Orlando stopped and pointed down a long hall lined with black plastic logs. "Down there, through those double doors. Just tell them what's going on. They won't care, as long as that truck moves out."

Orlando turned and jogged back the way they had come. Kevin turned the opposite way, down the hallway. A vile stench wafted through the hallway. Kevin's stomach roiled. Through the doors, on the open loading dock, he found a couple of guys loading more plastic wrapped bodies onto a very full truck. They were wearing plastic bunny suits, long gloves, rubber boots and respirator masks over their faces. Kevin noticed that the fresh outside air helped chase away some of the rotten smell.

Kevin greeted them and said he was here to move the truck. The guys hurrahed, slammed the back doors shut and told him the keys were in the ignition. "Vaya con Dios," they called after him, as they scampered down the walkway out of the dock area to the open parking lot and away from the horrid stench.

Kevin climbed into the cab and looked around. It was a typical setup, like the kind he had trained on in school. No sweat, for him.

Confluence

The gas tank was about half full. He also knew exactly where the city landfill was, so he didn't even bother setting the coordinates in the GPS device.

Kevin did the one thing he knew very well how to do: he drove the truck.

At the landfill, he pulled in and immediately saw a long row of dirt berm, with bays cut out by bulldozers. They reminded him of the medical bays he had just left. A man in a clerical collar and a full-face respirator mask approached the truck. The moment Kevin opened the cab door, the horrible rot smell invaded his nose and sinuses. In spite of that, Kevin stepped down from the cab to speak with the pastor. He explained that he had just come from the hospital. The man removed his mask to speak with Kevin. Then he nodded and motioned to several other people, who moved to the back to open the gates. The bodies had shifted around during the drive. A couple of them tumbled out when the doors opened.

Looking around, Kevin saw hundreds, maybe thousands more bodies stacked and arranged in the bays. Fires in many of them were sending up plumes of bitter dark smoke. Kevin gagged at the smell. His eyes watered. A few bays down from where he stood, a man was removing the plastic bag from a woman's body. The hospital gown she wore hitched up her side, revealing dirty underwear. Her flesh was darkening, purple and burgundy, due to pooled blood. Kevin turned away and retched, heaving up the thin acidic contents of his stomach. He couldn't remember when he'd last eaten, but he had been sipping from a water bottle in his pickup, earlier. The fluid came bursting out of him in waves, leaving him weak and shaking all over. He wanted to kneel, but didn't want to land in his own sick. So he struggled to stay on his feet.

After a few minutes, the preacher who had greeted him patted him on the back gently.

"Got it all out now?" he asked.

Kevin nodded. He was still struggling to get a solid breath of air into his lungs. Air that didn't taste of rot.

After an awkward moment of silence, the man asked, "Do you know how to unhook the cab from the trailer? The other trailer, over there, is empty and ready to be taken back to the hospital." He pointed at a trailer down the way.

Kevin looked at it, looked at the connections between the one he just driven. The trailer was refrigerated, with connections to the cab's fuel supply to run the generator that ran the coolers. Yeah, he could unhook those too.

For a few brief moments, while he focused on the hoses, wires and gears, he almost forgot where he was and what was going on around him. Then a shift of wind brought a fresh wave of stink over him, making him dry heave again. His stomach cramped. He clenched his hands on the tools and gears and separated the truck from the trailer. He climbed back in the cab, drove it forward and carefully maneuvered it to hitch it up to the empty trailer. He climbed back down and repeated the connection steps, in reverse. Once the cab was reconnected to the empty trailer, he looked around.

The preacher had been watching the maneuvers. He walked up to Kevin and spoke, "If you drive this back to the hospital, they'll fill it up again. You wouldn't happen to know where there's more refrigerated trailers we could use?"

Kevin thought. There were plenty of empty trailers at the depot where he coordinated a lot of his trips. Some of them had cooling equipment on board. They would work. He nodded to the preacher. He couldn't speak yet because his throat still burned from the bile.

"Okay, then. Can you please help us? None of us here knows how to drive these things, or hook them up."

Kevin nodded again. "Good man," said the preacher. "Thank you." He nodded, patted the truck cab's door and stepped back. Kevin climbed back in, released the brake and drove the empty trailer back to the hospital.

No one was on the dock when he first backed in, so he honked the horn a few times. After a few minutes, several new people came through the doors to see what was going on. They thanked him for bringing the trailer and said they'd start filling it up. There were plenty of bodies still waiting in the hallway. The odor continued to make Kevin's stomach roil.

Kevin had spent the entire day running around town and then at the hospital. Somehow, without his noticing, dusk had arrived. Kevin explained to the dock guys that he'd exchange the full trailer for an empty one the next day. They nodded in agreement. Lacking any better options to get home, he unhooked the cab and drove it to his house about ten miles away from the hospital.

It was actually his Dad's house. He and his brother Kaden still lived there, though. And their roommate, Bruno. So far as they could say they lived anywhere. Kevin spent about 90% of his time on the road. The three of them had their very own tiny trucking company: "Korey & Sons." They owned three rigs. They had been talking about buying a fourth and hiring on another driver. Bruno was their mechanic, doing maintenance when they were in town. For Bruno, it was a side gig. His day job was in a regular repair shop working on mini-vans and sedans. The Wilson men took contract jobs that had them driving stuff all over the western half of the country. Sometimes Kevin even took routes east of the Mississippi. His Dad claimed they were modern day cowboys, herding their stock to market.

Kevin flopped down on the worn sofa in the living room. He realized he'd not even tried to see Kaden or Bruno, after hauling the empty trailer back to the hospital. Nor had he told the preacher at the landfill about his Dad. What would he have done, even if they could locate his Dad's body? What would Kevin do with a body that was six days into decomposition? He'd figured he would have just arranged to have it cremated, anyway. Did it really matter if it was done in an oven at a mortuary or in an open pit? And what would he do with the ashes? Just set them on the mantle and stare at them forever?

"Fuck that shit," Kevin mumbled to himself. Stupid Superflu.

He thought about getting up to see if there was any food left in the fridge. But thinking about food made his stomach lurch again. So instead, he just tilted over sideways onto his good arm and fell asleep.

Chapter 6

Rochelle stared at her phone. Facebook's most recent post was four days old. Instagram's was three days. She thumbed through the list of contacts in the address book. How many were in there? She started counting them, but lost track when she reached the low hundreds and had only gotten to the letter "J." There were people in there from her high school days, study buddies and group project members. There were college friends, colleagues from her internships, companies and services she'd used. People she had met during the two short years she had spent in Chicago. She wondered if she should set up some groups and segregate them. Could she just delete them? It seemed kinda harsh to do that, without confirmation they were actually dead yet. She wanted to reach out to people, but it seemed incredibly awkward to send a text to someone she hadn't seen in three or four years, saying, *Hey, you dead yet?*

Rochelle was still curled up on the couch in George's office. She really wanted to just slip back into the fugue state, awake without really being conscious. Just waiting for the Superflue to come for her as well. But her hips and back hurt. Her bladder was full and her stomach was empty. So she sat up.

She took care of basic needs in the washroom next to the employee break room. She splashed water on her face and ran a brush through her hair. She wondered if she should go home to shower and change clothes.

Downstairs, she peered out the front windows. Yesterday's drizzle had developed into a full fledged rain, pattering down relentlessly. She didn't want to bicycle home in it. Then she remembered George's truck parked out back. Even that seemed like too much effort. Maybe if the rain stopped. So she turned the TVs and the lights on. One station just had a logo displayed. The other was silently streaming web cam coverage of mobs of people milling about outside a major hospital somewhere in the world.

Rochelle set about tidying up the bar. She threw out the dried up sliced lemons and limes from the day before. She put away a dishwasher load of glasses. She moved some stock from the basement storeroom up to the main bar. She picked up soiled napkins and tablecloths from the wait stations and dumped them in the bin. The bin was actually getting pretty full. She wondered when the linen service would come to pick them up and drop off a fresh load. That was one of the many things she did not actually know about running the bar, in spite of George's assumptions about her knowledge base. She was thinking about going upstairs to look up the paperwork for it when the chimes over the front door rang.

One of the regulars walked in and nodded at her. He stamped his feet to shake off the excess water, and hung his rain coat on a nearby hook. She recognized his face, but wasn't immediately sure what his name was. He took a seat in the middle of the long bar, where he could see both TVs easily. Rochelle walked around the end of the bar to meet him in the middle.

"What can I get for you?" she smiled at him.

"You still have Molson on tap?"

"Sure do."

The man nodded, so Rochelle pulled a mug for him and set it down on a paper napkin. The man handed over his credit card to her and said, "Don't close out the order yet. I might have a few."

"You got it," she said. She blatantly looked at his card and added, "Gary."

Gary nodded again and took his first sip from the foamy top. He was not wearing a surgical mask. Neither was she. "How's things going in here?" he asked her. Rochelle was wiping up the overspill at the tap.

She wobbled her hand. Paused. "Not sure how to answer that. George is gone." Her voice only cracked a little bit at saying that out loud.

"I'm sorry to hear that," Gary replied neutrally.

They both lapsed into silence for while. Rochelle returned to basic chores. She set the tables on the other side of the room with the dwindling supply of fresh linens, wrapped bundles of silverware and freshly filled condiment jars. While she worked, one of the TVs snapped over to a live broadcast. An anchor appeared and started reading the latest updates.

The World Health Organization has increased it's latest overall mortality calculations to 89%, it stated in a press release today. They also indicate that mortality rates for distressed populations, such as children and the elderly, is likely to be much higher. They caution that this information is still an estimate and they won't have final calculations for several more weeks yet. Unfortunately, this station was not able to reach officials at the WHO for further comment.

Rochelle had returned to her position behind the bar, a few feet away from her customer, but close enough to be in conversation range.

"You know, that estimate is way off," Gary suddenly announced.

Rochelle glanced at him. "Which?" she asked.

"The mortality estimate."

"How so?"

"It's much higher. Could go as high as 95%, maybe even more."

Rochelle's eyes popped. She stared at him. "How do you know that?"

"I know a guy at the CDC. Good friend of mine, actually. I talked with him last night. Said our goodbyes." Gary looked down at his beer and drank deeply. He held out his empty glass to her. She refilled it and set it back in front of him.

"Are you saying that 95% of people who are infected will die, or 95% of *all* people, regardless, will die?" Rochelle finally asked him.

He stared at her for a long moment. He finally answered, "The latter. Some people will be naturally immune to the virus. And I've heard there's a few people who recovered. But most of us..." He set his mug on the bar with a thunk.

"What about the ones who self-quarantined?" Rochelle asked. "Do they have any hope?"

Gary tilted his head. "Maybe. If they isolated back in June."

The TV news anchor was still reading stories.

Congress has declared a freeze on all consumer prices, including gasoline, effective immediately. This is intended to combat spiraling inflation, which has led to widespread looting.

The White House also reminds all citizens of a nationwide dusk-to-dawn curfew. Citizens should stay in their homes after dark, unless they are directly involved in healthcare, police or first responder operations.

Rochelle suddenly wondered aloud, "How can the White House announce anything? I thought the President died. And didn't they evacuate the rest of the government? Isn't that part of continuity-of-government plans?"

Gary answered, "What makes you think they haven't? You seen any Congressman around here lately?" He glanced meaningfully around the bar and out the front windows.

Rochelle frowned. The pictures that had supplemented the newscast showed politicians in indoor settings. They looked like normal briefing rooms. Those could be easily replicated anywhere, including an evacuation site.

Gary added, "Why do you think I'm sitting in a bar in the middle of the day, drinking beer? All the bosses have disappeared. There's no adult supervision at the moment."

Rochelle considered him. "Where did you work?" she asked.

"HUD. I'm - was - an assistant deputy director. Not high enough up the chain of command to rate evacuation. Which is pointless anyway. As they've said," he gestured his mug at the TV, "we're all probably already infected. Most likely." His glass thunked back down on the bar, empty again. Rochelle refilled it again.

Gary slurped his drink some more. Rochelle wondered if she should offer him some food. The restaurant's chef had not come in for days and she was no cook. So, she rummaged under the counter for the little bowls and salty snack mix. She poured out some for Gary and set it in front of him. He smiled at her in thanks and starting munching on the peanuts and pretzels.

The TV broadcast widened its reporting scope.

In international news, dozens more countries have announced they are closing their borders to all travel. Airports have been closed indefinitely to all commercial travel. China has stationed its naval fleet at all major ports of entry, to prevent unauthorized entry or exit from the country. International aid groups are protesting this blockade, as shipments of antiviral medications have been delayed.

Gary glanced at Rochelle and said, "If there's anything left on your bucket list you want to do, better do it quick."

Rochelle was stymied. She opened and closed her mouth a few times, but couldn't think of anything to say out loud. She had a million things on her bucket list. Her whole life was on her bucket list.

Finally, she asked, "What's on yours, then?"

Gary raised an eyebrow, thinking. He rubbed his chin. "Well, obviously, Machu Pichu is out of the question. Among the things that I can actually still do, I supposed I could climb the Washington Monument. I always did want to see the view from up there." He glanced out the front windows, where it was still raining outside. "But not today, not in that crap. Maybe tomorrow."

Rochelle nodded in agreement.

They heard the back door of the restaurant open and close. A gust of cool damp breeze wafted through the main room. A vaguely familiar, unmasked face appeared where the back hall entered the main room.

"Hey, is George around?" the man asked.

Rochelle shook her head and said, "Sorry."

The man looked a little stricken, but not surprised.

"Oh. Okay. Just wanted to check on him. I'm Bill. I work at Whigs, up the street." Rochelle was familiar with the place. It was a restaurant just a block away. It focused on casual fare, especially barbecue. Their logo featured a pink pig dressed in an old fashioned Tory wig, like a British barrister. Their emphasis was on food rather than drink.

Rochelle introduced herself, "Rochelle. Good to meet you."

Bill looked about a little forlornly. He nodded at Rochelle's customer.

"What can I do you for?" Rochelle asked, in the tone she'd heard George use to greet his local colleagues. He had known most of his business neighbors and they were friendly competitors.

"Uh, well, not sure how to ask this…" he trailed off, while he tried to find the right words. Rochelle waited patiently.

"I guess I'll just have to say it. How are you guys fixed for food? Are you still serving?"

Rochelle shook her head. "Cook hasn't been in for days. I'm pouring drinks, but if you're looking for a real meal, I don't think I can help you."

Bill's face actually brightened at this. Rochelle studied him. He was probably a few years older than she was, maybe more. His head was shaved clean. His forearms appeared to be tattooed, based on the complicated bit peaking out from under his lightweight jacket. He was wearing a chef's jacket under the windbreaker. He was thick chested, with a slight stomach bulge. Probably a chef who regularly made sure his food was up to standard.

"Okay. Actually, that could work out. What would you say to some mutual assistance? One of my waiters and I just made a big supply run, but we're running out of freezer space. Do you think your freezer could hold some overflow?"

Rochelle shrugged. She hadn't actually spent much time in the kitchen. "I don't know. Let's go take a look."

Gary seemed content to continue watching the TVs, so she led Bill back to the kitchen. There were a pair of walk-ins, a refrigerator and a freezer, side by side. Both had steel shelving racks lining the walls inside. The freezer was about half full with vacuum sealed meat, bags of vegetables and a few large cartons of ice cream. The fridge was also about half full, but some of the items were not in good shape. Lettuce was wilting and tubs of chopped onions were giving off a powerful smell. The dairy products looked a little curdled too.

"Uh, yeah, you're gonna need to throw out any of the produce that's gone bad," Bill said.

Rochelle wrinkled her nose at the smell. "Sorry, I didn't even think about what's going on in here. I'm not a cook. I have no idea what the rotation cycle is on this stuff."

Bill nodded sympathetically. "Well, I can help you sort it out, if we could store some extra stuff in the freezer? Would that be okay? It's getting harder to find stuff, but the butcher at the restaurant supply store sold us most of his stock. If we freeze it right away, it will keep for a while."

Rochelle didn't have any objections to the plan, in concept. But the assumptions underlying it all confused her. What if Bill got sick? Who would cook the food? Who was going to eat it?

"So, can you help us out?" Bill prompted her. When she still hesitated, he added, "We'll steer the drinkers to you, if you steer the eaters to us. Quid pro quo. I'll feed you, too. Is there anyone else still working here, besides you? We can feed them, too."

That sounded reasonable to Rochelle. Did she know enough about this guy to trust him to do as he said? What if something happened?

Rochelle decided she'd just have to take a chance on things. She could run a bar, but food was not something she was properly trained for. She knew health codes were a thing, but she didn't know much else about them. Finally, she nodded.

"Its just me, at the moment. So, yeah, that sounds like the best deal I've had in a while." She held out her hand to him and he shook it, smiling broadly. Then she wondered if hand-to-hand contact was safe or not. Well, too late now.

Bill said, "Okay, let's start by clearing out the bad stuff and making some room in here." He grabbed the large rolling trash cart from the corner of the kitchen and started heaving boxes of wilted salad greens and slimy peppers into it. Cartons of milk and cream were tossed, but the cheeses were re-wrapped in fresh heavy duty plastic and stored neatly, labels facing out. Root vegetables like potatoes, carrots and onions were sorted through. Any that were getting mushy were tossed, but the good ones were put back on the shelves. Bill said he'd come back the next day and cook them so they could be frozen to keep for long term. He also pointed out that the hamburger buns in the pantry were getting moldy and needed to be tossed, as well.

Bill invited Rochelle to accompany him back to Whigs, to help sort things out. Seeing their activity, Gary told her to close out his bill for the day, he was heading into his office, now that he was sufficiently fortified. That meant she could lock up for the afternoon.

Confluence

She left a sign in the window, saying "Be back soon."

Bill and Rochelle spent the afternoon reorganizing things. In addition to the pickup truck's worth of meat to be frozen, Bill also brought her several cases of liquor and wine. They used the restaurant's old fashioned electric dumbwaiter to lower stuff to the basement. After several hours of running back and forth between the two restaurants, up and down the hill a couple of blocks and then up and down the stairs, Rochelle was shaking with exhaustion. The rain had slowed back to a drizzle, but she was still soaked. Bill insisted that she return to Whigs for a final trip so he could feed her a proper meal. He quickly gathered together a plate of pulled pork, reheated beans and a side of freshly made coleslaw. His own sandwich buns were gone as well, so she just forked up the saucy meat.

They chatted cautiously as they ate. She told him the basics of her background, that she was a grad student, had grown up in Manassas and came from a large family. He explained that his dad was the owner of Whigs and he was preparing to take over the family business. They carefully stumbled around discussion of how the Superflu was affecting their families. Instead, they lurched into the safe topic of favorite movies, which lead to a discussion of all time greatest hits. For just a brief few minutes, Rochelle almost felt like a normal human being again, having dinner with a nice person, talking about normal things. Then she looked around his dining room, where only one other table was occupied. She made the standard excuse that she should really get back to the bar and fled.

The evening crowd at the bar was thin, but committed to their drinking. Most customers appeared to have given up on wearing the face masks, but Rochelle put one on after getting back from Whig's. One of her evening customers was the military commander she'd seen a few days ago. Or was it weeks? It was getting hard to keep track. He was talking with another middle management type she didn't recognize. The second guy was in a shirt and loose tie, his blazer on the empty stool beside him.

The commander said, "I'm glad they got the nuclear plants shut down safely, but that's actually going to cause more problems in the long run."

The second guy answered, "Had to be done. We can survive without power a lot better than we can survive radiation poisoning."

The commander grimaced. "What about the fuel reserves? Is anything being done to release those into the pipeline?" he asked.

"Well, the emergency declaration means that yes, they are allowed to do that. But it's a question of who's actually going to turn the spigots on, physically. People are dropping like flies. I'm not sure there's anyone there who can physically do that," the man answered.

The commander said, "If you want us to keep rolling, keep moving the National Guard around, we need that extra fuel. Everyone topped off their cars and little mower gas cannisters, when prices started to go up…"

Rochelle was called away to the other end of the bar and didn't hear the rest of their conversation.

Throughout the rest of the evening, drinkers came in, poured beer or liquor down their throats until they were numb and then stumbled home. At midnight the bar was empty, so she locked up. She rode her bicycle home on the wet streets. She realized she'd never gotten around to showering that day. She'd been in her clothes for 48 hours straight. And had spent the day working hard. She could see her mother's nose wrinkling in disapproval at the smell. So once she got home, she immediately stripped the clothes off and hopped in the shower.

***

The next several days followed a pattern. She checked her phone in the morning. When she saw there was still no texts from either Paige or Nerissa, she had a crying jag. When that was done, she cleaned herself up and set herself in motion for the day. She rode her bike to the bar, where she waited patiently, reading, listening to the TV, or a radio station, if they were broadcasting. In the afternoons, she traded resources with Bill and his lone surviving waiter, Chuck.

Bill processed the rest of the surviving produce in Paulbicki's fridge. He cooked the pototoes and vegetables and froze them in small serving sizes, carefully lableled. He also had Rochelle collect bag after plastic bag of ice from the bar's maker and store that in buckets and boxes on the freezer's shelves. He said it was just in case they lost power. He said the freezer would stay frozen better in the long run, if it had more mass in it to insulate everything.

In exchange, if any of Rochelle's few customers wanted more food than she could provide, she sent them up the street to Whig's. Later in the day, after his own small dinner service was over, Bill would come in and sit at the end of the bar, nursing a soda. He said he worried about her customers getting too drunk to handle. He said he was there just in case anyone need to be bounced out.

There were few day drinkers, but Gary continued to come in for his liquid lunch every day. He made a new friend when Martin started coming in. Martin was a similar middle management type, working for the Office of Performance and Personnel Management, which was a unit of the OMB. He was frustrated because their database systems were breaking down and they didn't have anyone left who could get the servers working again. So he was escaping his frustrations with a long lunch break. After introducing themselves, Gary declared he was going to call his new friend "Marty" because it rhymed with "Gary." Sort of.

They traded shop talk and dropped names, figuring out who they knew in common. The conversation turned loopy, though.

Marty asked, "So what's next then? Where do we go from here?"

Gary glanced sideways at his new friend. "I don't know about you, but I'm just waiting for the zombies to rise up."

"Seriously? You don't think things are bad enough as is?"

"Things can *always* get worse."

"Okay, so if they do rise, are you joining up? You going to be the zombie, or the zombie killer?" Marty asked.

Gary looked thoughtful and said, "Geez, that's almost Shakespearean. 'To zombie, or not to zombie.'"

Marty prodded, "So, run the ROI. What are the pro's and con's?"

Gary considered the question. "Well, let's see. The pro's are that once you're turned, you don't seem to feel much pain. No more caring about what society thinks of you. You can let your personal hygiene standards go to hell. You don't need to worry about making the mortgage payment anymore. On the other hand, there's all that unrelenting hunger to deal with. And you'll never have the satisfaction of telling your boss to go to hell."

Rochelle had been casually listening to their conversation, without participating. She pursed her lips in disgust at the turn this was taking.

Marty saw her gesture and said, "What about you? Zombie or not zombie?"

Rochelle looked up at them. She drawled, "Well, if there's zombies, somebody's gotta be zombie chow, don't they? I guess that's me. Not fast enough to run, not bad-ass enough to mow them down."

The guys chuckled at her. But that sent them off into a comparison of the various types of zombies in movies and TV shows. Then they grabbed for the TV remote, which Rochelle had left on the bar. They wanted to see if they could find any episodes of the *The Walking Dead* on the cable channel archives. Rochelle snatched it out of their hands and put her foot down. No, they were not getting into a walker-stalker marathon, she insisted.

They were still pleading with her jokingly, when they were all distracted by the rumblings of large vehicles on the elevated highway outside the front door. They slid off their stools and stepped outside, looking up. A long convoy of military trucks and tanks was rumbling along the freeway above their heads, moving eastward. They held their hands over their eyes to shade out the sun as they stared up.

Gary asked, "Where do you think those came from?"

No one answered.

Marty asked, "Where do you think they're going?"

No one answered.

When the last truck had rolled slowly by, they went back inside. Rochelle poured them new beers. They did not go back to talking about zombies.

***

Later that evening, Rochelle told Bill about the convoy. He suggested they were probably parking on the White House front lawn. There might be more that had deployed on the National Mall, which had rolled in from the Pentagon. Rochelle asked him why.

Bill speculated, "Probably to restore order. There's been a lot of damage from the riots at the White House and the Capital. Haven't you noticed all the vagrants wandering around? I think there's a lot of people from the 'burbs wandering in. Their houses are getting unlivable, so they're hitting the road."

"I haven't really been over to that part of town. If it's not here or my apartment or on the drive to Manassas, I haven't been there in weeks," Rochelle said. "I know it's not far, but I've been pretty tightly focused here." She waved around the bar.

Bill was seated in his usual spot. A few other drinkers were scattered about, alone or in pairs, talking quietly. They weren't wearing masks anymore, so Rochelle had given up on hers too. The others were too far away to eavesdrop on at the moment.

Bill studied her. He twirled the glass in his hands in circles.

"I know we don't really know each other yet, but can I ask you something?"

Rochelle looked up at him, wide-eyed. "What?"

"What are you doing here? You have to realize this city is going to fall apart. Things are going to get a lot worse, before they get better."

Rochelle wanted to look away, but she felt pinned. "I could ask you the same thing," she finally said.

Bill wasn't talking fast, but he didn't hesitate, either. "I'm waiting. I'm waiting to see if I'm going to get sick or not."

Rochelle finally managed to tear her gaze away from him. "Yeah. Me too," she finally said. Then she added. "Besides, I don't have anywhere to go. Where *would* I go?" she asked plaintively.

Bill shook his head. "I don't know. Me, I was born and raised here. I don't have anywhere to go, either. But couldn't you go back to your family's place?"

"To all the dead bodies?" The words were out of her mouth before she could slap her hand over it. She shook her head. Her throat closed up. It had been hours since her last crying jag, but the dam was starting to leak.

Rochelle swallowed hard to clear her throat and said, "I think my sister died at home. I don't know what to do. The funeral homes are all full and can't keep up. I tried to call them. I tried to call the police to do a welfare check. I should really drive out there, but I guess I'm afraid of what I'll find…" her voice broke in a soft crack. She looked away, took a deep breath and wandered off to wipe something clean. Bill didn't say anything, but his quiet, solid presence radiated calm.

An hour later, Bill watched her carefully as she cleaned up after the last customer left. Once she locked the front door and turned off the neon sign, she turned to face him. He was actually a decent looking guy. She'd gotten a better look at the tattoo sleeves on his arms now and liked the art. He was stocky through the shoulders and his head was rounded, like a bowling ball. It made it seem like he had no neck, at a glance. But that didn't detract from his appearance overall. Rochelle wondered what her mother would think of him. And then immediately shut down that line of thinking.

Bill said, "Come on, I'll give you a ride home. It's not really safe to be riding your bike out there, this late. Technically, there's a curfew, you know."

"Yeah, nobody has tried to stop me, though. Can't remember the last time I saw a police car around the area."

They stowed her bike in the back of his truck and locked the back door. They headed northwest through the heart of Georgetown. Since she was just the passenger, she could focus on the buildings around her. When she was riding, she had been too focused on the road, avoiding potholes and other cars, to pay attention before. Now she noticed that many buildings had their windows smashed in. Some had already been boarded up, but many stood gaping open. Pharmacies, convenience stores, electronics and other high end merchandise had all been vandalized. They passed a corner gas station, which was brightly lit.

"That one is still working," Bill said. "The owner has a few friends helping him guard it. They're heavily armed. As long as you have cash, you can get gas there. How are you fixed for that, anyways?" he asked.

"Uh, my car at home is full. I'm not sure how much gas George's truck has at the moment. I've been riding my bike for the past week."

Bill nodded. "Check it tomorrow. Go to that place, if you need to top off. Take cash from the bar's till. They're not accepting cards." He pointed at the working gas station.

"Why not? Cards are still going through at the bar."

"Yeah, but then what? Money from the card goes into the bar's bank account. How you going to get that money back out? Are you on the bar's bank accounts?"

Rochelle shook her head and frowned. She'd not thought about that before. Crap. She'd have to start steering the customers into paying for their drinks with cash.

When they reached her apartment complex, Bill insisted on circling the neighborhood and the complex's parking lot, checking out the environment. He rolled down the windows and listened. He blatantly sniffed the air too.

"What are you doing?" Rochelle frowned at him.

"Checking for body decomposition smell. I've heard some people are dying at home since the hospitals are full and out of supplies. If somebody dies at home, alone..." his voice trailed off.

The dam around Rochelle's reserve cracked a little more.

Bill didn't notice.

"Okay, I think it's safe here, for the moment. Do you need me to walk you in?"

Rochelle looked at him silently for a moment. Did she? She decided the better verb was "want," not "need."

"Sure. Why don't you come up for a bit." The decision was made in a split second and she did not regret it.

She led Bill to her third floor apartment and showed him in. One dim lamp in the living room had been left on, but otherwise the apartment was dark. She offered him coffee, but he declined, saying he didn't want caffeine at this hour. She stared at him for a few moments.

Finally she took the few steps across the open space between them, to stand within touching range. He smiled a little bit. She smiled back at him, her lips only trembling slightly. He put his hands on her hips and pulled her to him. She tilted her head up, stood up on her toes and met his lips. They kissed for a moment. Then Rochelle s brain flashed back on the crazy day, the crazy week, the crazy month. The dam burst. She let her feet go flat again and pressed her head into his chest. She tried to suffocate the sob that was errupting out of her, but that just made her whole chest vibrate. Bill wrapped his arms tightly around her, gripping her hard. He bent his head over the top of hers.

They stood that way for awhile, while Rochelle sobbed out the latest flood. She felt a few tears land on the hair on the top of her head, too. When she was done, a minute or a year later, she pulled back and looked up at him. She knew her eyes were red and puffy. It was too dark in the room to see him well. She took his hand and led him to her bedroom. In the dark, they slowly removed each other's clothes. Once they were undressed, they slid under the covers of her bed and explored. They made love slowly, carefully. It was plain vanilla, ordinary. And Rochelle was fine with that. She'd had other lovers before. She was not averse to having one night stands or weekend flings once in awhile. She'd learned a few things, had even had some really amazing sex in the past. But right now, all she wanted was his firm solidity next to her, on her, in her. They fell asleep spooned together.

Meanwhile, somewhere in Chandler, Arizona...

Kevin spent several days ferrying truck loads of bodies to the landfill. He couldn't believe how many bodies kept pouring out of the hospital's bowels. The dock workers told him they had been piled up in the morgue rooms, as those entire rooms were completely refrigerated. The rooms had been filled up like a giant walk in freezer, bodies stacked upon bodies. The ones that had been there the longest were wrapped in black plastic bags, but then the hospital ran out of those and started wrapping the bodies in sheets. Except, they didn't want to run out of linens, so word had been sent to the preacher running the cremation pits to retrieve bags for reuse. So the bodies were removed from the bags prior to burning. The bags were rinsed out and sent back on the empty trucks that Kevin moved about.

To Kevin, the landfill was an unspeakable horror. Every time he opened his cab door to step down, he was hit with a wave of sickening smell that had him retching up the contents of his stomach nearly instantly. Bitter black smoke billowed into the sky that could be seen for miles around. Flies buzzed about, creating a faint humming sound. In addition to the burning organics of flesh and hair, any clothing the bodies wore was burned as well. Plastic buttons, hair clips, temporary medical bracelets, all contributed a toxic chemical odor to the miasma that made Kevin's subconscious hind brain scream *Danger! Run away! Don't breathe it in!*

Sometimes, the workers at the hospital gave him piles of documentation to take to the preacher. Lists of names. He handed these over to the preacher and switched trailers as quickly as possible, so that he could mount up and quickly drive away again. After an initial burst of activity to clear out the morgue, the routine settled into just two trailers making the loop; one at the landfill, being emptied, one at the hospital, getting filled. After the fourth day, it took the hospital a whole day to fill the trailer, so he only had to do one trip.

Kevin visited his brother and roommate too. They had been checked into a room, shared with two other people, the beds side by side, with only inches of room to maneuver between them. The noise of so many patients, visitors, hospital staff and machines was overwhelming. Smells of sickness and cleanser mingled. If Kevin's stomach wasn't already empty, thanks to the landfill stops, he was sure he'd leave a deposit on the floor right next to his brother. The smells and noise didn't seem to bother them, though. The day after they checked in, they were so delirious from fever that they were sedated to keep them calm. On the next day, they were nearly comatose. And on the third day, they were dead. Kevin discovered their cooling bodies before the nurses did. Staff shortages meant it took hours for anyone to respond to his requests to come take care of things.

Silent as a stone on the outside, screaming on the inside, Kevin watched the exhausted hospital orderly shove the bodies into bags. The bags had just been hosed out only hours before and not very thoroughly. They were still damp and probably still smelled. But by this point, Kevin couldn't separate any specific individual smells. New bodies, old gunk in bags, floors that hadn't been mopped for a few days, smoke at the pits, it was all just a toxic stew now. His nose felt singed to the point of no longer having any working nerve fibers

Kevin followed the orderly as he wheeled the latest two bodies down to the loading dock. Two more guys grabbed the bags at head and feet and swung them sideways onto the growing mound in the trailer. Cool air circulated from the front of the trailer, over the mound and out the open back doors. Kevin stood in the wash of air conditioning from the interior of the trailer, with his eyes closed. He focused on the feeling on his skin, trying to ignore the smell and lingering taste of bile in his mouth.

One of the dock workers nudged his arm gently. "Dude, you okay?" he asked.

Kevin nodded. "Yeah," he mumbled. He shrugged his shoulders.

"You look kinda green. You been able to eat? My buddy out at the pits says you've heaving your guts up."

"Yeah," Kevin mumbled again.

The guy held up a small zip lock bag, filled with a dozen joints. Kevin raised his eyebrows and looked sideways at the guy.

"For your appetite. You can't go on not eating, just so you don't puke. You gotta eat something, keep the blood sugar stable and all that."

Kevin eyed the guy a moment longer. "Go on. You can have it. No charge. Another buddy of mine raided a dispensary. It's good stuff," he said.

Kevin shrugged, nodded his thanks and accepted the bag. He stuffed it into his jeans pocket for the moment.

The guy pulled out another single joint from his shirt pocket and lit up. He smoked quietly for a moment, looking up at the slice of bright blue desert sky they could see from the dock platform.

The guy abruptly said, "You heard they're having a meeting soon? Downtown. Next weekend. Anyone who's left. Going to talk about what comes next, what needs to be done to clean up."

Kevin shook his head. "A meeting? Who? Is the government finally coming? Is FEMA or the CDC or whatever finally going to send us a cure?"

"Nah. There isn't any cure. It's too late to get a vaccine out. This is just local people. About keeping things functioning for the ones that are left."

"Is there going to be anyone left? Aren't we all just waiting our turn to get heaved in there?" Kevin tilted his head at the open trailer.

The guy shook his head. "Nope. They say some people are naturally immune. And some people just get better on their own. If we're not sick yet," he gestured between the two of them, with the lit joint in his hand, "there's a good chance we might not get sick at all. We're survivors."

"Huh," Kevin said. He thought for a moment. "Well, if we're survivors of the Superflu storm, then doesn't FEMA or someone need to come rescue us? Open up some camps, get us food and blankets and crap?"

The guy frowned back at him. "Dude, it's frickin' Arizona. What would we need blankets and camps for? I haven't even turned off my air conditioning at home yet! Long as the power stays on, I'm fine right where I am." He pulled one last lungful of smoke in and dropped the butt to the ground, where he crushed it under the toe of his boot. Then he kicked it to the bottom of the loading bay. He patted Kevin on the shoulder and went back to the double doors, where several more gurneys with bagged bodies had appeared.

***

Kevin thought about what the guy had told him, for the next few days. Fliers were posted about the hospital, announcing the city meeting to be held in the downtown park in a few days. When he wasn't actually hauling a trailer between the hospital and the landfil, he wandered aimlessly about town. Thanks to the one joint per evening that he smoked, he was regaining some of his appetite. When the last boxed frozen dinner was gone from the freezer at home, he drove to his nearest grocery store. He'd planned on just getting some microwave burritos, but there was no one manning the registers, even though the doors were open. He saw a stranger wandering the aisles inside. The stranger nodded at him, but pushed his overflowing cart away and out the doors without paying. Kevin shrugged and decided if they other guy could do it, so could he. The store was about half full. And what was left on the shelves was disorganized, shoved out of order, spilled on the floor. The perishable produce like lettuce had been removed, probably to a backroom cooler. Or a dumpster out back. The plastic milk cartons in the racks behind glass doors were looking slightly green. A rotten odor, different from the dead bodies, was wafting from the dairy area, so Kevin steered well clear of it. He decided that the entire perimeter of the store, from produce to meat and fish was best avoided. He stuck to the aisles of boxed, bagged and canned food instead. The freezers were still on, so he grabbed more microwaveable meals, enough to fill his freezer at home.

When he got home, he picked one of the boxes of a frozen tray of food, warmed it up and plopped on the living room sofa to eat it. He stared at the big screen TV mounted on the wall. It hung slightly crooked. They had never been able to get it to stay level. It'd be level for a day or two and then when they looked again, it would be slightly off-kilter. Bruno had pointed out that their heavy duty truck cabs made so much noise and vibration, that it was shaking the house, enough to un-level the TV. When not in use, they parked the rigs on the back half of the dirt acre that was their property. It meant they had to drive past the house, just 50 feet from the outside wall of the house. At the time, Kevin had just shrugged and decided to live with an unleveled TV.

Now, the TV was a symbol of everything that was fucked up. The world was supposed to be right, full, level and broadcasting. Sports, movies, cartoons. Kevin would watch just about anything, if it meant he could sit still for a few hours after a long bouncing vibrating haul. But now, nothing was on. He flipped channels, moving up and down the dial. In the really high channels, music stations were still playing. Some of the movie channels still played, too. But there were no commercials during the breaks, just long blank pauses. Once, he stumbled onto a news broadcast, where some girl was reading out Superflu statistics. She was just wearing a t-shirt, her hair combed, but obviously no makeup. Her microphone was clipped to her collar, blatantly obvious. It was clear she was just some studio employee they had grabbed and stuck in front of the camera, because all the professional on-air talent was gone. Sick or dead, likely.

Kevin watched her mumble and stumble through content she was obviously reading from a teleprompter. She cited quantities of known dead in major US cities. She listed which nuclear power plants had been shut down. She announced the deaths of major government officials, movie stars, sports heroes and random celebrities.

Through it all, Kevin kept wondering, *Who's going to fix this? Who's going to clean this up? Where are we supposed to go?*

Years ago, on an old console hooked to an old TV, he and his brother had played a video game about battling zombies. In video-gaming terms, it had been rather primitive, living on the bleeding edge of a growing technology field, back then. The back story to the game was that all players were part of tribe that had banded together to survive. The tribe had to find food, water, weapons and safe places to hide while recovering from injuries. The main story arc within the game had been to retreat from a major city and cross hundreds of miles to a hidden canyon in the mountains. All while fighting off ravening hordes of undead who wanted to feast on their flesh. Kevin and Kaden had learned all kinds of interesting game hacks for survival. Like, if they were short on water, to tap household water heater tanks, which usually held a decent supply in a closed environment. Or, that super glue could be used on minor cuts to hold them together. And of course, they learned to always make sure the zombie got a double-tap head shot.

To Kevin, now, that game seemed like a good model for the current situation. He spent half a day pawing through old piles of game cartridges and CDs, looking for it, to see if he could play through it again. Maybe it had been modeled on a real world location? Maybe the game designers were part of a real life group and had a real hide-out somewhere? If he could just find it, look through the documentation, or maybe find their website, there might be a clue about where the survivors could go. But he couldn't find the old game. His brother must have traded it in for newer titles.

Finally, he flopped back on the couch, frustrated, thinking. Okay, so he couldn't go through the game, but he was a modern day cowboy, right? That's what his Dad had said. He lived in the storied American West. There were canyons all over the place. Canyons were magical places. Carved out by flowing rivers, so they almost always had water at the bottom. And high rock walls for protection. So, which one? Not the Grand Canyon, of course. That was too deep, too remote, no way to drive to the bottom. The only way to get down there was by helicopter or mule. The upper end of the canyon was hundreds of miles up stream and was flooded by Lake Powell. The lower end of the canyon was Lake Mead. In between was hundreds of miles of rugged, dry, inhospitable country and Indian Reservation lands.

But there were other canyons around. Oak Creek Canyon was his personal favorite. Before he'd started trucking, he'd spent goof-off time during the summer at Slide Rock State Park. Cold water flowed over slick sandstone rock, warmed by the sun. High cliff walls rose on either side. Up the road from Slide Rock, cute little markets sold ice cream cones and fishing bait. Hiking trails wound up through the pine and oak tree forest. The West Fork of Oak Creek was especially scenic. The only problem with the place had been the crowds of tourists doing all the exact same things he wanted to do.

Besides Oak Creek, there was Sabino Canyon in Tuscon, Canyon de Chelly and several others around. He'd heard they were just as beautiful, if not more so. But Canyon de Chelly was on the Navajo Reservation and was sacred to them. Visitation was strictly limited, so he had not been there yet. Sabino was tiny, with virtually no habitation inside the canyon and a very uneven, rocky floor. Not good for long term sheltering, probably.

Of course, Colorado wasn't that far away. There were probably dozens, if not hundreds, of fertile, welcoming mountain valleys and canyons that could protect and support small groups. But it got cold in the Rocky Mountains. And if it snowed, they were nearly impossible to get in and out of.

Kevin nodded to himself. Oak Creek Canyon it was, then. It was fertile, sheltered and had running water. That was the place to go. Get people to bug out there. Assuming FEMA or whoever, didn't have a better option. Maybe they did? Maybe they'd ask him to haul a zillion tiny houses and livable trailers from some storage depot somewhere, to wherever everyone gathered. He'd run back and forth and they'd build a new city. He'd be one of the modern cowboys, driving the cows to market, only houses, not cows. Well, maybe later on there'd be cows. Because everyone wanted milk and cheese and burgers, too. Eventually.

Kevin drifted off to sleep, envisioning his 18-wheeler driving slowly behind a heard of gable roofed cows, painted yellow and white, with bright flowers in window-box necklaces. He tooted his air horn at them, to keep them flowing across a cactus-filled prairie.

Chapter 7

The morning after their first night together, Rochelle woke to find her bedside alarm clock blinking 12:00 at her. That was odd. She sat up and fumbled her phone out of her jeans pocket on the floor. The phone said 8:37. She reset the alarm clock. The movements had woken Bill, so she explained it to him.

"Huh. Must have had a power outage during the night."

Rochelle frowned. "How long do you think it lasted?"

"Dunno. Maybe a second. Maybe an hour. Check your fridge. Is anything warm?"

Rochelle fumbled a robe on and went to check. The apartment fridge and freezer were small, so her supply runs from days before had stuffed it to bursting. She had plenty of pickles, eggs, cheese and root vegetables on the fridge side. They were still cold.

Bill put his jeans back on and followed her into the kitchen. Morning light was streaming in through the windows.

"Bill, what's going to happen to the power, long term?"

Bill was eyeing her coffee maker. "Not sure. Actually, that's another reason why I haven't left town, besides not having anywhere to go. If any town is going to get restored, somewhere on down the line, it'll be this one. But we might lose power for awhile in the short term. That's why I stuffed the freezers so full."

Rochelle frowned at him in confusion.

"Huh?"

"A full freezer will do better at staying cold in the short term, than a half empty one will. The more mass there is, the longer it takes for that mass to absorb heat and come up to room temperature. And those restaurant grade freezers are better insulated than residential ones. That's why I told you to bag up the cubes from the ice maker and store them in the freezer, too. The freezer won't stay cold forever, obviously. But they'll do better than these." He patted the apartment fridge.

"In fact, I was thinking we should increase the mass in each of our walk-in freezers even more…" he added.

Rochelle frowned at him. "How? Another supply run?"

"Yeah. But we should also start freezing water solid, not just making cubes. Use it to fill all the gaps. Make ice blocks. Stack them, like an igloo, around the walls of the freezer. For insulation. How are you fixed for plastic containers? Any size, that we can fill with water and then freeze? It would be good to store the extra water, in a frozen state, too. You can thaw it for drinking, later on, too, if the city loses water service, along with power."

Bill was still eyeing her coffee maker longingly.

Rochelle started a pot for him. "I don't have a lot of plastic containers, but I can scrounge up whatever I have…"

Bill nodded enthusiastically. "You should stop in one of the grocery stores and grab as many plastic bags as you can. Freezer bags, shopping bags, whatever you can get. Layer a few together, if it's a thin grade of plastic, so the water can't leak out and use that to line cardboard boxes and freeze that. Keep them small, to start, so they freeze faster and then pull the blocks out of the boxes and do it again. Work in small batches. Space them out around the freezer, so they can freeze as quickly as possibly. Then move them to the outer walls and stack. Repeat and make as many blocks as you can, while the water and power are still working."

Bill's speed and energy were picking up, as he sipped his fresh coffee and thought out his new project.

"In fact, Chuck and I were talking about making another supply run this morning, to see if we can find more food that can be frozen, before it's all gone. We'll look for freezer bags and more containers, too," he said.

Rochelle sent him to shower in the tiny bathroom. When he was cleaned up, she sent him off with a goodbye kiss. He promised to come by the bar later with more supplies, after his own dinner shift was done, same as he'd done for the last several days.

***

Confluence

Rochelle didn't need to be at the bar until around 11 a.m. or so. After another quick check of the immediate surroundings earlier, Bill had told her it would probably be okay for her to ride her bike to the bar again.

In her neighborhood, it was fairly quiet. The huge old trees in the park next to her complex were starting to turn colors. The day was sunny but chilly, with some puffy white clouds that looked like they might clump up and turn gray later on in the day. Rochelle took the path through the park area and enjoyed the moment of sunny clarity. After the crying episode and the sex, she felt cleansed, empty and refreshed. Ready for the next challenge. When she reached the southern end of the park, she glimpsed a stream of people flowing past on the road above her. She was cruising downhill to the tunnel under the road. In the quick glimpse, she realized there were more people up there than there should have been. She was in and through the tunnel in a moment and then pedaling eastwards along the forested trail that followed the river. On the road above to her left she noticed more people, walking in small groups, carrying backpacks, folded up tents and poster-board signs on poles.

Rochelle frowned. What was going on?

She had to weave her way through several more groups of people on the main lower road, in order to cross their stream. Then back up the hill half a block, to Paulbicki's back entrance. Then she realized there were more clumps of people streaming up the hill, so she circled around and loitered in the back alley until no one could see her pull into the tiny back lot behind the bar. She brought her bike inside, instead of locking it to the lamppost outside. There were too many people about who looked footsore and exhausted, to leave a bicycle out, chain or not.

None of her regular customers were waiting outside the bar's front door, but people were wandering the elevated highway above, as well as the ground level street. She wondered if she should unlock the doors for customers or not. There were so many of them, hundreds, after weeks of quiet sparse activity. She wasn't sure she could handle a huge rush of new customers at the moment. She hovered at the back of the room, no lights on, hoping they couldn't see through the outside window glare into the dimness of the interior.

Rochelle waited for over an hour, before a familiar face appeared. Gary knocked politely on the front door, shaded his eyes against the glass and peered in. She moved forward and unlocked the door for him. Once he was inside, she quickly locked it back up again behind him

"What is going on out there?" she asked him frantically.

"Mass migration of the lemmings," he quipped.

"Seriously. What happened? Where did all those people come from? Where are they going?"

Gary seated himself in his customary spot at the bar and folded his hands in front of himself. She grimaced at him but poured him his beer. He took a long swallow and answered.

"They were the protesters at the White House and the Capital building. The military rousted them out this morning. That's what that convoy we saw yesterday was doing. Told them that FEMA was opening a camp at Great Falls Park. And a couple other places, too, but this crowd," he waved to the windows, "is probably heading to Great Falls. They were ordered to pack up their tents and clear out. They fired warning shots over their heads to get them moving."

Rochelle stared at him. "They fired on U.S. citizens?" She was appalled.

Gary blinked at her. "Well, *over* them, not *at* them. As far as I know, no one was hit. They were just trying to light a fire under their butts. Told them if they didn't have a home to go to, they should head for the camps. Food, water and beds would be provided. They should also expect to have to work to help set the place up."

Rochelle thought about that for a few moments.

"Do you think I should open up the bar? I'm not sure I can handle a huge rush, all by myself."

"You could make a lot of money today, if you did," Gary pointed out.

Rochelle nodded and a waggled her eyebrows at that. She

diverged, "Oh, by the way, I'm only taking cash, from now on."

Gary looked hurt. He'd been paying via debit card. "What? How can you do this to me? My card is good!" There was a teasing tone in his indignation.

"It's not your card that's the problem. The problem is that I'm not on George's bank account. You're paying and the bank is receiving, but I have no way to get to that." Thinking about that made her wonder how any of the bar's bills would be handled. Was anything on auto-pay?

Rochelle's thoughts returned to the immediate problem outside the door. "Hey, Gary, run up the street to Whigs and see if they're open yet. They might want to sell lunch to this crowd. Might be better to offer everyone solid food, not booze."

Gary nodded and slipped out the front door again to run the errand for her. While he was gone, she dashed upstairs to pick over George's paperwork again. The linen was really getting piled up. She wanted to find out if the linen service was still in business. Could they come pickup? Could she pay them in cash? She located their invoices and found a phone number. She dialed repeatedly with no answer. Crap. That meant they were probably not open any longer.

A couple hours later, Gary returned with a clamshell tray of lunch for her, a chicken sandwich and fries. Bill had sent it to her with a thank you note for the warning and said if she wanted to lock up and come help them, he'd be thrilled. There was safety in numbers.

Gary was slightly put out at having his drinking routine interrupted, but conceded he could drink at Whigs just as easily as he could at Paulbicki's. He explained that he liked the view of the river better at the bar. But today, people watching was a good alternative.

At Whigs, Bill quickly oriented her to his setup and she got to work waiting tables. They had a medium sized rush of weary protesters who had not eaten a decent meal in days. Rochelle eavesdropped on the conversational chatter around her.

"It's not right, what they did, forcing us out like that."

"I just want the President to come out and tell us what happens next."

"What President? I heard the new one died a few days after being sworn in."

"Do you think they'll have hot showers at the camp?"

Rochelle moved from table to table, refilling drinks, delivering food. As the rush wore down, Rochelle was able to draw some of the lingerers into a bit of conversation. A large group was seated at a series of tables pushed together. Telling them she was taking a short break, she pulled up a chair and sat with them for a moment.

"So, I don't really understand what anyone expected to accomplish, at those protests. Seems counter-intuitive, to gather a bunch of people together in tight, when everyone should really be staying home in self-quarantine. What was the primary goal?" she asked gently. She raised her eyebrows. The answers were all over the map.

"Well, we had to show them that we matter."

"They need to get the cure out to everyone, not hoard it for themselves."

"I'm just trying to support my fellow citizens."

"Self-quarantine is a joke, a fallacy. There was never any hope of containing this thing."

"I really didn't have anywhere else to go. My apartment building in Baltimore burned down. So I came here. And now we're going to the FEMA camp."

The Great Falls Park was about 10 or 15 miles away. A very long walk, for those not conditioned to it.

Rochelle asked the man next to her, "How long have you've been camped out on the Mall?"

"About a week. My car got stolen. All I have is this tent, bedroll and some clothes, rolled up in there." The man was African American, older, maybe 65ish. It must have been a hard slog, spending a week on the Mall in autumn, in just a tent.

Rochelle studied the man. Before she could ask another question, he went on. "Seems like they could have helped us out more, maybe provided transportation in all those personnel trucks they had there. Or at least grouped us together, given us directions. I'm not even sure I know exactly how to get to the park."

Confluence

A man seated on his other side patted him on the shoulder and said, "I know how to get there. Stick with me and we'll make it."

A woman a few seats away was still on Rochelle's original question.

"The real problem is that the government needs to be held accountable for what happened. Someone, somehow, let that virus loose and then they lied to us about it. Its a weapon, I know it. And we're not going to let them get away with it."

Rochelle squinted at her. "How exactly will you do that? Hold them accountable?"

The woman just stared back. The whites of her eyes shone clearly all the way around, as her eyes bulged slightly. She didn't answer the question.

Rochelle added, "I mean, they evacuated Congress days ago, maybe weeks ago. They're not even there. And the President died, too. Thankfully, he did that after he declared the state of emergency for the whole nation. That's what made it possible to setup these camps outside the urban areas. Seems like it might be safer and more sanitary, to spread them out, so they don't have too many people clustered in one location, until they're sure they can keep things running."

The woman glared at her. "What about the Vice President? He should have been sworn in."

"He died, too. Before the President, even. I don't think anyone is President now."

The woman didn't have anything to offer, after that.

The African American man next to her said, "All I know is, I don't think I can walk all that way. Why can't they just put us in the houses around here? People are dying all over the place. There's plenty of empty houses all around."

Rochelle answered, "What if people died at home?"

The man looked confused for a moment and then nodded in understanding. People who died at home would have to be removed, before someone new could move in. Rochelle heard the "order up!" bell ding behind her. "That's my cue. Gotta go. Thanks for talking with me." She nodded at the cluster of people together and scurried off.

***

Rochelle returned to Paulbicki's much later, but did not open for business for the evening. She updated the sign on the door to indicate that it would be open the next day. There were still a few people wandering about, people who did not look like locals just walking home from work. Some looked drunk already, stumbling and weaving. They must have found liquor elsewhere.

Inside the bar, Rochelle packed up a bundle of the dirty napkins and tablecloths and quickly loaded them into George's truck, along with her bicycle. She kept a careful eye on things around herself.

At her apartment, all was quiet again. She gave a silent mental thanks to Apurva and her parents, for insisting on selecting the complex for its isolated, quiet location. She carried the load of linen to the basement laundry room and started the load. It looked like no one had done laundry down here in weeks. Some of the machines had a light coating of dust on them.

Bill met her at the apartment after closing up his restaurant, as they had arranged. They shared a late meal and a bottle of wine that he had brought along. Then they went to bed together again.

For the next couple of days, they followed the same routine. They worked their respective establishments. She made ice and built an igloo in the freezer. In addition to the solid blocks, she also bagged more cubes from the bar's ice maker and piled them in the freezer, too. Bill reported doing similar things for his own restaurant's freezer. Each evening, he came to Paulbicki's after he closed his own place and stayed until she closed up for the night. Then they went home together.

The dispersed protesters flowed out of the city. The city grew quiet again as the resident locals maintained their self-quarantines, waited to get sick or just waited to see what happened next.

On the fourth day of their brand new arrangement, Rochelle awoke in Bill's bed, in his own apartment over his restaurant. They had selected the change in location, in the spirit of fairness and balance. His apartment was larger. It had been his dad's, before he had taken over. His dad had died in the hospital several weeks before.

When Rochelle came to consciousness, she realized she was hot. She kicked the blankets off, trying to cool herself down. Then she realized the sheets between them were damp. There was an odor of sweat in the air. She rolled over to look at Bill. He was still asleep, but his face was flushed and his breathing was labored, hoarse. Beads of sweat dotted his bald head.

Rochelle patted him on the face. "Bill! Bill, wake up. What's wrong? Do you feel okay?"

Bill groaned and rolled over on his side. He calmed after rearranging himself.

Rochelle tried again. "Bill, can you hear me? Wake up!"

"Mmph. I'm awake," he slurred, not opening his eyes.

"Bill, you're running a fever, I think. How do you feel?" A panic tone was creeping into her voice.

Bill blinked his eyes and looked up at her. He glanced around. "What time is it?" he slurred. Then mumbled, "Crap, I feel like I've been run over by a truck. What the fuck happened?"

Rochelle jumped from the bed and stepped to the bathroom. "Do you have a thermometer? I want to take your temperature."

"Dunno…" he mumbled again. He closed his eyes and slumped his head into his pillow.

Rochelle rummaged around in his bathroom and then the hallway linen closet, but couldn't find a thermometer anywhere. She went back to the bed. She tossed him a fresh pair of undershorts and said, "Come on, we have to get you to the hospital. Get dressed."

Rochelle looked frantically about for her cell phone. She thumbed it on, but there were no signal bars. She flung it back down on the pile of clothes on the floor and looked about. She spotted a regular phone sitting in a charger on the dresser. She picked it up. There was a dial tone, miraculously. She pressed the buttons for 9-1-1. The line rang and rang, but no one picked up. She smashed the phone down.

"Come on, Bill! You have to get up!" She envisioned herself driving him to the nearest hospital.

"Noooooo," Bill mumbled from his pillow. He turned his face upwards again. "Just leave me be. We both know what this is. Hospital isn't going to help."

"Bill! We have to do something!" She nearly wailed.

He reached out his arm and looped it around her. He pulled her down horizontal onto he bed. "I'm sorry," he mumbled again. He maneuvered her around to spoon her back to his chest and hugged her for awhile. His breathing calmed for a bit. She thought maybe he even slipped back to sleep for a bit. But then he started shivering and his skin went clammy cold. She squirmed out, to find the blankets that had been kicked to the floor. She piled those on top of him and climbed back under with him. When the chill passed, she got up and showered for the day.

He could get over this, couldn't he? Some people did, right? Some people got better. Maybe he'd be one of them.

By the time she'd showered and gotten dressed, Bill had truly fallen back deeply asleep. She made sure the comforter and blankets were well tucked. She wrote out notes explaining where she'd be. She left Chuck's note on the back door of the restaurant. The one for Gary and Marty she left on the front door of the bar. She advised them to do their drinking elsewhere for a few days.

For the next four days, Rochelle took care of Bill as best she could. She brought him batches of soup, made up from a packaged mix in Paulbicki's pantry. She sponged him down with cool water when the fever spiked. She turned on heating pads under the blankets when he got the chills. She held his hand while he shivered. She listened to his muttered hallucinations. But in the end, it did no good. The fever burned hotter and hotter, until his brain seized up. He trembled, his body held rigid and stiff for an eternity. Then his body slumped into relaxation when his heart stopped.

Rochelle went into another tail spin. She had no idea what to do. In a fresh state of numb shock, she picked up her purse and walked out of Bill's place. She returned to her own apartment and curled up in her own bed. It still smelled faintly of him. The good smell, when he was clean, not the stink of fever sweat. She knew she hadn't been in love with Bill. But she had certainly been in like with him. The sex had been good. He was kind. He knew how to run a restaurant. He would have made a good partner to face the Apocalypse with. And suddenly, just like her Mom, just like her sisters, just like her friends, colleages and the rest of her family, he was gone. Before she had barely even gotten to know him, he was gone.

Chapter 8

Rochelle might have stayed in a semi-conscious catatonia for days, mourning for Bill, if possible. But a day after his death, someone pounded on the apartment door. She thought about ignoring it. Tried to, even. But they kept on pounding. When she heard a key turning in the lock, she got up and flung on a robe. The room was cold. Why wasn't the furnace running?

She emerged from her bedroom, to find a stranger pulling a key from her open front door. Adrenaline flooded through her. "What the hell? Get out of here!" she screeched.

The stranger looked up. "Oh! I'm sorry! I didn't think anyone was in here! We've been going door to door, checking on the residents."

Rochelle reached furious in record time. "Get the fuck out of my house!" she screamed.

"Sorry! Sorry!" The man backed out and closed the door after himself. He had not been the super, nor any of the maintenance staff, she was pretty sure. She knew them all by face, if not by name and he wasn't one of them. Why had he come in? How had he gotten keys? She had not requested any services, so no one should be just walking into her apartment, without her consent.

The adrenaline pumping through her body was making her shake. She felt light headed and her vision was blurry. Her breath was heaving her chest in and out. She reached out a hand to grip the arched doorway to that led to the bedrooms. She forced herself to take a deep breath, from the diaphragm, slowly. Then again.

She walked to the couch in the living room and sat down carefully. She leaned over her lap, bending her head down, gripping her head, elbows on knees. After a few minutes, her breathing stabilized and she sat back on the couch.

Rochelle wondered if she should get a weapon of some kind. George had said there was a shotgun in his office. She had not pulled it out yet. She didn't know how to use it. She had no idea where she'd get a hand gun either, for that matter. Maybe a knife?

Who had that guy been? Why was he coming into apartments? What happened to privacy?

When she could manage to get up without fainting, Rochelle took a long hot shower and dressed in warm clothes. The apartment was still cold. She tried dialing up the radiator positioned under the living room window but nothing happened. Normally, it would start hissing and clanking, when someone turned it on.

After fortifying herself with a cup of coffee and a bowl of instant oatmeal, she pulled out her winter coat and walked over to the complex's management office.

She pulled open the glass door and heard the little bell above tinkle. Inside, she immediately saw the same man who had barged into her apartment, talking to another man seated at the reception desk. The second one looked familiar, a maintenance staffer. She glared at both of them.

"Why were you entering my apartment?" she blurted out.

They looked at each other, chagrined.

The first man spoke, "I'm sorry. I knocked and knocked, but you didn't answer. I thought the place was empty. We've been going door to door, seeing who's still here and who's not. It's the third of the month and rent is due. We need to check on people, to see if…"

"See what?" Rochelle snapped.

"Uh, well, to see if any bodies need to be removed."

Rochelle stared at them for a moment. "Not in my unit, they don't." She turned to leave, but the second guy behind the desk spoke up, "Uh, wait. Rent is due."

"What?" Rochelle whirled around and stared at them. "I'm on auto pay," she declared.

The guys looked uncomfortable. The desk guy said, "Uh, we need cash."

Rochelle was fed up with them. With everything. She was fed up with people dying, She was fed up with money that didn't mean anything. She was fed up with waiting for the stupid Superflu.

"No, you don't," she told them. "I'm sure plenty of other

apartments are empty. You can get what you want from those. But mine is off limits. So stay the fuck out of my place!"

Rochelle whirled around and marched out. She wished she could slam the door behind her, but it was on a spring hinge that closed slowly, gently.

Then she remembered the furnace. She gritted her teeth and marched back inside.

"And why isn't there any heat coming from the furnace?" she blurted out. The men were still staring at her.

The man behind the desk answered, "We had to shut down the steam boilers. Orders from the city. Not enough fuel or electricity to run them."

Rochelle shook her head in bafflement. "What the fuck? How the hell are we supposed to keep warm this winter?"

The guys didn't answer right away. She could read the message on their faces, *Uh, put a sweater on?*

Instead they said, "You need to make sure any other appliances you're not using are turned off, too. Lights, TVs, computers, stuff like that."

She stared some more. It seemed like they were speaking two different languages. Neither side was fully comprehending the other.

Finally she asked, "Why?"

"Rolling blackouts. Power is getting weird. They're not sure how much power we're going to get, during the next few months. So, if you don't need it, unplug it so it doesn't get damaged when power comes back on."

Rochelle nodded slowly. "Got it." She started to turn back to the door and then thought of one more thing. "Is the city still picking up trash here?"

The guys frowned at her. "Uh, I think so. They did last week."

Rochelle nodded. She'd try calling the city department, to see why the bar's trash had not been picked up.

With a final whirl, she indignantly stalked out of the office again, for good this time.

Back in her own building, she folded a load of linens from the bar. She'd accidentally left them in the dryer for a couple of days and they were wrinkled. At least no one had stolen them from the laundry room. In the apartment, she unplugged appliances. Toaster, microwave, coffee maker. The hair dryer she and Apurva had shared. Apurva's machines too: computer, alarm clock, cell phone charger.

At the bar, she opened up for the day. She cleaned up the bathrooms, which had been neglected for just a little too long. She cycled another round of ice blocks out of the box molds and set more water to freeze. The freezer barely had room to move now. The ice blocks lined the wall and were mounded around the frozen food. Everything was as well insulated from temperature changes due to power loss, as it was possible to make them. She checked the walk in refrigerator, but all the spoilable perishables had been removed, or cooked and frozen. The remaining things would keep for while yet. She carried out bags of trash. The dumpster in back was nearly full.

Marty was the first customer to walk in early that afternoon.

"Hey, doll. What's shakin'?" he greeted her cheerily. "Haven't seen you in a while. Been worried about you."

Rochelle glanced up. There were lines around the corners of Marty's eyes.

"Sorry," she said. She took a deep breath. No point in holding it in. "Bill got sick. He died. Yesterday." She stopped, thinking. Had it only been a day? It seemed longer.

"Oh, kid, I'm so sorry." Marty's face fell in disappointment. "I was hoping he might be one of the immunes, like us."

Rochelle stared at him for a moment. "Are you sure we're immune? Seems like it hasn't been long enough, to be sure."

Marty gathered a trembling smile and plastered it on. "Sure I'm sure. Have to be, right?"

Rochelle nodded once and let it go. They waited patiently for Gary, but he did not arrive that day. At dusk, Marty strolled out to be alone with his own grief. Rochelle realized she had never asked either of her most regular regulars about their own families, if they had recently lost spouses or children. She couldn't imagine bringing it up now, after all that had happened.

A few other customers wandered in for their evening drinks. This night, they were mostly solo drinkers, so there was no interesting conversation to eavesdrop on.

The only moment of curiosity was when a man sprinted past the front windows. A moment later, an olive drab military humvee with red and blue lights mounted on top whizzed by, siren blaring. One of the customers stepped out the front door and looked up the street where man and car had gone. After a moment, he stepped back in and returned to his stool at the bar. He shrugged and said, "Just making an arrest."

"What for?" Rochelle asked curiously.

"Don't know. Couldn't tell." He went back to his drinking. Rochelle didn't press for further details.

***

After several more days, Gary shocked them by returning to the bar. He was grinning broadly, his arms spread wide when stepped in the front door.

"You miss me?" he asked brightly.

Marty was seated in his usual spot. The TVs were on. One showed only a logo. The other was tuned to the classic rock music channel. Rochelle and Marty had been quietly working crossword puzzles from a pile of old books Marty had brought in.

"Gary!" Marty cried out in shock. "I thought you were done for!"

"I almost was! But divine providence must have smiled down upon me, because here I am! I woke up from the fever two days ago!"

Gary thumped his chest proudly.

The two new friends quickly caught up on recent news. Rochelle poured Gary his beer and listened to them chatter about his recovery for a bit. When they had calmed a bit, Rochelle asked, "Gary, did you ever get around to climbing the Washington Monument yet?"

He frowned at her a moment and then grinned. "Nope, not yet, but I definitely will now! As soon as I have fully recovered my strength. I will dedicate the climb to my successful recovery."

Marty asked, "Are you sure you can even get inside? Didn't they lock up all the monuments and museums, especially when all those protesters were there?"

Gary's face fell. "Huh. That's a good question. Hmmm…" he trailed off, thinking it over. "Anyone got any bolt cutters?" he wondered aloud.

At that moment, the power in the bar snapped off. The lights went dark. The TVs shut off. The hum of the beer and wine coolers under the bar ceased. Rochelle had never fully realized how much background noise the machines made until they were gone.

The three of them looked around at each other. It was broad daylight outside. Plenty of sunshine filtered down from the second floor skylight, through the stairwell in the middle of the room. They could see each other clearly.

"Oh, crap," Marty said softly.

"Now what do we do?" Rochelle asked the room, softly.

Before anyone could answer, the power snapped back on. The TV's restored their pictures. The coolers started humming again. The clock on the coffee machine blinked.

Everyone breathed a sigh of relief. But Rochelle's brain was moving in top gear. She'd stocked up on supplies at home. She had a mother-lode cache of toilet paper in the study den, so long as the maintenance guys didn't sneak into her place while she wasn't there. But she didn't have many flashlights. Or batteries. Some, but not a lot. Should she bring what she had left to the bar?

Gary spoke up. "You don't happen to have a generator here at the bar, do you, Roche?" he asked.

Rochelle shook her head.

Gary and Marty looked back and forth between themselves.

"What do you think of maybe trying to make a supply run? Check the nearest Home Depot, see maybe any are left?" Marty asked.

Gary shook his head. "I doubt there's any generators left. They probably all got snatched up when people bugged out. Besides, where would you get fuel to run them? But you might find some other stuff still in the stores."

Rochelle wondered aloud, "Can space heaters run on batteries? Is

that a thing? All the ones I've ever seen have to plug into an outlet."
She was thinking about how it was getting colder. The trees had
mostly turned brown and were halfway through with shedding their
leaves.

Gary and Marty shrugged in unison. They were desk jockeys.
They didn't spend their free time camping or roughing it.

Gary spoke up. "If you want to try a supply run, I'll go with
you," he said to Marty.

"Not sure what else you can find that hasn't been picked over, but
it wouldn't hurt to look, I suppose," he finished. They looked at
Rochelle, to see if she also wanted to come.

Rochelle considered. The bar was well stocked with bar things,
like booze. But she had not made any effort to collect other kinds of
supplies.

"Yeah, I suppose," she replied back. "We should go first thing in
the morning. Can you meet me here early?"

"Where do you want to go? I think the stores inside the D.C. city
border will probably be really picked over. We should try going
farther out," Marty said.

"I guess," Rochelle said doubtfully. She was wondering if she
should look up the restaurant distributor stores, instead of
conventional retail spots. But those fell into two distinct categories.
Suppliers providing food and suppliers providing cooking equipment
and paper goods. And liquor suppliers were a completely separate
thing all their own. None of those would have generators, batteries
or solar powered equipment. The camping supply places were
probably very picked over by this point, too.

"I guess we should try for a Costco or a Sam's Club. Even if they
don't have any more generators, they might have other stuff we can
make use of." She looked at the guys and they nodded.

They arranged to meet very early at the bar and try for a large
shopping complex in Sterling, Virginia. There were other locations
closer but they figured those would mostly be picked over by now.
They hoped the ones farther out from the D.C. metro core would still
be stocked, somewhat.

Confluence

***

Early the following morning, they squeezed into George's little pickup truck and set out. As Bill had advised her, Rochelle had topped off the gas tank days before.

The drive out to Sterling was uneventful. They saw a few cars moving about on the roads. Most of the trees were fully turned and were faded to a boring brown, if they even still had leaves on at all. Drifts of leaves were piling up along side the road, caught up on bushes or fences.

At the Costco, they were disappointed. Most of the useful gear had been taken already. Aside from some broken packages, most of the shelf-stable food was gone. Camping gear, tools and cold weather clothing was completely gone. In the back of the store, the decomposing produce was stinking up the cold storage room. Moldy dry bread was scattered about the bakery department.

They picked over the broken up packages and managed to salvage a few undamaged containers of pasta, bottled mayo and canned jalapenos.

Afterward, they prowled around the sprawling interconnected shopping centers nearby. Most stores had broken glass at their entrance doors. There were few cars in the parking lots. When they cruised past a Total Wine and More store, Gary insisted they stop.

"You know, if we can't get what we need on our own, we can trade for it," he announced.

Rochelle asked, "What do you mean?"

"How's your booze supply at the bar? How full is that basement store room?" he countered.

So far as Rochelle knew, neither of them had ever been downstairs at Paulbicki's. The sign on the door said "Employees Only."

"It's still pretty full, I guess. We're not exactly moving inventory like we used to," she answered.

Marty's eyes were lighting up, too. He was studying the broken doorway, trying to see inside the store.

Gary said, "Why don't we see what they have in there anyway and take back as much as we can carry? You can start asking for barter stuff, in exchange for beer and booze."

Rochelle frowned. "How is that going to get us a generator? I can see trading a pack of batteries for a beer, but not a whole generator."

Marty shrugged and said, "Let's go in anyways. May not be what we want, but we just might find what we need. Don't know until we try."

They parked the car in front of the store and trooped inside. They took care to stay clear of the jagged glass still poking out from the door frames.

Inside, it stank like skunked beer. Cases and bottles had been smashed, leaving sticky dried puddles. Their shoes stuck in the tacky residue, making it hard to walk.

But in spite of the damage, there was still a lot of unopened, undamaged product left at the backs of shelves. The really high end liquor was gone, smashed or stolen. But there was a decent amount of mid-grade wine and bottled beer. They grabbed shopping carts and filled up the truck's flatbed as much as it would hold safely, bemoaning the fact that they didn't have a bigger vehicle, or a tarp and tie-downs so they could load it higher. Gary and Marty were excitedly talking about coming back the following day for a second run when an unfamiliar car screeched into the shopping complex, rushed up to them and stopped in front of their truck.

"What the hell do you think you're doing?" the guys piling out of the car shouted.

Gary, Marty and Rochelle froze in shock. They didn't say anything.

"This here is our territory. We claimed it!" The strange men were strutting forward, puffing up their chests to make themselves look bigger.

Marty said, "Look, we don't want any trouble."

The lead guy sneered, "Oh, you're already in trouble."

Gary spoke up. "The door is wide open, there's no sign. There's plenty more to go around in there. This isn't even a fraction of what's left in there." He gestured back inside the store.

"Uh, no, I don't think so. Unload it, right now," the lead guy gestured at the pickup truck.

Gary made a motion with his left hand, to Rochelle, waving at her from behind himself. He was standing between Rochelle and the strangers, with their pickup truck in front of both of them. He was waving her closer, to get into the driver's seat.

Gary said, "Uh, no, *I* don't think so, or I'll be unloading this." He brought his right hand up, showing a metallic colored pistol, pointed directly at the strangers. Everyone stared at each other for a moment. He brought his left hand up to steady his aim.

"Ah, fuck it!" the second guy said. Then he added to his companion, "Dude, totally not worth it. I *told* you we should have posted a guard."

Rochelle's heart was pounding. Where on earth had Gary gotten a gun? She'd had no idea he was carrying.

The two guys looked back and forth at each other, at the store entrance and then at Gary. The first guy repeated, "Fuck it," and got back in his car. The second guy did the same and they peeled out, squealing their tires.

Gary relaxed a tiny bit and said, "Come on, we better get out of here before they come back."

They left the shopping district and headed back towards D.C. Rochelle had been hoping for a chance to stop in a clothing store of some kind, or maybe a shoe store. She thought it might be helpful to get some new pairs of jeans and sweaters, maybe a new winter coat if the stock was out on the store floor. And new winter boots. But the experience with the strangers had soured everyone's mood. They just wanted to get back to the bar.

Less than a mile away from the bar, they were stopped by a new military road block. It appeared suddenly when they rounded a slight bend in the road. A humvee and regular large pickup truck were parked kitty corner to each other, blocking the road. There was a large plastic tank on a cart hooked up to the pickup truck. To Rochelle, it looked like the kind that landscaping crews towed around to spray large quantities of weed killer or fertilizer.

Rochelle stopped her vehicle about a hundred feet away from the blockade. There were several armed, uniformed men behind the vehicles. They walked out and motioned to everyone in Rochelle's pickup to get out.

"What's going on?" Rochelle asked, when they were in talking range.

"Ma'am, I'm sorry, but we're under orders to confiscate all fuel supplies. We're going to have to siphon out your gas.

"Excuse me?" Rochelle's voice rose an octave in outrage.

Gary and Marty spluttered too, "What the…"

The head guy in uniform waved to someone behind him, who wheeled out a dolly, with a small portable generator, a fuel pump and a five gallon cannister stacked on it. One guy quickly slipped into the driver's seat behind Rochelle and turned off the truck. Another snaked a hose into the newly opened fuel port. They started up their pump, which began sucking fuel out of the pickup. It deposited it into the cannister. Rochelle thought the pickup held about fifteen gallons. It had been full before they started on their excursion. The pumpers might need two trips.

"What the hell are you doing! That's my gas. You can't just go and take gas from people!" Rochelle yelled. One of the nearby guards gripped his service weapon tighter.

The head guy said, "I'm sorry, but we're under orders to confiscate all fuel for conservation. It's going to be rationed out. Here, go to this website, to request an allotment." He handed her a business card with a website address printed on it.

Gary and Marty spluttered some more, too. They were just as angry.

"How are we supposed to get home?" Rochelle wailed.

"How are we supposed to get on the Internet?" Gary grumbled. It had been gradually fading from everyone's devices for weeks.

"There will be some fuel left in the lines, enough to go a couple more miles. That should get you where you're going." The head guy said.

Gary interrupted, "Who authorized this? Where's this coming from? Who's in charge here?"

Rochelle looked around. The two guys running the pump did not look at her. Two more guys were on the opposite side of the pickup, with machine guns pointed at Marty, Gary and herself. Marty was staring them down, but Gary was focused on the head guy in front of them. At least he'd had the sense not to pull out his hand gun.

The head guy said, "U.S. Army, acting on orders from Homeland Security."

Gary threw up his hands. "Seriously? Since when does the Army report to DHS?"

The head guy said, "Sorry, that's above my pay grade." He did look genuinely regretful, Rochelle observed. He didn't like having to do this. He knew it was pretty messed up. But he was just a grunt who had to follow orders.

They all watched while the pumpers filled the cannister, took it over to the big tank on the cart, emptied it and came back for another round. When they finished, they closed the fuel port back up and quickly moved back behind their vehicles. The other guys, aside from the head guy in charge, would not look Rochelle, Gary or Marty in the eyes.

Rochelle announced, "This is highway robbery! You should be ashamed of yourselves! There's plenty of abandoned cars laying around you can siphon from. You don't need to steal from living people who are just trying to survive."

The head guy's lips curled, but he managed to say calmly say "We're done. You can go on your way." He walked back to his humvee, started it up and backed away from the blockade just far enough that they could squeeze through. The road beyond was empty.

Rochelle, Gary and Marty got back into the truck and started it up. She watched the fuel gauge needle immediately drop to "E."

"Come on, we better move while we can," Gary said.

Rochelle shifted into gear and drove through the opening.

They made it the final mile to the front of the restaurant, but the engine was coughing and spluttering. Rochelle pulled to a stop in front. "I don't think it's going to make it to the back entrance. We'll unload it here and push it over to the parking spaces across the street," she said. She was frustrated by the disappointing day.

Confluence

They unloaded the truck and stashed the new beer and wine in the basement. Then they settled in at the bar to sample one of the bottles they had brought back. The guys urge Rochelle to share a glass with them. Rochelle didn't drink wine very often, but she didn't have the heart to turn her friends down. They drowned their sorrows together and wondered aloud when the zombies would come to put them out of their misery.

Inside her head, Rochelle toasted Bill's memory. She was grateful for his foresight on how to keep her freezer stocked and insulated. She just wished he could have survived longer to help with all the other crap she could sense was coming soon.

Meanwhile, in Oak Creek Canyon, Arizona…

Kevin drove his Jeep Wrangler up Arizona Highway 179, to the intersection with Highway 89A. It was a roundabout, those newfangled things that always confused him. Of course, there wasn't any competing traffic to cut him off, so he slowed down and steered to the right. He glided around the curve and within moments, he was on the slope the angled up to downtown Sedona. Piles of red rock rose up to the east and west. Behind the red rocks, buff cliffs dusted with sage green sloped up to Munds Mountain on the east and more unnamed wilderness on the west. The old town area of Sedona lined the street with art galleries, fancy coffee shops and jeep-tour outfits.

Kevin idly wondered if he could pick up some more detailed maps of the area in any of the tourist spots. Maybe if he had to come back through, he'd stop to check. But for now he wanted to get into the Canyon proper. No one in Chandler had listened to his ideas about bugging out. He'd asked at the town meeting. He'd asked the work crews. He'd asked at the cremation pits. No one had listened. So he'd come to check things out on his own and report back. With pictures, with information, maybe he could still convince them that this was the place to bug out to.

Kevin drove north. After less than a mile, the city stopped and the wilderness came right up to the edge of the asphalt. On his right, below the main highway grade, through the yellowing cottonwood trees, he caught glimpses of denser green foliage and flashes of water. Oak Creek was down there, he knew. For a creek, it was pretty big. As far as rivers go, it was pretty small. It tumbled and chattered over rocks the whole way down the canyon. A few side streets branched off the highway to wander the floor of the canyon. A few cabins and small homes were scattered about, too.

Official highway signs had identified the canyon as a national recreation area. But posters had been mounted over the signs saying,

"Canyon Closed. Turn Back Now." They were hand lettered, black paint on white cardboard. That didn't look very official to Kevin. He kept on driving.

About a mile north of the Sedona city limit, the Midgley Bridge appeared in gaps between the foliage and cliffs. Kevin slowed down even further. Just before the bridge, the highway cut through one of the smaller red rock formations, forming a narrow gap with thirty foot high walls on either side. Before entering the rock cut, a white bed sheet, with more hand lettering, was staked to the rock. It said the same thing in foot high words: "Canyon Closed. Turn Back Now."

Kevin frowned. There wasn't a good place to turn around, in front of the rock cut, but he knew there was a scenic pull out on the far side of the bridge, where tourists could take pictures.

Kevin slowed his Jeep to a crawl and drove around the slight bend through the rock gap. As he cleared the bend, he saw that a makeshift gate of steel poles had been erected in front of the near side of the bridge. Several cars were parked on a small patch of level gravel to the left of the gate. On the right, a low, old rock wall tried to keep cars from going over the cliff and into the creek below. As Kevin rolled to a stop in front of the gate, two men opened the doors of the nearest pickup truck and stepped out. They were carrying guns; one had a long rifle and the other had an AK-47 cradled in his arms, strap over his shoulder.

Shit, Kevin thought. What had he gotten himself into?

Kevin rolled down the window of the Jeep and waved to the men approaching him. They stopped about twenty feet from the truck. The one with the rifle was fairly tall, stocky, with a thick mustache and stubble on his cheeks, dressed in jeans and a padded denim shirt layered over a t-shirt. The man with the AK-47 was dressed the same, but was shorter and no mustache. They both wore baseball caps and dark sunglasses to shield themselves from the sunlight. It was a chilly but clear winter morning in the Canyon and the sun was bright. They also both had medical masks tied around their necks, ready to pull up over their mouths and noses.

Machine gun man spoke first, "Son, did you not see the signs?

The canyon is closed. You need to turn around and go back."

Kevin stared at the men for a moment. He had to work hard to bite back a sarcastic reply, so he didn't say anything at all for a moment. The man's assault rife had been crossed over the his body, pointing downward at nothing in particular. When Kevin didn't answer right away, the gun came up, leveled at his Jeep.

The man repeated, "You need to turn around and go back the way you came."

"Uh, I can't really turn around here. No room," Kevin finally said.

"Then drive backwards until you get to one of the turn offs," said the man.

Kevin looked forward over the gate in front of the bridge. In the distance, behind one of the hills, he could see a thin plume of white smoke trickling up through the still air. Camp fire? Maybe a fireplace in one the cabins by the creek bed?

He looked back at the two men. Behind them, he could see several more men getting out of their trucks, with assorted guns in their hands.

Kevin finally spoke, "Yeah, why is the Canyon closed? I just wanted to take a look around? It looks to me like there's still people up there."

Machine gun man said, "That's none of your business. Now backup and get gone."

Kevin scowled suddenly. "Now wait a minute. Who the heck are you guys? What gives you the right to tell me I can't drive on state land? You don't look like no park rangers to me. I got just as much right as anyone else to go visit Slide Rock or West Fork, if I want to."

Machine gun man took a few steps closer to Kevin. He raised the gun and gripped it two handed. He gestured with it. "This gives me the right," he said. "And I say, 'the Canyon is Closed'!" he snarled.

Kevin felt beads of sweat pop out in his hair line. He forced himself to sit still.

The man with the rifle spoke up and said, "Javier, take it easy." He took a couple of steps closer as well and looked at Kevin.

"Look, kid, we got here first. We've claimed the Canyon for our people. Some of us own property here, from way back when. Been held in the family since before this became state forest land. Others... well we just came here to get away from the Superflu. Self quarantined. I'm sorry, but you're going to have to move along and find someplace else."

Kevin was thinking, *This is all bullshit* and was struggling not to shout it out loud. It was just like it had been in Chandler. People telling him what to do, without any explanation, any reason. Without telling him *why*. His right hand gripped the steering wheel hard. He kept his left hand on the window sill, trying to appear relaxed and non-threatening.

Finally, Kevin said, "You can't possibly be full up. Surely you need more people. I can help. I can work hard."

Don't say 'bodies.' Please don't ask me to haul any more dead bodies around....

"I got skills. I can contribute," Kevin added.

The two men looked at each other.

The tall man asked, "You wouldn't happen to be a dentist? Dental technician, maybe?" He looked momentarily hopeful. He turned to the other man, the one called Javier. "We still need more medical skills in the group," he commented.

Kevin's face fell. "Sorry, I'm not a dentist," he said.

"So what exactly can you do?" asked Javier.

"I can drive!" Kevin exclaimed excitedly. "I'm a trucker. Long haul big rigs. But I'm trained on other rigs, too. Construction vehicles, bull dozers, cranes, all kinds of stuff." He smiled at the two men. Javier frowned, but the other man looked thoughtful.

Javier had lowered the AK-47 to point at the ground. "No, we don't need any construction work done at the moment. We can drive trucks, too. It's not that hard. Especially with no traffic around anymore."

Kevin's face fell again. "Surely there must be something you need."

At that moment, a car appeared from around a bend beyond the bridge ahead. It sped up to the bridge and drove straight up to the

124

gate blocking it's way. A pretty young woman jumped out from the passenger side, waving frantically.

"Dad! Dad, come on! Its Mom. She's having seizures! You have to come. Its time!" Her tone was high pitched, tinged with panic.

Kevin looked back at the two men she had been gesturing at. The tall man with the rifle sagged a little. Then he started running toward the woman, leaving Javier behind. He squeezed through the side gap in the gate, just wide enough for a body, but not a car. He climbed into the back seat of the car. The driver, who Kevin could not see clearly through tinted glass and sun glare, reversed the car and backed off the bridge. He swiveled the car around in the larger turn-off on the other side and then peeled out at speed, spitting gravel and fishtailing back up the highway. Within moments, they were gone.

Kevin looked back at Javier, who had been joined by two more armed men from the other pickup trucks.

Javier looked back at Kevin. "So, as I was saying, it's time for you to be on your way."

Kevin stared back, trying to think of how to salvage his plan. He'd been so sure the Canyon would be the safe place, a place to hide out, until the Superflu was gone. But it seemed like the disease was in there, too. Wasn't there any place people could go, to get away from it?

He sat in silence for a moment, not doing anything, just thinking. A loud bang sounded from above, behind and to the right of his Jeep. A scatter of gravel clattered down the rocks to the right side. Kevin started, looking around wildly.

Javier spoke up. "That was a warning shot, from my man up on the rocks up there." He pointed at the taller cliff wall, to Kevin's left, behind the Jeep. Kevin had not noticed any men on the rocks above, before.

"And there's more up in the hills all over here. We're watching everything that goes on in this canyon, from Sedona northward. We don't want to hurt you, but we'll defend our families. We don't need what you're offering, so you need to move on."

Javier stepped back a few feet, to give him room to turn the Jeep around. It took Kevin a few back and forths, before he got the snub nose of his vehicle pointed southbound again. The sun glared in his face, so he put on his own sunglasses. He put the vehicle in gear and slowly drove back the way he came, thinking hard.

Kevin drove back through Sedona, but on a whim, he impulsively took the turn off to go up Schnebly Hill. The first short segment was paved, but that quickly gave way to a gravel path, which turned into a rutted track. The road was notorious as one of the most difficult, hazardous wilderness trails in the state. Good thing he had picked out a Jeep Wrangler with high clearance at the dealership. One of the crew guys in Chandler had told him the doors to the dealership were unlocked. Anyone could take anything they wanted. Nobody cared anymore about little details like bank loans and vehicle registrations. He'd needed a new small vehicle, after totaling his pickup. The Jeep was sturdy, powerful and could carry enough extra fuel along with camping gear and supplies for a few weeks on the road.

He navigated over boulders and across ravines, eventually climbing thousands of feet up the cliffs to a scenic overlook above Sedona. The little tourist town was scattered below him. Downtown was reasonably tidy, with streets and buildings laid out in an organized grid. But the west and south sides sprawled over the hills. Large tan and white houses dotted hillsides along winding black asphalt roadways. Churches, resorts and shopping plazas lined the major streets. A small airport claimed a mesa top to his southwest. To the north, the canyon wound into the hills. The burbling creek had cut a deep path through the soft land over many millenia.

Kevin put the Jeep in park and climbed out to study the view. He was pretty sure he was too far away for any of Javier's men to see him. He leaned his butt on his bumper and thought.

It was so frustrating, to get turned away from what he wanted. He'd been so sure that the canyon would be the safe place, the place to hide out, until things got better. But obviously, other people had also realized the same thing. And they'd gotten here first. Why hadn't he acted sooner? Why hadn't he come here weeks ago?

Well, duh. He'd been tied up with the last few runs. Their clients had begged him to make one last run to deliver some critical shipment to some warehouse in Seattle. On his the run, he'd watched the traffic disappear off the roads, as people got sick. He'd rushed frantically to get back to Chandler, racing through Oregon, California and across the desert, hoping to get to his Dad before it was too late. But of course it had been much too late. He should never have taken that last run in the first place. If he'd just passed on the job, he would have still been at home.

And then what? He'd have been the one to take his Dad to the hospital? And then taken Kaden and Bruno next? Would that have changed anything? It was pretty obvious now, that it wouldn't have stopped them from dying. Of course, they would have *known* it was Kevin looking after them. That might have counted for something.

But it was all just shit now. It wouldn't have changed the course of events, no matter what he had done. They'd been infected and almost nobody got better. What had that doctor said? 3% survival rate? It was probably a miracle he hadn't gotten sick himself. Maybe he still would get sick. But so far he felt normal, as healthy as he ever did. He'd never really thought much about his own health, didn't pay attention to minor details. But others had said that getting the flu was like being hit by a truck. Came on sudden and knocked you flat. If he had it, he'd know when it started. But until then, there was nothing to do but just keep on truckin, as his Dad liked to joke. He just had to roll with the punches, flow with the stream.

Kevin sighed and climbed back into his Jeep.

Chapter 9

November was an ugly month. It was gloomy and rainy. It was cold. It was lonely. It was boring. Aside from Gary and Marty, few customers were wandering into the bar. Each day was a struggle. All Rochelle wanted to do was stay curled up under the warm blankets. Her apartment had grown distinctly chilly. It was getting hard to get hot water out of the taps, too, because the maintenance guys were not keeping the centralized water heaters fully powered. She considered relocating to the bar permanently and sleeping on the couch in the office. The bar building seemed to do a better job of regulating it's internal temperature, with minimal help from the central heating system. The thick brick walls and adjacent buildings kept it well insulated. If the sun shone, it warmed up the front bar area pleasantly during the day, making it easier for the central heating to supplement it after hours. But so far, she couldn't find the internal motivation to make the effort to move her stuff from the apartment to the bar yet.

Rochelle's car at the apartment still had gas, but she was too scared to take it out, afraid that another military raid would leave her stranded much farther from her stomping grounds. So she had resorted to riding her bike almost everywhere, in spite of the cold and the rain.

About a week after the fuel seizure, Rochelle was cruising down the main thoroughfare, heading downhill. A few blocks before reaching the bar, she noticed the sound of a large vehicle behind her. She stopped, turned and looked. It was a big garbage truck, backing up out of an alley, beeping its warning.

"Hey!" she yelled at it. She waved her arms, yelling louder, "Hey! Hey!"

The truck was several city blocks away, so she turned her bike around and rode back up the hill towards it. She waved one free arm as she approached, still calling out.

The truck stopped. Rochelle could see a driver inside the truck, staring out at her. She rode up to the driver's side. He rolled down his window.

"Are you doing pickups?" she asked, slightly out of breath.

The driver stared at her with that "Well, duh!" expression.

Rochelle added, "The dumpster behind my bar is full and stinking to high heaven. Can you come empty it? Please? Pretty Please?" She tried smiling, but the expression felt foreign on her face.

"Yeah. Where?" the driver asked.

"Can you follow me? It's just a couple blocks that way," She pointed downhill.

The driver waved at her to lead the way. She circled her bike around and headed back downhill. The truck finished backing out of the alley into the main street and shifted into forward gear.

Rochelle pulled into the alley behind Paulbicki's and waited for the truck to catch up to her. She looked around, making sure the garbage truck could approach the dumpster easily. One of the most recent bags of trash had fallen from the top of the pile in the dumpster and was sitting on the ground in front of it. Rochelle hopped off her bike, grabbed it and quickly heaved it up to the top again. A wash of sickly sweet stink erupted. Rochelle could see some dark fluid sloshing around in the bag she had just tossed. A flash of motion at the base of the dumpster caught Rochelle's eye. A rat scurried away from her, running farther along the alley.

The garbage truck made the slow turn into the alley and lowered its overhead arms. They inserted into the dumpsters brackets, lifted the container up and over and let the contents fall into the open truck bed behind the driver's compartment. Bags and loose bits tumbled quickly out. The gripper arms gave one quick jerk, to make sure everything was dislodged and then set the dumpster back down.

Rochelle stepped around into the driver's view. He was already backing up, warning sounds beeping. She shouted "Thank you!" several times. She wanted to tell him to come back later, for free beer, but the noise was too loud. The driver just waved. He didn't back all the way to the main street, though. Instead, he straightened the truck and continued forward down the alley, following the direction the rat had taken. Rochelle watched him drive a few buildings down and then stop at another dumpster. He repeated the maneuver, emptying another container that was only half full to start with. The truck proceeded on down the alley, emptying several more, before making a right turn on the next street over and disappearing from view.

Rochelle wondered if he was city service, or private contractor. There had not been any labeling on the truck. She wondered if he would have gone down her alley and picked up, even without her hailing him down. Mostly, she was just grateful that that particular problem had been solved for the moment. She was still staring down the alley after the disappeared truck, when she heard a scuffle and then a soft squeal. A moment later, a medium size dog appeared from behind a section of privacy fence several buildings down, with the rat in its mouth, legs dangling limply. The dog glanced her way, then turned in the opposite direction and trotted away. Rochelle shuddered and went inside.

Hours later, around dusk, a familiar face popped in the front entrance. Chuck, Bill's waiter at Whig's. She hadn't seen him in days, since before Bill had gotten sick. She was only casually acquainted with him, so she greeted him awkwardly.

"Hey, Chuck. Good to see you."

He nodded at her. She had told him when Bill had gotten sick, but had run away after he died, without making any effort to notify Chuck, or anyone else. A wave of guilt washed over her. She should have done something more. She just didn't know what to do, then or now. While Bill had been sick, she'd tried 9-1-1 a few more times, with no success. She managed to find a coroner's office phone number in a old phone book, but no one answered that line, either.

"Hey, Rochelle. Listen, I wanted to let you know, we've got a new cook at Whigs, now. A buddy of mine, from another place I used to work at, awhile ago."

"Really?" Rochelle was surprised.

"Yeah, she's a good chef. Uh, I was hoping that the freezer arrangement is still in place?" He raised his eyebrows, asking.

Rochelle nodded. "Yeah, I don't have any problems with that. It's mostly Whig's food in there. I can't cook it. But will the other part of the deal still apply? Can you send drinkers and any excess booze over here after they've eaten? And maybe some food for us?"

"Yeah! Sure, we can do that. Any time you want. Or you can come over to our place, too, you know." Chuck nodded back, relieved that she was cooperating. "She starts tomorrow. She's gotta get her stuff. She was living over in the Southeast side. But she's going to move into Bill's Dad's place upstairs."

"Uh…" she trailed off, not sure how to ask what had happened to Bill's body.

Chuck nodded at her. "Yeah, I know. The body removers came and took him away."

Rochelle frowned in confusion. "The what?"

"The body collectors. They've got trucks going around, picking up the people who died at home. Hopefully before they start to stink too much."

"Oh." She squinted at him. "How does that work, exactly? How did you notify them?"

"Uh, I don't know. They came walking in the front door of the restaurant, a couple of days after he died. Told me what they were doing and asking if there was anything or anyone they needed to take care of in the area," Chuck answered. "So I sent them upstairs. Presto, body is gone."

"Huh. That's kinda weird. Nobody's come in here, with that offer. Awfully convenient timing."

"Hey, I can't explain why, I can only tell you what," Chuck finished. He nodded, patted the edge of the bar and turned to walk out the door. He was gone before Rochelle could ask what the collectors were doing with the bodies, after picking them up.

***

One evening, Rochelle was serving the usual assortment of three or four isolated customers, when the military commander she'd seen several times before returned. It had been a couple of weeks since she had seen him. The scene at the blockade, where her fuel had been stolen out of the truck, right in front of her, replayed in her mind's eye. She was angry all over again.

He took an open stool at the end of the bar. Rochelle picked up the bottle of bourbon that he liked and a clean glass. She set the glass in front of him, but did not fill it. She set the bottle on the bar between them, but held her hand on it. He looked up at her, eyebrows furrowed.

"I've got a bone to pick with you," Rochelle announced.

He raised his eyebrows at her. He was dressed in camouflage fatigues. There were patches on his chest, but she didn't know how they translated to rank. There was a name badge, too, that said "Wenrick."

"Can I help you?" he asked her cautiously.

She wasn't sure there was a polite way to ask, so she decided to just bite the bullet. "What's your rank, soldier?"

He stared at her and cocked his head. "I'm Colonel Derrick Wenrick, U.S. Army."

Rochelle considered. "Colonel" sounded pretty high up to her. She wasn't sure if the guys who had seized her gas were Army or not.

"My friends and I were stopped by a military blockade a week ago. They stole all the gas in my truck." She glared at him.

She could sense the cringe in him, even though his face did not move.

"Is this an ongoing, authorized practice?" she asked him tightly.

The colonel thought for a moment. "Technically, yes. An ill-conceived, poorly executed one, but a legitimate operation." He paused, then asked, "Can you tell me what happened in detail?"

Rochelle explained. He nodded and grimaced. "Yes, they were following protocol. As I said, it's not being handled well. Not my division. I argued against the operation, but they went ahead with it anyway. We're in a major fuel crunch and we're scrambling to move resources around. Collected fuel is being routed to the remnants of FEMA, the National Guard and others. They're trying to get food and supplies out to more remote locations that got caught short handed. But they're running out of fuel faster than anything else. They've got tons of MREs to deliver and some medicines, too. But not enough fuel to get the trucks around. So they've taken to siphoning fuel from civilian vehicles. Inside the city limits here, the thinking was that people can walk to wherever they need to go."

Rochelle thought about that for a few moments.

"And is that how you get around town? Walking? Last time I checked, the Pentagon is a couple of miles away."

"Actually, yes. I live in one of the condos on the next block over. I jog over to the Pentagon in the morning, for exercise and walk back at night. Unless one of the patrol groups is heading out in this direction and the weather is bad. Then I catch a ride with them."

He looked a little sheepish, apologetic. "Hey, you weren't hurt in the stop'n'seize, were you?" he asked her.

She shook her head. "No. Just scared. And pissed. We were moving more resources around ourselves," she answered. She waved the bottle in her hand to demonstrate what she meant.

The colonel looked down into his empty glass. "I'm sorry they put you in that position. I wish it could have been handled better. With the collapse of the news services and social media sites, we don't have a good communications tool to let survivors know what's going on." He looked like he wanted to say more, but didn't.

Rochelle continued to eye him for a moment longer. She finally poured a finger of bourbon into his glass. She put the bottle away and turned to finish unloading a fresh tray of glasses. Out of the corner of her eye, she studied him.

The commander downed his drink in one swallow and then rubbed his thumbs over his low-ball glass, studying it. Finally, he gestured for her to pour another.

The colonel pursed his lips for a moment and then spoke again, "So, I don't mean to pry, but I gotta ask. How are you fixed for things here? These glasses look fresh. I mean, that's good. It's great, in fact. It's good that you're keeping up with basic hygiene."

Rochelle frowned. "I just ran the dishwasher last night. There's a big industrial one in the kitchen. Heats up to sterilization temperatures. You're not worried about catching the flu *now*, are you?"

"No, no, that's not it." He hesitated. "Listen, if you've got any way to store some extra water in empty bottles or buckets or things, you should fill them up."

Rochelle looked at him, confused.

The colonel continued, "I've heard through the grapevine, that city water is compromised. The blackouts we've been having? It's affecting the pumps. There's a good chance that water pressure is going to drop to almost nothing in a few days or weeks. And even if you can get water from the taps, there's a chance it might not be as clean as it used to be."

He waited for that information to sink in. The gears in Rochelle's head started to turn over. George had left several stacks of old buckets in the basement storeroom. They used to hold pickles, condiments, sour cream, etc. When emptied out, George would wash them carefully and then stack them in the basement. He had said, 'you can never have too many clean buckets.'

Rochelle had not used them for the ice block igloo project, because they were too large. It would have taken too long to get five gallons of water to freeze solid and even when it did, the pressure of the expanding ice would have cracked the buckets, making them useless for the next round. It was actually more efficient to use the smaller cardboard boxes, which could flex with the pressure and freeze their plastic lined contents more quickly. But she had not thought about filling the buckets and leaving them liquid. Even just cold in the refrigerator, they could provide some insulation, she supposed.

The commander went on. "I've noticed the toilets in back are not the tank kind. It's going to be a real pain to flush them, if the water runs dry. If you pour extra water into the toilet, when it's flushed, it keeps the pipes lubricated and you can keep stuff moving along into the sewers. But you gotta do it as soon as someone flushes. Don't let things sit around and dry out or get hard. That will make it much harder to flush them." He paused, letting that sink in.

After a moment, he continued, "Worst case, you could haul river water from out there and keep that to flush the toilets. Real pain in the rear, but it would work. Then you can keep cleaner water for washing. And water for drinking or ice cubes in drinks should be boiled, too, just in case."

Rochelle nodded. She finally responded, "Is the water in the taps right now okay?"

"For the moment, for flushing and washing, I believe so." The colonel nodded.

"What about ice cubes made weeks ago?" She was thinking of Bill's instructions to build up as much ice reserve in the freezer as possible.

"Weeks ago? It should be fine," the colonel confirmed.

Rochelle nodded back. She went downstairs and located the stacks of buckets. Some were round, some were square. The round ones came in two sizes, three and half gallon and five gallon. Most buckets were white, but a few were green or blue. The oldest buckets at the bottoms of the stacks seemed slightly yellowed and brittle with age. A pile of lids sat on the shelf nearby.

Rochelle started pulling buckets out from their nested stacks. She carried sets of five or six upstairs and set them in the kitchen sink.

The colonel got up from his bar stool and came into the kitchen with her. He told her he'd fill them up, while she continued hauling more of them up from downstairs. In a fairly short period of time, they had filled more than 60 buckets. She put a couple of the square buckets in the restrooms, for flushing. The rest were stacked in the nearly empty walk in refrigerator and storage pantry. Lastly, she filled up a big soup pot and set it on the stove. She would start boiling batches and filling empty liquor bottles to store for drinking tomorrow.

Colonel Wenrick returned to his bourbon. When he finished his drink, he put a twenty on the bar. He stared at the paper for a moment, deep in thought, but did nothing. He got up, nodded to Rochelle and left for the evening.

***

Confluence

The following day, Rochelle passed word around to Chuck, Gary, Marty and the few other bar patrons who stopped in, about the coming problems with city water. Chuck nodded understandingly, agreeing that yes, boiling water for drinking purposes was a good idea. Gary and Marty riffed on ideas of where to get more buckets. Buckets were awkward to carry, without a vehicle. And they didn't have gas in their cars anymore. Well, Gary's car had gas, but he was keeping it hidden inside his garage, in fear of having it seized.

They were brainstorming ideas when a new customer entered the front door, letting in a gust of chilly wind through the vestibule. Both Gary and Marty raised their voices in startled "Hey's!" at the chill and turned to look at the newcomer. A man, dressed in khaki pants and a bulky ski jacket stood looking around the large room. His gaze settled on Rochelle behind the bar and the two men seated on the middle stools. He pulled his hands from his coat pockets, waved and nodded at them. He approached a few steps and asked hesitantly, "Would George happen to be around?"

Rochelle shook her head slowly and said, "Sorry, no. He's gone."

The man's face fell. He glanced down at the floor for a moment and shoved his hands back into his pockets.

Gary frowned at the newcomer over his shoulder. "You look kinda familiar. Are you from around here?"

The stranger looked up again, shifting back and forth on his feet. His eyes were a little bloodshot. There were dark bags under his eyes, too.

"Uh, not exactly. Sort of. I grew up around here, but I've been living in Boston. George was my older brother. I'm Frankie Paulbicki."

Gary swiveled around to face Frankie, a look of surprise blooming on his face. "Oh! Hey! You're a long way from home! Or maybe back at home. I don't know. Uh, are you okay?"

The man shook his head and stepped forward to the empty bar stool one away from Gary. He hitched his hip onto the stool, he leaned his arms on the bar and faced Rochelle, as did Gary and Marty.

"I just drove down here. Well, I had to walk the last ten miles.

136

Some goons in Army fatigues jacked my car! What is going on with that?"

"Yeah," Marty answered. "It's a thing. They're consolidating all the gas. They took the gas right out of the truck we were were driving, just a few days ago." He nodded at Gary and Rochelle. "Barely had enough left to coast home."

Rochelle interrupted them, "Can I get you something? Beer? Wine?"

Frankie shook his head, "Nah, it's too early to drink. Got any hot coffee?" He glanced at the beer bottles in front of Gary and Marty, but didn't say anything else.

Rochelle nodded and poured him a cup from the coffee pot under the bar. She only kept it about half full, since few customers came to a bar for coffee. But it had been freshly made with newly boiled water, a few hours ago. She grabbed a little container full of packets of sugar and powered creamer and set it down near him, as well. Frankie ignored it and drank the coffee black. He nodded gratefully at the first swallow.

Finally he asked, "So, what happened to Georgie?"

Rochelle glanced at Gary and Marty, who just shrugged back.

Finally she answered, "Same as what happened to everyone else He got sick. He gave me the keys, walked out the door and went home, I think. That's was a few weeks ago."

Frankie just shook his head. "I guess I kinda knew that. I've been calling him, at home and on his cell, for weeks. I thought for sure that if I wasn't sick, if I'm immune, then he must be too. A good strong immune system, that's gotta be a genetic thing, right? Gotta run in families, right? Both of us, we hardly ever got sick when we were kids. At least, not that I remember. Georgie was ten years older than me, so we didn't hang out a lot when we were really young. By the time I got old enough to have much in common with him, he was off doing his own thing. He was in the Marines for awhile. And by the time he got out and came back here, I had finished college and grad school. I was teaching sociology for a living. I was in California for a while and then moved to Boston about ten, twelve years ago. But I always came down here for Thanksgiving." He sighed, reflecting on his memories.

"And I made it. I had to leave early, I wasn't sure what road conditions would be like, so I gave myself extra time. It's already snowing up north. And it was really hard to find gas. All the stations are closed. Normally, I would have taken the train. That's what I used to do, before. But that's gone now."

Frankie stopped cold. He sat in silence for a few moments, staring at the steam rising from his cup.

Finally, he added, "I guess everything is gone now. I made it in time for Thanksgiving, but there is no Thanksgiving anymore. It's all just gone to shit! Fuck!" The last word burst from his lips as a strangled shout.

Frankie abruptly wheeled about and hurled his half full coffee cup at the half wall behind him, the one that divided the bar from the dining area. The cup crashed and shattered, splashing dark liquid over the wall and floor.

Rochelle stepped back in shock. The man had been so calm, sad calm. The sudden burst of rage had startled her. She exchanged glances with Gary and Marty.

Gary spoke first. "Dude, it's not *all* gone. This place is still here." He waved around at the bar.

Marty nodded enthusiastically. "And since you're probably George's last surviving relative, that makes it your bar now, I think." Then his face fell too, as he looked back guiltily at Rochelle.

Rochelle wasn't sure what to make of the situation. She didn't precisely think of herself as the owner now. She was more of a caretaker, she thought. But she wasn't sure what she would do with herself if she just handed the bar over to some stranger. And how did she know if he was really George's brother? Would it be rude to ask to see some identification? He did look like a younger version of George, Rochelle admitted to herself.

Frankie looked around. He looked back at the mess he'd made on the floor. "I'll clean that up," he said apologetically. He stood up and made a beeline straight for the closet down the hall, where the cleaning supplies and tools were kept. He came back with a handful of paper towels, a whisk broom and a dust bin. He soaked up the wet coffee puddled on the floor and then rubbed at the dark spots with more paper towels. He emptied the broken shards and wet towels into a large garbage bin stashed just inside the kitchen and returned to the main room.

He looked at Rochelle. "I'm sorry about that. I shouldn't have taken out my anger on you like that. I hope I didn't scare you too much." He had a hang-dog look on his face. Genuine contrition.

Rochelle shook her head. "No worries. It's okay. And I think he's right. I think this is your bar now. I've just been working here."

Frankie shook his head back at her. "That's fine. I'm not really ready to take over the family business. I think I need to deal with some things first. I need to go to George's house, see if maybe his body is still there." He paused, then asked, "Do you guys know if any funeral homes around here are still operating? Anyone doing burials or cremations?"

Everyone shook their heads. Marty offered, "The city is doing mass body pickups now. They're going door to door, in my neighborhood. I heard, if you put a red 'X' on your door and leave the door unlocked, they'll come in and take whatever bodies they find. Just tape up a piece of paper on the door or a front window. No need to ruin a perfectly good door with paint."

Frankie stared at him. "And then what?"

Marty stared back at him, confused.

Frankie elaborated, "What are they doing with the bodies?"

"I don't know. Mass burial, I guess? I'm not sure."

Frankie harrumphed and shrugged. Sadly, he said, "Doesn't seem very civilized, not having a place to put a marker in remembrance."

Gary frowned and asked, "And how civilized is it going to be, when things warm up in the spring and all that decomposition makes the air so foul you can barely breathe?"

The two men stared at each other coldly for a moment. Then Gary sighed. "Sorry, didn't mean to be rude. But it's a public health issue. Decomposing bodies are a health hazard to the survivors. Gotta move them away from the populated areas. Or move the surviving people away from the bodies. One or the other, take your pick."

Frankie frowned back. "Did you guys hear any final survival rates? I heard 3%." He arched his eyebrows at everyone. They nodded. One of the last TV news broadcasts they'd seen had said the last word from the CDC and the WHO was that only about 3% of the population was expected to be either immune or to recover from the Superflu. And there might be some variances within sub groups of the general population.

Frankie nodded back. "Well, this is right fucked."

Everyone nodded glumly.

"Okay. Well, I'm gonna go take care of business." He opened his mouth, as if to give more instructions to his newly inherited employee, but then closed it again. He waved again, shoved his hands back into his coat pockets and then turned to shoulder his way out the front door. Outside, he turned right and walked with grim determination away from the bar.

Rochelle stared thoughtfully after him. After a moment, she asked, "Did you guys know it's Thanksgiving?" She had lost track of the days. Date and day of the week, they were all a blur to her now.

Gary shook his head. But Marty piped up. "Yeah, I knew. It's tomorrow, actually. Chuck said he's thawing a couple of turkeys. They're going to roast them tomorrow. Said the restaurant is open for the holiday, for anyone who wants a good meal."

Gary mumbled appreciatively at that. They'd been eating meals at Whigs, in addition to their liquid lunches and were relaying information between the two businesses. They had more or less given up on going to their respective offices in downtown D.C.

***

Thanksgiving was yet another surreal experience for Rochelle, alien and familiar at the same time. Chuck waved her down, as she rode her bike down the hill past his place, heading towards the bar. He insisted that she come in and meet his new cook. Her name was Cherry, he said. They shook hands and smiled. Cherry was a plump woman in her early forties maybe, dirty dark blond hair held back in a pony tail. Chuck pointed out that Rochelle had waitressing experience and Cherry immediately seized on that, asking if she could help with the holiday rush. Cherry explained that she'd spent the last two days scavenging supplies from homes in her old neighborhood and had hauled everything over here in a little cart towed behind her bike. Thanks to Whig's own pantry and freezer and her own scavenging, she had supplies enough to feed maybe a hundred people. She and Chuck had been telling anyone they saw on the streets, about their plans for a holiday meal. They had even decided the meal would be free, since they hadn't really paid anything for the food, themselves.

Cherry concluded by saying, with the crowd they were hoping for, they would need serving help and could she please join them?

Rochelle heard the "Sure" coming out of her mouth, even though the thoughts inside her head were protesting: *So, is this a charity thing, like serving meals to the homeless? Only, there's plenty of homes around, just no people. Are we the people-less now? Is that a thing? And what the hell do we have to be thankful for anyway? The whole world is gone and now we're having a big feast?*

Rochelle believed that if she said anything aloud to Gary, Marty or any of the other customers, they'd tell her to be thankful she was alive. Only she wasn't really sure that she was alive. What was being alive, when no one else was? Yeah, technically, her customers and neighbors were, but her family was gone, her closest friends were gone. Did that mean she was gone, too? She felt like she was trapped in some kind of limbo, a purgatory, just waiting for the Superflu to roll her, just it like it had everyone else. Bill and Gary were the last people she knew to get sick. It seemed like most everyone else she knew either wasn't going to get it or had recovered already. Were there still new cases happening? How long was she supposed to wait to see if it was really done? When would the waiting be over? And if it was over, what came next?

Rochelle posted a handwritten sign in Paulbicki's window, directing customers to Whigs. She piled a few items from her own freezer and pantry into a hand cart and walked it back up to Whigs.

There, she helped Chuck set up tables on the little front patio, just in case they needed the overflow space. Chuck demonstrated a new skill she'd been unaware of when he picked the lock on the door of a another restaurant a few doors up the street. That one had been closed for weeks. One at a time, Chuck carefully loaded tall space heaters and propane tanks onto a hand dolly and wheeled them to Whig's front patio. He stashed a few extra propane tanks in Whig's enclosed dumpster space in back too. They were reserved for future use with the portable grills or space heaters, if necessary. Then they set the tables with clean silverware and glasses. While they waited for the crowds to show up and the food to cook, they helped Cherry in the kitchen, chopping vegetables and stirring sauces.

As she worked, Rochelle couldn't stop her brain from wandering back to holidays with her family. In the Tylin household, holiday meals were a command performance. Catherine had always insisted on serving a large formal meal on the good Wedgwood china and everyone dressed up. In addition to her daughters, husband and any other close relatives in the area, she frequently invited friends or her charity colleagues. If the head count was over a dozen people, she hired caterers to prepare and serve the food. And the food was always based on the latest trends in fine dining: brined turkeys, braised brussel sprouts, salads of bitter greens. Never did a gloppy casserole or canned cranberry jelly grace her table.

One year, when Rochelle was sixteen, she wandered to the back sun porch, to find Hollan and Paige hiding out from their mother's dinner guests. They had found a bottle of mixed margaritas and were indulging. Paige, who was still under legal drinking age, had justified it as practice for the future. She insisted that Rochelle also start practicing. The girls had giggled and laughed for hours, while hiding from their mother. That was when Rochelle developed her taste for the tart beverage.

Even though Chuck and Cherry had told everyone they'd start serving at 4 p.m., people started arriving at noon. At first, it was just early bar patrons who had seen her sign at Paulbicki's and had no where else to be until 4 p.m. So they hung out on the patio and Rochelle brought them drinks from Whig's small supply. It was a mild day, relatively speaking. No rain and not too terribly cold. A few people bemoaned the lack of football games to watch, so Chuck pulled out some decks of cards and a few board games and set people to playing. A few people suggested a round robin tournament, just to make things competitive. The games kept people from drinking too much and getting too maudlin with their own thoughts and memories.

Around 3 p.m., Colonel Wenrick walked up the street, with a couple other uniformed men. Their uniforms differed from each other, so Rochelle was pretty sure they were from different services. But apparently, they were working together at the nearby Pentagon.

During a lull in the game playing and drink serving, Rochelle had a few moments to sit and watch Gary and Marty playing gin rummy with two women she didn't know. The military brass were seated behind her and she could hear their conversation.

Wenrick was asking the man in the dark blue coat about logistics. "What about Dalton? Is he ready to start flying real planes yet?"

Rochelle thought the guy in the blue coat was Air Force, but she wasn't completely sure. The name badge on his windbreaker said "Padgett." He responded, "Dalton is spending nearly sixteen hours a day in the flight simulators. But flying cargo transports is very different than flying fighter jets. He's nowhere near qualified, according to the rules. However, if you don't care about enforcing those rules any more, I can send him up tomorrow."

Wenrick nodded. "I think we really have to. There's a surviving general and several other high ranking personnel still on base in Germany. And another one in Kuwait. We need to get them home, along with all the equipment the plane can carry. The airfields there are still stocked with aviation fuel, so he can fill up when he gets there. Once the generals are back home, they can direct further missions."

The other guy at their table snickered at them, "What, you actually want to be outranked? Promotion by Superflu survival not working for you?"

Wenrick shook his head.

"Not much of a promotion, when you're just last man standing.

hill." He grimaced and took another swallow of his beer.

Padgett asked, "I heard there's some civilian survivors on base over there, too. You're also bringing them back, right? I've got an officer who was stationed in Germany, but was on a short term training assignment in California. His family got stuck in Germany. Apparently, he's got a fifteen year old son that survived there."

The third guy whistled. "Shit, I didn't think anyone had any immediate relative survivors."

Wenrick responded, "Yeah, its pretty rare, but not impossible. And yeah, if they're part of that group, then yes, they'll be on the plane. Do you know the kid's name? I can check and make sure he's accounted for."

Padgett nodded. "Yeah, I'll get that for you tomorrow." Wenrick nodded back.

Wenrick turned the third guy and asked, "Hey, Stossel, any progress on your projects? Did you ever hear from that sub?"

Rochelle's eavesdropping was interrupted by a call for more drinks from one of the tables inside. Another flurry of activity consumed her.

A short while later, Chuck whistled on his fingers to get everyone's attention and told them they were ready to start the buffet service. Cherry appeared in the doorway to the kitchen and took a quick bow when everyone started clapping and whistling their appreciation. Anticipation had been growing all afternoon as the wonderful aromas wafted from the kitchen.

Rochelle helped hand out plates and napkins, answered questions about where to get soft drinks and generally made herself useful. Once the customers were seated, she assembled a plate with a few slices of turkey and a small mound of stuffing and mashed potatoes. At her Mom's fancy dinners, potatoes were always something elegant, like piped rosettes, crusted over with a tiny blow torch to form crispy edges. Or they were sweet potatoes. Never just an ordinary pile of plain white mashed potatoes, with gravy to ladle over them.

The tables were nearly full, so Rochelle set her plate on the small side bar, where lone diners could eat and watch the TVs. Those were turned off, of course. She sampled a few bites. It was unfamiliar, but good. It did not taste like the Thanksgivings she had experienced before. And for that, she was grateful.

Before she could swallow more than a few bites, though, she was called away to ferry a fresh round of drinks to a table. And then an accidental spill needed to be cleaned up. And empty plates were ready to be bussed away. And before she knew it, the dinner was over and people were moving onto dessert or wandering away. Several people asked if she'd be opening Paulbicki's afterward, so she made her excuses to Chuck and Cherry, skipped the pies and slipped out to help the hard core drinkers drown memories of their own past family Thanksgivings.

Chapter 10

After Thanksgiving, the weather shifted to truly become winter. All of the leaves were gone from the deciduous trees. The sky was almost always overcast and snow started to sprinkle down occasionally, when it was cold enough. It didn't stick to the ground, at least not right away.

Riding her bike from her apartment to the bar became grim. Rochelle rarely went through the park anymore, as leaves and branches knocked down by the wind littered the pathways, making a wipe-out far too likely. She really wished she could go back to driving her own car, or George's little pick up truck, but the military check points around the city were still in operation. She usually cruised past one on Wisconsin Avenue near the Naval Observatory. They didn't harass her, because she obviously wasn't using any fuel to get around town. But not using a car was making it hard to get things she needed. Like more warm clothes and better boots.

Rochelle had discovered that several clothing boutiques scattered about Georgetown were unlocked. Someone had taken to leaving small cards posted in windows, with locked/unlocked symbols on them, to indicate if a store was open for scavenging or not. This cut down on the amount of glass breakage. Most people had realized that there was tons of stuff still left in the stores and they could take what they wanted with no consequences. Any glass smashing that was still going on had more to do with rage at their personal situations than a need to get at the stuff behind the glass. The lack of working vehicles kept people from taking more than an armful of stuff at time.

Meanwhile, power in the city was getting wonky. Daily and nightly blackouts were occurring with alarming regularity. Rochelle had shut off or disconnected as many appliances and lights as she had access to, to conserve the power and so they wouldn't be damaged by a surge when power came back on. The freezer and fridge at the bar managed to maintain their cold temperatures, thanks to her water and ice insulation project. Whigs was very carefully managing their stockpiles of frozen meat. Everyone figured they'd have enough to last until spring or summer, at which point, they could see about finding some wandering livestock or small farms outside the suburban regions that might still be operating and offer to trade.

This had been another of Gary and Marty's wild brainstorming ideas on survival. But when Rochelle asked them what exactly they planned to offer to trade for the butchered livestock, the brainstorming session came to an abrupt end. Aside from their personal scavenging efforts, they weren't doing much of anything except sitting on their butts. They both lived in cold but otherwise comfortable homes elsewhere in the Georgetown area. Each day, they would spend a few hours in their own neighborhoods, picking locks (a skill they learned from Chuck) and checking the inside. They turned off and unplugged appliances. If there were still dead bodies inside, they posted a hand drawn red "X" on paper in the front windows. If bodies had been removed, they made sure the red "X's" were taken down, too. Then they made detailed lists of things that could be useful in the future, like cars in garages, batteries, packaged food. And they collected more bottles of booze. Sometimes they even packed up cases of wine or beer and wheeled it on dollies into the bar with an air of smug pride. They offered their deliveries as credit to Rochelle to serve it back to them and other customers.

Rochelle was satisfied with this shift in currency. Everyone was running out of cash and she wouldn't take cards anymore. She had plenty of cash in the till and in the safe in the office upstairs, but she had nowhere to spend it. She had not found a working laundry service. Instead, she was carrying small batches of linens home to wash in the apartment basement. There was no mail being delivered, so if there were any bills for what little electricity they were using, she had no knowledge of it. And there didn't seem to be much else that needed to be purchased for the bar. She didn't need any more wait staff; there weren't enough customers to justify it. And she didn't need a bouncer, either. The patrons were pretty good at policing their own ranks. If anyone got too drunk and turned belligerent, they were politely escorted out the door. If it looked like they might start harassing Rochelle personally, they were more forcibly kicked out and told not to return, ever.

Unlike the rare rude customer, Frankie Paulbicki returned to the bar a few days after Thanksgiving. But he didn't seem quite ready to shift into gear yet. He sat on the stools with Gary and Marty and listened idly to their chatter, without contributing much to it. Rochelle tested him by asking for his advice or preferences on small matters, like which brand of beer to make the "house" beer of the week, or if a glass of wine should cost one AA battery, or two. He declined to provide much input and left running the bar to her alone.

Late one afternoon, when the power had been out for hours, Colonel Wenrick appeared. He'd been a regular visitor for weeks, coming in about every other day or so. Gary and Marty said they'd also seen him at Whigs, getting dinner, several times, too. Wenrick greeted everyone with a nod and a smile and took his customary seat at the end of the bar by the window.

Rochelle brought him his usual finger of bourbon in a low ball glass and set it down.

"Seems especially chilly in here today," he commented.

Rochelle nodded. "Yep. Power has been out for hours. The furnace downstairs is electric," she commented. She was bundled inside three sweaters and had leggings on under her jeans.

Wenrick just frowned in response.

Gary and Marty stared at him from a few seats away. Gary spoke up first. "Any chance you know when the power situation is going to stabilize?"

They had both figured out by now that the military man was fairly high up on the ladder at the Pentagon. He sometimes held quiet meetings with other uniformed or suited people. Those meetings were held at the tables on the other side of the bar, where it was much harder to be overheard.

"Well, I don't have any direct control over the situation. But what I can tell you is that they're working on it," Wenrick answered calmly.

Gary pursed his lips for a moment and then probed. "Who is 'they,' and what kind of work are they doing?" he asked.

Wenrick sighed. "'They' is the U.S. Navy. They've recalled all the submarines and nuclear powered air craft carriers to their home ports on the east and west coasts. A lot of the sub fleet was ordered into quarantine conditions, back in August, when we first realized the nature of the Superflu. Dozens of boats, each with hundreds of seamen, were never exposed to the virus. They stayed quarantined through the fall, under water and are just now coming out of it. We're dosing them with the few small quantities of vaccine we got from the developmental labs at the CDC..."

Gary interrupted him, "Wait, there's a vaccine? I thought they didn't have time to develop one!"

"Well, the CDC developed the prototype of the vaccine. The pharmas are the ones who didn't have time to manufacture it in quantity and distribute it. The prototype is several thousand doses, though. Not enough for the whole country. But enough for some nuclear power engineers to come out of quarantine and get the North Anna power plant up and working again. The other sources of electricity most commonly generated around here is coal or natural gas. And the problems with getting supplies of coal to the generating plants are even bigger than distributing what little electricity there is."

Wenrick paused to sip his drink. When he had regained his stream of thought, he continued.

"So, the nuclear power plant techs from the subs are going to take over the North Anna plant and get that running again. It's going to take them weeks, or maybe a couple of months to figure out how a civilian operation works. It's not the same as on the subs. But if we focus the power it generates to here in the metro D.C. area, it can power most of the city. So long as there's no unnecessary drains by other communities, or stuff."

Marty nodded. "We've been shutting off and unplugging appliances as we go." He stopped, clearly wondering if he should explain his small scale neighborhood investigation project or not. It could be misconstrued.

But Wenrick just nodded. "That's good; keep doing that."

Gary redirected. "That's all well and good, but what about Rochelle here? It's freezing in here. We're coming up with plenty of small batteries, but no one knows how to connect them to an indoor space heater. The big heaters at Whigs are propane based, for outdoor use. We'd give ourselves carbon monoxide poisoning, if we brought one of those in here.

Wenrick looked alarmed. "No, no! Don't do that! Those kind are definitely not meant for indoor use."

Gary pressed, "Well, how about a generator that we could put out back, to run this place? And some fuel? When is that situation going to be resolved?"

Wenrick looked chagrined again.

"Look, I understand that hijacking consumer fuel right out of cars was a bad idea. It was just supposed to be a short term thing until they could get the federal fuel reserves opened and pumping supply out to everybody. And that's just a mid-term thing until they can get a refinery working again. And an oil rig. The biggest issue is finding people who know how to work the equipment. You don't happen to know how to pump gas out of a giant storage tank, do you?"

Gary and Marty both shook their heads, equally chagrined as well.

Wenrick looked thoughtful. "So, just out of curiosity, what do you guy know how to do?" he asked casually.

Marty piped up. "I know how to sit at a desk and push keys on a keyboard!" he said cheerfully. "I know how to do meetings and talk on the phone." Wenrick raised an eyebrow at him, not appreciating his sarcasm.

Marty added, "I was with OMB, before. Pushing numbers around. Not much call to manage a federal budget, at the moment. I think I've been retired."

"Do you think you could push those numbers around if they represented people, housing and supplies, instead of budget?" Wenrick asked.

Marty looked startled. "Uh, I dunno. He's the one with HUD."

He pointed at Gary, sitting beside him.

Wenrick was startled. "You're with HUD?" he asked Gary, astonished.

Gary responded, "Well, I *was*... but like he said, I think I've been retired now."

"Geez, man, they need you even more than they need a numbers pusher!"

"Who does?" Gary asked.

"FEMA! There's still a few people left over there, too. They're trying to figure out where to put all the displaced people. That camp out in Falls Creek Park was a bad idea all around. They're closing that, but they're not sure where to send everyone. The camp is full of people who got stuck somewhere far from home or whose homes are unlivable. Some apartment complexes got destroyed by fire. And there are more people migrating out of the north, where it's too cold, too snowy and no power," Wenrick explained.

Gary glared balefully at him. "Dude, there's empty houses all over the place. And if thats not enough, there's condos, apartment buildings and hotels everywhere, too. All they need is power!"

Wenrick nodded. "I know! They know that too, they just need someone to help them coordinate it all! Figure out which sites are habitable, collect data on what's available, what's occupied, who needs it. And then distribute that information. Can you help them?"

The two men stared at each other for a moment. Wenrick asked again, "Do you know where FEMA's offices are? Their headquarters? If you just show up and tell them what you can do, I'm sure they can put you to work."

"Yeah, I know where they are. I don't suppose you'll tell all the check points to leave me alone and not siphon the gas out of my car?"

And Wenrick was back to being frustrated. "Sorry, I can't do that yet. Maybe soon, we'll have some kind of pass or card that exempts critical personnel. And they're trying to get some simple bus service restarted."

Gary was still unhappy. "Well, if I have to walk three miles to get there, they better not expect me to be wearing a suit. They might be un-retiring me, but I'm not wearing a suit anymore, I've decided."

Wenrick smiled. "I really don't think they'll care about that. So you'll go help them?"

Gary grumbled in his chest. "Yeah, I'll help. Tomorrow. It's too late today, but I'll walk over there tomorrow." He glared at Marty, who added, "Yeah, I'll go too and see what they need. I'm sure they can probably put me to work too."

Gary directed his next comment back to Wenrick, "In the meantime, you need to get serious about finding a generator and a barrel of gas for this place. We need heat in here. Rochelle needs heat! She's got no meat on those bones and I can't have her shivering to death like some inbred chihuahua!"

Rochelle glanced up. She'd been listening to them, but not participating. Just a silent observer.

"I'll see what I can do about that. First thing in the morning." Wenrick swigged down the last drops from his glass and set it down on the bar. Then he stood up and pulled his coat on. He turned without a salute and strode out the door on a mission to find a generator.

***

Wenrick lived up to his promise the very next day. As far as Rochelle was concerned, it was not a moment too soon. Her apartment had been freezing cold. All she did there anymore was sleep under a dozen blankets and change clothes. She couldn't even heat water to bathe with and had been reduced to horrible, wet, cold rub-downs to wash herself. At the bar, if the power was on, she could at least heat water for washing in the kitchen. So she had transferred several sets of clothes there and stored them in the office upstairs. She still longed for a proper shower. But since that was not an option, hot water for the makeshift bird baths was better than cold.

An hour after she arrived for the day, two young men in plain military fatigues arrived in a green truck and quickly winched down a large generator. Using a hand pallet jack, they maneuvered it onto the small back patio, where it was hidden from casual sight. They also unloaded several barrels of gasoline and showed her how to siphon it out and fill up the generator's tank. They ran industrial grade electrical lines into the bar, with extensions to the main floor and the upper floor. They also gave her two small indoor room heaters; one for the main bar area and one for the office upstairs. They advised her to avoid connecting the walk-in fridge and freezer, until they had a better handle on fuel management. They were suitably impressed with her igloo insulation project and said that should hold things safely until grid power could be restored, or until the food was used up.

Thanks to the generator, Rochelle's daily routine shifted even more. She spent nearly all her time in the bar, only going out to walk up to Whigs for lunch or dinner. The crappy weather made riding her bike dangerous on potentially icy streets, so she stashed it away until things improved. She slept on the couch in the office, with several blankets piled on top of her.

Now that the bar was heated to a more tolerable condition, more customers started appearing, many of them uniformed. Wenrick and his colleagues hitched rides with patrol groups, who dropped them off in the neighborhood. They visited Whigs to eat dinner and then had coffee or beer at Paulbicki's afterward. They had quiet conversations in the corners, which sometimes grew tense and argumentative. Rochelle overheard stray comments like, "You can't merge the entire military into one unit, without Congressional and Presidential approval!" and "I heard the quarantine at Tuscarora failed; everyone got sick and died there too. There is no Congress left! And no President, either. No one cares if we reorganize. In fact, if the public benefits from the services we can provide as a combined unit, they'll support it."

As with all conversations that she heard accidentally, she kept her mouth shut and did not repeat anything to the other bar flies.

***

Confluence

A series of winter storms hit the D.C. area in quick succession. Snow piled up, three and four inches at a time, then developed a thin icy crust, before more snow piled onto that. The few military vehicles moving about the city just drove over the snow and ice mixture, which formed icy rutted pathways. After the third storm, a city snow plow pushed a furrow clear along the street in front of the bar, followed by a salt truck. They cleared just one lane only, before disappearing from the area. Later that day, one of the new military regulars posted a city map in the bar's windows, indicating which streets would be plowed regularly. It was just a tiny fraction of the main thoroughfares, forming a loop that circled around the Pentagon, the National Mall, Capital Hill, the White House and the main bridges over the Potomac. A note at the bottom of the map indicated that neighborhood streets would not be plowed, due to a lack of personnel and fuel.

Rochelle took advantage of the new snow to collect more fresh water. She packed it into empty wine, beer and liquor bottles, which had been stashed on the bar's tiny back patio, wedged between the dumpster enclosure and the building. It had been rarely used, even before the Superflu, so filling it up with trays of empty bottles had seemed like a reasonable idea to her. She still had plenty of good water in the buckets and ice blocks stored inside. But the urge to conserve and take advantage of the fresh clean snow was too strong to ignore.

Gary and Marty came later in the evenings now, after their new "office" jobs. They told Rochelle and any other customers about what was going on elsewhere in the city.

They explained that the FEMA camp in the Falls Creek park had been scaled back, to just serve transients, people who were on their way to other places. At the camp, people could get a cot to sleep on for as long as they needed to rest, and food and supplies to carry when they were ready to continue their journeys. If they had nowhere else to go and were looking for a permanent option, they were directed downtown.

Confluence

FEMA had taken over several downtown apartment complexes and hotels. They were directing anyone who couldn't live in their previous homes to take up residence there. This included the steadily increasing numbers of military personnel, who were being ferried back from distant overseas bases. Several small teams of pilots and support people were flying nearly nonstop to collect vital equipment and the few remaining survivors and return them home. Once back on American soil, they were either set up at the massive Naval Base in Norfolk, or at the Pentagon. At the Pentagon, they had set up tents as temporary structures, but anyone who planned to stay in the area long term was soon rotated into permanent housing. FEMA's job was to identify empty housing, clean it up and let the military and civilians know what was available.

In addition to the housing redistribution project, FEMA was also still redistributing emergency supplies, including more generators and fuel. They had eventually found people who could figure out how to get the federal fuel reserves flowing. And once the fuel starting moving again, so did the emergency food reserves. The product was starting to trickle through the distribution channels again.

Gary also reported that any stray children anyone found, but couldn't care for could be turned over to FEMA. They were setting up a massive orphanage in one of the nearby hotels. Most kids were ten years old and up; it was rare to find anyone younger than that, who had survived without any adult intervention. FEMA had put out urgent calls for anyone with child care and teaching experience, to help them.

The volunteers at FEMA seems to be determined to prove that the Superflu couldn't kill bureaucratic lunacy. To communicate all this information, FEMA had redesigned their website. Thanks to the work of a couple of web developers, they had overlaid a rudimentary set of web pages on top of their old site, to list housing options, job skills needed and status of supply caches. The site was hosted on a massive Internet service provider stationed in a nearby suburb. The data center had a priority supply of fuel for two massive generators. The Pentagon was one of the provider's many customers, so they

155

made sure the site stayed operational.

Of course, as with any website, just building it was not enough to get people to visit it. Thanks to the lack of power, almost no one had access to the Internet. So Gary and the team he had joined resorted to developing printed fliers to post around town, wherever survivors were congregating. Like Paulbicki's. Rochelle designated the back hallway as the community cork board, for posting of messages, announcements and services available.

***

The winter nights were long and the days were dim. Winter weather systems kept the skies overcast almost daily. Sunshine was rare. It was making Rochelle feel like she was simultaneously hibernating while still walking around upright.

After one particularly long night of serving drinks to the usual handful of customers, Rochelle shut down the lights. Someone had brought in several battery powered LED camping lanterns, which she used to supplement the few lamps connected to the generators. She usually kept the lighting minimal to conserve on either power source.

Even without the electric light, the room was not completely dark though. It was snowing outside and dim light scattered through the falling flakes. Rochelle wondered if perhaps the cloud cover was thin and moonlight was refracting through the clouds. Inside the bar, a very faint glow filtered down from the skylight above the stairwell.

Rochelle unlatched the thin chain that blocked the central stair case to the upper dining room. They hadn't used that room for months now. She sat down on the fourth step up and faced the front of the bar. From this level, she could just see over the tops of the trees to the river beyond. Or she would have, if it wasn't snowing. The trees were slowly being coated in white fuzz again. Wind had drifted off the earlier layer of snow and the new snow falling now was not yet crusting over the skylight, sealing them off in darkness.

Frankie was the last patron in the bar that evening. He had

upturned all the chairs and barstools onto the tables and counter so that she could mop the floors in the morning. When he finished, he came and sat on the stairs with her, two steps below her.

After a moment, he said, "It's really pretty, watching the snow fall like that. Very peaceful."

Rochelle nodded, but didn't say anything.

Frankie tried again. "You know, you're doing a good job here. I can see why George let you take over the bar."

Rochelle nodded again, but added, "Well, it's not like he had many choices. I was basically last woman standing when he got sick."

Frankie relaxed on the wide stair, spreading his legs wide, elbows on thighs, hands clasped but hanging calmly in front of himself. "So, tending bar is not your life goal, then?" he asked sardonically. He swiveled his head towards her, so she could see his upraised eyebrow.

She shook her head. "I have no idea what my life goal was, actually."

She thought for a moment. "I was in grad school, for an MBA, with a concentration in marketing and packaging. I wanted to help businesses deliver their products with less packaging and be better for the environment. That seemed like a worthwhile thing to do at the time. Now, it just…" Her voice trailed off.

Frankie echoed her. "And now, you just have no idea what to do next, right?"

Rochelle nodded, "Right."

They watched the snow fall for a few more minutes. It was mesmerizing. Rochelle thought she might be falling into a trance.

Frankie broke the silence again. "Did I hear people saying it's winter solstice, earlier?"

"Yeah," Rochelle answered.

He scratched at his chin for a moment. "Well that seems fitting, for a dark and snowy night, then."

Rochelle didn't say anything to that.

Frankie added, "That means Christmas is in four days."

"Uh huh."

"You could close up the bar, if you wanted. Maybe Whigs will do another holiday meal?"

"Yeah, they're doing that. I'll probably go help them out; close the bar and send everybody over there."

"Well, that's good. To celebrate with people, I mean."

Rochelle pondered that. "Is it? Good to celebrate, I mean? What does Christmas even mean anymore?" She paused, but Frankie just looked confused. She elaborated.

"Everyone used to complain about how commercialized Christmas had gotten. Well, that's not an issue anymore. Everyone also said it was supposed to be a time to spend with family. But my family is all gone. I liked spending time with my sisters, but our mother used to make Christmas an absolute nightmare. Everything had to be so damn perfect, the perfect decorations, the perfect clothes, the perfect gift. If we screwed up anything… well, it was just a nightmare. All I can remember about family Christmases now, was my sisters and me complaining about Mom."

Frankie had turned sideways to watch her as she spoke. "Didn't your Dad do anything?"

Rochelle frowned. "It's weird. I can't really remember him doing much of anything. It's like he was just a guest in the house. Like he was just staying in a hotel. It's not like he was actually *there*, there."

"I'm sorry to hear that." Frankie responded automatically.

Rochelle waived the comment away. She asked quietly, "So, if you had a suckey family history, then what does Christmas even mean?"

"Uh, the birth of our Lord and Savior? You know, there's a church a few blocks away that's got a few people cleaning it up. They're going to do a Christmas Eve prayer service…"

Rochelle waved a flattened hand back and forth. "Mom stopped dragging us to church when we were teenagers. We got too rebellious for that. She only went herself for the social standing it gave her; she was involved in some of the church's charities. I don't think she ever believed in any of the teachings though. It was just another place for her to be seen by her peers."

"Hmm," Frankie said. He wasn't sure what else to say to that.

Rochelle went on. "So I guess I kinda lost my faith when I realized that. Well, you can't really lose what you never had in the first place. I guess I just kinda saw through all the bullshit. I heard someone say once, that religion is just a way to get people to behave in a consistent way. That's a paraphrase, mind you, not an exact quote. But the point is, religion was invented as a social construct, an organization, a set of rules on what is acceptable behavior and what is not. Don't steal, don't kill, don't fuck around."

Frankie was still watching her.

"So if you discard the formal structures that make up religions now, if you set aside the formal organization and all their trappings, then what's the point of Christmas? If you discard the religion, then religious holidays are meaningless too. The only thing left is to spend time with friends and family. And now that's gone too."

Rochelle's face fell as she concluded her logic loop.

Frankie looked around the dim bar, thinking. After a few moments, he said, "Societies have always celebrated things. Births, deaths, marriages. Good harvests. Solstices, equinoxes." He gestured his hand towards the front windows.

"You know, Christmas co-opted a lot of early pagan religions. The Christmas tree? It's a highly pagan symbol, borrowed from Norse mythology. A tree that stayed green, full of life, all year round? That was a very powerful symbol of hope. Moving the date to wintertime, even though Christ was born in the spring? They tied the event to the winter solstice on purpose. The early Christian Church was trying to convert people who already had a set of built-in holidays. They couldn't just completely discard them; they had to incorporate existing traditions into the Christian calendar. My point is that there's always something to celebrate and people to celebrate with. You're not completely alone. You have new friends. Why do you think all these people keep coming here?" He waved an arm around the empty bar.

"They're willing to be your friends, to help you, if you just let them in," he finished.

Rochelle stared back at Frankie for a few moments. It was an incredibly kind offer. But she didn't know what to do. There wasn't any "in" inside of her for them. She was empty, hollow, waiting. Finally, she shrugged. "I guess all I really want for Christmas is some peace and quiet. Like this." She gestured at the falling snow outside again.

Frankie smiled gently. "Well then, I guess you can say, 'mission accomplished!'"

He stood up, put his coat on. "I'll check in on you tomorrow. But for now, I'll leave you to your peace and quiet. Merry Christmas, Rochelle."

Rochelle nodded back to him. She sat on the stairs for a few more minutes or hours. She wasn't really sure how long. She thought about his original question, about what her life goals were. Wenrick and Gary had asked her the same thing, more or less, as well. She had absolutely no idea what to do next. She felt like she was a piece of driftwood, caught on a sandbar in the middle of the river. She was inert, just waiting for rising flood waters to tug her loose and carry her onwards, with no control and no choice.

She watched the snow falling. The flakes grew larger and softer, coating everything in thick fluff. Then they petered out. A few small bursts of flurries started up and died down. Rochelle sat on the stairs until she got uncomfortably cold. Then she went upstairs to the warm office, laid down on the sofa and dragged the blankets over herself.

Chapter 11

The wintry weather continued for several weeks into the new year. Snow or rain fell. Thanks to the piles of old rutted snow, it was nearly impossible to ride a bike anywhere. Walking was nearly the only way to get around. But that made customers complain about wet feet, wet socks and how difficult it was to move around the city

Inside the bar, those complaints were directed to Colonel Wenrick, whenever he happened to visit. His usual routine was to stop by the bar sometime after the dinner service at Whigs. Sometimes they saw him being dropped off by the patrols. He'd drink one or two shots of bourbon, chat calmly with anyone who wanted to say anything to him and then leave on foot. He suffered the seasonal inconvenience along with everyone else.

One evening, Gary pressed him. "So, I know the rest of us can't drive cars around, but I'm surprised you're coming all the way here from the Pentagon, on foot, in this crap." He gestured at the gray fog outside. "Where do you even live, anyway? I heard most of the military were taking up places in the Southwest Waterfront area."

Wenrick glanced at Gary. "Which is exactly why I'm not. Gotta have a little balance in my life. A little privacy. I live in one of those condos a couple of blocks over. Seems like only a couple of them are still occupied at the moment. I'm surprised more of you haven't moved in there."

Marty shook his head. "Why would I move? I've got a great place already. It's not that far. And the walking is good for me."

Wenrick glanced at Rochelle, who was hovering in her usual post behind the bar, monitoring the room. "You know, Rochelle, you might think about claiming one of them, for yourself. It'd be a lot closer to this place and better than sleeping on some couch."

Rochelle shrugged. "How would I move my stuff from my apartment? And is there more power there, than anywhere else?"

Wenrick grimaced. Electricity was becoming a sore topic.

"Actually, we're talking about having an amnesty day, on the fuel thing. We realize a lot of people still have cars with gas in them, parked in garages. It's not good to let them sit too long without being turned on, without moving. We're just trying to work out the best day for that with the remnants of city management.

Gary said, "There's a city management? Since when? I thought you guys were in charge now. You've brought in so much personnel, you're practically running the place now."

"That's really more about reorganizing. It was never anyone's intent to take over this city. We're just consolidating all our resources to a few select locations - Norfolk, the Pentagon, a couple other bases. When we have all the people and equipment together in just a few locations, it's easier. We're doing a lot of skills retraining, so they can handle more situations. The goal is to send them back out to help other communities, eventually."

Gary asked, "And is that what you're doing, personally?"

Wenrick answered, "Not quite. I'm more focused on logistics. Checking in inventory, seeing that it gets stored correctly. Seeing that people get where they need to go. Kind of like what you're doing, Gary." He stared pointedly back at Gary. Gary just grumbled into his beer.

Marty spoke up. "I'd really be in favor of that gas amnesty day, you know. It'd be nice to make another big scavenging run and collect stuff from my personal investigation list. Even though we're working for FEMA right now, I'd rather not draw down on their supply stash. There's so many other people who need more than I do right now. I know where to find enough food and water for myself; I just need to be able to carry it all home; more than just a walking cart's worth, that is. I need to drive my car!"

Wenrick nodded. "Okay, I'll keep pushing for it in our daily meetings. It'll probably be on a Sunday. Not this Sunday, but the one after." That was about ten days away, Rochelle thought. She was still having a hard time keeping track of the date. She was encouraged, though. If the snow would melt just a bit, she could ride her bike home, load up her own car and then drive it back to the bar. She was getting low on a few things herself and would like a few more changes of clothes.

***

Wenrick lived up to his word and the powers that were decided that for one day, the military check points and gas collection crews would rest and not stop civilians who were motoring about town. Fliers were posted around town. Word was spread from mouth to mouth. Best of all, the weather cooperated. A few days before, a warm rain system moved through the region, melting most of the snow and compacted ice on the roads.

Rochelle made a point of recharging her phone and setting an alarm to wake up early. It was jarring to be woken up by a clock again, after several months of waking up naturally at around 10 or 11 a.m. But once her body recovered from the rude shock, her brain kicked into gear. She was eager to get back to her apartment again.

As soon as it was fully daylight outside, she wheeled her bike out of the storage closet and locked up the back door behind her. She strapped on her helmet and mounted up, riding uphill away from the river.

At that early hour of the morning, there was was no traffic moving about, even with the amnesty. Rochelle assumed that would change later in the day. She knew that Chuck and Cherry had plans to make a run to a small farm they had heard of outside the city, which had some hogs they were hoping to barter for. And of course, Marty and Gary had ambitious plans to round up large quantities of wine and liquor for the bar.

Rochelle's apartment complex looked more or less the same as it always had. Ugly aging boxy buildings shaded by huge trees, which were leafless at the moment. Leaf litter was scattered about and bags of trash were piled in front of the overflowing dumpsters. It seemed the maintenance guys still on the property had not figured out how to contact city waste removal services to request a new pickup. Thankfully, it was still too cold for there to be much smell yet. Rochelle resolved to let them know how to get a trash pickup.

Rochelle eagerly bounded up the stairs to her floor, two at a time. She happily unlocked the front door. And immediately, her heart sank. Debris was scattered over the living room floor. The shelving unit on one wall was canted at an odd angle. The high def flat screen TV had been knocked to the floor and was bent oddly, clearly broken. Pillows and a blanket from the couch facing the entertainment center, were scattered on the floor. One pillow had a dark stain on it. Rochelle guessed it was soda, from the empty can laying on its side nearby.

The den that she and Apurva used as their study room, was torn apart. The neatly stacked bales of toilet paper were mostly gone. A couple of broken bundles had scattered individual rolls about. The cardboard boxes of canned soup and crackers were gone, too.

Rochelle wandered the rest of the apartment. Both bedrooms had clothes pulled from their hangars and scattered on the floor. In her own room, underneath a pile of dropped clothes, she found a large shipping box filled with bundles of tampons still intact. A plastic tub on the floor of her closet held more toothpaste, deodorant and moisturizer. A flat pack tub that she had hidden under Apurva's bed was still there. It contained more food odds and ends: jerky, protein bars, granola bars, some packets of oatmeal.

Rochelle was devastated. All the careful work she had done to collect supplies for herself was nearly destroyed. The bulk of the useful items had been taken, leaving only scraps and partially empty containers.

After absorbing the shock for a few minutes, Rochelle leaped up and strode out of the apartment, slamming the door behind her. She pattered down the stairs, out the building entrance and marched across the complex, to the main management office. The office door wasn't locked, so she stepped inside. No one was manning the small reception desk. A door led from the reception area to the apartment unit behind it.

"Hey! Hey, anybody around?" Rochelle yelled and thumped on the apartment door. She had to yell a few more times, before she heard a fumbling thump coming from the other side of the door. After a moment, the large maintenance guy she'd seen before came shuffling out, pulling on a bathrobe over saggy gray sweats and a t-shirt. He hadn't shaved in days and bed head hair was sticking up all over his head.

"What?" he mumbled, staring at her blankly.

"Where's my stuff?" she demanded angrily. "Who looted my apartment?"

The man blinked at her for a moment.

"What stuff?" he asked dumbly.

Rochelle announced her apartment number. Then she added, "You know, the one I specifically told you *not* to go in, last time we talked. I told you to stay out of my apartment."

A shifty grin spread over the man's face, as he matched the apartment number to the physical location. "Oh yeah, the one with all the toilet paper. Dang, you had a lot! What on earth does a little thing like you need with that much?" He shook his head and waved his hand. He didn't expect a real answer.

"It was my stuff! You had no right! I told you not to go in there!"

The man went back to staring blankly at her. After a tense moment, he said, "We thought you moved out. You ain't been around for weeks. Finders, keepers." He shrugged, turned away and stepped back into his own apartment, closing the door behind him.

Rochelle's eyes bugged out. "Hey!" she shouted again. She gritted her teeth and shouted again, even louder, "Hey!"

She heard a muffled "Fuck off" come through the door. She shook her head in disbelief. She thought about shouting some more, maybe even a full body scream. She thought about pounding on the guy's door. But clearly, that would not achieve the desired response. She doubted if her supplies were even still around. They had probably either been consumed or traded, by now. Maybe some of it was hidden in other units. But she doubted she could get the guy to cough them up, now. She wondered if his partner in crime was around. She wasn't sure if the other guy the maintenance man had been working with was actually an employee of the complex or not.

Frustrated, incensed, Rochelle returned to her own apartment. She felt violated; her privacy had been invaded. She couldn't stay here any more. Clearly, the maintenance guy was not going to respect her space and stay out. Worse, now that he knew she'd come back, he'd probably come sniffing around again, to see if she'd brought anything new. He'd go pawing through her stuff, touching her clothes, maybe worse.

Rochelle took another look around the place, to figure out what she could salvage. Then she set to work. She pulled out the couple of suitcases she owned and stuffed them full of the clothes that had been dumped on the floor. Then she used the sheets from her and Apurva's beds to make bundles of the remaining supplies and clothes. She hauled arm loads of bundles out to her car, huffing and puffing up and down the stairs. She transferred load after load, until her little Accord was stuffed to the roof. Then it occurred to her that maybe she should have checked the car first, before loading it. If the battery was dead, all that work might have been for nothing. In a brief moment of good fortune, the car only coughed a couple of times, before turning over and rumbling to life. She let it thoroughly warm up, before driving it back to the bar.

It took her only moments to make the drive back down the hill, which astonished her. The bike rides usually took 20 or 30 minutes. Once there, she unloaded the car, but was faced with a new problem. The office was not exactly set up to become a mini apartment. There was no dresser or closet for her things. The couch was admittedly becoming pretty uncomfortable. She was starting to long for a proper bed. Maybe the Colonel had had a good point, about claiming one of the condos on the next block over?

She decided to walk over to the condo complex and have a look around. It was just a block west of the bar. A narrow alley led to an unloading area, but several other gated entrances faced the surrounding streets. The gates were only wide enough for foot traffic, not cars. Rochelle guessed that residents probably leased parking places in the nearby underground garages. Inside the gates, a series of small narrow courtyards wound through the two and three story units. They were all surfaced in red brick, with tiny wrought iron balconies on upper stories. Security glass fronted most windows, many of them bayed out for extra light. Small landscaping planters dotted the courtyards, although the small bushes and trees were brown or leafless at the moment. Rochelle was sure it would be a lovely place in the spring or summer, when everything was green And if there was anyone to provide landscaping services, of course.

Rochelle studied the front doors carefully. None of them had any red "X"s, indicating body removal was needed. Nor did they have the little locked/unlocked cards she had seen in the retail stores nearby. Without those clues, it was hard to tell which ones were occupied. She supposed if she came at dusk, she could see if any had lights on inside and then she would know which ones were occupied. But she didn't want to wait that long. She wished she knew Wenrick's phone number. She wished there was a working cell phone tower nearby. That service had disappeared weeks ago, along with the cable TV programming and social media websites.

Rochelle decided the only way to find out if anything was occupied was to try some doors. She didn't have lock picking skills yet, although she figured Chuck would be happy to show her the basics, if she asked. She picked a door on a whim and walked up to it. She tried the handle. It was locked. She tried the next unit and it was locked as well. Feeling a little like Goldilocks, she tried a third door, to find it opened easily at the turn of the door handle.

She gently pushed the door inward and sniffed the air, parsing the faint aromas. Just dead leaves, rain puddles from the outside. Maybe a faint whiff of river muck a few hundred yards away. No rotten-body smell came from the interior at the moment. The small entrance opened into a cold, slightly messy living room. Newspapers and magazines were scattered on a table in front of a wrap around sofa. Dust coated the TV mounted on the wall, the books on the shelves, the dining table set with a basket of plastic fruit. In the kitchen, the counter tops were cluttered with small appliances, pottery jars holding utensils, half empty bags of gourmet coffee, dirty mugs and a couple of spoons. A pile of old mail and a sweatshirt sat on the counter that divided the kitchen from the dining space. The window over the sink had a few dead potted houseplants on the sill. She peeked into a few of the cupboards. Plates, cups, bowls. The dishwasher was about half full with more of the same, gunk permanently crusted onto the surfaces.

Confluence

Rochelle looked up the stairs leading to the upper story. She wasn't quite ready to try that area yet. Instead, she returned to the living room. The bookcase that faced the sitting area was full of books and knick knacks. She examined the contents more closely. Small ornaments. Pretty rocks. Bookends. Small frames filled with pictures. The pictures showed smiling happy people. Kids with mouse ears. Birthday cake smeared over a toddler's face. A young woman wearing a graduation cap and gown. An old man with a pipe clamped in his mouth, staring serenely off into the distance.

Rochelle felt her stomach turn over. This had been someone's home. She was invading a stranger's privacy. She'd hated knowing that nasty maintenance guy at her apartment had invaded hers. How could she do the same to this person? Were the pictures of the kids this homeowner's own children? Grandchildren? The graduation picture was old, faded. Maybe that was the homeowner herself?

Rochelle bolted out the front door, pulling it firmly shut behind her. How could she even think of taking over someone else home? What gave her the right to just shove that other person's things aside and dump her own in there? She didn't even know the owner's name. She needed a sign, she needed permission. If only the owner had made it clear that it was okay for someone to borrow her space. For the greater good. For safety. Convenience. But there was no sign, no mysterious communication from a stranger. The owner had just disappeared. Just like a million, billion other people. Lives interrupted in the middle of living.

Rochelle returned to the bar, shivering a little, her head spinning. She needed to get the rest of her stuff out of her apartment. She needed a safe place to live. There wasn't space or amenities enough at the bar, for that to be a good long term solution. Her car would only hold just so much stuff. She needed to stash what she had and make at least one more run up to Glover Park.

She finally decided to just unload her car and put the stuff in the storage room inside the bar, for the moment. When she saw Wenrick next, she'd ask him for help on identifying an empty condo.

With that plan finally decided on, she quickly downed a couple of the granola bars she'd grabbed earlier and drank some boiled water. Fortified, she returned to her tasks.

***

When Wenrick came in the following evening, she practically pounced on him, in her eagerness to find a condo. She quickly explained the situation to him. He was delighted to help.

"Of course I can help you pick one of the condos. I checked most of them out myself months ago. I made a list, in fact. We can go over there right now, if you want!"

He looked around the bar, which had the usual assortment of a half dozen or so customers. Gary and Marty were playing Scrabble with a pair of women at a table on the other side. The women came in together about once every other week and were looking for anything to occupy their minds. Frankie was sitting on his usual stool at the bar, though. Rochelle looked at him and raised her eyebrows.

"Frankie, do you think you could handle the place for a little while, while I step out?" she asked him.

Frankie looked startled at the idea of stepping behind the bar, instead of sitting in front of it. He looked around, as if he had never seen the place before. "Yeah, I suppose I can hold down the fort for a bit."

He stood up and came around behind. Rochelle pointed out a few obvious things under the counter, like the wine cooler (which currently only stored red wines at room temperature). Then she took off her apron and handed it to him. Wenrick politely held the front door open for her and they stepped out.

At the condo complex, Wenrick pointed out the unit he occupied and unlocked his door. He had a decent view of many of the units, as he faced the largest courtyard. Inside, Rochelle found a neat, tidy living room and kitchen. Wenrick said he had a small office den upstairs and went to retrieve his notes. He came back with a small notebook. Inside, individual pages listed out the unit numbers, their status as locked or unlocked and interior conditions. Wenrick also explained that he had already red tagged the units he could get into and had arranged for the body collectors to come. That had been two months ago. He'd also taken out any trash and cleaned out fridges, to keep the rot and smell to a minimum. Otherwise, though, he had mostly left the homes as they were.

Wenrick flipped through his pages and selected one of the smaller two bedroom homes that was across the courtyard from his own. They stepped out and crossed to the home's front door. It opened easily and Rochelle scanned the main room. Like the others she had seen, the narrow condos made the most of the small amount of space they had, with large front windows. The entry way was minimal, opening directly onto a large main living/dining room area, with a kitchen area adjoining it. Stairs on the opposite wall led to bedrooms on the second story. This particular unit was cleaner than the one she'd seen earlier, but it too had been someone's home. There were not as many personal pictures, but there was a rather elaborate game console connected to a large screen TV and a long row of assorted video games on the shelf below it.

In the kitchen, everything was put away, but she noticed a pair of small metal bowls on the floor in the corner. Food and water for a pet, she realized. She looked questioningly at Wenrick. He dropped his eyes, rubbed his hand on the back of his head.

"Cat, I think. A couple of these places had cats; one had a small dog. The dog was dead, but the cats, uh, escaped outside. When I left doors open for them for awhile. If they could hack it, they went feral, I guess. Helps keep the rat population under control. Sorry."

Rochelle shook her head. Out of all the things she had to deal with, she was not going to worry about some cats turned loose to fend for themselves.

She took a quick tour of the upstairs. The master bedroom had a king sized bed in it, which was much bigger than her own little double. The bed was made, but she really wanted to wash the sheets, anyways. She checked the taps in the bathroom and as she had figured, nothing but a hiss of air came out.

Wenrick had followed her upstairs, checking for any un-escaped pets or other issues. "Yeah, water hasn't been pressurized in this area for weeks now. I've been melting snow for wash water. I want to get some barrels to collect rainwater, too. And I put a small generator out in the courtyard -"

"You did? I didn't see that!" Rochelle exclaimed.

"Yeah, well, I hid it in some of the bushes. Don't want it just walking off by itself, naturally."

Rochelle peeked out the front window, to where he pointed. Now that she looked, she noticed a patch of yellow that she had ignored before. Orange electrical lines snaked up to an outlet on the front of his unit.

Wenrick continued, "I'll set up the converters to draw power inside here too. It's good for a space heater, a lamp or two, a microwave or hot plate. But just like at the bar, you need conserve the fuel as much as possible."

Rochelle nodded her agreement. Conserving power was becoming second nature to her now.

"Any word on when that power plant will be back online?" she asked. He hadn't talked about that project the military had undertaken for awhile.

"Well, the work at the plant is coming along well. The technicians are re-educating themselves on civilian equipment and some initial testing has gone well. But those recent storms we've had have messed up some transmission lines and a couple of transformers. We're scrambling to find enough people with the skills and knowledge to repair those, or route around them. That could be weeks yet. Or more." Wenrick looked as glum as he sounded.

"And no running water, until the power comes back, right?" Rochelle asked forlornly.

He nodded, "Right."

Rochelle turned back to study the bed. She flipped back the comforter to examine the sheets. They looked pretty normal to her. Not hotel crisp, but not stained and no noticeable aroma, either. She decided she could wrap her own bedsheets, along with Apurva's, over the existing set, layering them to cover the entire mattress. That would keep the invisible stranger cooties off her, she decided.

"Okay, this will work," she told Wenrick. "I'll start moving my stuff in tomorrow."

Wenrick smiled at her. "Great. It'll be good to know I've got a neighbor to keep watch on things around here. We can look out for each other."

Rochelle nodded happily back at him.

Chapter 12

A few weeks later, a new stranger strode into the bar. It was another gray, rainy winter day in the city, otherwise known as "normal." Gary, Marty and Frankie were the only customers in the bar at the moment. Since it was a weekend, they were relaxing with some crossword puzzles, querying each other over difficult clues.

Rochelle heard the sound of a motor outside. There were few vehicles on the streets these days, so the sound caught her attention. It didn't sound like the grumbly military vehicles that occasionally roamed about. Instead, it was a deep throbbing roar. Rochelle and the guys glanced out the window just in time to see a Harley Davidson motorcycle cruise past the front. It disappeared from view when it turned the corner, heading uphill towards Whigs. Everyone shrugged and went back to their own puzzles.

A few minutes later, the front door opened, tinkling the little bell above and a man strode through the vestibule. The rain clouds above the city had parted momentarily, to let a brief ray of sunshine shine down through the center skylight. The stranger stopped right in the middle of the patch of light, like an actor hitting his mark. He looked about.

"So, this is the famous Paulbicki's that I've heard so much about?" he asked the room at large.

The guys on their stools turned to look at him curiously. Gary responded first, "What exactly did you hear?"

"I heard that this is the place to see and be seen, the place where the deals are done, where the decisions are made."

The bar flies glanced at each other and then at Rochelle. Small frowns were exchanged.

The stranger was a good looking guy. He was tall, wearing a long dark dress coat over suit pants and dress shoes. He carried a leather backpack on his shoulder. His hair was glossy, wavy, brown, clean, but about five months grown out from what had probably been an expensive haircut. When he spoke, he flicked his head slightly to toss back a long lock that wanted to fall in his face.

The stranger approached the bar and gestured at an empty seat. "May I join you all?"

The guys nodded and mumbled, "Sure."

Before sitting down, he extended his hand first to Gary, then to the others and introduced himself. "Gavin Sadler, from Petersburg, Virginia."

Everyone politely shook hands and gave their names. When he reached Rochelle, he studied her a moment. "Ah, you must be the requisite pretty barmaid. I gotta say, you are definitely rockin' the forlorn waif look." He winked at her as he shook her hand. To the side, the guys glanced at each other again.

Once Gavin had taken the open bar stool, Rochelle smiled and asked, "What can I get you?"

Gavin smiled back and asked, "Do you have anything on tap?"

"Sorry, just bottled or canned. But we have Molson, Fat Tire and some Coors."

"Molson's sounds good. What are you taking in payment?"

"What do you have?" she asked back.

Gavin open the top of his leather backpack and pulled out a sealed bottle of Absolut vodka. "Will this work?" he asked.

Rochelle nodded. "Sure. That'll keep you in beer for a while." She was running a one to one ratio on drinks; one shot of liquor was equal to one glass of wine, or one bottle of beer. An entire vodka bottle would keep the guy in suds for awhile. She set a paper napkin in front of him, opened a bottle and set it on the napkin. She gave him a quick nod.

"Thanks, doll." He smiled at her again.

Gary spoke up and asked "Well, you're a little ways away from home. What brings you to the big city?"

"Well, that's a bit of a story. I just came to see what's going on, who's in charge around here and how I can help." Gavin nodded enthusiastically.

Gary was still frowning slightly, as he parsed that opening statement. "Okay, I'll bite," he said, "Start at the beginning. What's your bit of a story?"

"Well, as I said, I'm from Petersburg, just south of Richmond. I was the mayor down there." He paused, waiting for everyone to show their impressed face. No one did anything.

Gavin's eyes flicked over the people seated beside him. Then he grew more serious. "So, everyone died of the Superflu. Except the ones that didn't. Me, I got sick, but then I got better. And once I got better, I took a look around. And you know what I saw?"

Gavin paused, waiting for his tiny audience to engage with his patter. The bar flies continued to stare at him silently. They were D.C. natives. They were immune to politician charm.

Gavin didn't let that stop him from finding his rhythm. "I saw opportunity. I saw resources. Sure, it looks like an empty world out there. Only, it's not completely empty. Its only mostly empty. There's still people about. There's still resources about. And that means there's opportunity out there."

He paused again, waiting for enlightenment to reach them.

Marty fed him the prompt he was so clearly waiting for. "Opportunity for what?" he asked.

Gavin smiled beatifically. Slowly, he explained. "Opportunity to rebuild. This is our chance to fix everything that was broken in the world before. To simplify. To streamline. To eliminate the waste, get rid of the clutter."

Gary was still skeptical. "And what kind of waste are you planning on eliminating, exactly?"

Gavin nodded at the question. "Anything that was slowing us down. All the bureaucracy, the details, the excessive rules. Once we simplify things, we can really see this country grow into what it was always meant to be."

Gary raised an eyebrow. "And what exactly are we meant to be? Exactly?" he repeated.

"The greatest nation on Earth. Land of the free. A place where a man can work hard and build a beautiful life." Gavin glanced at Rochelle. "Or a woman, of course."

"Of course," she murmured back.

Gary didn't let up, though. "How do you plan to do that?"

"Well, we need to gather up those resources, move them to centralized locations. We need to get people centralized, too. We need people to go door to door, remove all the bodies, bury them and clean out the housing. We need to pull together all the remaining food, water and medicine. We need to get the power turned back on. And the water."

Marty interrupted him, "They're already doing that."

Gavin was momentarily startled. "Who is?" he asked.

"FEMA. Volunteers. Some D.C. city people. The military. They're working on restarting the nuclear power plant."

"They are? Fabulous! That's wonderful news!" Gavin's startled enthusiasm had a slightly patronizing tone to it. "How did that come about?" he asked.

"They're doing their own gathering. They're bringing back all their surviving personnel from overseas bases."

Gavin was surprised. "Really? How? Planes? Ships?"

Marty shrugged and said, "Whatever works. They've got a few pilots. The big ships are docked, but they've got enough personnel back to run some of the smaller ships at half capacity, I think. Isn't that what Wenrick told us?" He directed the last question to Gary and Frankie, who nodded confirmation.

Gavin said, "Huh! I was not aware of that. Tell me, how do I get in touch with them? How can I find out more?"

Gary snarked, "Well, you could walk over that bridge out there, down the road and knock on the Pentagon's front door."

Marty asked, "How did you get here, anyways? Was that you on the Harley we saw a little bit ago?"

Gavin nodded, lifting his beer bottle to his mouth.

Marty followed up, "How are you keeping gas in that thing? There's checkpoints all over the city, separating people from their vehicles."

"Oh, I got an exemption. One of the military checkpoints farther out, in Springfield, stopped me. But since it's a motorcycle, it's not using nearly as much gas as a car or SUV would. So they gave me a little card to put on the windshield. Let's me drive about town."

Marty and Gary were astounded. "Seriously?" Marty asked.

"They took our gas right out of the tank under us! We had to wait weeks for an amnesty day, just to make another supply run."

"And see, that, right there, is exactly the kind of opportunity I'm talking about! Gas is the most critical resource of all. In order to move all that food and people around, we need vehicles. And vehicles need gas. There's plenty of idle cars sitting around in garages; we need to siphon that gas out and use it, before it goes bad. And there's private fuel depots around, too. We need people who can get those things pumping. Is the military doing anything about those?"

Marty mumbled, "I dunno," but Gary said, "Yeah, they're already siphoning from civilian vehicles. We just said so."

Gavin barely heard them. "And most important of all, we need the supply of oil to start flowing to the refineries again. And people to run the refineries!"

He paused, waiting for the gang to see the brilliance of his conclusion.

Frankie asked, "And how exactly is refining more oil doing anything to 'clean things up'? Isn't that what you said earlier, you wanted to clean things up? How is burning more fossil fuel going to help with that?"

Gavin waved his hand dismissively. "I meant, clean things up metaphorically. I meant, like, administration and rules and government."

The guys continued to stare at him. Gavin took another sip of his beer. He gestured with his bottle and continued his stump speech, "I meant, like moving to a more direct form of government. Putting major issues to a public vote. We'd have so much less arguing and controversy, if everyone could just vote directly for the laws they want enacted. We have the technology, if we can get the Internet up and running again. And see, that's another reason why we need power restored. Did you say they're restarting a nuclear plant? Man. I had no idea that was even possible!" Sadler shook his head.

He went on, "Anyways, that's the really big opportunity in front of us. Correcting the mistakes of the past. Fixing our form of government to use the current technology we already have. And we have to fix our technology, to restore our civilization. We've come too far to let it all slip backwards. We have to keep moving forward. And that is what I mean when I say that I see a future filled with opportunity. Opportunity to fix things, to get it right this time.

Gary was still skeptical. It was written all over his face. Frankie and Marty just stared at the brash stranger blankly.

Sadler swallowed the last of his beer. He pointed at the vodka bottle on the back counter and asked Rochelle, "Does that count as running a tab? Is that credit for the future?"

Rochelle nodded and said, "Yep. I'll keep track. You can drink on that for a while."

Gavin stood up. "Great! So. Can anyone direct me to the FEC offices?"

Marty asked, "FEC?"

Gavin answered, "Federal Election Commission. I'm going to register my intent to run for President!" He smiled cheerfully at everyone.

***

A while after Sadler's breezy visit to the bar, the weather cleared. Just a day before, yet another winter rain storm had blown through, but afterward, strong winds pushed the clouds away. The air was crystal clear, the sky a painfully bright blue.

Rochelle awoke earlier than usual and decided to take advantage of the sunny morning with a bike ride. Since retrieving her car and moving into the condo, she had been walking between her new home, the bar and Whigs. She hadn't seen any other part of the city in weeks. Some exercise and a change of view seemed like a good idea.

She dressed in warm layers, gloves and a helmet, and then headed south over the Francis Scott Key Memorial Bridge. From there, she followed surface streets and sidewalks south along the river. There was zero traffic moving about, so she ignored the right of way signs, rode the wrong way on one-way streets and hopped over curbs with impunity. She wanted to cross over to Theodore Roosevelt Island, but the foot bridge was nearly blocked with overgrown brush and downed tree branches. Rochelle figured the wooden planked trail that looped the island would probably be just as messy. And that was a hazard, a potential bike crash waiting to happen.

Instead, she continued south on the Mt. Vernon Trail, until she reached the four bridges spanning the Potomac, connecting Arlington to D.C. proper. The big bridges for the freeways were elevated and tricky to get onto via bicycle. She had to circle around a bit and carefully maneuver onto the I-395 bridge to cross over. On the other side, she took the first exit ramp that led to East Potomac Park, the other small island that bracketed the river. The island separated the Tidal Basin from the river. It also was home to a popular golf course, which was overgrown with unmowed brown grass. A narrow roadway circled the perimeter of the island, with a few parking spaces scattered about. Beside the roadway, a sidewalk with rail fencing on the water side rimmed the island. Rochelle followed this path to Hains Point at the southern tip of the island, where she stopped for a break. She took a seat on a nearby bench that faced the water. The tip of the island overlooked the confluence of the Potomac and Anacostia rivers.

Rochelle tilted her head back and enjoyed the warmth of the sun on her face. A breeze ruffled her hair. She drifted in a pleasant trance of no thought at all. She was just starting to cool off from the exertion of bike riding, when she heard the sound of a motor in the distance. It was a deep rumbling with a slight shushing sound layered in it. She opened her eyes, and looked around, trying to identify the source. Up the Anacostia River, a barge was motoring downstream.

Rochelle stood up and walked to the railing lining the island's river bank. She leaned on it, and studied the barge. It was small, as far as river barges went. If it had been loaded with standard cargo containers, it probably would have held only two, maybe three, end to end along it's length. But this one didn't have any cargo containers on it. It rode low in the water, its gunnels just feet above the water line. Rochelle guessed it must a have a sunken compartment on the inside. Maybe it was the kind that carried coal or grain down to larger dock yards? Except, neither river had any major dockyard facilities for industrial distribution. The Navy Yard was about a mile up river on the Anacostia. Any other docks or marinas on the water were for recreational boating.

The barge carried a pile of cargo that formed a long fragile pyramid stretching the boat's length and rising a dozen feet above the gunnels. The cargo appeared to be made up of short lengths of logs; roundish objects laid perpendicular to the boat's length and stacked high. Each log was coated in blue, black, white or yellow plastic sheeting. A few other spots of color showed here and there.

Rochelle's blood ran cold when she realized what she was looking at. They weren't logs. They were bodies. Corpses, wrapped in body bags or sheets, stacked like wood. Superflu victims.

Her heart thudded in her chest. She felt a wave of heat, then a sharp chill wash over her. Her stomach thought about throwing up. All she had consumed so far that morning was some boiled water from her carry bottle. She continued to stare in horror. A little voice inside told her to look away. It was rude to stare at other peoples' misfortunes. But she couldn't stop. The rational side of her brain pointed out there was no one to be rude to. The bodies didn't care. They were dead.

She didn't see anyone alive on the boat, but there had to be someone in the tiny pilot house on the back end, steering. The boat must have been moored and loaded at one of the Navy Yard docks. She wondered where it was going.

She watched in fascinated horror as the barge continue downstream. A gust of cold wind shifted direction and brought the sickening stench of rot in her direction. Her stomach immediately objected by hurling half a bottle's worth of tepid water outward to splash onto the concrete and rocks at her feet. She gave a tiny leap back, trying to avoid her own backsplash, while still hunched over in the cycle of heaves that emptied her stomach.

When she finished, she swished and spit out the foul taste from her mouth with a fresh sip from the bottle. She tried not to breathe too deeply. She pulled her t-shirt up over her nose and mouth, to block some of the smell. She waited a few minutes, for the horrible smell to drift away with the barge. She took another small mouthful of water and carefully swallowed, to soothe her burning throat. She sipped a little bit more, slowly. She didn't want to throw it back up too, as she would need the hydration to finish her ride back home.

When she looked up again, the barge had continued its way downstream, steadily growing smaller. Rochelle didn't want to have another crying jag, but the tears started leaking out slowly. All those people. Was there any chance one of those bodies was someone she had known? Bill? George? One of the hundreds of people in her phone contact list? An acquaintance? A former bar customer who had stopped coming in months ago? She thought she had finished all her crying, after the last of the close-up deaths, after Bill. But the more she tried to stop this round, the more it leaked out.

Finally she gave in. She backed up to the bench behind her and sagged onto it. She pulled her legs up and wrapped her arms around them. She squished her closed eyes into her knees, letting her jeans absorb the tears. She blubbered and let the drool drop from her mouth onto her legs. After a few minutes, the heaving sobs slowed and stopped. She took a few deep breaths, sniffled to clear her nose and looked up. The barge had glided around a bend and disappeared from view. The river had swept the horror away like it had never existed, leaving a calm, serene, glassy surface on the water.

When the numb state finally settled back onto her, Rochelle returned to her bike and mounted up. It was getting close to lunch time and customers might be looking around for her. She rode slowly back up the length of the island, the image of the barge and its contents popping into her head over and over. She had to focus hard on her immediate surroundings, to dismiss it from her brain. Once she reached the major streets crossing the island, she turned north. She crossed the National Mall, followed Constitution Avenue to Virginia Avenue and then up to the Georgetown neighborhood. As elsewhere, a few pedestrians walked about and offered cautious waves. But there were no normal cars moving about. Oddly, though, she saw a long dark limousine turn into the Watergate apartment and hotel complex, as she pedaled past. She wasn't close enough to see if there was an gas exemption card in the front window.

***

At the bar that evening, Wenrick made one of his regular visits. He came in alone and stopped at the bar to say hello.

He explained that a couple of his colleagues would be joining him so he was going to take a table seat once he had his drink. Rochelle poured him his regular bourbon. As she handed it to him, she told him what she had seen.

"I was out for a ride this morning on East Potomac Island. I saw a barge going down river. It looked like it was carrying bodies."

Wenrick listened attentively and nodded. His expression conveyed that he was familiar with the idea of barges of bodies moving about. He raised his eyebrows at her in question.

"So, where were they going? How did they even get on that boat?" she asked.

Wenrick studied her, assessing how much information she really wanted. "Well, they're going out to sea, for disposal. What's left of city management has been gathering up the dead bodies. But the crematoriums around the city can't keep up with the throughput. There's too many to bury, not enough coffins, no way to get that many of them embalmed. We could bury them in mass graves without coffins or embalming. But then decomposition fluids could contaminate the area, maybe get into the water supply. And then you've got a cholera outbreak. It's been too cold and wet to successfully incinerate them in the open, too. I've heard of a few places elsewhere using big industrial incinerators, like for burning biomass for energy. But that just seemed, I don't know… undignified. And none of those facilities are near here, so there's transportation issues. Burial at sea just seemed like the best way to go."

Wenrick paused and studied Rochelle. She was absorbing the information.

Wenrick added, "It's a nice day today, calm waters. That barge is seaworthy, so it will go out beyond the edge of the continental shelf in the Atlantic and unload there. They're removing them from body bags so they can reuse them and then weighting the bodies with rocks."

"So, they're just fish food, then? Is that really any more dignified than incineration?"

Wenrick looked at her. "They send a preacher, to recite a sermon as they unload. If you want to attend the group funeral on a future load, you can go along. It's a 24-hour round trip, though. And they only go out when the sea is calm. They pick up more barges in Norfolk, link them together and head out. They also pick up some troops in Norfolk, who can run the small cranes, as well." Wenrick made a motion with his hands, like a claw grabbing items from a pile.

Rochelle shook her head. She did not want to ship out on a barge full of bodies. She wondered how the workers could stand the smell. It had nearly knocked her over and she'd only endured it for a few minutes before it dissipated.

They were interrupted by Wenrick's colleagues entering the bar. He nodded to Rochelle, but moved off to the table on the other side that they had claimed.

A short while later, Gavin Sadler returned to the bar, a broad cheerful grin on his face. He took the open stool that Wenrick had vacated and requested a beer. Rochelle uncapped another Molson and handed it to him.

"So, how is everyone tonight?" he asked everyone pleasantly. Everyone murmured their generic greetings back.

Sadler followed up, "You know, I don't think I caught any of your names, the last time I was in here." He raised his eyebrows in question, so everyone provided their own names. Gavin shook hands with each as they did so. When he got to Rochelle, he smiled his high wattage grin and added, "And I'm *very* pleased to meet you."

Once he sat back down, he asked, "So, what's going on in here tonight?"

Gary shook his head slightly, to suggest 'not much,' but added, "Oh, Rochelle just learned about how the city is disposing of the bodies today."

Sadler looked curious. "And how is that?"

So Gary explained what Wenrick had just told them. Sadler nodded his head and confirmed that yeah, it was a sensible, if cold, solution to the problem. He added that in his travels about the state, he'd seen some places that were resorting to mass graves. If they could identify a good location, some place with a deep clay-lined pit that wasn't likely to contaminate their local sources for fresh water, they used that. Other communities were struggling with mass cremation. And there were pockets of locations, small towns and exurbs that were just avoiding the problem altogether by abandoning their homes and migrating elsewhere.

"So, have you been doing a lot of wandering, then?" Marty asked him.

"Yeah, here and there. Testing the waters, seeing what's what." Everyone stared at Sadler, mentally pressuring him to explain more. So he added, "I'm trying to see what this country needs to recover from this."

Gary put his head on his hand, elbow propped on the bar, leaning forward to look around Marty at Sadler. He asked, "Didn't you say you were Mayor of Petersburg, before?"

Sadler grinned. "Yes, yes I was. I was half way through my term there, when this Superflu hit."

Gary followed up, "And, what exactly did you accomplish in your time there, as Mayor?"

The grin on Sadler's face wavered. "Well, lots of things. I helped the city attract some new business startups to launch in our downtown incubator. I oversaw a 5.6% drop in violent crime in the city. Uh…"

Gary interrupted him. "I don't recall the exact statistics but I believe that Petersburg and the surrounding counties, were predominantly African American. Care to tell me how a white man managed to get himself elected Mayor of a black community?"

Sadler grinned again. "Hard work and perseverance. I grew up in that town, I went to school there. All of my friends, my colleagues, were African American. My mama taught me that it's not the color of our skin that matters, it's the quality of our character that counts."

Gary responded, "Uh huh. That sounds like a line straight from a stump speech."

Sadler nodded earnestly. "It is. But it's also true."

The conversation paused, but Gary continued to stare hard at Sadler. Finally he asked, "And when this Superflu hit, why didn't you help your own town recover? Why are you wandering about the state on a Harley? Why are you here? Don't you have work to do at home? Most places have zero management experience left in place, to guide the survivors in their recovery. D.C. doesn't have any of its old guard left. The military is effectively taking over and that's only because they're so anal-retentive about organizational control, that they were able to get enough people back from overseas bases. They managed to collect enough people who can get past their shock and figure out what needs to be done."

Sadler nodded. "And they're doing a fine job of it! I'm really impressed by how much they've gotten done so far."

Gary continued to stare at him.

Sadler squirmed a bit and added, "As for Peterburg; there wasn't much to be saved. A big fire got started accidentally, in the downtown area and spread to hundreds of buildings. It only died out when we got a bad rainstorm after a couple of days of burning out of control. Unfortunately, the place is completely destroyed. Anyone who was left has scattered to other places."

After a moment, Gary nodded and said, "I see." He faced forward again, ready to let his line of questioning drop.

Rochelle turned away to carry drinks to the pair of women playing cards at a back table. She also checked on Wenrick's meeting, who were fine with what they had. Back at her post behind the bar, she bent down to put away a half full wine bottle. When she stood up, she noticed that Gavin had been staring at her rear end. When he realized she'd caught him looking, he just grinned at her and winked. She turned away before he could see the tiny flicker at the corners of her lips.

Sadler turned back to Gary and Marty. "So, what are you guys doing to get by around here? How are you getting food, water,

185

heat?" he asked.

Marty piped up. "We're working for FEMA now. Back to being office drones. We tell people where to go to get supplies. And then we have to tell people to work together to collect more. And then we have to tell them what to do with the supplies once they haul it out of the warehouses. You know, all on spreadsheets and forms, of course."

Sadler nodded. "You mean, like those MREs and silver blanket things?"

Marty nodded back. "Yeah, like that." He pulled a folded flier from his pocket. "See, this is what we hand out, to let people know where to go to get stuff. If they don't have a place to live, we tell them to come downtown and we'll find a place for them. We're also working on clearing out some of the bigger apartment buildings around here, for permanent housing. No one wants to live in a cold tent, when there's a nice sturdy building available."

Sadler nodded. "Yeah, I know! I grabbed a place in the Watergate. I have to walk up six floors to get to it but hey, that's good exercise!" He patted his stomach to indicate how fit he was.

Marty nodded. "Yep, that's one of them. Only, FEMA, didn't claim that one. That one was just done by random survivors who wanted to live in a high rise by the water. But we're following that model. We pass the word around to any survivors we see about, ask them if they need help and can they contribute to a group. Anybody can help with cleaning out housing."

Sadler asked, "And everybody is just living on MREs and bottled water? What are you going to do when those run out? Are you making any plans to start growing food? There's good farm land all over the place, outside the city."

Gary and Marty nodded. Gary took over. "Yep, we're recruiting for that too. Anyone with any kind of relevant experience is encouraged to help out with new farm projects. There's teams about, who are going around, identifying good candidate sites, places with equipment, seed stock, fertilizer, you name it. Soon as spring gets here and it warms up, they'll start breaking ground."

Marty added, "As long as they can convince the military

186

checkpoints that their fuel usage exemption cards are valid." He glanced meaningfully over his shoulder at Wenrick's group, who were not paying attention. They were leaning into their own quiet conversation.

Gary and Gavin glanced at the table on the far side of the room. Gavin asked, "What do you think they're talking so hush-hush about?"

Gary shrugged. "Military stuff. Who knows."

The guys all sipped their beers. Gavin turned to Rochelle. "So, you don't talk much, do you?" he asked her directly.

Rochelle shrugged. "Nothing much to say. A bartender's job is to listen," she answered.

Gavin rubbed his fingers over his chin, thinking. "Not even a smile for a customer?" he asked. She smiled perfunctorily for him. He grinned back, still trying to draw her out. "Now, that's better! Doesn't that feel better, to share a little cheer with the gang here?"

Rochelle couldn't keep the fake feeling going. Her face fell back to neutral again. "What's to be cheerful about? Today, I saw a barge with thousands of dead bodies on it, going down river. Just another beautiful day in the Apocalypse!" She forced the fake smile again, for a very brief moment.

Gavin stared at her, drumming his fingers on his cheek, thinking. "You know what you need?" he asked. Then he answered his own question, "You need a day out in the country. Get away from the city. Go for a drive, look at some new scenery, get some fresh air."

Rochelle whirled to face him and glared. "What do you think I *was* doing today? I was out on my bike, riding around, sucking in all that fresh air. Until I choked on dead-body rot!"

Gavin got a little gleam in his eye. "Bike? You ride?" he asked.

"Bicycle, not motorcycle," she answered.

Gavin's face fell a little. Then he brightened again. "You ever been on a motorcycle? I could take you out for a ride. Could still do you some good."

Actually, no, Rochelle never had ridden on a motorcycle before. She contemplated the idea. Her mother would never have allowed it, had she been asked, when Rochelle was younger. But her mother would have liked Gavin Sadler very much. He was exactly the combination of handsome and charm that Catherine Tylin was drawn to and encouraged her daughters to pursue. In spite of the Harley habit.

While Rochelle thought this over, Gavin pounced on the opening. "So, what do you say? We could go out tomorrow. I can pick you up here at noon. Can someone run this place while you take a break?" He glanced around at the guys. Frankie, sitting in the farthest position away from Sadler, nodded and waved his hand. Marty also nodded, pointed at Frankie and said, "He can." Gary frowned a bit but didn't say anything.

Sadler grinned again. "Okay, it's a date, then! I'll pick you up here at noon."

Chapter 13

At noon, just as he said he would, Gavin Sadler pulled up in front of Paulbicki's on his motorcycle. He parked it, swung his leg off and came inside to retrieve Rochelle.

Rochelle had prepared for the excursion with some care. On the one hand, she was reluctant to go, but on the other, she was intrigued by the guy. She hadn't had time to truly develop a crush on him yet, but he was the kind of guy she normally would have been attracted to, before. So she selected her heaviest duty jeans, with leggings underneath, expecting it to be cold outside. She had a short sleeved t-shirt layered underneath a long sleeved t-shirt, under a bright sweater, under a short leather jacket. While she had dressed for the event, she was still uncertain whether she should actually get on the bike and go with him. She wasn't completely sure she hadn't been buttonholed into it, thanks to Frankie and Marty's easy complicity and Gavin's breezy conclusion.

Inside the bar, Rochelle greeted Frankie. No one else was in there. She showed Frankie where things were stashed and the keys to assorted locks. In spite of working in the bar during his school years, things had shifted around and he needed a refresher.

Rochelle gave Gavin a tentative smile when he strode in. Now that he was here, it was clear he had been serious about the proposed outing. He also wore sturdy jeans and a leather jacket. She gamely decided to give it try, in spite of yesterday's depressing experience on the river.

"Now there's a sunny smile to go with this sunny day out there!" he grinned at her. "And it's going to be a smashing day!" he added.

He explained that they were going to look about for a late lunch at a nice spot. Before Rochelle could ask what that meant, he waved to Frankie, who waved back. Frankie assured Rochelle that the bar would be fine in his care. Outside, Gavin handed Rochelle a spare helmet and helped her adjust the strap under her chin. Then he put on his own. They straddled the bike and she settled in behind him. She could lean back against the small back rest, or lean forward to wrap her arms around his chest. He encouraged her to hold onto him, as it would better balance the bike when steering around corners.

Gavin started the motor and the loud rumble drowned out all conversation. He pulled away from the bar and headed northward through Georgetown. After a couple of miles, he veered left on Highway 190 through the suburbs. Rochelle watched the land change around her. Dense urban city reduced to sprawling suburbs. Store fronts were replaced by houses and churches. Then the suburbs evaporated to rolling wooded hills. The trees screened the road so densely, it was hard to see what lay beyond. In a few places, the screen lowered to reveal open areas that used be golf courses, probably part of some fancy country club, Rochelle guessed.

After several dozen miles, Gavin banked the bike onto side roads, two lane black top roads lined with mail boxes and driveway turnoffs. He slowed down and studied the houses about. The motor was too loud for her to ask but she wondered what he was looking for. To her, the houses seemed cold, abandoned. She wondered if anyone was still living in them. Or maybe decomposing in them. She examined them more closely, looking for signs of life or death.

Gavin wandered the roads. The houses and the lots they were on grew larger the farther they went. They were set well back from the road. Decorative fencing and large mature trees lined the road, shielding the huge homes from prying eyes. A few times, Gavin slowed to a stop in front of a house and studied it. Rochelle opened a hand in flat gesture, asking him what was up. He just shook his helmeted head and drove on. Finally, after discarding several choices, he pulled into a driveway that was fenced on both sides, a lane threaded between two other properties on either side. The landscaping gave way to a stand of lightly wooded acreage. After a mile, the driveway made a u-turn, to face a wide gabled ranch house. White fencing that looked like it should have horses on the other side, formed a square around the home. The gate in the fence at the white graveled driveway was wide open.

Gavin drove about halfway up the driveway, stopped the bike and turned off the motor. Rochelle listened to the sudden silence, waiting for the vibrations from the bike to stop shivering her bones. Gavin slipped off the bike and turned to grin at her. He removed his helmet and gestured for her to do the same.

Rochelle asked, "What are we doing here? Do you know this place?" She looked about.

Gavin shook his head. "Nah. I'm pretty sure it's abandoned. But it makes a good place to take a break, doesn't it?"

"I suppose." She looked dubious. She'd thought maybe they'd visit some state park with a pretty overlook of the river or something, when he'd proposed the drive last night.

"How do you know it's abandoned?" she asked.

"Ah, well, there's a few tricks for that. Curtains are a big clue. You remember that blue house I stopped at before?"

Rochelle nodded.

"Did you notice the curtains in the upstairs window moved? Like someone was pulling them closed, or peeking out from the inside? That was an occupied house. Maybe the original owner, maybe a squatter; doesn't matter. But there's no need to mess with someone else's claim; there's plenty of empty ones to go around."

"So, if the curtains are moving, you move on?" she asked.

"There's more to it. If the curtains are closed, someone was in there, maybe still is. If they got sick and stayed home, they probably closed all their curtains, when they went to bed. Everybody does that. Block out light, create some privacy. Makes us feel safe. So, if the curtains are closed, there could still be dead bodies inside, if there's no living people about. But if they're open, they left during the day and just never came back."

"And is that all there is to it? To figuring out if a house is empty or not?"

"Nope. Cars are a clue, too. If they're parked about, you look to see if they've been driven recently. Are the tires starting to get flat from sitting still so long? Are they parked in a normal spot or are they just stopped wherever, like someone dashed in, during an emergency? If they're just sitting on the grass, I leave those houses alone. Whatever emergency happened there, nothing good would be left behind."

"What if the cars are inside a garage?"

Gavin nodded. "Right, gotta check garages, too. If there's cars inside and closed curtains, definitely leave those bodies alone. But if the cars are gone and curtains are open, then it's a pretty sure bet that whoever was living there, went to a hospital when they got sick."

"And that's it? Cars and curtains?"

"And you have to look for other signs, too. Landscape maintenance. Maybe equipment around. Newly installed solar panels or a wind turbine, maybe. Maybe a big rain cistern mounted on a roof that doesn't look like it should be there. Something useful, functional, but kind of unsightly, by the standard of these kinds of properties." Gavin waved an arm around. Rochelle didn't see any signs of recently installed equipment. The grass had not been mowed since late last summer and was winter brown. Sticks and piles of leaves were drifted up against the perimeter fence.

Gavin turned about on his heel and said, "Come on, let's go inside."

"How are we going to get in?" Rochelle was puzzled.

"Back door. Everyone always says they lock their doors, but there's always a back door that's 'accidentally' left unlocked."

They circled around the side of the garage. Gavin peeked into the garage window. "Yep, no cars!" he pointed out. Rochelle looked and agreed.

Behind the garage, they found a long concrete patio, stretching the length of the house with a wide roof providing shade. The patio was divided into sections. The first section held a collection of gardening equipment and supplies, piled on and under a counter mounted on the back wall behind the garage. Beyond the privacy wall that shielded the gardening workshop, planters and patio furniture formed pleasant little groupings. The outdoor sofa and chairs would have been a nice place to lounge and enjoy sunny afternoons, if not for the mold accumulating in the corners. The cushions were upholstered in fabric designed for outdoor use, but they were never meant to be left outside during an East Coast winter.

Gavin tried one of the sliding glass doors. It opened into a great-room area, next to an open kitchen. That door was locked. Gavin tried the next one, which Rochelle could see faced a home office, with a desk, computer and bookshelves. That door slid open with just a few firm pushes to clear the track of old leaves and dirt. Gavin and Rochelle stepped into the small office area.

"See? Told ya!" Gavin chortled. "Someone always forgets to lock a back door."

Rochelle took a quick sniff. A faint musty odor came to her, like the mold on the patio furniture. But she did not detect any dead body smell. That calmed her nerves a bit.

She followed Gavin into the hallway. The hallway was a tiled straight path through the center of the house. To their right, the hall was lined with several doors left open. She could tell at a glance those were the bedrooms and maybe a bathroom. On their left, they entered the great room they had seen from outside. The portion that faced the back patio was the "casual" part of the house. The formal living room faced the front of the house. Next to it, across from the kitchen, a formal dining room was separated from the living room by a half wall and support post. It was furnished with a huge glass table mounted on a sturdy pedestal and and storage hutch full of china place settings.

Rochelle heard Gavin whisper, "Jackpot!" to himself. She turned to look at him, but he was already moving towards the kitchen. He pulled open a few cabinets, to examine their contents. "Wonder what we can find for lunch..." he commented. "Ah, here we go. Wheat Thins!" He pulled a yellow box out of a cabinet which was filled with other boxes and bags of snack foods. He pulled open the tab top. It had been previously opened before, so he shook out a small handful of squares and sampled one.

"A little stale, but not too bad." He turned to a tall pantry closet, continuing to rummage about. From the pantry, he pulled an armful of treasures: jars of artichoke hearts, sun dried tomatoes, unopened mayonnaise, a can of olives, a can of tuna, a dry summer sausage vacuum sealed in heavy duty plastic. He piled the treasures on the wide kitchen counter and returned the cabinets. He pointed at things, mumbling to himself, "uh huh" and "that and that." Within moments, he had found a medium sized mixing bowl, a big platter and a large spoon.

"Pity we don't have any cheese, to round out this platter but we can make do," he commented.

Rochelle responded, "I can check the fridge…" and turned to it automatically.

Gavin leaped past her and pressed his hand to the surface of the refrigerator. He said, "No! What's in the fridge stays in the fridge! Seriously. Power's been out for months. No telling what mixture of meat, milk and produce is rotting away in there. As long as you don't break the seal, we can keep on breathing normally."

Rochelle flashed to her moment of up-heaving yesterday and quickly agreed. Pantry staples would be enough for their makeshift antipasto platter. She stepped around to the other side of the counter and took a seat on one of the tall chairs to watch Gavin work. Cracking open the sealed jars, he quickly assembled a simple tuna salad with the artichoke hearts and mayonnaise. He sprinkled in some dried onion flakes as seasoning, along with a sprinkle of salt and pepper from the shakers beside the stove. He piled the preserved tomatoes and olives into small bowls, along with more crackers and set it on the platter. He added forks and napkins and then said, "Okay, let's go sit outside. It's actually warming up some out there. It's getting nice, in the sun." He smiled brightly at her.

They sat down on the least mildewed patio furniture and shared the meal. They scooped up bites of the tuna salad onto the crackers and washed it down with room temperature bottled water. Rochelle had found several cases stacked in a corner of the garage.

"So, it seems like you do this a lot," she commented to Gavin. He raised his eyebrows at her, since he was still chewing on a bite of food.

Rochelle added, "Breaking into strangers' homes, raiding their pantries. Is this a regular thing for you?"

Gavin wobbled a hand. "Well, it's better than subsisting off of MRE's. You ever try those? Those things are nasty!"

"Yeah, but doesn't this ever give you the willies? I mean, this was someone's home!" Rochelle had avoided looking about the living room too closely. There were large framed family portrait photos clustered on one of the walls there.

Gavin shrugged. "Eh, not really. I mean, if they're gone, it's not like they can use the stuff anymore." He tapped his water bottle. "No point in letting it go to waste forever. Besides, I find it fascinating to look at other people's houses. How they decorated, how well they kept it up. How much space they thought they needed. I mean, look at this place, it must be 3,000, maybe 3,500 square feet. How many people do you think lived here? We should go check out the bedrooms, when we're done, see how many kids they had." He was waving a free hand around enthusiastically.

Rochelle glanced around the patio. It was a pleasant space. If flowers bloomed in the spring or if the planters were restocked, it might even be beautiful. The patio looked out onto a skinny patch of yard, bordered by the white fence and then the thin oak woods beyond. A flash of red darted past; a cardinal bird.

"I guess," Rochelle answered. "Did you live in a house like this, in…" She stopped because she had forgotten the name of the city he said he was from.

Gavin shook his head. "Nah. Much, much smaller. My folks couldn't afford much, when I was growing up. Dad was on disability and Mom was a secretary. But there were big rich houses all over the area. I'd ride my bike, the bicycle kind, down country roads and see these big huge old houses, the red brick, the black shutters. And I just wanted to know what they looked like on the inside. So, now, I'm finding out." Gavin shrugged and studied her.

After a moment, he asked, "Where did you live, growing up?"

Rochelle answered slowly. "Manassas. Colonial style house. White siding, not red brick. Just a square box with a pointy roof, really." She shrugged back at him. She didn't really want to elaborate, to explain that she too had lived in a big house and so had plenty of her friends. She'd seen the insides of many nice homes.

Gavin asked, "Didn't it ever bug you, how much some people had? The furniture, the new cars, the clothes, the club memberships, the perfect house, the perfect life?"

In a small voice she answered, "No, I never really thought about it." She'd spent her teen years wishing for a little less perfection than what her Mom had insisted upon.

They ate in silence for a few moments. Rochelle spoke again. "I guess I didn't really care about other people's lives being so perfect, because I was too focused on being the perfect daughter for my Mom. She was a real witch. Trust me, perfection is not all it's cracked up to be." She rolled her eyes for emphasis.

Gavin wiped his mouth with his napkin and sat back, spreading his arm over the back of the love seat he was on. Rochelle was on the opposite side of a low table from him, in a matching love seat. He studied her for a few moments.

"So, you're pissed off at your Mom. Did you ever get to tell her to go to hell? I take it she's gone now?"

Rochelle nodded around a mouthful of food to confirm her mother's absence. When she swallowed, she explained, "No, the last time I talked to my Mom, we were planning my sister's wedding. We all wanted to tell her to go hell, but couldn't. She was our Mom. She got sick that very afternoon, actually."

Rochelle pushed her own plate away, as well.

Gavin was still studying her. "Hmm. Wedding planning. There's some real anger-inducing moments."

"Well, it was my youngest sister's wedding. I'm the third of four."

"So let me get this straight. You had a witchy mother. Then you lose everyone to the Superflu. Your apartment gets ransacked. And now you're stuck running a bar, serving booze to a bunch of government hacks-"

"I wouldn't call it 'stuck'," Rochelle interrupted. "I'm actually pretty grateful to have the bar. Wait, how did you know about my apartment?"

Gavin wobbled his head. "The guys told me. Okay, so you're not stuck. But still, this is probably not what you'd thought you'd do with your life, right?"

"I guess," she shrugged.

"Girl, where is your rage stage? Why are you not screaming at the top of your lungs, at the injustice of it all?"

Rochelle stared at him blankly. "What good would that do?"

Gavin flopped his arms up and then back down. "The five stages? Denial, grief, bargaining, anger, acceptance? Doesn't matter what order you do them? You haven't done any of the anger yet, have you?"

They continued to stare at each other in bewilderment. Gavin suddenly leaped up. "Come on, let's get some of that anger out." He grasped her hand, pulled her to her feet and led her back inside. Once in, he let go and strode down the hallway, glancing into bedrooms. "Oh, perfect!" he exclaimed. He stepped into a bedroom that clearly had been occupied by a boy. He emerged a moment later with a wooden baseball bat in hand.

Gavin brushed past Rochelle and went to the main open area of the house. He studied the china hutch in the formal dining room. He opened up one of the cabinets and started pulling out piles of dinner plates. He set them on the glass dining table. He casually brushed aside the dusty basket of dried flowers that sat in the center. "We could take these outside, but I think this will work much better, right here," he announced.

Rochelle's eyes widened in alarm and she took a few steps backwards. Gavin gripped the baseball bat and pulled it over his shoulder. He stared at the pile of plates and then swung the bat like he was hitting a home run. Ceramic plates shattered with a loud crash, large chunks flying toward the big picture window facing the front yard. He had aimed his strike so that the debris flew away from both of them.

Rochelle jumped at the crashing noise. Her mouth opened in shock. Gavin picked up another plate from the hutch and tossed it the air, bringing the bat around one handed to smash it mid-air. Tiny shards scattered about the table and floor. "That's the ticket!" he shouted.

"Okay, now it's your turn!" Gavin announced. He grabbed a stack of three tea cups and set them on the table. He extended the bat to her, handle first. Rochelle automatically accepted the bat, but then just stared at it.

"Come on. Smashing things is the best way to get your rage out. Try an over-head swing, like an ax." He demonstrated the motion.

Rochelle looked about at the shards. She looked at the hutch still full of china behind him. Her mother would have had a fit, had anyone deliberately broken any of her own collection. Her mother had Wedgwood, inherited from her grandmother. It was only brought out for special holiday meals. Once, when Rochelle had been eight, Paige had accidentally dropped a creamer on the tiled kitchen floor. Their mother had snapped viciously at them, but quietly, since there was company in the front room. Then she had grounded Hollan, Paige and Rochelle alike.

Thinking of that creamer and her mother's potential for distributed punishment, Rochelle raised the bat. Her mother wasn't here anymore. Rochelle felt like she was outside herself, watching the bat rise over her head, then fall forward onto the stack of teacups. There was nothing her mother could do to her anymore. The bat moved with such speed and force that it went through the cups like they were delicate Christmas ornaments and hit the table. The table glass was half an inch thick, with green edges. The impact of the bat created a spider web of cracks.

Rochelle felt the blood rushing through her veins, pulsing in her throat. A wave of heat rolled over her face. Before Gavin could even set out a new batch of china, she raised the bat again and brought it down. This time, the corner of the table cracked all the way through and a large chunk fell to the wooden floor underneath, breaking into several smaller pieces.

"Yeah!" Gavin shouted. "That's the spirit! Here, try these!" Gavin put more cups onto the remaining part of the table. Again, the bat went up over her head, paused and came crashing down.

Stack after stack of china was laid before her. Salad plates. A sugar bowl. A teapot. Dessert cups. Strike after strike, she moved along the length of the table, breaking off chucks of glass along with the porcelain. The crashing shards rattled to the floor, almost drowning out the sound of her mother's voice inside her head. With each strike of the bat, her mother's disapproving face flitted about the periphery of her vision, impotent and silent.

Finally, Gavin set a huge soup tureen on the remnants of the center pedestal and said, "Here, give me that. I wanna do this one." She sucked in a huge breath, her chest heaving. Why couldn't she get enough air into her lungs? She reversed the bat to hand it back to him.

He squared up to his target and snarled, "Who the fuck ever uses a fucking soup tureen!" He swung the bat and smashed it, shards flying again. Rochelle felt a tiny bit graze her cheek, but paid it no mind. She was still heaving in great huge breaths of air, staring at Gavin. He stared back at her, grinning maniacally. His over-grown brown hair falling into his eyes. They both started laughing. Slowly, at first, then faster. Rochelle couldn't figure out how she could huff a laugh, when she could barely breathe, but the grin on her face made up for the lack of loud expulsion of air. Gavin crunched over the shards of porcelain and glass on the floor to put his hands on her shoulders. They continued to laugh hysterically for a few minutes, gripping each other for balance.

When the initial rush subsided, Rochelle looked up into his face. His blue eyes were gleaming and a smile still flickered across his lips. They stared at each other. Rochelle reached up a hand to brush away a broken piece that had landed in his hair. Under the dusting of grit, his hair was soft. His gaze intensified and he stepped even closer to her, moving his hands from her shoulders down to tighten around her back.

Rochelle tilted her head back to accept his kiss. Within moments, they were mashed together in a firm embrace. He backed her up, stumbling a little, to brace her against a support post behind her. They kissed, running their hands up and down each other for a few moments. The blood was still pounding inside Rochelle. When Gavin lifted his lips to move to her neck, she mumbled, "Bedroom!"

He gripped her hand and pulled her behind him, back down the hallway. He pushed open the last door on the right, to find a neatly made up king size bed. Rochelle didn't have time to look around, before he gripped her about the waist and awkwardly tumbled them both down on the bed.

They fumbled off their multiple layers of clothes, brushing away a few more bits of glass and ceramic. Stripped down to their underwear, suddenly noticing the cold air on their skin, they slowed down. A moment of awkwardness intruded, so they returned to kissing frantically before stripping off the last bits of clothing. Rochelle kept her eyes closed and focused on the feeling of skin on skin. A brief thought flitted through her mind: how long had it been since Bill? She didn't know; she hadn't been keeping track of the days of the week.

That thought was followed by another: where were her condoms? She kept a couple from the supply that Apurva had brought her, in her purse. But she had stopped carrying her purse around weeks ago, maybe months ago. She had a moment to be thankful for the supply of birth control pills that Apurva had also gotten for her. She took one religiously every morning when she brushed her teeth.

Then rational thoughts evaporated out of her brain, as Gavin's hands on her body reach an especially sensitive spot. She just knew that she liked this, liked skin on skin, liked the weight of a man pressing her into the bed. She willingly, gladly accepted him into her. She met his thrusts enthusiastically, energetically, working to find the perfect rhythm. He varied the pace, speeding up and then slowing down to kiss and caress her sensitive spots, stimulating her. She pressed her hands into his back, pulling him closer. She wrapped her legs around his hips, to get a better angle and grip.

Finally, after several rounds of teasing slow downs, he finally accelerated and pumped into her. She could hear the mattress squeaking under them. She felt her body spasm and then his. He straightened his legs and rolled off her, grinning and heaving for breath. He left an arm splayed across her body, not willing to let her go just yet. She was still struggling for breath, too, so she lay still and basked in the moment.

"Wow!" he mumbled into her shoulder.

"Yeah," she mumbled back.

He lifted his head, grinning. "Now, see, doesn't it feel good to get your anger out?"

Rochelle giggled and turned on her side to face him. She moved her fingers over his body, exploring more slowly. She wondered if he had the stamina to go again in a little bit. Turned out, he did. The second time was slower, but just as intense.

Gavin fell asleep for a while after that. But Rochelle found she was too energized to do the same. So once his breathing deepened, she slipped out of the bed and found her scattered clothes. In the master bath, she thought for a moment. It was unlikely the house still had running water, but there might be a little pressure and supply left in the pipes. She's probably only get a small amount so she'd better be prepared to catch it. She plugged up one of the matching sinks and tried the tap. As she had guessed, a weak flow of water poured out, filling the sink about halfway before it hissed and petered out. She wet down a washcloth and wiped herself off. The cold water completed her cool down, so she used one of the larger bath towels to dry off. Then she put her clothes back on.

After she was redressed, she wandered about the house. She crunched through the broken shards, to retrieve a couple more bottles of water from the garage for Gavin, when he woke up from the nap. She looked into the other bedrooms. In addition to the master bedroom, there were two girls' rooms and one boy's room. Plus the office where they had come in through the sliding glass door originally, which could probably be configured as a bedroom, if necessary. On the other side of the central open area, next to the garage, a mudroom/laundry branched off.

Rochelle looked about. Clearly, the casual great-room was where the occupants spent most of their time. The other rooms were too formal, too sterile, to actually do any ordinary living in. But the great-room had a huge soft sofa and big screen TV. Rochelle stopped herself before examining the rest of the rooms any more closely. If she looked any further, she'd discover that this had been a real family's home. Just like the condo she'd explored. And that just led down a dark path. She didn't want to think about the people who had been here, about the boy who played Little League, or the girls who rode ponies. Or the husband and wife who played golf. The couple in whose bed she had just banged a strange man.

Instead, she went back outside. There was a tiny bit of tuna salad left, which had not gotten crusty yet, so she finished it off. Then she curled her legs under herself and sat on the patio furniture, letting her mind drift. She didn't think she was returning to her previous state of walking catatonia. Now that she had uncorked her anger, she realized that that's what she'd been: catatonic. A walking zombie. Not feeding on brains, though. She'd been feeding on nothing at all. There was a certain bliss to nothingness. Like being in a bubble, caught in stasis. Maybe if she called it meditation, it was more legitimate?

Now, though, the sex had energized her. Not physically, just mentally. It made her feel alive, awake, for the first time in months.

She waited patiently for Gavin, who woke up from his nap about an hour later. She went back to the bedroom when she heard him call out and explained that she'd left some water for him. She also pointed out that it was getting late and the days were still pretty short, so they'd lose the afternoon light soon. Through body language, she made it clear that she was not up for round three at the moment. But a flirty smile told him that future dates could be arranged, if he wished.

Gavin graciously accepted the situation and cleaned up. They firmly closed up the sliding glass door they had been using, but did not lock it. Gavin said it was just a courtesy, for the next wanderer who happened to come through. They were leaving most of the supplies in the pantry, for whoever else might need them, since they couldn't carry much on the Harley. Rochelle did stuff a few more water bottles and some more granola bars into a backpack she found, though.

On the ride home, Rochelle wondered if they should have cleaned up the smashed glass and china. She figured that anyone who came through that area looking for loot, would have sturdy shoes on. They would not be in immediate danger of cutting open a foot. If anyone wanted to take up residence, they could sweep up the debris themselves. It wasn't like there wasn't plenty of smashed up stuff elsewhere in the world. In parking lots all over the city, cars had been crashed. Store front windows were shattered everywhere, too. After their own little hammer time, she understood now why someone would crash a perfectly good car into a window.

Chapter 14

After their date in the country, Rochelle felt more energized when she returned to the bar. She bounced a little on her feet. A small smile stayed on her lips, even when she was not doing much of anything at all.

The guys didn't seem very happy about it, though. They seemed a little more grumbly than usual. Gary's sardonic comments took on a slightly sharper tone than usual.

In spite of the guys' implicit criticisms of Sadler, Rochelle fell into the same natural pattern with him, as she had with Bill. Gavin started coming to the bar in the evenings and staying until Rochelle closed up. Then they went to her condo or his apartment in the Watergate for the night. This happened once or twice a week. Gavin didn't like to have sleepovers any more often than that, though. He was a restless sleeper, often getting up in the middle of the night to wander about, or tap on his laptop. One night, when his puttering about woke her up, Rochelle asked him what he was working on.

"Just drafting speeches that I'll need on the campaign trail," he said, glancing at her over his shoulder. He was seated at a small desk in his bedroom. Rochelle was still snuggled under the warmth of several layers of blankets.

Rochelle thought about that for a moment. "So you're really serious about this thing, then? You're really running for President?"

"Sure am," he said, grinning. "Filed the paperwork and everything."

Rochelle frowned. "With who? Is there anyone who can even do that filing? Process it, or whatever?"

"Well, there wasn't actually anyone physically there, at the FEC office. But I filled out the form and left it on a desk there."

"You left it on a desk? How does that count?"

"It was the desk of the head of the office, the grand pooh-bah over there. Whoever ends up taking over the operation will find it when they move in."

"That doesn't sound very official," Rochelle said slowly.

Gavin turned all the way around from his desk to look at her directly. The cheerful grin was gone from his face now. He stared at her for a moment.

"It's as official as it needs to be. Look, you know perfectly well that the government is in shambles. Your buddy Gary and the others over at FEMA? They're not doing anything the way they were supposed to, under the old regulations. They can't. But at least they're doing something. They're getting people mobilized, getting things cleaned up. The military, they're the closest thing we have to a functioning government at the moment, but no one wants to live under martial law indefinitely. Meanwhile, everything else, federal, state, municipal, everyone is just making up new rules as they go along. We get to rebuild the engine, make it better, sleeker, more efficient. We'll rebuild it to *look* a lot like it used to, because that's what everyone's familiar with. But it'll be better. It'll run smoother. You'll see."

Rochelle studied him. He didn't say it out loud, but she could nearly hear the words inside his head, read them written on his face, "And I'll be at the top of it all."

***

Gavin spent his days building up his campaign. He was recruiting people to help him. In various drinking holes and meeting places around the city, even just wandering the National Mall, he talked to people, looking for able-bodied people with skill sets. He negotiated with the military for permission to drive about the city freely. In exchange for their non-interference with his usage of precious fuel inside the city limits, he was helping coordinate some work crews who could siphon more fuel out of cars in the suburbs around the city. They moved it to big tanker trucks, which they then parked at various gas stations, to dispense into permitted vehicles. The military was thankful for the contribution and granted him his permanent exemption for any vehicle he moved about in.

Confluence

Gavin had explained this to Rochelle during one of their late night conversations, when his restless wanderings had awoken her again. He waved a hand, expanding on the complexities of fuel recovery. "It's an intermediate solution. Obviously, it's a finite resource. But there's no point in letting it go to waste just sitting in a garage somewhere. The long term solution is to get oil production back online. That's the major project I'm working on. Establishing lines of communication to places where oil is extracted and refined. Actually, I may have to make a trip to Texas in the next couple of weeks, to personally see what's going on down there."

He glanced about, thinking. "You know, you could actually help me. I need some supplies for the trip. I'm actually getting low on toothpaste. Do you think you could scavenge up some for me? The whitening kind?" He smiled at her hopefully.

She frowned back. "You need me to do your shopping for you? What are you doing all day? You can't just break into someone's house and grab a tube for yourself? I thought you were doing that all over the place?"

"Well, those FEMA work gangs have started going about clearing things out. Its taking longer to find a neighborhood that hasn't been scavenged yet. I need to spend my time focusing on the bigger picture."

Rochelle was still frowning. "Uh huh. So why don't you just get stuff from the FEMA cache? Gary says they took over an office building and are making it into a warehouse for stuff like that. He says anyone can take what they need from there."

Gavin was quick to respond. "No, no, can't do that. Can't have the voters thinking I'm a charity case. In order to inspire confidence, I have to project an image of having all my shit together, like I know what I'm doing. Uh, how can I put this?"

He came back to the bed and sat down next to her, his hand caressing her thigh through the comforter. "Okay, imagine this hypothetical situation. You're in high school and they're running a class president election. There's two kids running. One guy is the captain of the football team, he's tall, handsome, gets good grades. The other kid is the band geek, who's always carrying too many books and dropping them all over the place anytime he gets bumped in the hallway. He's a klutz, always fumbling, stumbling over things. Which candidate are you going to vote for? The one who has his act together, or the one who's falling apart?"

Rochelle didn't answer. She was thinking that the geek would never have gotten nominated in the first place, unless someone else was playing a cruel practical joke.

Gavin answered for her. "The jock, of course. The one who's got those pearly white teeth and can speak in complete sentences. The one who doesn't have to go shopping at the dollar store. And that's what I'm trying to show the world, that I've got my act together. That I'm the one who can lead the team to victory. So. Will you help me?"

Rochelle studied him. Getting toothpaste wasn't that big a deal, she knew. Gary would bring her some, if she asked. Heck, people were starting to trade all kinds of odd items for their drinks at the bar. She could probably just let it be known that she needed some and it would show up in a matter of days.

She nodded at him and added, "You know, a barber shop just opened, up the street from the bar, across from Whigs and a few doors up. Well, technically it was a hair salon, before, but the guy who's setting up in there is calling himself a barber."

Gavin's face brightened. "You don't say? That's fantastic." He patted her approvingly.

She hadn't wanted to tell him, because she actually kinda liked his long grown-out hair. It was soft and a little wavy. But she could sense that he would want something much shorter and sleeker for the sake of his campaign.

***

Spring was starting to show signs of returning. The days were getting longer. A faint green haze was appearing on the trees as new leaves started to bud.

Gary and Marty had gone all in with the remnants of FEMA. The Superflu pandemic no longer qualified as an ongoing emergency. So the few remaining people who had worked for the agency were actively recruiting more help from surrounding survivors, including Gary and Marty, to work on recovery projects. Gary was running numbers on spreadsheets, collecting data on available resources, identifying housing that could be cleaned up and re-occupied. Marty was coordinating with military units at the Pentagon to make sure they avoided duplication of effort.

The recovery projects sponsored by the agency included more body removal from the city and suburbs. As Sadler had said, they had basically decided to ignore municipal boundaries, unless a functioning city government could be identified. They considered the entire metropolitan area as part of their immediate domain. Trucks were rounded up, hazmat suits distributed and crews were directed to go house to house. They picked locks where they could or broke in when they had to. Bodies were wrapped, loaded and taken to one of several dock sites, loaded onto the barges and sent down the river. A few smaller municipalities along the river added their contributions to the grim tide as well. In Norfolk, the barges were lashed together and towed out to sea.

Once a neighborhood was cleared of bodies, they had to wait for the horrific odors to subside. Bodies that had been laying on beds or couches for months at a time, had seeped decomposition fluids into the furniture and floors. And flies laid eggs that hatched maggots which pupated into more flies, too. It took days or weeks for the odors and pests to disperse. In some cases, if the home had contained a large family, or lots of pets, the hazmat workers advocated for burning the bedding in a big street bonfire.

Gary was explaining all of this to Rochelle one evening after a chilly, rainy spring day. He was trying to convince her to join one of the secondary projects. He'd been watching her reorganizing some newly traded stock. That had involved moving some heavy cases up from the basement, repacking them and then carrying them back downstairs. She really missed the electric powered dumbwaiter that used to lift heavy stuff from the basement to the kitchen.

The lack of power was making her grumpy, too. The little space heater plugged into the generator didn't do nearly enough to keep the place warm. She was wearing three sweaters over a t-shirt and leggings underneath her jeans. Her feet were bundled up so tightly in two layers of socks in her winter boots, she could barely flex her toes. It seemed like once the chill seeped inside of her, she couldn't get warm again.

Gary said, "So, on the cleanups, you'd be going into an empty house. All the dead have been removed, sometimes weeks or months ago. This is just to straighten things up. Take out the trash, box up any food and water… and…"

Rochelle heard hesitation in his voice. "And what, Gary?"

"And check for stuff. Like, guns, drugs, valuables. Anything not locked away in a safe. Or safes that can be easily removed to break open later."

Rochelle eyed him. "Valuables? What kinds of valuables?"

Gary stared at her for a moment. "Cash. Coins. Gold and silver jewelry."

"What on earth for? What good is cash going to do anyone now? I take payment in bottles now." She thunked a sealed scotch bottle onto the bar counter. She was still huffing a bit from her recent exertions. She paused for the conversation, spread her hands on the bar and leaned forward towards Gary, waiting for his answer.

Gary squirmed a bit and looked uncomfortable. "It's about creating scarcity. In order to get an economy functioning again, money has to be scarce. If we collect a big share of it now, we can parse it out slowly, later on."

Sarcasm lit up her voice. "So this project is really just robbing the dead? Are the hazmat crews checking wallets before they wrap up the bodies? Are they taking wedding bands off of hands, too? How about gold crowns on their teeth?" Rochelle glared at him.

"No, no, no. Nothing like that. In the long run, it's actually okay if some wallet cash goes down with the bodies. That contributes to the scarcity too."

"How much scarcity do you really think you can create?" Rochelle asked, frowning and waving a hand emphatically. "There's cities all over this country. D.C. is in the middle of one long nearly continuous urban zone, from Boston to Atlanta. You going to clear all of that? This country was what, 300 million people? That's, what, 100 million homes? You really going to clear out the sock drawers of 100 million homes?"

Gary protested, "Rochelle, come on, you know that's not possible. And I think the population used to be closer to 340 million, with about 128 million households."

"Whatever! I'm not Wikipedia. My point is, it's not going to be possible to clear all that out."

"Look, we understand that we can't get everything. The point is to get what we can. To get loose guns out of circulation, restrict the drug traffic. Figure out a way to restore value to the American dollar. There's talk of going back to a gold standard. I don't know if that will happen. But if it does, we'll need to collect gold to reforge into coinage."

"Seriously? This is all the coinage I'm seeing these days." She picked up the scotch bottle, waved it at him and turned to put it away on the shelves behind her.

"Not very easy to carry around in your back pocket though, is it? And what about that pack of toilet paper Susan brought in last week for you? Are you really going to carry a bulk pack of TP to the farmers market when you want some fresh eggs? "

"Farmers market?" Rochelle asked, puzzled.

Yeah, that's another project we're working on. Marty knows more about that one than I do. They're getting some farms going, out in the countryside. Lots of old estate houses on huge lots. Used to be farms, fifty or a hundred years ago. Some even still have an old barn on them. Now they're just really big lots with really big houses on them. Marty's got teams out looking for equipment, gathering up seed, breaking ground. Once they can start harvesting things, they'll haul it into town to sell. You planning on trading scotch bottles for eggs? Wouldn't it be easier to use some coins?"

Rochelle frowned at him.

Gary went on. "So, eventually, if we melt down the gold jewelry, we can make new coins. We can pay the workers in coin, who then pay for their booze, here." He waved his arm to gesture around the room. "Then you can use the coin to go buy eggs."

Rochelle thought over what he had said. She got stuck on the farms project. "Where are you getting all these workers for the farms? Or the other recovery projects, for that matter? There seems to be an awful lot of work to do. Are the three percenters enough?"

"Well, if we're talking about just the three percent from D.C. only, then no. But there's survivors pouring out of the cities up north; heading south. Those winter storms we had here? Apparently, they were blizzards up north, in New York and Boston. And Baltimore is in a bad way, too. They had a real problem with lots of fires destroying stuff. But really, all over the east coast. So people are looking for somewhere better. The agency wants to salvage this town. Too much history, too much symbolism, to just abandon this place. We got lucky, that no major fires got out of control here. So there's still plenty of good housing, other resources. Anyone we find out wandering, we recruit. They set up recruiting stations along the I-95 corridor and some other major freeways. It's a sales pitch. Find out what they need, what they can do, then offer something that matches. Clean up, farming, driving trucks around, whatever."

At that moment, a soft pop sounded and an overhead ceiling fan/light fixture suddenly flickered on. The blades started moving around, gradually building speed to create a soft breeze.

Gary and Rochelle stared up at the fixture. Then Rochelle looked around. The little power indicator on the coffee maker in the corner was lit up. Its clock blinked.

Rochelle asked in wonder, "Did the power just come back on?" She felt a little silly for asking the obvious.

"Uh, yep, sure looks like it," Gary answered her. They looked at each other and grinned. Rochelle looked about the bar, thinking fast. Then she started to scramble. She turned off the generator to save on fuel. She turned off the battery powered camp lantern she'd been carrying down to the basement and back. She turned on the ice maker. The igloo in the big walk in freezer was gradually getting worn down. She'd love to replenish it with some fresh ice. She had to pour some boiled water from the kitchen stockpots, into the cube trays inside the ice maker, since the water wasn't running yet.

Once she had the ice trays loaded and cooling down, she looked around for other tasks she could do, now that she had power. She elected to start filling the stockpots with more water from the bottles in the storage room. As booze bottles had been emptied, she'd taken to filling them with fresh snow that had fallen weeks ago. The snow had thawed and was just water now. While it had fallen cleanly from the sky, she still wanted to boil it, before using it for washing or drinking.

In spite of Rochelle's quick thinking, the power only stayed on for about forty five minutes. The new ice cubes were only partially frozen. Their centers were still liquid. The five gallon stockpots had warmed enough to start steaming, but had not yet reached rolling boil, when the power blipped off again.

Rochelle grunted in frustration at losing power so quickly again. Gary commiserated with her. "Well, it was a good sign of progress, after being out for months now, right? I'm sure it will come back. It's a process and they're still working out the glitches."

Rochelle nodded, but she reconnected the generator so that she could run the stove to finish boiling the new batch of water.

Colonel Wenrick came in about an hour later and they reported the brief power surge to him. He grinned and said, yes, the team at the North Anna power plant was making progress on getting a steady flow of power outbound. The reasons it didn't stay on had more to do with transformers and distribution issues in the grid, than generation at the source. That was another thing that his team was working on. Wenrick turned to Marty, who had joined them earlier and asked, "Is that something you can pass word about, out to the recruiting camps? To be on the lookout for anyone with electrical engineering experience and steer them our way?"

Marty nodded. "We already are. Padgett told me to send them to his unit. I think a few dozen high qualifieds have been identified and maybe a hundred or more low qualifieds, like household electricians."

"Okay, but Padgett is Air Force and the unit at North Anna is Navy."

Marty stared at him, waiting for the punchline. "And?"

Wenrick grimaced, "And, I'm Army, so I have no idea how many engineers the Navy has at North Anna. I need them at the local electrical utility stations, to run the boards."

Marty continued staring hard. "Sounds like a real communications challenge, there." Communications, meaning phones, either land line or cellular, had been a real sore point for him, ever since he'd started helping the agency. He'd been pestering Wenrick and the other military personnel he came in contact with, for access to their radio equipment and satellite phones, as an alternative. Some had been distributed to him, but so far, the different branches had been very stingy which left big gaps in everyone's ability to share information efficiently.

Wenrick pursed his lips, acknowledging the ongoing challenges of trying to share out people, equipment and resources while they were still gathering it together. He glanced around at everyone, considering his next words carefully.

"Look, the brass, including me and the other guys you know, have been having some discussions about something. We haven't wanted to share it publicly before now, but I think its time to get some civilian input." He paused. Everyone was watching him expectantly.

Wenrick swallowed and asked, "What would you guys think if we joined all the branches of the military into one? Instead of this five branch stuff, we'd tear down all the barriers between us. Instead of the Navy hoarding it's communications equipment and the Army hoarding all the gas, it would just be one unified military."

Marty snickered. "One big happily family? Ha! Good luck with that!" He was well versed in the tricky dynamics of large organizational relationships.

Wenrick nodded, "Yeah, I know. It won't be easy." He waited to hear what the others had to say.

Gary frowned hard. "You need Congressional approval and possibly Presidential approval, to do that," he said. He left unstated the obvious, that there was no President and no Congress to give that approval, at the moment.

"What if we did it anyways and asked for forgiveness later?"

Gary flicked his eyebrows and rolled his eyes. "Well, I don't suppose there's any physical way to stop you. Who are we going to call? There's no police force big enough to intervene. No FBI, no Secret Service, no Homeland Security."

Wenrick nodded his acknowledgment of that. He looked to Frankie, who had been silent, but actively listening to the conversation. "Thoughts, Frankie?" he asked.

He pondered and spoke up, "Well, I can't help but bring a sociologist's perspective to the situation. That's a pretty major restructuring. I can't help but think that you're wiping out 250 years worth of military history and tradition. But on the flip side, the whole Superflu has pretty much wiped out everything else, so why not transform what's left of the military? The guys are reinventing FEMA and by extension, all the other federal agencies too. Sadler is running for President, without any competition or party affliation. Maybe we're not going to have a two-party system anymore. What would the new unified military's mission be?"

Wenrick answered promptly, "To protect and restore this nation. To serve the citizens, help everyone get back on their feet again. Like that, only, you know, in more formal language."

Frankie nodded again. Wenrick looked to Rochelle and raised his eyebrows.

Rochelle blinked, "Hey, don't look at me. I don't know anything about running a military."

Wenrick pressed her. "Would you have any objections, if we moved forward, without Congressional authorization?"

Rochelle shook her head. "Nope. I don't care. But, you know, you could ask Gavin what he thinks." She nodded at her boyfriend, who was seated with a few people at a table on the other side of the room, having an intense conversation of his own.

Wenrick glanced over his shoulder at the group. Quietly, he said to Rochelle, "He's not President yet. And, his ability to actually become President, will require the assistance of the military. Preferably a newly unified one that isn't bogged down with internal squabbles over resources."

Rochelle shrugged and said, "Chicken and egg. Let's get him over here and ask."

Gavin looked up from his own hushed conversation when Rochelle waved to him. At her gesture, he stood up and approached.

"What's up, babe?" he asked her, smiling at the others arrayed along the bar.

Reluctantly, Wenrick quickly outlined the proposal and leaned back. Without pausing to even think about it, Sadler grinned and slapped Wenrick on the back, "Outstanding idea! Absolutely brilliant! What can I do to help?"

The bar flies glanced back and forth between each other.

Wenrick said, "Well, I don't think there's anything you need to actually do at this point…"

Rochelle could practically see the wheels spinning in Gavin's head. He launched, as if he had not even heard what Wenrick had said. "This could seriously work. I need help to run this campaign and get the election launched. No one but the military has the power to distribute ballots and collect them. And I'll need a protection detail, on the campaign trail. My guy over there is getting a bus, but we've heard about some problems with gang violence - not around here, but elsewhere. So, if we work together, that will inspire public confidence, which goes a long way towards restoration. This could be a win-win for all of us! Yes, this is a terrific idea! What do you need to move forward?" He beamed at Wenrick.

Wenrick actually looked a little dismayed. "Uh, I think we've got this. It's really an internal matter."

"Great!" Gavin turned back to Rochelle. "Chelle, sweetie, could you bring over another round of beer, please?" He gave her that broad shiny grin that made her stomach flip over. She nodded and set to pulling more bottles out of the fridge.

Wenrick turned back to face the bar, parallel to the rest of the guys. His face was closed off, stoic. Gary prodded him, "What? You asked for civilian opinion, you got it. What are you so peeved about?"

Wenrick blew a breath between pursed lips. "Not sure. It kinda felt like I was getting his permission, not his opinion. Which is not what I needed. Except, we do need it. At least, some kind of executive authority blessing. But not his, because he's not the

Commander-in-Chief. Yet."

Wenrick sighed. After a moment he added, "This frickin' Apocalypse is so damn frustrating. Why couldn't it have just been zombies? Just double tap them in the head and boom, you're done."

The guys chuckled in sympathy.

Meanwhile, somewhere in the Ozark Mountains...

Kevin sat staring into his little camp fire, not thinking about much of anything. It had grown fully dark, too dark to write any notes in his little book. Too dark to stumble about looking for more firewood. He had finished eating his camp beans and weenies, but it was still too early to go to sleep. So he stared, watching the sparks swirl up and vanish into the sky.

He wanted to empty his mind and just absorb the nature around him. The Ozarks were beautiful, calm, peaceful. But images of his travels during the last few months slid about inside his head. He had spent months criss-crossing the southwestern corner of the country, pausing to return to Chandler to give his reports. All across the region, he saw empty towns. Burned cities. Billboards shot up with thousands of rounds of ammunition. Cattle lying dead in dry fields, stiff and dried out, nothing but skin and bone. In the larger towns, the smell of rotting bodies made him heave his stomach empty, every time.

But some places were doing okay, just like his own home town. Wind turbines were pumping ground water into troughs and pipes. Solar panels had sprouted on roofs. Lone farms thrived with huge vegetable gardens and goats in pens. People rode bicycles or horses or walked in small groups. Some stores still had useful goods in sealed packages. Some stores were so barren and clean, it looked like they were ready for a new owner to set up shop.

He thought about his recent trip to California. The Central Valley had been in good shape. People in the little farm towns said they had absorbed survivors from the bigger cities. But they had also said don't go north. A nuclear power plant had blown up, they said. He had listened to that advice and looped back south.

In Louisiana and Texas it was hard to find anyone who would talk to him. He saw people walking on roads, but when they heard

216

the sound of his vehicle, they ran off to the side and disappeared into the woods. The few who talked to him were cautious about sharing information. Some were driven nearly insane with shock and grief. They were caught in the grip of fear, wild eyed. If they said anything coherent, they said don't go east, that it was worse there.

The people on the Indian Reservations about the southwest seemed like they always had, just fewer. Moving along at their slow relaxed place. Suspicious of strangers, but not outright hostile. They would talk with him, but they didn't have much to say. All Kevin learned was that they were doing what they had always done; farming, raising livestock, keeping their ways.

Nowhere in his travels, did he find anyone with grand master plan to fix anything. Obviously, it was too late to bring back the dead, so a cure for the Superflu was beyond pointless now. But he still wished for someone to tell them all how to get things back the way they had been before, just with less people.

A noise from the woods behind him startled him out of his reverie. *Animal?* He wondered. He leaned back out of the light of the fire, craning his neck about, waiting for his eyes to adjust to the dark.

A man, a boy, really, stepped out of the woods behind him and spoke softly. "Evenin.' Sorry to startle you. Mind if I share your fire for a bit?"

Kevin sat upright, studying the stranger. He was dressed the same as Kevin: layers of jeans and coats, a thick hat, sturdy shoes. He wore a back pack on his shoulders as well, but his hands were empty and relaxed at his sides. After a moment, Kevin nodded, gestured and said, "Sure."

The boy walked around him, giving him a wide berth. He sat across from Kevin, on one of the logs arranged around the fire pit. The campsite was one of many scattered about the parks in the Ozarks National Forest.

The stranger nodded his thanks and said, "I'm Andy." He raised his eyebrows.

Kevin responded to the prompt automatically, "Kevin." The boy was too far away to shake hands, without getting up and stepping a few feet over, so Kevin figured that social nicety was optional.

Andy nodded again. "Where you from?" he asked pleasantly.

Kevin had had this particular conversation dozens of times now, since he'd started scouting about. "I'm from Chandler, Arizona, but that's just where I hang my hat in between times. Mostly, I'm on the road."

Andy whistled. "Arizona? That's a long ways away. You must be headin' north, then, somewhere cooler?"

Kevin shook his head and waved his flattened hand. "Nah. I'm going east. Just taking a little side trip through the Ozarks here."

Andy frowned. "East? Why you wanna go there? The whole East Coast is a mess."

Kevin frowned back at him. "How do you know that? Where are you from?"

Andy answered, "Philadelphia area. Trust me, it's fucked up back there. Do yourself a favor and go up to Minnesota or Wisconsin or something."

"Fucked up how?" Kevin asked.

Andy launched into his narrative, eager to share his own story. "Too many people died. The cities are turning into stinking rotting swamps. It wasn't too bad when the weather was below freezing. But it's warming up, so the bodies are decomposing. I hear there's mountains of bodies around the hospitals, just dumped there last fall. The smell is everywhere. And the flies and maggots? Don't even get me started about the flies. But there's nobody left to do anything about that now. And the power's gone off in most places too and the water is bad. A neighbor of mine, he survived the Superflu, just to shit himself to death because of bad water."

Kevin nodded sagely. "Yep. Gotta boil the water, unless it's from a sealed bottle. They been saying that for months now."

Andy became more animated as he talked. He gestured with his hands, waving them for emphasis. "And I heard the military took over D.C. They're taking everyone's cars away from them. They say they gotta conserve the fuel."

Kevin frowned again. "Where you there? In D.C.?" he asked.

"Nah, I just heard about it from others who said they went

218

through it or near it. We went really wide around it. Through the Appalachians. Don't want to tangle with the military. We're on a mission."

Kevin's frown deepened. "Who's 'we'?" he asked. He glanced about, but didn't see anyone else.

Andy didn't answer right away. After a moment, he said, "Kevin, I need to ask you something. Do you think life is sacred?"

Kevin stared back in confusion at the abrupt change in topic. "Uh…"

Andy didn't wait for a full reply. "See, my mama and my grandma, they took me to church every week. The preacher taught us that life is sacred. He said, 'everyone has a right to live their life. Every life is important.' But then this Superflu came along and well you know how that turned out."

Andy held his hands out to the fire, warming them.

"So, if God created all life, then it stands to reason that he created the virus too. Everyone said viruses are alive too. Just tiny little bugs, hopping around from host to host, living their own lives. But they must not have had a preacher and church on Sundays. Cause, of course, that virus killed damn near every host it ever touched."

Andy rubbed his chin thoughtfully. Kevin still didn't know what to say. His own Dad had said they were Christians, but he never took either of his boys to any church that he could remember.

Andy's friendly chatter slowed down to a thoughtful tone. "So was my preacher wrong? He said God created all life and that life was sacred and meant to be lived. But God created that virus too and that virus didn't respect any life. That virus didn't act like life was sacred. So what gives? Do you think God was wrong? Or maybe my preacher was wrong? After all, he was just a man and he died like everyone else, hallucinating, sweating, bleeding and shaking. It can t be that God was wrong, could it? God is infallible. God is om… omni… whatever, I can't remember the word. But what I mean is, God is all. Of course, that's just another thing my Preacher taught us. But if he got the other thing wrong, maybe he's wrong about God too. Heck, maybe he's wrong about all of it. Maybe there is no God Because why would God expect us to treat life as so precious and then go and let nearly everyone die? Maybe everything I was taught was a lie. How can I tell? How do I know?"

The stranger waved a hand to make it clear he didn't expect an answer.

"So my point is, if I set aside all that I was taught, due to overwhelming evidence to the contrary, then I have to conclude that, no, in fact, life is not sacred. And if life is not sacred, well, then, that just makes it a whole heck of a lot easier for us to do what we have to do here. And see, my thing is, I need to get to California. With my friends, here."

As Andy spoke, Kevin glanced around to see a new person, a boy, a little younger than Andy, step from the forest shadows to his right. Kevin had guessed that Andy was around 18 or 20 years old, so he estimated that this new kid was about 16. The kid was holding a semi-automatic pistol in both hands, pointed directly at Kevin's chest.

Kevin rolled his eyes and turned back to glare at Andy. "Really? You really going to do this?"

Andy's face hardened. "Yeah, I kinda gotta."

Kevin scanned farther about. He discovered yet another person, a teenage girl, also emerging from the woods to his left, also holding a pistol leveled at him.

Kevin flung his hands up in the air in a fatalistic gesture. "Seriously? What do you think you're going to get here?" He waved around the campsite.

"That Jeep looks especially nice," Andy said. The girl was walking around the Jeep Wrangler, looking inside the windows and at the half dozen gas containers strapped to the roof. She nodded at Andy and said, "There's food inside, too."

Andy grinned and replied, "Fan-fucking-tastic! Now, how about we do this the easy way and you just toss the keys over here?" Andy had pulled out yet another pistol from somewhere and also pointed it at Kevin.

"Are you fucking kidding me?" Kevin sat still on his log, not making any sudden moves, but he let his extreme annoyance show on his face.

Kevin added, "You realize you can get a car just about anywhere, right? You don't need to steal mine. You can walk up to practically any house and take the car! And the food! Nobody will care!"

Andy shook his head. "Did you not hear what I said earlier, about everything being fucked up? There's bodies everywhere. You don't have to drink the water to get sick. Just going inside and touching the bodies can make you sick."

Kevin scoffed. "Aw, that's bullshit. That's not true!" Then he wondered. "Wait, what kind of sick are you talking about? Superflu? Or something else?"

Andy shrugged. But the girl said, "Distery."

Kevin squinted at her. She was just slightly beyond the circle of light from his campfire, so it was hard to see her. "You mean dysentery? They talked about that at the meetings back home. And cholera." He sounded out the medical words slowly, unsure of them himself.

Kevin explained, "They said we should wear gloves and masks, when handling the bodies. And wash our hands really good when done. No one's gotten sick from dead bodies, if they follow the directions."

The three kids looked back and forth at each other, considering.

Kevin waited for them to see reason. Finally, he pointed out, "So if you find your own masks and gloves, you can go into a house, find the food, the car keys and take the car. For that matter, you don't even need to go near the bodies. Just break in, grab the keys and go. You don't need to take *my* Jeep!"

The boy on the right asked, "And how are we supposed to find gloves and masks? Ain't no hospitals anywhere near here."

Kevin shrugged. "Uh, try a Home Depot or any hardware store. You don't need a full hazmat rig. Just a respirator. Any kind of painters gloves or kitchen cleaning gloves will do, if you're raiding just one house."

"Ain't no Home Depot anywhere around here, either. Not for miles and miles," said the boy.

Kevin knew the boy was probably right. At the moment, they were in the middle of the Ozark Mountains. There were assorted little hamlets and towns scattered about, along with a few small stand alone farms here and there. But they were probably fifty or a hundred miles away from a city large enough to support a big box hardware store. Kevin was just trying to keep them talking, trying to convince them to not take his Jeep. He knew perfectly well he could do all the things he was advising them to do, to get their own transportation. He just didn't want to take the time. He'd already done his scavenging work. Why should he have to do it all over from scratch again?

Andy interrupted his train of thought. "Look, we don't mess with dead bodies and we don't go into houses with dead bodies. We have to get to California and that's a long ways away. We need the Jeep and you're out gunned. So toss the keys over." He gestured with his pistol for emphasis.

Kevin was thinking about his own pistol, tucked into his belt at his back, under his winter jacket. It would take him too long to fumble it out now. Any attempt to do so might upset the two teenagers on either side of him. He had to give them credit for setting up the ambush and trapping him on three sides. He'd not been paying attention and then had been nicely distracted by Andy's chatter. Could he still distract them in turn, get them to reconsider finding their own car? In desperation, he tried one last tactic.

"What's in California? I was there, a couple of months ago. I can tell you what I saw, what to expect, where to go, what to avoid."

Andy and his friends considered that, for a moment. The girl looked hopeful. But Andy reluctantly shook his head. "You can say what you want about California, but we're still taking the Jeep. As you said, you shouldn't have any trouble finding another car yourself." He gestured again with his gun, indicating he still wanted the keys.

Kevin considered his options. While he thought, the teenage boy took a few steps closer, squinting in determination. His hands shook a tiny bit. Kevin quickly became convinced that the boy would shoot out of stupid fear. He didn't seem to have much self control at the moment.

A gunshot wound out here in a very sparsely populated national forest would probably be the death of him, Kevin considered. It wasn't like he could pop back into the Chandler Regional hospital for another quick set of stitches. Of course, that was assuming the shot wasn't immediately fatal.

Good sense finally asserted itself over Kevin. He sighed. "Okay, okay. I'm gonna stand up - slowly! Slowly! The keys are in my pocket." He matched his motions to his words, keeping his hands wide and visible. All three kids watched him closely. He extracted his keys from his pocket and gently tossed them over the fire, to land in the dirt at Andy's feet.

Andy picked up the keys and nodded to his companions. The girl bent over to grab Kevin's bed roll, which he had already spread on the ground near the fire, preparing to go to sleep soon.

Kevin groaned, "Hey, come on! Not my gear! I need that! It gets cold out here at this elevation."

The girl ignored him, bundling the camp sleeping bag to her chest and climbing into the backseat of the Wrangler. She had to shove over a duffel bag to make room for herself.

Andy and the other boy took the front seats and had the vehicle started within moments. They pulled out of the campsite on spinning tires, spraying dirt and leaves behind them.

Kevin stared after them, dismayed, angry, pissed off. He let out a mighty roaring "Fuck!" Then he yelled a few more curse words. He wanted to whip out his gun and fire at the retreating Jeep. Instead of pulling his gun, he imagined Andy's face as his target and swung a full body kick at the rocks around the fire pit. His comfy athletic trainer shoes were not sufficient protection against rocks. The toes of his right foot immediately complained.

Kevin roared some more in pain and frustration. He sat back down on his log, lifting his right leg to his chest, to clutch his foot in his hands, trying to squeeze the pain out. He rocked and hissed while the pain vibrated through him. After a few minutes, he took off his shoe and sock, to inspect the damage. The nails on his first two toes were broken from the impact. He had been overdue for a trim anyway. He tore away the the loose bits, leaving jagged edges that would catch on his socks. Yet another annoyance. Then he realized his nail clippers were in the little pack of grooming supplies in his duffel. Which was still in the Jeep. He yelled wordlessly out loud again.

He didn't have an object as simple and ordinary as toe nail clippers. He had lost his sleeping bag, all his clothes, his crates of food and water. His Jeep. All because he had let his guard down. He had let a stranger's rambling chatter lull him into thinking he'd made a new friend.

Kevin let go of his own foot and wrapped his arms around his knees again, rocking. He put his head down over his arms, curled up in a fetal position.

Everything was gone. His gear, his Jeep. His childhood friend, Bruno. His brother, Kaden. His Dad.

No one was doing anything to fix it, either. No one had saved the world. No one had stopped the Superflu from spreading. There hadn't been any frantic chase through an airport or a busy downtown street, to stop a villain from hurling a vial of evil yellow liquid into a innocent crowd. There was no magical divine intervention. There was no hero to save the day. There wasn't even a grumpy but determined sheriff about to round up thieving punks.

Kevin wept, feeling sorry for himself, his foot still throbbing gently. He missed his Dad. He missed his brother. He missed traffic. He missed watching sports on TV. He missed eating in restaurants, where a waitress brought out hot plates of salty, rich food.

Kevin's pity party didn't last long. Even though he missed his Dad, he also knew Dad would have smacked him upside the head for sitting there, whining and sniveling like a little boy. When he finally lifted his head, he started assessing the situation.

He still had his own gun, untouched under his jacket. The stupid kids hadn't even thought to check him for weapons. He had a swiss army knife in his pocket, too. A flashlight still lay on the ground, next to his own backpack of essentials. The pack contained a few nutrition bars, a couple of bottles of water, a small first aid kit, his maps. And he knew there were some houses a few miles down the road; he'd passed them on his way here. The same ones he'd been thinking of when he'd tried to convince the kids to do their own scavenging.

He'd been wandering about the Ozarks for a couple of days, just enjoying the scenery. He'd always wanted to see more of this part of the country. He'd driven I-40 through the area in his big truck plenty of times, but that was only a tiny slice of the region. On this journey, he had the time to wander the back roads, wherever he wanted, exploring. Just as he had advised the kids, he'd been scavenging as he went, siphoning gas from parked cars.

That gave him a chuckle. The hand held fuel pump he'd been using was packed away in a case under all the other boxes in the back of the Jeep. It might never occur to them to even look for it. They might not even recognize it for what it was. And the cans on top of the Jeep were almost empty. There definitely wasn't enough gas to get all the way to California. They'd be forced to go raiding anyway. Raiding places that might potentially still be filled with dead bodies, to get more fuel and food. Or else go back to walking when the fuel ran out.

Kevin laughed a little to himself. Then he sobered, when he realized that nah, they'd just find some other idiot to rob, just like himself.

Kevin put his sock and shoe back on, kicked dirt over the remains of his little camp fire, pulled on his backpack and set off down the road in search of better things.

Chapter 15

Rochelle resumed her morning bike rides around town for exercise. She avoided the river areas, not wanting to subject herself to the miasma of odors from more river barges. With the warming weather, the smell of decay was getting stronger and spreading over the city. So she rode north, exploring the nearby Maryland suburbs of Chevy Chase and Silver Springs. She used her cell phone to take pictures of un-looted retail spaces and homes. When she found an interesting street or neighborhood, she would stop and assess. If the horrible dead body stench was in the air, then it was clear the body collectors had not yet been through. If the air was reasonably clear, she'd try the doors of a dozen or so homes. If the doors were still all locked, it was likely they had not yet been checked for bodies, or valuables. She made notes of locations and addresses. In the evenings, she passed the information to Marty so he could send out the crews.

In spite of Gary's pitch to get her more directly involved, she still just couldn't bring herself to actually start taking things from people's houses. It felt like stealing to her. She had a deeply ingrained aversion to doing that. She wondered why she even felt that way. It wasn't like either of her parents had ever been involved in law enforcement careers. They hadn't strongly preached any particular position regarding criminal behavior, other than the basic, "don't take other people's stuff." Rochelle figured, to her mother's point of view, it would just be rude. Her mother was all about socially correct behavior.

So instead, Rochelle did her part by providing preliminary scouting information on the neighborhoods she rode through.

One warm and sunny spring morning, Rochelle noticed that the scattered cherry trees were starting to bloom. The downtown area had many of the trees, especially around the Tidal Basin and East Potomac Park. The trees had inspired many people in the region to plant them in their residential landscapes. Rochelle was overjoyed to see the light pink fuzz developing. In a few days, the sweet floral aroma might even overwhelm the dead body miasma.

***

One evening when the cherry trees had reached full bloom, a new person came into the bar. The middle aged man was slightly portly, gray haired, balding on top. His clothes seemed a little over-sized on him, as if he had lost weight in the last few months, but hadn't found smaller clothes yet.

He walked into the bar and looked about curiously. Frankie, Marty and Gary were seated at their usual stools at the bar. When the man didn't move away from the entrance, Rochelle called out to him. "Welcome to Paulbicki's. You can take a seat where ever you like."

He nodded acknowledgment, looked about again and elected to take one of the bar stools, the one at the end by the window, where Wenrick liked to sit. The colonel wasn't there at the moment.

Rochelle gave the counter in front of him a fresh wipe, even though she knew it was clean and set a coaster down in front of him. She didn't want to use paper napkins anymore, if she could avoid it, because that just generated trash, which filled up the dumpster and she was trying to keep pickups to a minimum, to go easy on the few trucks still cruising about town. The cardboard coasters could be dried and reused.

"What can I get you?" she asked in the casual sing song rhythm of all professional waitstaff.

The man thought for a moment, looking over the shelves behind her, stocked with a wide assortment of bottles. Finally, he asked, "Do you have any tonic, for a gin'n'tonic?"

Rochelle nodded. "Some." Tonic water had not been a top priority in Gary and Marty's scavenging efforts to keep their favorite watering hole stocked, but there were still a few bottles left. "Sorry, no limes, though."

The man nodded at her, to indicate he wanted the drink, even without the garnish. Rochelle added ice to a glass, mentally giving thanks for another burst of power that day to make fresh ice. Then she poured in the gin and tonic water, which was still somewhat fizzy, even though it had been opened weeks ago. She set the glass in front of him with a smile.

Ritual completed, Gary offered his usual opening gambit for any stranger who came in the bar. "So, where are you from?" he asked pleasantly.

The stranger glanced at Gary and the others beside him and then looked down into his drink. "Where am I from? Where am I from? He mumbled softly to himself. Then in a normal conversational tone, he answered, "Well, originally I'm from Wisconsin."

Gary waited a moment, to see if the man would explain further. When nothing more came, he prompted, "So did you spend the winter there in Wisconsin and just now came down here?" He raised his eyebrows expectantly. Of all the strangers wandering through the city, they had yet to encounter anyone from so far away.

"No, no, that's just where I'm from originally. Not where I was, before. Or during." The stranger slowed to a stop and took a sip of his drink. He savored the piney astringent flavor, as if he had not tasted it in a very long time.

Gary and Marty were giving each other the look, the one that meant this guy might be in need of more than just casual bar conversation. The one that meant they might need to usher him over to the agency offices for more urgent assistance.

But the man continued in a normal tone, "No, I just came back from Tuscarora. I just got back to find my apartment has been ransacked. So I went to my office, but it's locked and I don't have the keys. There doesn't seem to be anyone about. So I walked up the Mall..." He trailed off for a moment, lost in his own thoughts. Gary and Marty were staring hard at the new person, when they weren't glancing meaningfully at each other.

"And there's this smell in the air outside. Not the body smell. I've been smelling that for days, for weeks. But something else. Not the cherry blossoms either, although those are wonderful. But as I walked along the river, I could smell something else. It smells like...

228

like roasting pork. And I'm so afraid it's not pork. And then I saw the light in here - you have light! How can that be? And I thought maybe you're cooking food in here. I used to come here, before. My wife liked this place. But now that I'm inside, I can't smell the pork anymore. But it's out there, outside. That smell, like an old fashioned barbecue. Please don't tell me they're turning cannibal around here. Because that's what humans smell like, when they're cooked. Like pork. At least, that's what I read somewhere." The man's face looked about ready to crumble into grief.

Marty, sitting closest to him, reached out an arm and patted him gently on the back. "Don't worry, it's not. It really is pork that you're smelling outside. They're smoking half a pig, up at Whig's. Up the street. They just pulled it out of the freezer a few days ago. We can take you up there, if you want. Are you hungry?"

The man stared at them in astonishment. "Really? Seriously?"

Gary nodded. "Really," he affirmed.

Marty asked again, "Are you hungry? When did you last eat?"

The man nodded, then shook his head. "I'm not starving. I mean, not starvation starving. I've been on light rations for a while now. They had MREs at… at the place… Anyway, yeah, I'm hungry, as in, 'yeah, I could eat,' but not starving. If there's others who need it more, I don't mind. I've still got calories on board." He patted his pouchy stomach under his loose shirt.

Marty smiled, "Don't worry, there's plenty for everybody. They're a long way away from being out of food. It might be served with some odd side dishes and there's no fresh vegetables left. But they've got plenty of meat. And rice and pasta. They reacted quickly last fall and got lots of stuff frozen. Come on, why don't we walk up there? We'll show you where." Marty stood up, followed by Gary.

As they were coming to their feet, Gary held out his hand and introduced himself. "And what's your name?" he asked.

The man shook hands and said, "I'm Henry Livan." Gary's eyes widened slightly, but he just nodded. Henry took another swallow of his drink, left the half filled glass on the bar and followed Gary to the door. While they were facing away, Marty turned back to Frankie, who had not gotten up, and Rochelle. He leaned toward them and hissed softly, "He's a Congressman!"

Frankie startled at the news and looked over his shoulder at the departing men. Rochelle raised her eyebrows. Once the door had closed behind them, Frankie said, "Well, he *was* a Congressman. Not sure if that still applies now."

Rochelle shrugged. "Not sure it doesn't, either." She paused, studying him. "You're not going with them?"

He shook his head. "Nah, I ate already. I'm fine right here." He continued to nurse his own drink.

***

Gary, Marty and Henry returned about an hour and a half later, bringing a plate of pulled pork with a pickle, a bag of chips and a packet of sauce for Rochelle. Gary and Marty had back filled the Congressman on what had been going on in town, in his absence. When Colonel Wenrick came in for his evening nightcap, they introduced him to Henry, including the explanation of his former occupation. Wenrick smiled warmly and welcomed him back to D.C. Rochelle listened in as Henry told Wenrick about his experiences.

Tuscarora had been the secret evacuation site for what remained of the former federal government. However, most of the people who had been taken there had succumbed to the Superflu, including the last President, who had only served for five days, before his own death. After him, there had been no one left in the chain of succession, so the position had been vacant for months. Henry, a few other Congressmen, a handful of family members and a couple of young Marines were the only ones who were naturally immune or had recovered. The Marines had been in facility and communications lock-down mode. They refused to contact the outside world to find new orders, until it was clear that the survivors were not going to get sick. Until it was clear that no additional help was going to come to them.

Once released from lock-down, the few survivors had taken a couple of the military vehicles parked in the compound outside the bunker and returned to D.C. Inside the city limits, members of the small group had peeled off one by one to return to their homes. They were unsure what they would find, but were eager to be surrounded by familiar things and spend some time alone, after being trapped in close quarters for so many months.

When Livan finished his story, Wenrick offered his apologies that none of the remaining brass at the Pentagon had even known about the evacuation site, let alone thought to send a retrieval team. They had been too busy with their struggle to bring home survivors from overseas locations, communications issues, securing weapons depots and assorted other logistical nightmares. Whoever had been responsible for monitoring the evacuation site from the outside had died without passing on the communications protocols.

Livan waved the issue away, saying isolation was kinda the whole point of a secret bunker that no one knew about.

Later, Rochelle told Gavin about the Congressman's return, during one of their late night after-sex conversations. Gavin was thrilled to discover that some high level government representatives had survived and returned. He immediately made plans to pounce on them in order to make allies and legitimize his candidacy.

***

A few days later, Gavin put his plans into action, when he made a splashy arrival at Paulbicki's. The guys, including their new friend, Henry, had arrived shortly after the normal dinner rush at Whigs and had settled into their drinks. They were talking jovially, drilling into post-Superflu stories about who was doing what, where more things needed to be done and so on. Henry was pleasantly surprised at how quickly people adopted a barter economy. In addition to their drinks Paulbicki's handful of neighborhood survivor regulars paid for hot cooked food at Whigs by trading packaged food to Chuck and Cherry, to be used in future meals.

Out of the corner of her eye, Rochelle saw a long black limousine glide up to the curb outside the bar. She turned and frowned at it. Thanks to Wenrick's haranguing of his colleagues at the Pentagon, they had discontinued almost all of the fuel seizure operations around the city. The checkpoints were still manned by guards, but that was mostly to direct the erratic streams of refugees wandering into the city. They screened for potential troublemakers and steered them clear, or otherwise provided such aid so as to eliminate the need to cause trouble.

The guys noticed Rochelle's attention and turned to gaze outside as well. The power was back on in the area and orange sodium street lights were lit, for the moment. The dark car gleamed with reflected light. The driver hopped out and came around to the near side to open the door. Gavin Sadler stepped out, followed by two more men. All of them were dressed in slacks and suit coats, but with open shirts, no ties. One of them opened the main door to the bar for Sadler, who strode through confidently, pushing the inner vestibule door open on his own.

Inside, Sadler waved about to greet everyone, nodding and smiling. In addition to the usual bar flies, a few tables were occupied by some of the less-regular regulars.

"Hey, everyone! How's everybody this fine night?" he called out loudly.

Rochelle frowned. It was not actually a very fine night at all. Clouds had moved in during the afternoon and a light misty rain had started to wet the streets. She suspected it was going to get worse before it got better.

Bar patrons murmured their greetings, knowing Sadler by face and reputation.

Rochelle piped up, "What's the deal with the limo? What happened to your Harley?"

Sadler had been about to make a beeline for the Congressman, spotting him instantly at the end of the line of bar flies. But Rochelle's question stopped him cold. He frowned at her. "What do you mean?" he asked.

"Kinda ostentatious, don't you think? And aren't they gas guzzlers? We only just barely got back the ability to drive around town. You don't want to spoil it for everyone by wasting so much gas, do you?" The words popped out before she could think much about what she was saying.

232

Sadler frowned even harder, but just for a moment. In that brief instant, Rochelle abruptly realized she had displeased him. He was giving her that look her mother always gave, whenever Rochelle or one of her sisters had disappointed Catherine. The look that said, 'How dare you do this to me front of others?'

Rochelle froze, not sure how to take her words back, or what to do next. Sadler narrowed his eyes at her, but didn't say anything. Gavin had told her a couple of nights before about how he wanted to approach Livan. He just hadn't said anything about a fancy limo.

In the awkward silence, Gary spoke up, "So, I suppose you'd like to be introduced to the Congressman." He gestured at Henry, who stood up, preparing to shake hands. "Sadler, this is Congressman Henry Livan, from Wisconsin. Henry, this is Gavin Sadler."

Sadler squared his shoulders up and faced Henry, plastering on a cheerful smile. Henry took a couple of steps forward. The two men shook hands and grinned at each other.

Henry spoke first, "Mr. Sadler, I've heard so much about you. It's a pleasure to meet you. I understand you want to run for President."

Sadler beamed back, "Well, yes, I *am* running for President. I was hoping I could count on your support."

Livan nodded and said, "Let's talk a bit."

The two men adjourned to a side table, with Sadlers' two assistants in attendance. Rochelle overheard brief snatches of Gavin's usual campaign schtick. She understood that he was recruiting Livan's support. The conversation lasted until Wenrick arrived. The Colonel and Livan had already had a lively discussion about the current status of the nation. They had agreed to meet back here tonight, to followup on several topics that each had spent the day investigating, within their respective spheres of influence.

When Livan saw Wenrick enter, he waved and then stood up. He made his excuses to Sadler, shaking hands again and giving him a pat on the back. Gavin seemed a little annoyed to be put on the back burner. Wenrick suggested that he and Livan go upstairs, for more privacy.

That startled Rochelle a little bit, because no one had used the upstairs dining room in months. The staircase was right in the middle of the room, but everyone seemed to ignore it like it's only purpose was to collect the sun's rays from the skylight above it. She hadn't swept the dining room floor or wiped the tables up there in months.

She quickly gathered together a glass of Wenrick's favorite bourbon, a refill of Henry's gin-and-tonic and a damp rag. She pattered up the stairs after them and found them in a corner, settling in for an intense talk. She wiped off the table for them and set their drinks down. They thanked her and she trotted back down the stairs.

Gavin grabbed her arm before she even landed on the ground floor. "What are they doing up there? Are they talking about me? Are they going to provide the resources I need for the campaign?" he hissed at her softly, so as not to be overheard.

Rochelle frowned at him. "Gavin, calm down. They just sat down. I have no idea what they're talking about. They're not going to tell me."

Gavin let her go, but followed her up to the bar, as she retreated behind it. He glanced at Frankie, Gary and Marty, who were all watching him curiously. The rest of the bar had returned to it's usual conversational volume level.

Gavin joined the bar flies, while his people remained at their table on the other side, scanning the room.

After half an hour, Wenrick and Henry clomped back down the stairs, empty glasses in hand. They looked about and spotted Sadler at the end of the bar. They approached him. Livan spoke first. "So, to recap what you were saying earlier, a major platform in your campaign is encouraging people to get back to work, to get goods and services flowing again. Is that correct?"

Gavin had stood up. He nodded vigorously. "Indeed, it is. I've been planning on a recruiting trip to Texas, to see what conditions are like down there."

Henry nodded. "Uh huh. And do you think you can get the oil industry restarted? If there's only 3% of the population left in the area, that might not be enough to handle the rigs or refineries."

Sadler had a answer ready for that dilemma. "Well, if I recruit more people along the way and send them there, they can make up the workforce. The existing experience in the area can train new people. It'll take a little time, but it's worth doing."

Livan raised an eyebrow at him, cocked his head to the side, studying him. He glanced at Wenrick. "Will that work for you?" he asked.

Wenrick nodded. "As you know, we're still going to be in a major fuel crunch, sooner or later. According to our calculations, based on incoming data, there's enough gas left in the distribution network to last until it starts to go bad, at current usage rates among civilian and military alike. There's no point in letting it go bad, which is why we're lifting the civilian restrictions on driving in this region. But we need production up and running and ready to deliver product when the current supply is gone. Preferably before that happens. If you bring back solid evidence that fuel production is getting restarted, we will provide military resources for security escort, logistics and communications, to your campaign over the summer and fall."

Henry nodded and added, "Likewise. If you provide solid evidence that oil production is getting restarted, I'll grease the wheels administratively, here in D.C., for a legitimate election. I'll oversee ballot production, recruit more people to run for Congress in their own states, all that. I'll also handle what little administrative direction is needed, until you are elected President. Or anyone else. I won't stop anyone else from also running against you, if they step up. I'm just saying, I'll make sure that what remains of a national government in this town, works to run a valid election. But there's one more thing we want from you, for this support." He stared intensely at Sadler.

Sadler frowned. "What's that?"

Henry responded immediately, "We want to name your Vice President, after the election is complete and you're sworn in. You don't get to pick a VP. We do."

"We, who?" Sadler asked, his eyes flicking back and forth between Livan and Wenrick.

"The rest of the surviving Congressmen and myself. This is a new kind of 'check-and-balance.' We'll place a Vice President. Just in case… something should happen. Naturally, it will be someone we can trust."

Sadler's lips pressed together in a thin line. He wasn't happy about that requirement. He considered his options for a few moments.

"Very well," he said finally. "We have a deal." He held out his hand to shake. Livan accepted it and they shook firmly.

Rochelle looked about at everyone else. Gary was frowning a bit, while Marty and Frankie watched the impromptu deal with intense curiosity.

Business concluded, Sadler signaled to his two men, who quickly followed him as he strode back out the door. They climbed into the limo, which smoothly drove away into the light rain. Henry and Wenrick thanked each other, said their good-nights and disappeared shortly afterward as well. Rochelle was left to wonder about what had just occurred, right in front of her eyes. She wasn't sure what to make of it, but she had a feeling she had just witnessed a tiny slice of history unfolding in front of her.

Chapter 16

Within days, Gavin was ready to leave for his trip south. He pressured Rochelle to come with him.

"Seriously, babe, you should really come. You're wasting your time here. What are you even doing here, just tending bar? It's not even *your* bar." He seemed to have completely forgotten about her jibe at the limo scene.

Rochelle shrugged. "What would I even do on your trip? It's not like I have much to contribute to a campaign, either."

Gavin shrugged too. They were laying in bed. He had his arm around her shoulders, her head resting in the crook of his arm and chest. His shrug jiggled her.

"You went to college. You could write speeches for me."

"I'm not a speech writer. My degree is in business administration. My MBA was focused on marketing. I don't know anything about politics."

"But that's perfect! A campaign is just another kind of marketing operation. You'd be selling me. Build the brand, design the website, introduce me on stage, that kind of thing."

Gavin rambled on, talking about the kind of wholesome image he wanted to present, how they could gather crowds for campaign speeches. And, oh, maybe they should stop by his family home on the way, to pick up old photos they could scan and make into a presentation or something.

Rochelle stopped listening to his rambling stream of consciousness. She wondered if she really could leave town. Frankie was slowly coming out of his own walking catatonia; maybe taking over the bar would help get him right with the world again?

But Texas? She'd never had any interest in going to Texas before. There were other places she'd wanted to see around the country, before going to Texas. She wanted to see the Rocky Mountains. And Seattle. And the Grand Canyon. She'd been to Florida for a few college spring breaks with friends. And she'd been to California to visit Paige a couple of times. Sometimes, during high school, her mother had taken the girls to New York City for long weekends of shopping and theater. And of course, she'd lived in Chicago for two years. That had been a great city, before. But Texas? And it probably wasn't going to be the nice parts of Texas, either. It was going to be the industrial parts, the oil refineries and chemical plants. She'd heard that oil refineries smelled bad, too. Could it be worse than dead body rot? Were they even doing anything to clean up the bodies down there? The heat and humidity would probably make things ten times worse down there, she figured.

She mentally prepared her rationale for politely declining Gavin's offer. But his ramblings had wound down and he was rapidly falling asleep, not even waiting to hear her final decision. When his arm relaxed and slumped off her shoulder, she sighed and rolled over, spooning her hips and back to him, pulling a sheet over both of them.

***

The cherry tree bloom peaked and fell, leaving a new bright green haze of tiny leaves on the trees. Without the blossoms to overcome it or at least fight back, the dead body stench was thickening in the city. Some days were better than others. If the wind was blowing, the smell was dispersed. Other days, when the spring warmth spread into the previously frozen homes, the smell blossomed just like the flowering trees and perennials. Now that spring was here, flowers were popping out everywhere. Tulips, daffodils, any kind of bulb flower was blooming. So were other trees, aside from the cherries. Apples, dogwoods and magnolias were all putting on a fuzzy coat of white or blush pink flowers. The horrible smells emanating from the abandoned homes and hospitals overwhelmed the visual beauty, though.

Rochelle wondered if things were better out in the country. Maybe out there, the smell wouldn't be as bad. She still thought about that house she and Gavin had broken into. There were so few houses around that area, that even if they did have any bodies left in them, maybe the smell would be contained inside them. She hoped that she and Gavin could go for another motorcycle ride out in the country, when he got back in a few weeks. Gavin had left town without even saying a final good bye to Rochelle, after she had finally told him that she had to stay where she was. That callous, thoughtless, abrupt disappearance almost sent her back into a tailspin. She told herself that it was just because he had been frantically busy with the trip preparations. He'd be back in a few weeks. Then they could have some time together, she assured herself.

In the meantime, she coped with the horrible miasma of rotten, fetid odor in the city by dabbing ointment under her nose to block, or at least reduce, the smell. Vicks Vapor Rub had become a hot commodity about town, scavenged from empty houses and looted from drug stores. It was being traded for all kinds of things, including drinks at the bar. It was one of many new alternative forms of currency Rochelle was accepting. The most common form, aside from liquid supplies to be served, was MREs.

The newly unified military announced they had rechristened themselves the United States Armed Military Forces, or U.S.A.M.F. Then they set out to prove to the civilians that their reorganization was a good thing for everyone. They expanded their clean-up program to the surrounding suburbs. Teams of newly combined low ranking personnel were sent about in hazmat suits and trucks, collecting anything that could rot, from bad meat in refrigerators, to dead pets, to bodies still lying abandoned in bedrooms and hospital morgues. The operation was a massive search project, training exercise and shake down cruise combined into one. Low ranking soldiers, sailors and airmen had to get over old fraternal rivalries and forge new working relationships, while hauling leaky bundles wrapped in sheets and bags. The new U.S.A.M.F. also coordinated with the remnants of FEMA to recruit more civilian volunteers to help with the projects, paying them in MREs and housing.

Those MREs circulated and turned into an informal currency. They were being traded in a small impromptu market that had sprung up in the courtyard of the shopping complex a block down the street from the bar. It was just a collection of random people putting up a table and a 10x10 tent canopy, on days when the wind was strong enough to blow the bad odors out, but not so strong that the canopies were at risk of being torn away. People traded items they had scavenged, like chapstick, hand lotion, disposable razors, condoms, batteries and bars of soap. At the bar, Rochelle accepted MREs and even more oddball items from random customers, including cans of Ensure, packets of taco seasoning, baby formula, canned water chestnuts, ramen noodles, and boxes of soup stock. Several female customers made a special point of discretely bringing her boxes of tampons and pads, too.

Power was getting more consistent, but city water still wasn't working. So the new military mounted an operation to address that too. They already had plenty of small scale water purification systems running in their camps around the Pentagon. Each mini water plant could provide drinking water for a few thousand people at a time. But the city refugee population was growing faster than they could keep up with. The military had already cleared smaller bases in Virgina and Maryland, gathering all the surviving enlisted personnel, officers, equipment and weapons, and settling them at the Pentagon, or at the Norfolk base. Now they expanded that evacuation process to bases in Pennsylvania, Ohio, West Virginia and the Carolinas. They prioritized water purification systems, communications equipment and light duty weapons, along with surviving personnel. The only exceptions were weapons depots with enough heavy duty equipment to be a problem if it fell into the wrong hands. It was too much stuff to move easily, so those were left in place, with a minimum guard force.

The mini water plants were distributed to stations about the city, along with cisterns to collect rainwater and large water tanker trucks that pulled their source supply from municipal storage tanks or rivers and creeks that were not too polluted with runoff. Civilians carried buckets and jugs to the stations, filled up and carried them home again. Even though the water had gone through minimal treatement, everyone was strongly advised to boil it again, just in case.

Confluence

Wenrick and Livan were especially informative sources of information on what was going on around the city. They both tended to come in late, after 9 p.m. or so. Both had one, sometimes two drinks. They never had a enough to get drunk, just enough to help them get to sleep. They would talk quietly, exchanging information about various projects. Gary and Marty contributed their perspectives as well. Frankie sat quietly at the end of the bar, listening, observing, but not talking.

One calm warm evening, Livan asked Wenrick, "Have you had much problem with deserters? I always heard that could be a big problem, in large scale disaster situations. People abandoning their posts to be be with their loved ones?"

Wenrick shook his head. "If there's deserters, we don't really know about it, officially. Anyone who's not on base, not reporting for duty, is assumed to have died of the Superflu. When we find survivors on a base, we assess their fitness to serve. Sometimes they're too broken up over what happened, about losing all their people. If they're too broken to do their jobs, we're, uh, releasing them from service."

He paused, unsure if Livan would insist upon more formal procedures for entering and exiting service. Livan didn't say anything. He just waited patiently for Wenrick to go on.

"Most soldiers just want a job to do, something to keep busy with. They do better in small teams, when they have a mission to accomplish. A goal, a purpose. It helps bring them out of the depression, if they can see that they're helping others, helping civilians. If they're contributing to a mission that serves the greater good."

Henry nodded sagely. "Everyone seems thrilled to have the power back on. It seems to be getting more consistent."

Wenrick agreed. "Yeah, we've collected enough Corp of Engineers personnel and civilian engineers, to finally get that working again. It really helps that Marty's teams have been turning off appliances." He nodded to where Marty was seated a couple of stools away. Marty waved his acknowledgment back.

Henry asked, "What about water? If that could be stabilized, then

241

this could truly become a functioning city and not just a widely distributed refugee camp."

"Yeah, that's next on the list as well. We've been so focused on electrical engineering experience. We haven't really recruited for civil engineering. Those purification systems have handled drinking water needs. But man, I really miss hot showers."

Everyone nodded. Marty offered, "So, should I start sending word about, to find skills? That's kinda out of my personal range of experience? What do you need? Plumbers?"

Wenrick answered, "More than just plumbers, although they'll need that too. I suggest talking to your contacts over at city management. I think that first they need to get the city water plants turned back on. They'll need anyone with civil engineering, construction, pipe laying experience. Maybe even someone with agricultural water management experience could contribute."

Gary pointed out, "Municipal water plants are about pumping and purifying. There's a lot of chemical processing that happens, to turn raw water into clean city water. They'll need chemical supplies."

Everyone fell silent. Without a functioning transportation grid in place, it was going to be very difficult to get chemical supplies from source to destination. They didn't know exactly what kind of chemicals were needed or where to find them. And even once they found out, it would mean using precious fuel to truck stuff around.

Finally, Wenrick said, "Well, just like everything else, I guess we'll have to figure that out too."

Rochelle had been silently monitoring the conversation. She spoke up now. "Couldn't you ask Gavin to help with that too? He's investigating all kinds of manufacturing, on his trip. He could probably find out where there's stockpiles of chemicals. There's probably lots in Louisiana and Texas."

Gary snorted. "Oh sure, just let me whip out my cell phone here and call him up." He matched motions to words, bringing out his dead phone and pretending to tap at the screen. Everyone still carried their phones around out of habit, more than any real functionality.

Rochelle rolled her eyes. "Didn't you guys give him some radio equipment?" She looked at Wenrick.

"Yeah, he's got a satellite radio," he admitted. "Might take a little time to get a message to him, but we can put it on his list of objectives.

"Well, there you go!" Rochelle beamed at them, satisfied with her contributions to their problem solving.

Wenrick looked at her for a few moments. "Rochelle, can I ask you something? Are you sure you know what you're getting into with this guy?"

"What do you mean?" she asked back, a note of alarm creeping into her voice.

"It's just…" He paused, fumbling for the right way to say it. "I just don't think this guy is all he's making himself out to be."

Rochelle stared at him. She tossed her head. "And I still don't know what you mean."

He didn't respond, so she added, "He's a great guy! He's got plans, he's going places. He wants to fix things. What's wrong with that?" she asked plaintively.

"Lots of people want to fix things. They just don't spend a lot of time talking about wanting to fix things. They just go out and fix things."

Rochelle thought about that for a moment. She retaliated, "Gavin has bigger plans. He's aiming for more than just heaving body bags onto a barge. He's working on the big picture. He wants to be President. What's wrong with having a little ambition?"

"Nothing, nothing. It's just…" Wenrick paused, then tacked. "Rochelle, what's your ambition? How do you want to see this country recover from the Superflu?"

She recoiled, startled by the question. She'd never thought about it. She had no idea how to map out a recovery from a virus that had wiped out 97% of the population. She didn't know if it was even possible. And did she even have any ambition to try? Did she have any ambition for anything?

She'd had ambitions of completing her MBA and getting a job in marketing for a Fortune 500 company. Or maybe one of those high powered boutique companies where all the others outsourced their marketing efforts. Something in a big city, like New York or San Francisco. Or Europe would have been wonderful, too.

Of course, now that all seemed like pointless nonsense. So now what was her ambition? To tend bar for the rest of her life? Hardly. But if not this, then what?

Once again, she realized she didn't have a clue what to do next. Become Gavin's First Lady? Stalk about the White House in dress suits, planning parties and holiday decorations? Yeah, that didn't sound like anything she'd be proud of, either. Her mother would have been thrilled. But picturing it in her head made her feel like a little girl playing dress up, stumbling about in shoes too big for her feet.

What else then? Half a dozen other images and job roles flitted through her brain. Account manager. Website designer. Media producer. Journalist. Nothing that was viable in the reduced economy. They were jobs from the old world.

What kind of jobs would the new world need in the future? Farmer? Oil rig worker? House cleaners? Would they get bonuses for handling dried up mummy corpses in houses that hadn't been opened in five years?

She snorted to herself. What was Wenrick getting at? What was the point of the conversation? Oh yeah, he was questioning Gavin's suitability. She glanced at him. He was studying her, while she thought things over. She scowled.

"I have no idea. Look, you're not my Dad. You don't get parental approval rights over my dating choices. I'm not 16 anymore. I don't need you sitting by the door with a shot gun in hand, waiting to turn on the porch light when I get home."

Wenrick held up a hand. "Hey, hey, ease up. No offense meant. I'm just asking some tough questions. I realize this is none of my business. But I gotta wonder, what would your Dad have thought about Gavin, had he ever met him?" he asked.

Rochelle was again startled by the question. Her Dad rarely ever had an opinion that her mother didn't give him. He'd met plenty of her boyfriends, shook hands, made small talk. And then said absolutely nothing about them when they disappeared and were replaced by someone else.

Her face falling, she wiped at the counter, stalling for time. When she couldn't think of a better answer, she admitted, "I don't know what he would have thought about Gavin. My Dad… well, I guess he just wasn't much of a presence in my life. In our lives. My sisters' and mine, I mean."

Wenrick nodded his understanding.

Gary just had to go and add his two cents worth, though. "Rochelle, the Colonel has a valid point. Sadler is not the great guy you think he is. I realize you can't see it yet, but the guy is all flash, no substance. I can't find anything to trust in him."

Rochelle was back to scowling. She'd been aware that the guys didn't think much of him. She had assumed that situation would correct itself in time, probably once Gavin won the election.

She pointed a finger at Gary and said, "You're not my Dad, either. You don't have to trust him. You just have to trust me. I'm not a little kid, I've had plenty of boyfriends before. I can handle myself."

With a huff, she grabbed her damp rag and moved off to wipe down a table on the other side of the room.

Meanwhile, elsewhere in Virginia...

After the ambush in the Ozarks, Kevin regrouped. He decided it was time to get serious about his own mission of getting to D.C. As he had tried to convince the idiot kids to do, he raided several empty houses nearby. He quickly located a sedan car and then clothes, food and water. He drove to the nearest major metropolitan area eastward on his journey, and found the standard collection of car dealerships located on the perimeters of any major city. To his immense satisfaction, he decided that upgrading to a Jeep Rubicon was an excellent way to make lemonade out his little handful of lemons. It was much bigger than his Wrangler. From there, he set about scavenging for more supplies. He replaced his clothes, toiletries, camping gear and hand-held fuel pump. He raided houses for more food, too. As he had seen back home, some houses had very little food, some had some and some had lots. Different people kept different amounts of packaged food around. Some of it required little or no cooking, like pop tarts and jerky. Some of it required extensive preparation and cooking, like pancake mix and pasta. He wasn't much of a cook, so he stuck to granola bars, canned beans and Slim Jims, whenever he could.

Fortified, he made a beeline for Washington D.C. Just as he had wanted to spend time in the Ozarks, he also wished he could spend time in the Appalachians too. It was another place he'd only seen from the highways passing through. He consoled himself with the idea that maybe on his way back, he could take some time there. His only deadline was to be back in Chandler around July 1st, roughly. But first, he still had to find answers to his questions: why hadn't anyone cured the Superflu? Why hadn't anyone fixed things to stop the disaster from happening? Why wasn't anyone putting things back together now?

Kevin considered what Andy had mentioned, about cars being seized from people around D.C. He wasn't sure if that was true or if it was still true. He decided to err on the side of caution. After crossing the Appalachians, he elected to follow highway 81 north, to route 66. In the exurbs around D.C., he veered off and wandered about Gainesville and Chantilly. He saw few people about and most were on bicycles or on foot. They were mostly in areas where the air seemed fairly clear. Anywhere that he could smell that intense dead-body odor, he did not see any living people moving about. When he did see people, they did not react badly to his Rubicon driving by calmly, which he took as a good sign.

Even so, he decided that stashing the Rubicon would be his best option. He found a quiet neighborhood of larger homes. Some doors were marked with giant red "X's", which he assumed was about body removal. He selected a home with no "X" on the door, and easily broke in through a back door. From there, he manually opened the house's garage door, finding it empty of cars, but with several mountain bikes hanging from ceiling hooks. He grinned at his good fortune. He pulled the Rubicon in, closed the roll door, and inspected the bikes. He lowered one that appeared to be the right size for him, and tested it out. The tires were still springy.

Kevin spent a day outfitting himself for cycling into the city. He reorganized his backpack and reviewed his maps carefully. He'd be going on surface streets mostly, not highways.

The following morning, a clear and sunny Sunday, he set off for the final leg of his mission. Chantilly was just over ten miles from the river that bordered the city. He encountered his first military checkpoint well before that, stationed at a major crossroads of state routes in Arlington. He approached cautiously, and stopped when they waved him down.

The lead soldier politely asked him for his identification and where he intended to go. While the soldier studied his Arizona driver's license, Kevin looked about. A pickup truck hitched to a huge plastic water tank on a wheeled platform was parked to the side. A short line of four or five people waited patiently, while a uniformed soldier filled a five gallon jug from the tank's spigot.

Kevin wasn't sure if he should answer the guard's original question with his real reasons. So he just said he was going downtown. To his shock, they just smiled, and said, "okay." His ID was handed back, the gate was pulled open in front of him and the men stepped back.

"Wait, that's it?" he stared at the soldiers.

The one who had been questioning him smiled blandly. "Is there something you needed? Directions? Food? Water?"

Kevin frowned. Basics weren't what he needed. He needed answers.

An idea came to him. "Are you guys taking reports of problems? Like, I was robbed. Got ambushed. They took my Jeep."

The lead soldier frowned. "Where was this? Arizona? When did it happen?"

Kevin answered, "In the Ozarks. About ten days ago, I think?"

The soldier peered at him in confusion. "The Ozarks? That's a long ways away from here, to get here in ten days on a bicycle." He studied the bike that Kevin was straddling.

"Oh, no, I, uh, found another car and drove that most of the way here. But I ran out of gas. So I got this instead." It was only a little white lie. Kevin hoped it wouldn't be a problem for the guard.

The guard studied him some more. "Did they hurt you, when you were robbed? Did you get any names? Descriptions?"

Kevin shook his head, but said, "No, I'm not hurt. The one kid said his name was Andy. And they were just kids, teenagers. White. But I couldn't really see them very well. It was after dark, when this happened. Oh, they said they were going to California."

The soldier pursed his lips. After a moment he said, "I don't think there's much we can do about that, given how far away things are now. If you really want to make a report, I can get a form…" He was looking at a nearby store front, where a few more uniformed soldiers sat inside at desks.

Kevin shook his head. "Nah. You're right. It's too far away and they're long gone. If it's okay, I'll just be on my way." The guard nodded and stepped back. He pushed off on the bicycle. The soldiers cleared the path through the checkpoint barrier for him, letting him pass.

Kevin followed the route through Arlington, trying to keep one eye on the skyline, looking for major landmarks. But the tall office buildings all around him blocked his distance views. He had to weave about a bit, when he reached the river, to figure out which bridge to take. He ended up finding the Francis Scott Key bridge and crossing over on that one. Once he reached the other side, he turned east, intending to head for the Mall. It had taken him all morning to get this far, and he was getting hungry for a lunch break. The strip of park land on his right side looked overgrown, but pleasant enough, so he stopped, thinking to sit for a moment on a random park bench. He looked about, observing his surroundings. He realized that the smell of dead bodies was not nearly as strong here, as compared to other places he had passed through in the last few days. It was almost… minimal. Unnoticeable.

Across the street, a man walked along the street and turned into a storefront. Kevin frowned, wondering what was going on over there. The elevated highway above the street blocked his view, so he had to maneuver a bit, to see the sign above the front door the man had walked into: Paulbicki's. Kevin shrugged to himself, parked the bike and approached.

Kevin opened the bar's front door and stepped in. Inside, a bright beam of sunlight streamed down from the upstairs area. After his eyes adjusted to the interior, he noticed the long bar to the right side and tables to the left. A couple of people were seated at the tables, engaged in serious, quiet conversation. They ignored Kevin's entrance. So he turned to the right. One man was seated at the end of the bar, by the windows, nursing clear liquid in a short glass. Kevin took a seat several stools down the row from the man, placing himself about midway along the counter. He waited patiently for a few moments, keeping an eye on the gentleman, wondering if he should speak up.

After a moment, a young woman appeared through the doorway to a back room. The kitchen? Storage? She was carrying a plastic tray filled with brown beer bottles. Kevin studied her. She had medium length raven-black hair, dark eyes and pale clear skin. She was skinny and short, but with a few nice curves. She smiled at him.

"Hey!" she greeted him. She set down the tray of bottles on the counter and turned to him. "Welcome to Paulbicki's. What can I get you?"

Kevin smiled back. "Is that really beer?" He flicked his eyes at the tray she had just set down.

"Yep. Bud Light. It's getting a little old, but it's been kept cold, so it's not too nasty yet. Want one?"

Kevin nodded and said, "Perfect!"

The woman selected a bottle, snapped off the cap and set it on the counter in front of him. Kevin immediately lifted the bottle and swallowed a mouthful. It was indeed cold and tasted exactly as it should.

"Aaaahhhh" he sighed appreciatively.

The woman smiled but turned away to put the rest of the bottles into a small fridge underneath the bar. When she unloaded the tray, she picked it up and headed back to the storage area. Kevin admired her rear end. Not huge, but it had a nice subtle curve that he appreciated. The girl was hot. Which meant he probably didn't have a chance in hell with her.

Kevin glanced around again and saw that the man at the end of the bar was looking at him. Kevin realized he'd been caught ogling a woman's rear end. He shrugged sheepishly.

The other man smiled and spoke up, "Where you from? I haven't seen you in here before."

Kevin shook his head. "Nope. Not from around here. I, uh, just came to see the sights." He wondered if he really should get dragged into a long drawn out conversation.

The man didn't respond right away, so Kevin added, "I'm from Arizona. Just out driving around. Well, riding, really. On a bicycle. Someone told me they're confiscating cars around here, for the gas, so I switched out."

The man nodded. "Yeah, the military was doing that for a bit. That was a pretty terrible idea. But they've managed to move some fuel supplies around and are letting people drive their own cars now."

Kevin took another swallow of his beer. How long had it been since he'd had beer from a bottle, so cold the glass was getting those little water droplets? They had good beer at the brew pub at home, but that was draft, in glass, with a foamy head on it. A completely unrelated experience, compared to cheap beer in a bottle, in his opinion.

The man didn't want to let the conversation drop, though. "So, Arizona? You're a long way from home. Mind if I join you? I'd like to hear how things are out there." He raised his eyebrows questioningly, turning his body towards Kevin.

Kevin shrugged and said, "Sure. Whatever. What do you want to know?"

The man stood up, stepped closer and took the stool next to Kevin. He held out his hand. "I'm Henry Livan."

Kevin was a little surprised; not many people freely offered him a hand shake these days. He wished he'd made an effort to shake hands with Andy. His Dad had said you could get the measure of a man from handshake. Maybe if he had shaken hands with Andy, he would have realized the kid was a jerk.

Kevin took the older man's hand, squeezed firmly but not painfully and said, "Kevin Wilson."

Henry said, "So, did you drive most of the way here and then switch to a bicycle, or what?"

"Pretty much. Been driving around all over the place, actually, seeing what's what. But been wanting to get here to D.C., ever since things went to shit last fall."

"Why?" Henry asked, mildly curious.

Kevin thought for a moment.

"Well…" he stalled. "I guess you could say I was on a mission. I guess I still am, but I'm not so sure it matters anymore."

"And what mission was that?"

Slowly, Kevin answered, "Well, at first I was trying to find a safe place to wait things out. But it turns out, that wasn't really necessary. So, then I guess I was trying to find out where everything went, where all the people went, where the fixers went. I mean, yeah, I know almost everyone died, and we're just 3% now. What I mean is, I wanted to know where the government went. I want to know what happened to the people who were supposed to stop this thing. Why

251

didn't they stop it? Why didn't they fix it? Where's the cure? Where are they hiding out and why didn't they take more of us with them?"

Kevin sighed. He'd been asking these questions for months. He wasn't sure they even made sense anymore. Most people looked at him like he was crazy when he said them out loud.

Henry Livan did not look at him like he was crazy. Henry Livan smiled sadly at him, and said, "Son, what makes you think they didn't try to fix things, before? How do you know they didn't come up with a cure?"

Kevin turned to look at him, flabbergasted. "There's a cure? Why doesn't anybody know? Where is it? Why didn't they save more people? What happened?"

Henry was still smiling gently, but it didn't reach his eyes. His eyes brightened with unshed tears, turning a little red around the rims.

"Son, the Superflu was a virus. The process for identifying a virus and coming up with vaccines to neutralize the virus takes time. It takes months. And this particular virus was too ornery to cooperate. The scientists told us it probably mutated and started circulating in animal populations more than a year ago. Probably somewhere in southeast Asia. It moved to humans sometime in May or June, and started spreading. But it stayed hidden for a really long time. People were walking around with it, in their bodies, in their lungs, and spreading to everyone else, for weeks before they got sick. It took more than two months for the viral load to grow enough to sicken the patient. By the time the doctors identified the strain in August, it had already spread all around the world."

Kevin listened intently. He'd heard all this before, in different ways. But the way this man was saying it finally made sense to him. The man was speaking calmly, knowingly. He went on.

"Once they were able to isolate the strain of virus, from other versions - and there were other types of flu also going around, mind you - then they could start making a vaccine. It takes four to six weeks just to make a prototype of the vaccine and test it to make sure its effective. So that puts us into mid-September. By that point, lots of people were already getting sick and hospitals were getting flooded. Normally, once they have the prototype, they start distributing it out to the pharmaceutical companies who manufacture it in large batches for public distribution. It gets cultured, packaged and then shipped out. That process can take another six weeks to six months. Normally. Only, there was no normal about this virus. By the time they had the prototype, everyone was already getting sick. The lead scientist on the development team actually died of a seizure at his desk, just two days after signing off his final approval."

"Wait, how do you know this? What scientists?" Kevin interrupted.

Henry paused, looking at him. "Sorry, I guess I didn't explain that part, did I? I am - was - a Congressman in the U.S. House of Representatives. I sat on the committee that was briefed by the CDC. Their virus investigation team was briefing us weekly from early August onward. They were requesting all kinds of exemptions to FDA policies on vaccine development. Normally, there's a lot of checks and balances built into the process, which adds time. They were asking to fast track this one, skip the double-blind testing, use the version developed by the B team, etc. Which we approved."

Kevin was stuck on the word, "Congressman."

"You're a Congressman?" he spluttered.

Henry paused. He could see the wheels turning in Kevin's head. He waited for Kevin to catch up.

"B team?" Kevin asked.

"Yes. Normally, multiple independent teams work to identify and isolate the virus, and then develop a vaccine. Then they compare results, correct errors and test to make sure it's working as it should. However, this time the other teams lost too many people, getting sick, before they could complete the normal cycle. B team was the only one that came up with a viable vaccine. The House committee approved their exemption to go into mass production immediately, so they started sending out prototypes, about late September. The problem was, everyone was already getting sick by then. The airlines were canceling flights and then the FAA shut down most airports for commercial travel, trying to prevent the spread of the disease. Package shipping was still permitted, so the CDC tried to ship out samples. Except the drivers and pilots and delivery people were also getting sick and dropping out of the transportation network. The CDC asked the military to help, so they got Army units to pick up packages in Atlanta, to drive them to various places. Except those drivers got sick, too. A few actually made it to their destinations, but the pharma plants were closed up, or didn't have enough people around who could get the production going. Or they didn't have enough of the growing medium on hand to make enough. Or if they were able to make even a little bit of vaccine, which also takes weeks to grow, there was no one left to package it again and ship it out to hospitals and doctors. And by that point, at the end of October, almost everyone was sick or already dead."

Kevin stared at him, dumbfounded.

Henry searched for the point he had been trying to make. "So, there was a vaccine. It was just a problem of distribution. And timing. But they did try. They really did. A lot of really good people worked really hard to fix this. But real life is not like the movies. Sometimes, the hero doesn't save the day."

He smiled sadly again, and waited for his story to sink in. They sipped at their drinks for awhile.

Kevin understood about supply and distribution chains. He'd had made pickups and deliveries from pharmaceutical plants before. He knew that it all relied on other humans waiting on loading docks, wrapping pallets in shrink wrap, counting off boxes on clip boards or tablets. And then he drove the truck to another place, where more humans drove fork lifts to take the pallets off the truck where they were unpacked and divided into smaller sets, to be carried in smaller trucks to corner pharmacies, doctors offices and hospitals. And if those drivers were sweating and shivering in bed at home or in the hospital, well, the work didn't get done.

After a time, Kevin asked, "And what about the government?"

"What about it?" Henry asked back, calmly.

"Everyone always talked about doomsday bunkers under a mountain somewhere, someplace safe to take the President, if there's nukes incoming. Was any of that true? Did you all hide out, waiting for the dust to clear? Did you get those few vaccine doses they did manage to make?"

Henry snorted softly. "Son, the President died days before they even finished the prototype. Since the VP was already dead, they swore in next surviving person in the chain of succession, but then he died a few days later, too. Yes, they evacuated what remained of Congress, the Supreme Court and the top levels of most federal agencies. They took us to an isolated location..."

"Was it Greenbriar?" Kevin interrupted.

Henry shook his head sadly. "No, not Greenbriar. That was decommissioned years ago. Too many people knew about the place. No, they took us to Tuscarora, in Pennsylvania."

"Never heard of it," Kevin said.

"Well, of course not. Wouldn't be much of a secret hideout bunker, if everybody knew about it, would it?"

Kevin wobbled his head in acknowledgment. "I guess not."

Henry continued his explanation, "Turns out, though, that evacuation and quarantine was completely pointless. By that point, we were all infected already and just waiting to get sick. Vaccines don't work if you're already infected. They have to get into your system before the live virus does. They trigger the body to build the antibodies to fight off the virus. They need time to do that, before the virus shows up. And, as I said, the virus was already spreading like wildfire long before anyone even identified it. They didn't know to look for something in people who showed no symptoms. They don't start looking for it, until the first few people have gotten sick."

Henry took another swallow of his drink. The pretty bar maid came back, raised her eyebrows at him and nodded at his glass. He nodded back, so she poured him another two fingers of whatever he was drinking. It smelled like pine needles to Kevin. The girl made the same gesture at Kevin, so he nodded as well. She set another beer bottle in front of him.

Henry murmured "Thanks," to her. She wandered back to the kitchen or whatever was on the other side of the door.

After a few moments, Kevin asked, "So, everyone just sat around in that place then, waiting? What was the plan?"

Henry sighed. After a moment, he answered, "Son, there wasn't much 'sitting around' going on. Mostly people were dying. We didn't have enough medical personnel to take care of the sick, so we did the best we could to take care of people ourselves. They were our families, too. I mopped up floors, I made beds, I washed laundry, I held my wife's hand while she died…" His voice croaked on the last part, and he stopped for a few moments.

When he could speak clearly again, he continued. "We dug graves, too. There were about a dozen of us immunes left, at the end. And another ten or fifteen people who recovered from the fever. Out of over a thousand people who had been evacuated. A couple of the Marines who were guarding us were survivors, too. Big strong young guys. They were just kids, really. But they didn't have a chain of command left. They tried to keep us locked up inside the compound because that was what their commanders had told them to do - to keep us quarantined and safe. Except, they didn't say for how long. But eventually, they realized it was all over and there was no point in staying put. We finally convinced them that some elected officials and appointed bureaucrats outranked them and could countermand their orders. And we may have had a couple of weapons of our own, too. Eventually, they just unlocked the gates. We took the few remaining vehicles and headed out. I didn't see any point in going back home to Wisconsin. It was still winter. So I came back here. My apartment here is still okay. It was ransacked for food, but they didn't destroy anything."

Henry stopped talking and waited patiently.

After a moment, Kevin asked, "So now what?" He glanced around the bar. "What comes next?"

"Well, what do you want to come next? You're the one on the quest to find a cure, to find rescue, to find answers."

Kevin pondered that. "Well, I've pretty much figured out that I don't need to be rescued. Obviously. I guess I never did. And clearly, it's way too late for a cure. I guess I'm just wondering how we go forward from here."

"One step at a time," Henry said. "One step at a time."

Kevin nodded at that. He pondered his situation. He'd always figured this phase of his quest would end with him bursting in on

256

some secret meeting of guys in suits in the Capitol building, or maybe the White House. He had pictured himself slamming open a door, demanding, "Where's the cure!" or something. An alternate version of the fantasy had him breaking into that secret bunker. He never imagined the quest would end with a simple conversation while sitting on a bar stool, sipping beer.

Kevin wondered how he could tell if the old man was being truthful. He seemed to have a kind and honest face. But he was a politician. And nobody trusted politicians. Maybe he should verify what the old man said?

"So, you just abandoned that bunker? Is it still open? Do you think you'll ever go back there?"

Henry shrugged his shoulders. "I can't imagine why I would go back there… Except maybe to have my wife exhumed and cremated. She never wanted a traditional burial. We just didn't know what else to do and those guards wouldn't let us out of the compound, at that point. Can't just leave bodies laying about. You noticed that smell out there, right?" Henry nodded out the window and shuddered.

Kevin nodded back, shuddering also.

Henry added, "It's actually not that bad, today. It's getting better. The U.S.A.M.F. is in high gear on their clearing project."

"The what, now?"

Henry gave him the detailed explanation about the military. Kevin only half listened. His mind was still wondering about that bunker.

When Henry finally wound down, Kevin circled back. "So, do you think you could tell me where that bunker is? Would it be possible for me to go see it? It's not that I don't believe you or anything. But I just gotta see for myself. I think I really have to see this thing through to the very last end."

Henry studied him. He took another sip of his drink. Finally he said, "Sure, kid. You can go see it. We left it open. Even if anyone locked up after us, it's probably no harder to get into than anything else. A good pair of bolt cutters oughta do the trick. You got a map?"

Kevin pulled his backpack around to his front and pulled out his packet of maps. Henry spent a few moments pointing out the location and tips on the best route to take. The most obvious one was actually not a good choice, he said. A minor bridge had been damaged during one of the ice storms last winter and was in a danger of imminent collapse.

When he finished, he also recommended that Kevin go up the street for a meal, and maybe to one of the nearby hotels for the night, before setting out the next day. Kevin was surprised at his suggestion.

"The Watergate?" he asked. "As in... *the*...?" Kevin stumbled. He didn't know much about modern history, but everyone had heard that word before.

"Yes, that Watergate. It's a very nice place, actually. Great real estate. Some people are working on getting it cleaned up. It was part hotel and part apartment complex, before the Superflu. They got all the bodies and trash out. Power is on, but water isn't yet. Still working on that. But you should check it out."

Kevin nodded his thanks. It suddenly occurred to him that he should pay for his beers. And he had no idea what they were accepting for currency. He looked at the hot bartender, who had just returned from a back room. He pointed at his beers, and mumbled, "Uh...?"

The girl looked back and smiled. "Oh, don't worry about. Henry brought in several bottles this morning. That covers everyone's tab today, I think."

Kevin looked back at the man beside him. Henry said, "Sure, that's fine. Your story buys your beers. I still want to hear about how things are in Arizona."

Kevin smiled and obliged. He spent a very pleasant hour talking about his home town before heading out to find hot food and a comfortable bed.

Chapter 17

Spring was well on it's way to summer. Trees were fully leafed out. Weeds were popping up all over the parks and residential landscaping, but barely anyone had time to even think about cleaning them up. Everyone was too busy with other projects. Without much official direction from the shreds of city administration, the sole remaining federal agency in town, or the reconstituted military, people were taking on their own restoration projects. A mini Renaissance was emerging, as small bands and groups formed, making friends and finding things to do that were useful, helpful and constructive. Everyone had looked about, wiped the last of the tears from their faces and realized they didn't want to live in a dump anymore. Everyone wanted a nice place to live. So they boarded up the gaping holes in the storefronts. They pushed or pulled wrecked cars out of the streets. They welcomed refugees coming from surrounding regions and directed them to where they could find housing, food and ways to contribute. There was even a small group of people dedicated to reopening the assorted Smithsonian museums.

The spontaneous market place down the street was growing. Community organizers emerged and declared that it would be a weekly event on Saturdays. Gold coin, both old and new, started to appear, offered as currency. Vendors shrugged, asked their neighbors how much they thought they should charge for a box of q-tips and set rates as they went. Everyone acknowledged that rates would fluctuate for a while, until someone figured out a better way. Most people treated it like a game. They knew they didn't *have* to trade a gold Krugerrand they found in a grandmother's jewelry box. They knew they *could* spend half a day to drive out to Reston, break into some house and grab a twelve pack of toilet paper, siphon half a tank of gas from a car in a garage and drive back. But it was a heck of a lot easier to give up the Krugerrand for a bottle of laundry detergent.

So they did.

Not everything was getting easier, though.

Gavin returned to D.C. about five weeks after leaving. He strode into the bar with his usual swagger, his pair of male cronies and a new person. A beautiful, tall blond woman dressed in elegant slacks and a simple blouse. The kind of outfit Rochelle's mother wore when she went out to lunch with her friends from the charities she had worked with. Gavin was holding hands with the woman.

Rochelle felt a rush of cold shock prickle over her skin, when she saw the clasped hands. Gavin nodded cordially at her, but didn't make any effort to talk to her, or even come within speaking range. He took a seat at a table on the far side.

Sadler waved at the usual crowd of bar flies and semi-regulars. It was a medium sized crowd, by post-Superflu standards. It was Saturday, so many people were taking a day off from their self-imposed work. But it was also a beautiful day outside. Without a baseball or basketball game to watch on TV, there wasn't a lot of reason to sit around inside a bar, so early in the day. Rochelle had been thinking about bringing out the plastic tables and chairs that were in the storage basement and putting them on the front sidewalk, but hadn't yet done so.

Rochelle still didn't have any official waitstaff on the payroll. She wondered if she could call it a "barterroll" now? She knew that was a wildly irrelevant thought. She wished she had a bouncer. She wished she had a waiter so that she could send him over to take the drinks order. She wasn't sure she could speak coherently, if she had to go over to Gavin's table herself. She wasn't sure she could even walk straight. Clearly, things had changed and no one had thought to inform her about it.

She stood behind the bar, hands curled over the edge, gripping it tight. Her knuckles were turning white. Gary and Marty were watching her with growing alarm. They kept glancing over their shoulders at Sadler's group and then back at her.

Gary finally addressed the white elephant in the room. "Uh, Rochelle, you okay there?"

She clenched her teeth and shook her head to dismiss the

situation. "Yeah, I'll be fine," she finally snapped.

After a few minutes of no service, one of Sadler's companions got up and came to the bar. "Uh, could we get a round of beers?" he asked, straight faced.

Rochelle stared at him silently for a long moment and then plastered on her best customer service smile and Southern Virginia Belle voice and drawled, "Sure thing, hun! Be right over."

The man returned to Sadler's table and sat back down. Rochelle pulled out the oldest, warmest Pabst beer cans she had in the little fridge, snapped open their tab tops and set them on a tray. Then, she added a small bowl of very stale, unsalted peanuts. She took a deep breath and let it out. She picked up the tray, walked around the end of the bar and over to Sadler's table. The four people were talking quietly.

Gavin looked up when she approached and smiled calmly. He smiled the basic smile he gave to anyone who provided a simple service. Not the LED bright smile of a campaigning politician. Not the secret pleasure smile of a man who had fucked her on his kitchen table. Not the gentle smile of a man who recognized how much grief and pain a human being could endure and still smile back at him. No, it was the smile that meant, Y*eah, that service is worth about 15%. And I'll probably round down, depending on what the final bill is.*

Rochelle stared at him, not moving, not setting the drinks down yet, watching as the cheap smile faded into a frown. He glanced at the woman beside him. His arm was resting along the backside of her chair and he was leaning slightly towards her. He glanced back at Rochelle and then at the cans of beer on her tray.

"Pabst? You don't have any Molson's left?" He raised his eyebrows.

When the rage finally boiled over in her, her vision narrowed to a tiny field of view. All she could see was Sadler's face. He'd gotten another hair cut. Another completely irrelevant detail to notice, but there it was, blocking some of her comprehension of what was she was actually doing. Moving like someone was controlling her hands for her, like a puppet, she picked up the cans of beer, one by one.

She thunked them down on the table. Hard. Hard enough to make the beer splash and fizz out of the openings. Beer started to spread over the table, running over the edges, dribbling into laps. After the first can, the strange woman uttered a startled "Oh!" of dismay, pushing back. She didn't move fast enough to avoid the splash of the second can. Or the third.

"Here's your beer!" Rochelle hissed at Gavin. She gave the fourth and last can a good hard shake, before slamming it on the table in front of him. The beer sprayed and splashed over everyone, herself included. She turned about and started to stalk away. And then thought better of it. The group was frantically looking about for napkins to soak up the mess.

"You know what?" Rochelle asked rhetorically. "I changed my mind. You don't get beer. You can get out of my bar!" she shouted at him.

Sadler tried to recover his dignity, which was difficult, as the liquid running off the table had managed to land right on the crotch of his pants. "Is this really necessary?" he asked.

The strange woman added her two cents worth to the fray, "What is going on? What is your problem?" She was indignant.

Rochelle glared at her. "He's my problem! And he is no longer welcome here. All of you, get out." They stared at her in disbelief, so she roared, "NOW!"

The foursome shuffled around the table, past her and out the door. The last man glanced at her with a hurt look on his face, like he was being punished for something that was not his fault. She did not relent, scowling at all of them.

When the door finally closed on them, Gary let out a boom of cackling laughter and slapped his palm on the bar. Marty followed his lead, grinning too. In between huffs, Gary pointed out, "You are covered in beer!"

Rochelle looked down. Her own shirt was damp. The stink of crappy beer rose up. She plucked it away from her skin, full of revulsion at the sticky wetness clinging to her.

She pointed at Marty and said, "You're in charge! I'm going to go change clothes." She didn't have any spare clothes left at the bar;

she'd moved all her personal possessions to the condo around the corner. And Frankie hadn't shown up yet today. He'd probably be in later.

She marched out the door and turned right, heading home. At the condo, in the middle of her kitchen, she stripped out of her jeans and t-shirt. Even her underwear and bra were uncomfortably wet, so she shucked out of those too. They stank of bad beer. She dropped them on the tile floor to deal with later.

Wishing that city water service was restored, even if it wasn't fit for drinking, she marched upstairs to her bathroom. She had a few inches of water left in the plugged up bathtub, laboriously hauled, bucket by bucket, from one of the small rain cisterns.

While Wenrick put in 80 hour work weeks at the Pentagon, he still managed to make a little time for minor improvements to the condo complex. They had a couple of new neighbors now so he was coordinating small projects with them. Several weeks ago she and her neighbors had scavenged and installed an assortment of large plastic water barrels under the buildings' roof gutters. They used that makeshift cistern water for washing.

The water in her bathtub was sepia colored, like an old photograph, from running down the roof and through the spouts. She had boiled it, but that did nothing to remove the faint rust color. And of course, it was just room temperature. Even so, she lathered up a washcloth and scrubbed herself down. Then she rinsed by pouring cupfuls of the rusty water over herself. The beer smell persisted, so she knelt on the tub floor and washed her hair, turning herself nearly upside down to wet, lather and rinse her head.

The exertions distracted her enough from Gavin's betrayal, so that her rage calmed down slightly. Whole minutes went by when she wasn't screaming, *How could you?* inside her head.

Once she felt cleaner, her damp hair combed out, she put on fresh clothes. Downstairs she found the pile of wet dirty clothes she had left behind and carried them up to the bathroom. She dunked them into the soap and shampoo infused water and swished them about. Between the beer and cleansing products now dissolved in the water, it was difficult to get the clothes thoroughly rinsed clear. Normally she kept an extra bucket of clean boiled water handy for this, but she had used the last of it up on herself, converting it into the washing water at the bottom of the tub. So instead, she used a laundry basket to carry the damp pile out to the rain barrel she and Wenrick had designated for additional rinsing, just for situations like this. She squeezed out as much excess water as possible out of the laundry and took it back upstairs to be arranged on drying racks. She opened a window to catch a light breeze, hoping that would help speed things up.

Once finished with her impromptu laundry chore, she sighed and sank down on her couch for a moment to catch her breath. Hauling wet laundry up and down and around was heavy work. The rage at Gavin had already had her heart pounding. But something else was bugging her, too. She looked about. The light in the room was all wrong. She realized that she was sitting in her new home at a time of the day, mid-afternoon, when she was never at home. She never saw the house with the sun streaming in through the windows from this angle. It threw weird shadows about, in the wrong places. The glare was too harsh. The furniture was casting sharp shadows, everything haloed with golden sunlight.

The effect made her feel like a stranger in her own home again. She'd worked hard to claim the space for herself. And now she was weirded out by her observations all over again. Rochelle leaped up, grabbed her keys and dashed out, slamming her locked door closed behind her. She strode back to the bar, moving at her top walking speed. The afternoon sunshine pouring down was actually hot. She worked up a light sheen of new sweat by the time she strode back into the bar.

She'd been gone less than an hour. But Frankie had come in while she was gone. Gary and Marty were telling Frankie the story of her evicting Gavin, with grand dramatic gestures and loud guffaws of laughter. Part of her wanted to laugh with them. Part of her grew angry all over again. She knew they weren't laughing at her, but at Gavin for being an idiot asshole. They even chided her for it.

Gary tried to cheer her up, but failed miserably. "Come on,

Chelle, we did you warn you that the guy was an a-hole."

She nodded her acknowledgment. Yeah, they had told her. Or tried to. She stood in her customary place behind the counter, arms wide, leaning on her hands on the bar.

She thought about her first date with Gavin, when they'd gone "smashing," as he called it. She realized it was actually the *only* date they had gone on. Since that one, they hadn't actually gone out, anywhere. He came to the bar and when she closed up, they went to his place or hers. They had sex. Lots of great sex. Really hot sex. Rochelle admitted it to herself. She liked the sex. But did great sex make him a legitimate boyfriend? Had he ever said he loved her? She knew she'd never said it to him, not even a casual friendly version, let alone a serious heart-to-heart version. She'd been kind of thinking that she might be on her way to being in love with him. But was she, really?

No. In hindsight, in clear sight, she realized now that she was just infatuated with the idea of him. She loved the sex, not the person. She'd been hoping he'd step into the mold of her idea of the perfect boyfriend. One who took her out on official dates once in awhile. Of course, dating in the aftermath of the Apocalypse was a tricky thing. But it was not like she expected limo rides and caviar. A nice walk, or a DVD on the TV at home. A personally prepared meal. He'd demonstrated that he was a decent cook. Was it really too much to expect him to do that again? Apparently, it had been. Clearly, he had no intention of living up to her version of good boyfriend material.

So, what had he expected of her? He'd asked her to do minor things, like find him toothpaste, or straighten up his apartment. And if she hadn't managed to accomplish those things, he'd been annoyed. He'd been annoyed when she questioned his use of the limo, that evening weeks ago. He'd been annoyed when she refused to become his campaign manager. Other little moments like that, had made it clear that he didn't think she was girlfriend material, either. How could she have been so blind then and only see the truth now? Why had she ignored the signals?

The rage started boiling up in her all over again. She really didn't want to get soaked with beer again, but she didn't want to just squash the rage down inside, either.

A scene, a picture of shattered china in a stranger's house, flitted across her brain. She looked about the bar, under the counter. At the far end, there were several plastic trays of coffee mugs, stacked on top of each other. She picked up one of the mugs and hefted it, judging its weight in her hand. It was just an ordinary ceramic mug, straight sides, plain white, simple handle. Probably mass produced in China. She turned and walked out from behind the bar and out the front door. She looked left, looked right, looked down at the concrete sidewalk. The building was fronted with Georgian red brick, with windows set in frames of thicker brick.

Stepping a few feet away from the front door, Rochelle lifted the cup above her head in both hands, paused, inhaled deeply. Grunting out the breath, she brought her arms down fast, flinging the cup on the concrete sidewalk. It shattered into a million shards, spreading in a star pattern, until they washed up against the brick wall. The tinkling sound of rattling continued to ring in her ears for moments afterwards.

Rochelle went back inside. The bar flies were staring at her, befuddled by her behavior. She marched behind the bar and picked up an entire tray of mugs. It held two dozen, normally. This one was missing just one. She carried the tray outside, and set it on the ground. She picked up a mug. She looked inside of it.

Speaking directly into the mug, she said, "This is for all of your shit, Gavin Sadler." She raised it above her head and hurled the mug onto the ground, right where the shards of the first one still remained. It too shattered.

She picked up another mug. To this one, she spoke a little louder, "And who the fuck runs for President in the middle of an Apocalypse!" She smashed that one to the ground.

Mug after mug, she yelled her rage into the cups, and then smashed them.

"And this for your stupid frat boy hair cut!" Smash!

"And this is for asking me to get you toothpaste!" Smash!

"And this is for driving fucking limos around town!" Smash!

"And this is for not saving your own home town!" Smash!

Confluence

About the time she reached the seventh or eighth mug, a man turned the corner behind her. She saw him out of the corner of her eye, as she was bending over to pick up another mug from the tray. She pulled up and whirled around, startled. She stared at him, wide-eyed, a little out of breath from yelling at the cups.

The man stared back at her.

"What?" she asked, nearly shouting. The man looked vaguely familiar, but not one of her regulars.

They stared at each other in silence for a moment. The man's eyes flicked to the ground behind her, at the shards sprayed over the sidewalk, at the partially full tray of mugs at her feet.

"Uh, they're not really bombs, you know," he said carefully.

Rochelle heaved in a new breath and huffed to blow a lock of hair out of her eyes. "What?"

The man waved a hand. "Never mind. You had to be there. Uh, are you okay?"

"I'm fine!" she snapped. Then it occurred to her he might be a customer. So she pulled open the front door, whirling around because the door opened the opposite way. She gesture expansively with her arms, waving him inside, but spoke fiercely, practically shouting, "Welcome to Paulbicki's! Have a seat where ever you like!"

The man circled around her, giving her a wide berth and went inside. Rochelle let the door close behind him.

Inside, she vaguely heard the man ask the bar flies, "Do you guys understand women?" That was followed by loud gales of laughter. She ignored them. She picked up another mug and growled into it.

"And this is for doing me in some stranger's bed!" Smash!

"And this is making me give you a pedicure!" Smash!

"And this is for being my mother's perfect idea of a perfect boyfriend!"

Rochelle stopped, cup in hand. She stared into it, shocked at her own words. Where had that come from?

Yes, her mother did like good looking men. Charming men. She'd always encouraged her daughters to pursue successful men: doctors, lawyers, businessmen. Politicians would have been fine with Catherine, too. She would not have made any distinction between the successfulness of a politician and a doctor. Yes, Catherine would have liked Gavin Sadler very much indeed.

Rochelle let the cup fall gently out of her hands. Even without the applied force of an arm swing, it still shattered when it hit the concrete. The shards just didn't spread as far and wide.

She picked up another cup and looked inside it. She spoke softly into the cup. "Fuck you, Catherine."

She raised her arms up a little farther and swung them down, hitting the growing shard pile.

She repeated the motion, saying loudly, "Fuck you, Mother, and the horse you rode in on. Fuck your stupid, narcissistic, selfish, scheming, manipulative, demanding…." She ran out of adjectives to describe her mother, so she hurled the mug, sentence unfinished.

She picked up one more. This time, she spoke quietly into the mug. "I love you, Mom, but I'm done. I'm done with your idea of the perfect man. I don't need a man to survive in this world. I'm not going to be the perfect daughter you think I should be. I'm not going to live in the big house. I'm not going to have the high powered career. I'm not going to be who you want me to be. I'm going to be someone else." She dropped the last cup. It broke into pieces.

Rochelle took a step back and surveyed the damage. White ceramic shards had scattered and ricocheted off of each other and the building. They littered the entire sidewalk. They crunched under the heel of her loafer shoes.

Rochelle took a deep breath and raised her head. The sun was blocked by the elevated highway above the street, but it was still a lovely day. Light puffy clouds in a blue sky. Gentle breeze creating ruffles on the river water. She took several deep breaths, filling her lungs and exhaling slowly. She wanted to feel the sun on her face. She could go across the street and sit on one of the little park benches. But first she needed to clean up the mess she had made. Someone could cut themselves. If they were stupid enough to walk around barefoot. The shards could cut a bicycle tire, too.

She went back inside. Frankie had taken up position behind the bar. The stranger who had interrupted her smashing session was

268

seated next to Marty, a cold bottle in front of him. The spilled Pabst cans had been cleared away from the table on the other side of the room. Rochelle nodded to the guys, retrieved a broom and dust bin from the storage closet and headed back out front. About half way, she realized it would be more efficient to bring one of the trash bins with her too. So she turned about and dragged that with her outside. She carefully swept up the smashed pottery and dumped it. Then she hauled the trash bin back through the bar, out the back door and heaved the heavy bag into the big dumpster. Tomorrow, she would put up the sign that signaled the roving trucks that the dumpster was full enough for a pickup.

With a sigh, she walked through the bar one more time. She paused when she realized the guys were still carefully watching her. Frankie waved a flattened hand side to side, dismissively. "It's just a few cups. I'm not in any position to be critical," he said.

Rochelle went through the front door. She walked across the street, sat on a bench in the sun and lifted her face one more time.

Chapter 18

Rochelle sat on the bench in the sun. For just a moment, she found a tiny piece of peace. A slice of nothingness. It reminded her of the time from months ago just yesterday, when she had been waiting for the Superflu to take her too. She'd been numb. Stuck in a bubble. Somewhen, the bubble had burst. Or maybe it had evaporated? She wasn't really sure, but she'd been out, living, experiencing emotions, enjoying things. There was even a fierce awakening joy inside the rage she had just processed.

She sat on the bench, savoring the nothingness, until the sun moved low enough in the sky to be shaded by the trees and office buildings across the river. Without the direct sunlight to warm her skin, the air started to turn cool. She opened her eyes and looked about. The river lay before her, calm, flat, flowing steadily, just like her heart rate, finally. A soft glow from the last rays of sunlight reflected off the upper stories of nearby buildings, the highway, the river. It was a pretty town, she decided. Except for all the weeds. It was slowly getting cleaned up, though. But it still didn't feel like her home town. Even after three years and the nearly complete destruction of humanity, she was still just a tourist in this town. But where else was she supposed to go?

With a sigh, she stood up and walked back into the bar. Frankie was stationed behind the bar. Gary and Marty were on their usual stools and the newcomer was seated to Marty's right side. So, for a change, she took a seat at the end of the line of bar flies, next to the stranger who had interrupted her smashing. Frankie smiled at her and asked, "What can I get for you?"

She grinned back at him and then popped her eyes in surprised realization. She hadn't had a drink at this bar in months! She used to enjoy a midnight margarita or two with the rest of the former waitstaff. When had that last been? When George had gotten sick? After George and everyone else disappeared, she'd forgotten about her midnight drinks. She'd been surrounded by every kind of alcohol she could ever possibly have wanted. And she used to enjoy the nice buzz. Heck, she'd even been known to get completely plastered once in awhile during her college days. But in all these many months of waiting for the Superflu to come for her, she'd completely forgotten that she could have turned off her heart and brain with a few inches in a glass. A bartender who didn't drink! How crazy was that?

Marveling at her own obtuseness, she looked Frankie in the eye and said, "Margarita, please! On the rocks, with salt."

Frankie nodded to her and set to making the drink. While she waited, Rochelle glanced at the guys, who were pretending not to watch her. The stranger next to her was less subtle about it, glancing sideways at her.

Frankie set the drink in front of her with a flourish. She eagerly lifted the glass to her lips and sipped. The salt, tart and sweet flavors mingled pleasingly. The sharpness of the tequila made her cough a little bit. She nodded and smiled at Frankie, to let him know it was perfect.

Gary and Marty resumed their normal chatter. They had actually spent their Saturday morning doing some personal scavenging and then trading at the market. They were reporting on what was circulating about.

The stranger seemed not to be paying attention to the guys. He was still glancing at her. She finally asked him, "So, you probably think I'm completely crazy. That little scene out there..." She turned her head to look at him.

The guy shook his head, waved his hand. "Hey, glass houses..."

Rochelle frowned, confused.

The guy elaborated. "What I mean is, guys who wrap their trucks around light poles, are not in any position to complain about broken cups. I get it. You had to do what you had to do. Not the first time I've ever seen pottery get smashed."

Rochelle was stuck on the truck around the light pole. "Wait, I don't get it. Did you wreck a truck? Because you were mad?"

The guy grinned at himself. "Heh, I was beyond mad. I was practically on fire! I could barely see, I was so angry."

Rochelle turned slightly on the stool to face him. He responded automatically to the gesture and turned to face her as well.

She asked, "So, what happened? Were you hurt?"

The man launched into a story, explaining exactly how he had crashed his truck. He twisted around, pulled up the sleeve of his t-shirt and showed her a ragged red scar on his left bicep, as proof of his mis-adventure. When he mentioned his home state, Rochelle interrupted him. "Arizona? You're a long way from home!"

He paused, nodded and said, "Yeah, I get that a lot."

Rochelle envisioned a scene from the old cult classic movie, *Raising Arizona*. She and her sisters had watched it a couple of times. She visualized the seared dry landscapes of the movie as backdrop to the man's story about driving his pickup truck into a light pole.

Just as he was winding up his story, the bar's front door opened and Henry Livan joined them. He took a seat to Rochelle's right. Then he leaned forward to get a better look at the man her to left and grinned.

"Kevin! You came back! Did you find the place?"

Kevin waved to Henry and they leaned back to shake hands in greeting behind her. Kevin immediately switched gears, to report on his experiences.

"Yes, sir, I did. Your directions were perfect." The initial smiles of greetings slowly faded to somber expressions.

Henry asked, more calmly, "And were you able to get inside? I wasn't completely sure if the last two guards locked up after we left or not. But I figured you could probably get in, even so."

Kevin nodded. "Yeah, it was just a lock on a chain. The bolt cutters took care of that. I got in and was able to look around like you said. I found your cemetery. And I'm very sorry about your family." He looked sadly at the Congressman.

Henry nodded his acknowledgment. "And did you find everything else you wanted?" he asked simply.

Kevin shook his head. "Eh. I guess everyone was right. There is no hero, there is no magic cure, no secret community waiting to reboot the world. I'm not really even sure why I ever thought there was. I don't even know where these ideas came from. It just seems like these things were always inside my head, that the government was here to protect us, to tell us what to do, where to go, how to be. But at the same time, no one ever liked being told what to do, or where to go. Everyone always complained about the government and the politicians - oh, sorry, sir..." His voice trailed off as he glanced sheepishly at Henry.

Henry waved it off. "No worries, son. I did my share of complaining, too. Keep going." He gestured back to Kevin.

Kevin looked about, thinking. "So, I dunno. I guess... I guess it's not like a nuclear holocast, where there's so much destruction and so little stuff left. There's plenty of stuff left all over the place. Hey, did you guys know there's a little market place over there..." He gestured out the window, roughly in the direction of the shopping complex down the street.

Gary and the guys nodded, but waited for him to continue his train of thought. Rochelle interrupted him, though. "Caust," she said. "It's nuclear holo*caust*."

Kevin frowned at her in confusion.

"You said 'holocast.' Not quite the right the word."

Kevin's face fell. He said, "Oh. Sorry. I guess I'm not very good with big words."

Rochelle touched a hand to his shoulder, "No, I'm sorry. I didn't mean to be critical. I just couldn't help it." She smiled to take the sting out of her rebuke.

Kevin shrugged. He perked up a bit. "Anyways, this situation isn't like any of the movies I ever saw. It's the people that are gone, not the stuff. And it's just most people, not all people. There's still people left. You know, back home, they're doing some really great things. There's this whole group and they're getting everyone together and cleaning things up, making sure the power stays on. I helped out some, did a little bit of cleanup, too. But I got, what'd she call it, a case of wanderlost?" He looked about, searching for the correct word.

Rochelle offered, "Wanderlust? You like to travel around?"

Kevin nodded vigorously. "Yeah, that the word! Wanderlust.

That's what I do. I travel around, look at things. They asked me to get information about what's going on elsewhere, bring it back. So that's what I'm doing. In fact, does anyone know what the date is? I gotta be back home by July. They're having an election."

Henry looked startled. "Wait, an election? That's not until November."

Kevin looked equally confused. "No, this one is in July. It's just for mayor and City Council."

Henry nodded his understanding. "Ah, a local election. I get it."

Kevin was still confused, though. "Why did you think it would be in November? What's happening then?"

Henry replied promptly, "Presidential election. There's a guy…"

Gary, Marty and Frankie all looked suddenly alarmed and hissed at Henry, "Shhh!" and "not now!" They glanced apologetically at Rochelle. Rochelle just picked up her margarita and took a big swallow. It really was very tasty.

Henry looked at the other guys. "I don't get it. What happened?"

Marty said "Never mind," while Gary said, "We'll explain it later."

Rochelle spoke up. "It's okay, guys. I was right there. It's not a secret." She turned to Henry. "Let's just say, Gavin Sadler is persona non-grata around here, from now on."

Henry was puzzled. He mumbled, "Uh…" and thought about things for moment.

Finally he said, "Okay, so, moving on… What's everyone else been up to today?"

Gary jumped in. "Hey, I got an idea. I found a pool table in this house in the Adams Morgan area. We should bring it here, put it upstairs! Maybe get some dart boards, too. Nobody ever uses the upstairs room anymore. If you put some games and things up there, maybe more people would come?"

Rochelle looked about at the guys, startled at the idea. Frankie spoke up. "Uh, how do you plan to get it up there?"

"It can be taken apart. The legs can be unbolted from the main table. Carry it up in pieces, assemble it back together again up there."

Frankie rubbed his hand over his whiskered chin, thinking. "Still awfully big, heavy and awkward. I dunno…"

Gary wasn't giving up on the idea. "Do you think we could get some of Wenrick's soldiers to help? The big strong young ones? Or maybe we could find a crane, a little one, like they use for moving pianos, to lift it up through one of the windows upstairs?"

The guys started drilling into the details of their hypothetical project. Paper and pens came out and sketches were made. Frankie threw up objection after objection, while Gary and Marty found ways to work around them. The talk finally coalesced into a plan to go hunting for a moving crane at a regional moving company headquarters. They even roped Kevin into helping, when they realized he had experience driving a variety of heavy duty vehicles. Kevin seemed confused by the zig-zagging conversation, which had veered away from him and then back again.

Rochelle sat back, drinking her margarita. She kept her eyes tightly focused on what was in front of her, thinking very hard about not thinking at at all. When the first drink was finished, a new one magically appeared in front of her. She never felt any impulse to remove her empty glass and put it on a tray, waiting to load into the dishwasher. At some point, a plate of food from Whigs was set in front of her. There was salad on the plate! She asked where the lettuce had come from and Marty explained that Chuck and Cherry were trading with a small farm that had started up out near Potomac Hills. Spring vegetables were just starting to be harvested. Rochelle savored the new tastes and textures, welcoming back a tiny bit of normality.

The conversation ebbed and flowed over her. The guys pressed Kevin for more stories about his experiences since the Superflu. Wenrick appeared for his evening bourbon. Sitting in the middle of the row of bar flies, Rochelle's effort to not think at all turned into random wanderings.

Had this breakup happened before the Superflu, her sisters and probably Apurva, would have flocked to her side. Or at least spent hours on the phone with her, consoling her. She pulled out her phone. She'd taken to recharging it, now that power was mostly back on. She could look at pictures, play games or thumb through old text threads. She scrolled through her list of hundreds of contacts. If the Superflu had left 3% behind, surely a few of her contacts must be among the survivors? Where were they now?

Idly, she pushed the call button on a few of them. But nothing happened. There were no signal bars. Even though her phone had power, the nearest cell phone towers did not want to connect her to the stray three percenters she might know.

Rochelle set her phone down. A new drink had appeared in front of her. She swirled the ice around. She gently picked off grains of salt and licked them from her finger nail. She could feel the eyes of the new guy next to her, but she didn't turn to face him.

She wondered why she was surrounded by men. Where were all the women? Months before, her life had been filled with mostly women and the men were just the minor bit players. Now the situation was reversed.

Of course, Cherry the cook was up the street. And there was the pair of irregular women regulars who came in, sat at the back and played cards or Scrabble. They were a little older, probably closer to Gary or Marty's age. She didn't know their names.

But there was no females her own age for her to talk to. No one who knew exactly the right way to console a friend after a breakup. No one who knew the exact right ratio of ice cream, chocolate and alcohol to fast track the break-up recovery process. Rochelle imagined how the potential conversation would go. Nerissa would say there were plenty more fish to be fried. Hollan would say there was nothing wrong with being single for while. Paige would say that getting under a new guy was the best way to get over a previous guy.

Rochelle downed drink after drink steadily. The food had slowed down her progression to drunk status a little bit, but she made up for it. By 10 p.m., she couldn't feel her lips anymore and the room was spinning a little bit, even though she was sitting up straight. Except maybe she wasn't, because the guys grabbed her by the shoulders, saying, "Whoa, there…" and "Okay, I think it's time to send her home."

Outside, the cold wash of air made her perk up a bit. She realized that Kevin and Wenrick were each supporting her by her arms as she stumble walked home. Wenrick fumbled open her door for her, when she couldn't figure out how to put the key in. They led her to her sofa. "Come on, lie down here; on your side, not on your back..." And that was good, because lying on her back really made the room spin.

A moment later she heard someone say, "Come on, I'll let you into one of the empty condos. You can stay there. But you gotta give her some space, okay? Check on her, to make sure she gets up okay in the morning, but you keep your hands to yourself, you hear?"

That was followed by a mumbled, "Uh, yes sir."

And then she knew nothing else, but the softness of a blanket draped over her shoulders and the sweet bliss of sleep.

Chapter 19

Rochelle awoke to a screaming headache. Her teeth felt like they were wearing tiny little sweaters. Her shoulder ached from sleeping on it for hours without moving.

She sat up slowly and then remained still for long minutes, just breathing, waiting for her head to stop throbbing. When she could finally open her eyes, she looked about. She was on the couch in the condo's living room, a throw blanket bunched in her lap. Morning sunlight streamed in, mostly at familiar angles.

There was a trash basket lined with plastic bags next to the couch, where her head had been. To her relief, it was empty. Two bottles of water stood on the coffee table in front of her, one half empty, the other still sealed. And oddly, a half a bag of Hershey's Kisses sat next to them. *Where had those come from?* she wondered. She didn't recall getting any chocolate in the scavenge that was traded in at the bar.

She opened the half bottle of water and finished off the remaining amount. Then she opened the bag of chocolate and extracted one. She carefully peeled off the silver foil and little paper tag, letting them fall to the table. The candy was coated in white powder, which was perfectly normal for old chocolate. She nibbled off the tip of the cone. It tasted just as it should. Even better, her stomach didn't complain about it. She popped the rest of it in her mouth and let it melt slowly on her tongue. She sat back, savoring, wondering where it had come from.

Finally, her bladder let her know it was time to get moving. Moving in extra slow motion, she made her way to the bathroom. The stinky, no-longer-clean water was still standing in the bottom of the tub. She really wanted another wash, but she wanted cleaner water for it. That would require hauling several more bucketfuls from the rain cisterns, which seemed impossibly tiresome at the moment. She was still sitting on the toilet, contemplating her options, when she heard banging on the door downstairs.

She pulled up her pants and slowly made her way back downstairs, wondering who would actually be knocking. She didn't know the new neighbors very well yet and Wenrick would be at the Pentagon by now. Or would he? Was it Saturday or Sunday? Or Monday? If it was Sunday, he might take a day off and do his own chores about the complex.

Thinking the knocking was most likely Wenrick, she opened the door. To her surprise, the stranger from the bar last night stood there, a covered plate in his hand. What was his name again? Kevin! That was it.

"Uh, hi…?" she asked.

He smiled tentatively. "Uh, hi! I just wanted to check on you, make sure you're okay. I went to that restaurant over there," he gestured vaguely in the direction of Paulbicki's and Whigs's. "They gave me this, to bring back to you. It's scrambled eggs."

Rochelle glanced at the plate. The bottom plate was covered with another plate inverted on top, hiding the food. She glanced back at Kevin's face. She studied him a moment. He was not classically handsome, not politician handsome. He wasn't even cute by high school boy standards. But he wasn't ugly, either. Plain brown hair. Ordinary face. Brown eyes. Kind of forgettable, unless she made an effort to memorize him. He was dressed in jeans and a plaid shirt over a t-shirt. Not dirty enough to be considered 'grunge' fashion.

"Fresh eggs?" she wondered aloud. Then she frowned. "Did someone feed me salad last night? Real salad?" she asked.

"Uh, yeah. They said something about trading with a farm… I don't know who's who around here yet, but yeah, it's all fresh. They chopped up some green onions for the eggs, too." He gestured with the pair of plates again. "And eggs are good hangover food." He smiled at her encouragingly.

Rochelle shrugged and opened the door wider, waving her free arm toward the small dining table.

Kevin entered and politely set his present at the head of the table. He looked about awkwardly, unsure what to do next. Rochelle decided that, yes, she did want to eat the food, but first, she needed to get the chocolately sweaters off her teeth.

"Stay here. I'm going to brush my teeth. I'll be right back."

Once again, she climbed the stairs to her bathroom. In addition to brushing her teeth, she also scrubbed at her faced with a damp wash cloth, using the last of her upstairs bottled drinking water to moisten it. She shook out two ibruprofen pills out of a bottle and carried them back downstairs.

Kevin was looking about the room, reviewing the CDs lined up in the rack next to the entertainment center. Rochelle grabbed the other unopened bottle from the coffee table and snapped it open. She swallowed the two tablets with the water and then turned to the dining table.

"Uh, did you want something to eat, too?" she asked awkwardly.

Kevin shook his head, "Oh, no, I ate already. That guy, the Colonel, he told me to make sure you got something to eat this morning, is all."

"Oh." Rochelle couldn't think of anything else to say, so she grabbed a fork from the kitchen and sat down. She uncovered the bundle and found a fluffy mound of yellow, dotted with bits of green onion. It smelled delicious; delicate and light. She tried a forkful. It tasted as good as it smelled. It wasn't exactly hot anymore, after the walk over, but that was okay. In addition to the eggs, there was also a small mound of mashed potatoes, maybe from one of the batches that Bill had cooked up last fall. She swallowed a few more bites carefully, enjoying the flavor and directing her stomach to also enjoy the idea of neutral food, instead of the remains of tequila acid.

Finally she spoke to Kevin, who was floundering about, trying to find something useful to do or say. "So, I must have been a real mess last night," she said.

"Oh, no worries," he said. "Those guys, they were all just worried about you. The Colonel especially said I was to make sure you ate something. He said he had to go to work, but since I was going to be around, he asked me to look in on you."

"Around?" Rochelle wondered.

"Oh, he said I could stay in one of the condos, a few doors over." He pointed outside.

"Ah," she replied. She thought back on their conversation yesterday, on the sidewalk in front of the bar. She frowned. 'Hey, what did you mean when you said the cups were not 'bombs.' What was that about?"

Kevin looked up from the CDs. "Oh, that! Yeah, there was this thing a couple months ago. I was checking on a group of preppers and they thought all the pots in my Jeep were IEDs, so they smashed them on the road."

Rochelle frowned even harder, even more confused.

Kevin shrugged. "Okay, that didn't make sense, even to me. I guess I should start at the beginning." He walked over to the table and sat down with her. Rochelle continued to slowly take small bites of the food, interspersed with swallows of water from her bottle. Kevin told her a long rambling story about a group of militia-minded preppers who had claimed a tourist canyon in Arizona and did not appreciate his arrival on their proverbial doorstep. For the second time. He explained that he'd been hauling hand-made pottery urns as trading gifts, but the preppers had been very suspicious. Just to make sure the urns were not some kind of explosive device and to convince Kevin that his presence was unwanted, they had smashed them all on the blacktop roadway. Then they had wrapped his wrists in zip ties and held him in a dark room for a day. After a day of internal squabbling, the leaders of the prepper group had dragged him back to Chandler, intending to warn everyone that Sedona was claimed territory and they should just stay clear. The conversation had not gone exactly as planned, when they discovered that, aside from Kevin, the people of Chandler were not especially interested in Sedona.

Kevin wound down his story. "So, she basically told them they could go to hell. Only she did it really nicely. She said they could trade, or they could leave us alone, it didn't much matter to her, but that we were not a threat. So after that, I just took off again, to head here. To the East Coast, I mean."

Rochelle had followed his story closely. "So, this 'Maggie' person, she's your girlfriend? You seem to think pretty highly of her."

"Girlfriend? Oh hell no! Ew." Kevin scoffed at the idea. "No, she's more like a sister. I mean, she's great and all, but kinda bossy, too. Not as bossy as her friend, Ariana. But those two together, oh man... I just keep my head down, do what they say and don't tangle with them." Kevin rolled his eyes.

"So, after the thing with the preppers, you just wanted to get away from town for a while? Lay low?"

"Kinda. But really, it's more a fact finding mission. Gathering evidence. They want to know what's going on elsewhere, if anyone is going to be making more gas in the future."

Rochelle winced slightly, but rather than picking at the fresh wound in her psyche, she asked, "So they're the ones that sent you on this wanderlust mission, then?"

"Yeah, kinda. Plus, I got my own reasons." He looked at her expectantly. Rochelle thought back. Hadn't he been talking about something, last night? Had she already been too many margaritas gone to remember? Something about a place in Pennsylvania?

She prompted him. "And those reasons are...?"

So he retold that part, the part she had only half paid attention to the night before. In much more detail, he described how he had wanted, needed, to find out what had happened, why everything went to shit, in his words.

Rochelle had finished her food, so she leaned back to listen. The guy waved his hands a lot when he talked. He rambled and went off on tangents. Clearly, he was one of those types that when you got him talking, he could just go on and on and on. Rochelle let him. She was partly thinking about maybe one more piece of chocolate, too.

He concluded by admitting, "So, I guess there really isn't any magical savior, no cure, no hidden government waiting to just pop out and tell us what to do. Everyone, we're all just figuring it out as we go, making up new rules as we go along."

Rochelle thought about Henry's condition to Gavin, that Congress would be appointing the next Vice President. That was a new rule they were just making up.

"Somewhere along the line, the new rules will have to get

formalized, I think," Rochelle offered.

"Yeah, probably," Kevin nodded. They sat quietly for a moment, each thinking about the difference between before and after.

Finally, Kevin stood up. "So, I think my little mission here is accomplished." He smiled at her empty plate. "Your friends at the bar asked for my help with moving a piano. I think it's about time for me to go meet them." He pulled his cell phone out of his pocket and glanced at the time.

"Pool table," Rochelle corrected.

Kevin nodded. "Right! Pool table. See? You were paying attention!"

Rochelle grinned. Maybe more information had slipped in than she thought. She stood up to walk him out the door. She glanced about and her gaze fell on her coffee table once more.

"Hey," she asked, "Where'd the chocolate come from? I'm pretty sure there wasn't any in here, before last night."

Kevin turned back, "Oh! I found that in the condo the colonel let me into. You were mumbling about chocolate, last night. I thought you wanted some, so I brought it over." He smiled at her.

Rochelle was astonished. She had no memory of talking about it out loud. She barely remembered even making it to the couch.

"Uh, thank you! That was really wonderful of you." They smiled at each other some more, shyly.

Kevin waved, stepping out the door. "Okay, so maybe see you later, at the bar?"

"Yeah, I'll be in later. Let the guys know. But I gotta take care of some chores around here first." She closed the door gently behind him.

***

Rochelle spent several hours on her housekeeping chores. She hauled buckets of water to wash herself, do laundry, and flush the toilet. She carried trash out to the communal dumpster. Like others around town, the dumpster was only emptied when it got full and they put a sign out on the main roadway, to alert the city trucks.

Word about dumpster locations had to be passed from person to person, back to the shreds of city management who could then alert the half dozen or so remaining drivers that a pickup was needed. Rochelle wondered if Kevin's home town city management team had a better way of communicating things, as it sometimes took days for the information to be passed around. Maybe they should setup some kind of messengering service? Teenagers were running around; she'd seen them, although none came into the bar. They seemed very gun-shy of adult interference in their new freedom. But maybe someone could recruit them to be bike messengers? Rochelle filed the idea away to share with Marty and Gary when she saw them in a few hours.

Rochelle arrived at the bar that afternoon to find the guys had succeeded in their own mission. A small crane truck, the kind used to lift roofing materials onto houses, was parked in front of the bar, it's arm extended to an open upstairs window. Rochelle didn't think those windows opened. In fact, she was pretty sure they were solid plate glass.

She pushed open the front vestibule door to hear the clatter and click of pool balls from upstairs. She climbed the stairs, following the sound of voices. Tables and chairs had been moved out of the way, stacked in a back corner. The guys had managed to maneuver and reassemble the desired pool table in the front corner of the upstairs dining room. The main large front window was dislodged, turned sideways and leaned against a wall, suction cup handles protruding from it, waiting to be reinstalled. A light breeze was blowing off the river into the room. Dust bunnies were getting swirled into small clouds under the other tables. She made a mental note to get a broom and dust bin up here.

The guys were still trying to level the table, testing it with a small tool and by hitting balls and watching how they rolled. There was a fair bit of banter tossed about regarding anyone's ability to judge the levelness of a table just by looking at it and playing on it.

Frankie was right in the middle of the group, rubbing chalk onto a pool cue, so Rochelle just watched them for a few minutes, halfway up the stairs. Technically, it was his bar and if he wanted to remove plate glass windows, it was up to him to get them reinstalled afterward. She saw Kevin on the opposite side of the room and he noticed her as well. He smiled at her, but didn't say anything to the rest of the guys, who were deeply engaged in what they considered a very important project.

Rochelle went back downstairs. Behind the bar, everything was in tidy order. In the kitchen, she rotated a new batch of water from the storage buckets into the stockpots to be boiled for drinking water or icecubes. The power was on most of the time now, but the city water was still iffy.

Rochelle paused for a moment, to be thankful of all that Bill had taught her about food safety and preservation, in the short time she had known him. He had been instrumental in helping everyone and making sure there was plenty of food that was stored to last during the difficult winter.

Of course, that supply was dwindling too, as Whig's slowly used it up. She had to give them credit. They had managed the supply very well while feeding their local community. The meals had been heavy on protein and carbs and light on vegetables. But they had not allowed very much to go to waste. She supposed if there were any health inspectors around, they might have complained about health code rules not being followed. She knew that unfinished serving trays of casseroles had been wrapped and chilled, to be portioned out as left overs the next day. Before, that would never have been permitted. Old rules said that once something had been prepared, cooked and offered to the public, it had to be disposed of to prevent the spread of food borne illness. That had been horribly wasteful. Cherry had been very diligent about keeping food hot or cold and not letting it sit around at room temperature which was perfect for growing bacteria. But she also never let anything go to waste, either.

Rochelle puttered about cleaning up the kitchen. They hadn't done any real cooking in Paulbicki's own kitchen since last fall, but they did sometimes put out snacks. And if anyone carried in food from Whig's, they collected the dishes until a full tray was cleaned and ready to carry back to Whig's.

Eventually, Gary and Marty came back down to refill their beers.

Afternoon merged into evening and Henry and Wenrick appeared as usual. Wenrick asked her how bad the hangover was.

Once again she had the sensation that she just passed through another bubble of time. Had it only been yesterday that Gavin had shown her that he was dumping her by walking in while holding hands with another woman? It felt like it had been months ago, years ago. She could barely remember last night's drinking binge. And the hangover was a fading memory too.

"Actually, I'm feeling better already. Food and Ibuprofen did the trick. Thanks for making sure Kevin fed me. That helped." She nodded at him.

"Glad to help," he smiled back at her.

Gary and Marty seemed happy to see the last of the politician, too.

Gary pounced. "So, what's next, Rochelle? Now that you're not just sitting around here, waiting for that schmuck to get back?"

Rochelle looked at them quizzically. "Not really sure what you mean?"

"Well, I keep saying you should get more involved in some project around here, around town."

"Like what?

At that moment, Frankie and Kevin came down the stairs. They had managed to re-seat the plate window in it's frame, but they had to head out immediately to find new window caulking. They set off to see if anyone in the trading market down the street had any. If not, then they would have to find a hardware store that had not been too badly looted. *Really, who would loot window caulking?* Rochelle wondered.

Rochelle turned back to Gary. "You mean, I should take on projects like window installations?"

Gary shrugged, "That's one option. Or maybe you could open a distillery, or something. Someday, we're going to run out of scavenge. Sooner or later, someone's got to start making more." He tipped his glass from side to side.

Rochelle cocked her head at him quizzically. "I don't know anything about distilling liquor." She thought for a moment. "A school friend of mine wrote a paper on liquor advertising. About segmenting and targeting the right markets, how to position the brand, types of advertising that work best, that stuff. And that's all I know about liquor. I know how it's marketed - or *was* marketed - and how to make the drinks. But I don't know how to make the stuff that goes in the drinks."

Gary harrumphed and thought for a bit.

Marty spoke up. "So what do you know how to do, then?"

Rochelle rolled her eyes. "Not much." She thought for a moment. Her current work experience consisted of waitressing and tending bar. Her schooling had been preparing her for a career. During her two years in Chicago, she had worked in the marketing department of a medium sized agricultural business, as a glorified assistant. She'd coordinated graphic designer projects, written a little bit of ad copy and placed advertising insertions in trade magazines. She'd helped the department prepare for major conferences, too. It was not the kind of experience that translated into the business of rebuilding society.

"You know, I don't really know much of anything," she replied aloud to Marty's question.

Marty consoled her. "That scouting you've been doing, in the suburbs? That's been helpful. That's a good project to keep working on. I could place you with some advance teams. It'd be safer, too. Sometimes they find survivors that have been locked up in their houses for months. They stocked up when the crap got started last fall and are still doing fine. But they've spent so much time alone, they're not really responding well, when healthy people show up on their doorstep. Sometimes those interactions don't always go so well. I worry about you getting caught up in something unexpected."

Rochelle nodded her thanks for his concern. "I was really just doing that for the exercise, the bike riding. I don't knock on doors. And I didn't really think of it as a systematic project. I can keep on doing it, though."

Marty repeated, "It'd be safer if you went with someone." He paused, glanced at Gary. "Maybe you should take Kevin out with you on your rides."

Rochelle frowned. "Kevin? What for? Didn't he say he needs to get back to Arizona? I don't think he plans on staying in town for long."

Marty shrugged. Gary raised at eyebrow at his friend. "Maybe he's not staying for long. But while he's here, he could be helpful. He's doing his own information reconnaissance, you know." Rochelle nodded. She'd picked up that part from his stories earlier that morning.

Marty went on, "So, he's learning what to look for, too. You two could help each other out, share tips and tricks or something."

Rochelle was still confused. Wenrick was staring hard at Marty. After a moment Wenrick asked, "Are you sure that's such a good idea? Do we really know anything about this kid?"

Marty was mildly affronted. "Hey, you're the one that put him in one of your condos. And you told him to get her food this morning. You must think he's okay at some base level."

"Well, that's different!" Wenrick spluttered. "I'm just saying, we don't know that he's any better than Sadler-"

Gary scoffed, "Anybody is better than that prick!"

Marty, seated in the middle, looked back and forth between his friends on either side of him and pointed out, "We spent the whole day with him. He was real helpful on the pool table project. He knows trucks and vehicles. He knows how to handle himself in situations, too. He told us a couple more stories. He's gotten into some trouble, out on the road. But he got himself out of it, too. I know the kid runs his mouth a lot, but it comes from a good place."

Gary looked at Marty and pointed out, "But don't you think you're just rushing them into things? Isn't that the whole problem, going too fast?"

Marty shook his head, "Nah. It's not the speed that's the problem. It's the quality of character. And we've just vetted the guy."

Rochelle exploded. "Hey! Guys! I'm standing right here! Don't talk over me like that! I can make my own decisions! You guys are *still* not my Dads!"

She glared at the three men seated in front of her. They leaned back, startled at her outburst. Wenrick looked sheepish, realizing he had overstepped a boundary. Gary just raised an eyebrow at her again.

Rochelle wanted to scream some more. She wanted to huff in indignation. She wanted to storm out of the bar. She wanted to hurl a few more cups. But she recognized that would be a childish thing to do at this point. Even more than venting her frustration, she wanted to be a grownup too. So, in a calm but very firm voice, she repeated, "Guys, I can make my own decisions. If Kevin wants to go for a bike ride, I'd be happy to show him around town. Not because you guys say so, but because I want to. Now, don't you have something better do with your own time?"

They looked at each other in confusion. They were sitting on bar stools, drinking. It was dark outside. This was the best thing they could be doing, at this time of the evening, they clearly thought.

"Like playing pool, upstairs?" Rochelle prompted.

Gary said, under his breath, "Oh yeah..."

Marty added, "Come on, Colonel. Let's see those pool shark moves." The three men headed upstairs and within moments she could hear the clacking of pool balls being racked.

Kevin and Frankie returned hours later, several tubes of caulking in hand. But it was getting very late and they were tired. They briefly explained that the informal market was closed up for the day. So they had to drive out to a Maryland suburb east of the city, wander about, flashlights in hand, searching a half ransacked store and then drive back. That had taken them most of the evening. They decided they could finish the project in the morning.

When they finished their tale, Rochelle informed Kevin, "So, the guys said you're interested in seeing more of the city. I can take you on a bike tour, show you the sights, the monuments and stuff. If you want. Be here at 9 a.m." Inwardly, she cringed at how imperious she sounded.

Kevin looked confused. He glanced at Frankie, who was equally confused. Kevin said, "Uh, okay, sure, I can do that..."

Frankie added, "Yeah, sure, Rochelle, I can caulk that window by myself..." with only the slightest bit of sarcasm in his voice. They clearly realized something had transpired in their absence, but they didn't know what.

Chapter 20

A few minutes before nine the next morning, Rochelle stepped out her front door, to find Kevin waiting in the condo courtyard, holding up a sturdy mountain bike.

"Uh, I thought I said we'd meet at the bar," she said.

"Well, yeah, but I'm staying right over there. Seemed kinda silly to go to the bar." He pointed at a door a few units away.

"Oh. Right. Uh, how did you know I was still here?"

"Your bike is right there." He pointed again. Her own bike was chained to a decorative light post in front of her own door.

"Oh. Right," she said again. She was a little baffled and discomfited. She didn't know how to handle herself. She had no idea what she was doing here. Butterflies flipped about in her stomach. She unlocked her bike and pulled it away from the post. She straddled it and started to position her feet.

"Uh, should we have helmets?" Kevin asked.

"Nah. Those are just for traffic. And there's no traffic. Well, hardly any. I'm not worried."

Kevin shrugged and latched the helmet he'd been holding to a small rack on the back of his bike. They pushed off and headed towards the river.

Rochelle led them through parks and shopping plazas along the Potomac River. They cruised past the Kennedy Center and then turned left at the National Mall. Along Constitution Avenue, she stopped periodically to point out the landmarks and monuments.

Kevin insisted on getting off the bikes to examine the Vietnam War Memorial in more detail. He explained to her that his Dad's older brother had been killed in the war. He didn't know much about his uncle, other than that his name was Kenneth. Kevin thought he might have sort of been named in honor of his uncle. They both wondered if they could locate his uncle's name etched onto the rock wall. But there were thousands and thousands of names. It would take all day to read them, looking for just one name. Kevin stood in silence for few moments, thinking about his Dad, wondering about his Dad's relationship with his own brother. Rochelle waited patiently for him.

After contemplating the Memorial for awhile, they continued on. At the Washington Monument, Rochelle stopped to consider. She realized that, as far as she knew, Gary had never checked off his bucket list item of climbing the Monument. She'd have to give him some flak about that, when she got back to the bar.

Then they cruised around the enormous building of Capitol Hill. Rochelle pointed out buildings around the perimeter of the Mall, mostly museums and federal buildings.

"Which one is your favorite?" Kevin asked, when they paused for a drink of water in front of the Smithsonian Castle.

"Geez, I dunno. I've actually not been inside many of them." She paused, wondering at her own words. "You know, that's really weird. I've lived in this town for three years and I've lived in Virginia my whole life, but the only time I've seen these museums was on class field trips in school!"

Kevin grinned, "Kinda like living in Arizona my whole life, but only seeing the Grand Canyon once?"

Rochelle grinned back at him.

Kevin added, "And once is better than some people. There were plenty of 'Zonies who never saw the Canyon. Before." His face fell on the last word, as he remembered where and when and why.

Starting to pedal forward again, Rochelle commented over her shoulder, "You know, I always wanted to see the Grand Canyon."

They resumed the ride. Rochelle detoured away from the National Mall, turning south for a couple of blocks. The area was filled with large office buildings between five and fifteen stories tall. Several buildings had been under construction when the Superflu had started and had left open concrete floors exposed. Equipment was scattered about behind chain link fencing. After circling around the unfamiliar territory a couple of times, Rochelle found the FEMA agency's federal headquarters. Several heavy duty tents were set up outside the front entrance. People were seated at tables, equipped with computers powered by thick cables running inside the front doors of the building. Short lines waited calmly at a few tents, while individuals were seated across from staffers, talking calmly.

Kevin stared in astonishment. "What are they doing? Has this been going on all along?"

Rochelle shook her head. While this was the first time she'd seen the operation in person, she'd heard all about it from Gary and Marty. "Nope. Only for a few months now. They're doing intake or outreach, or whatever. Any refugees coming into the city, they get directed here. And from here, the staffers direct them to places where they can stay, short term or long term. They're screening for skills, finding out what people can do to contribute. There's a loading dock in the back too, where they've got trucks of supplies and stuff. They'll hand out kits. Small kits if you just need a little something, bigger ones if you're going to stay in the city and pitch in."

Kevin continued to stare about him. At a nearby table, a middle aged woman in a clean polo shirt and khakis was seated at one of the computers. Across from her sat a teenage girl. She looked thin under her dirty clothes. Her hair was lank and greasy. The girl put her hands to her face, sobbing quietly. The middle aged woman stood up, came around the table, knelt and put her arms around the girl. She held the girl, rocking gently, for a few moments. Neither Kevin nor Rochelle could hear what either of them said to each other, but the girl's sobs eased, while the woman just patted her back. After a few more moments, the woman said to the girl, "Come on, let's get you some food and clean clothes in back. It's all going to be okay." She led the girl inside the building, while another staffer took her place at the computer.

Kevin's face screwed up, anger clouding over. "And where the heck were they last fall? Where were the camps out West, when we needed them?"

Rochelle wasn't sure if that was a rhetorical question or not. At that moment, she noticed Marty walking down the shallow steps at the front of the building. Marty had already seen them and was beaming, heading straight for them. He waved a hand in greeting.

When Marty got close enough, he said, "Hey! I'm glad to see you two! Are you doing the city tour, then?" He looked at Rochelle hopefully.

"Yeah, pretty much," she answered.

Kevin spoke over her, though, "Where was all this, out in Arizona?" His tone was distinctly angry. He added, "Why wasn't there any outreach out there?"

Marty's beaming smile dimmed. "Uh, we kinda talked about this already. You said your town didn't really need the help after all?"

"Yeah, I know what I said. And I meant, *I* didn't need it after all. I just wished... I just wanted to know someone was there to help. Back then." His tone went from angry to sad in a few words. "I just wish someone had been there to tell everyone what to do."

Marty said, "Kevin, the old FEMA had ten different regional offices. The one for the West Coast region was in San Francisco. That office probably did run some kind of camp or assistance program, back then. Were you anywhere near San Francisco, to take advantage of that? Before they all got sick, too?"

"Uh, I guess not."

"And didn't you say that your own people figured out what to do for themselves?"

"Well, yeah, they did... eventually."

"So what makes you think these people here could do any better job at helping than your own people did?"

Kevin was baffled.

Marty went on, "Most of the people here, they're not the original FEMA employees. I'm not, either. FEMA lost 97% of it's people too, just like everyone else. The ones you see here, they just stepped in and took over. There's documents and binders full of instructions all over the place inside, but these people are just figuring it all out too, just like your people. We're just making it up as we go along. There's no plan for how to hand out apartments to teenagers. All those binders are about setting up trailers for people trying to leave a city after a hurricane or an earthquake. They don't cover situations where there's excess housing and too few people."

Kevin squinted, still watching the interviews happening in front of him.

Marty extended an arm in a conciliatory gesture. "Look, if you think your home town still needs help, we can probably get a truck load of stuff together. You could drive it out there. Is that the kind of help you need?"

Kevin waved a hand, "No, no, that's not what I meant. They're fine. They consolidated supplies, they're growing food now."

"So what did you mean?" Marty asked gently.

The anger had drained out of Kevin. "I don't know. I guess it's the same as what Henry told me. There's no magic solution, no cure, no hero in a cape. It's just regular people doing regular work. We all have to help ourselves. And I guess most people are doing that."

Marty studied him thoughtfully for a few moments. Then he looked about the streets around them. He pointed at the shell of a partially constructed building just across the street from the FEMA building. "Kevin, you see that construction crane on top of that building over there?"

Kevin was puzzled at the change in topic. "Yeah?"

"See how it's swiveled slightly over to the side, like it was hauling up stuff to the top?"

The crane's long beam was fully extended, with a cable dangling from its tip along the side of the open building.

"Uh huh?"

"People around here are worried that that crane could topple over, if a big storm comes through here. Sometimes the summer storms can be pretty strong. In fact, we're lucky it didn't fall over in one of the winter storms we did have. If it does fall over, it could take down a lot of that stuff up there. Like that partial concrete wall there? It'd make a mess of the street, maybe hurt someone. It could also fall right into our loading dock in back. That would make it really hard for us to keep stuff moving in and out of here."

Kevin studied the crane and the building. He held his hand up to forehead, shielding his eyes from the sun. He stepped a few feet to the side, to get a better angle on the scene. Marty and Rochelle followed. After a moment, Marty asked, "Do you think you could get up there and move it?"

Kevin continued to stare, studying the situation. Finally he said,

"Well, if there's keys for the ignition, I could probably get the arm folded down. I can't actually get the crane back down on the ground. That would take another crane to do that. I don't see what actually lifted it up there in the first place. Some of those construction things are built in place and then disassembled to take back down. Or they're even left in place, to use for window washing, after the building is finished. Kinda depends on the project, how big it is."

Marty nodded. "I think if the arms just got folded down, maybe if it was moved to the center of the structure, it wouldn't be in danger of coming down the wrong way."

Rochelle gaped at the two men. "How's he even going to get up there?" she asked Marty. Without waiting for answer, she asked Kevin, "Do you even know how to work that kind of equipment?"

He responded promptly, "Yeah, sure. No big deal."

Kevin flicked down the kick stand of his bike and parked it on the sidewalk. He started walking down the street, crossing over to the other side. Marty whistled back towards the tent, waving at someone else. A large black man came over at a jog. Marty quickly explained to the newcomer that he had found a crane operator and could he go show Kevin how to get up to the top floor.

When the black man jogged after Kevin, Marty explained to Rochelle, "That's Jonas. He's been up there, checking things out. He'll show Kevin where the hole in the fence is and the stair well. And the construction office - there's probably keys to the equipment in there."

Rochelle stared at him. "You couldn't have found someone with construction equipment experience to do this, before now? With all the refugee screening you've been doing here?" She waved her arm at the tents.

Marty quirked a side smile at her. "Oh, I probably could have, had I thought of it before now. I guess the job just needed the right hero to come along at the right time."

Rochelle looked back at the building. Kevin and Jonas had disappeared from view for the moment. She counted the open concrete floors. Twelve stories. It was going to take awhile for them to climb the stairs. She looked around, decided there was nothing wrong with sitting on the ground to relax for a bit and folded her legs.

After few minutes, Marty exclaimed, "Damn, I should have sent one of the walkie talkies with Jonas. Well, this is going to take while. You know, you could go inside, say hello to Gary, if you wanted, see his office."

Rochelle looked up at him. "I've seen offices before. Anything special about this one?"

Marty shook his head. "I suppose not."

After a few moments, he wandered inside. He must have told Gary and plenty of others what was happening outside, because small groups of people started strolling out. They lined up on the sidewalk, staring up at the building shell.

After a little bit of time, Rochelle thought she could hear the sound of a motor coughing and rumbling, but then it spluttered out.

Gary appeared with Marty. They both stared back up at the building. "No change?" Marty asked.

Rochelle shook her head. "Not yet."

Marty said, "That motor in that crane hasn't been turned in on more than six months. They might need a mechanic up there."

The faint sound of an engine coughed to life again. As they watched, they saw Jonas's figure lean over the scaffolding around the roof perimeter and wave to the small crowd below. People waved back. A few shouts of encouragement rose up.

After a few more moments, the dangling cable slowly started to rise up, reeling back in to snug up to the extended tip of the arm. Then the arm rose up slightly, to a sharper angle. The movement was a little jerky, making it bounce slightly. It rotated away from the wall, circling around a pivot point they could not see, to return it's center mass to middle of the building's roof. When it stopped rotating, Rochelle could see only a portion of the arm. Then the arm started contracting on itself, as it's extensions were withdrawn. The small crowd of people on the street started cheering. When they could no longer see anything on top of the building, they turned to each other, huge smiles lighting up their faces. Slowly, they returned to their own work, chattering happily to each other.

Fifteen minutes later, Jonas and Kevin reappeared, strolling back up the street. When the scattered crowd saw them, they pointed. Jonas waved at his friends, pointed at Kevin and raised his arms, grinning broadly, encouraging everyone to praise him. For a few moments, people cheered and clapped.

Kevin waved bashfully, slightly confused by all the attention. When the moment passed, he returned to stand in front of Marty, Gary and Rochelle.

"Okay, it's secured now. Or, as much as it can be up there. The arm is fully collapsed and level to the ground, in the lowest possible position. And the cab's stabilizers are out, too. It's right in the middle of the roof, so, even if a tornado comes along, it would have to roll over at least twice, before it fell over the side of the building. And, well, if anything is strong enough to make it do that, it's probably going to take down the whole building, not just the crane."

Marty beamed. "That's perfect, Kevin! Thank you so much for doing that."

A woman carrying a pile of folders was moving from the tents to head indoors, but she veered to the side to approach them. She laid a hand gently on Kevin's shoulder and said, "That was a really wonderful thing you did up there. You may have saved some lives. Thank yo so much." She beamed at him, patted his arm and then continued to make her way inside the offices.

Kevin looked after her, confused. "All I did was push a few levers. It's not that big a deal."

Marty said, "To them it is. We're all just regular people, doing regular work. We all have to help each other."

Kevin squinted at him thoughtfully, but didn't say anything else.

Chapter 21

After taking their leave of the crowd at the FEMA building, Rochelle and Kevin rode back up the Mall and past the Tidal Basin. She elected to circle around East Potomac Park again. They took another short break at Hains Point on the southern tip of the small island. She had not been back to this park since the day months ago when she had seen the river barge. Like that day, the river water was calm. The confluence of the Potomac and the Anacostia blended together seamlessly. A small sandbar had formed a few hundred yards off the point. A tree log was lodged in the sand, pointing bare stick arms up to the sky.

They sat on one of the park benches to munch on granola bars and sip from their water bottles. Kevin stretched his arms out, flexing his back. He rested his arm on the back of the bench behind her, not touching her, but somewhat enclosing her. There were still empty inches of space between them on the seat, though.

Happily, there were no river barges visible on the river today. The dead body smell seemed nearly gone now, Rochelle noticed thankfully. She explained how the barges had been carrying thousands of bodies out to sea and how it had made her sick to her stomach. Kevin nodded in vigorous agreement with her.

"Yeah, I'm right there with you. It makes me sick, too. Physically. I drove a few truckloads from the hospital morgue, to the pits. Hauled some out of houses, too. I tossed my cookies every time. I can't handle it, either."

Rochelle nodded back. "The guys keep talking about how there's all these projects going on, to clean things up. I just can't quite bring myself to step up to volunteer; not if it means going near the dead bodies. It's just so… horrifying." She shuddered.

After another moment, she asked, "Do you ever wonder why we do that? People in general, I mean. Why we are so grossed out by dead bodies. I mean, sooner or later, everyone dies. We're all going to, someday. Sooner or later, we all have to pick up someone and do something with the body."

Kevin shrugged. "I dunno. Once I heard someone say something about how throwing up is a natural reaction. It's our body's way of warning us to stay away from things that might hurt us. You know, diseases and things. It's instinct."

Rochelle didn't say anything to that. Kevin finally asked "So, who did you lose?"

Rochelle paused, wondering how much detail to share. Finally she answered, "Everyone. My sisters, all three of them. My nephew. My Dad. My Mom."

"The same Mom you were yelling at in the cups the other day?"

"The same one." Rochelle nodded and smiled a little bit.

The conversation paused again.

Kevin suddenly said, "Same here. My Dad. My brother. My friends."

Rochelle wondered, but couldn't bring herself to ask him what had happened to them, beyond the obvious, beyond dying of the Superflu.

Instead, she asked, "Doesn't it make you mad, sometimes?"

In the back of her mind, she was thinking about Nerissa, how she had just stopped texting and calling. She hadn't been able to bring herself to go out to Manassas, to check on her. Well, to take care of the aftermath. A pang of guilt washed through her. She clenched her jaw for moment, fighting to distract herself.

Kevin answered, "Sometimes. It used to. Not as much anymore."

Rochelle mused. "It's such a stupid grief. I don't know how to describe it better. All the dying, the Superflu, it's nobody's fault. You can't get mad at anyone, because there's no one to be mad at. I just *am* mad. I feel *stuck*. You know what I mean?"

Kevin nodded, "Yeah."

"It was just a mindless little virus. Just a scrap of genetic code wrapped in some proteins. Its an utter waste of time and energy to be mad at a virus. It's not sentient. It doesn't have any will, any desire. It just replicated. And then it interacted badly with its host. Its probably killed itself off, too."

Kevin nodded again.

Rochelle thought about her next question carefully. "Okay, so here's the thing that has me stuck. The dead bodies gross me out so much that it makes me sick to my stomach. But I miss my family and I want to make things right. I think my sister might still be at home. I know my mom was buried - we had a funeral and everything - it was early on, back then. And I'm pretty sure my oldest sister, Hollan, got transferred to a morgue, when she died in the hospital. And my other sister, Paige, she was out in California. I can't do anything for her. But my youngest sister, Nessie..." Rochelle's voice broke. She blinked rapidly to clear her eyes that suddenly filled with tears.

When she could speak again, she continued, "I think I need to go out to Manassas to bury her. I shouldn't have left her for so long. I should have done it long ago, but it got cold and dark and I've been stuck. It's going to be so gross, but it has to be done. I don't think I can get moving, until that gets done."

Kevin responded promptly, "Yeah, sure, I'll go with you. I'll help." When a few tears trickled down the side of her face, Kevin lifted the arm that was behind her, to gently nudge her neck and upper back. He awkwardly patted her shoulder. His jaw moved a couple of times, but no more words came out.

Rochelle nodded and sighed. "Thank you. Okay, first thing in the morning, then? We'll drive out there."

Then she stood up abruptly. Gently she said, "Come on, I need to get back to the bar."

Kevin nodded and stood up as well. Together, they followed the river upstream. Behind them, the tree log on the sandbar finally broke loose and was carried away by the flowing water.

**

Rochelle met Kevin outside her condo door the next morning, the same as the day before. She handed him a plastic bag filled with a respirator, gloves and a small bottle of vapor rub. She kept a bag for herself. He looked inside and nodded his understanding.

Assorted customers sometimes traded in items like these for their drinks. She called them the "one hit wonders," because they came in, traded in their gear, drank their fill and then walked out, never to be seen again. Sometimes she traded the gear back out to others at the little market down the street. Others she piled into boxes in the storage closet. These sets came from that stash.

Rochelle drove her own car, Kevin in the passenger seat, his knees slightly hunched up. It was a small car and the seat didn't go very far back. They didn't talk much on the drive, until she got very close to her home town. Then she started pointing out major landmarks, like the schools she went to and the church her mother had dragged them to during her youth.

At her mother's house, she easily unlocked the door. Her house key was still on the same ring as her car key. She paused for a moment before pushing the door open, wondering if she should put the mask on right away or wait and see. Or wait and smell.

She glanced at Kevin, but he didn't say anything. He just waited patiently for her lead. He gave her a small smile of encouragement, though.

Taking a deep breath and holding it, she pushed the door open. The weather stripping around it's edges was slow and sticky to release, after being sealed tight for so long. Inside, it was dim, the curtains drawn closed. Rochelle led the way inside, moving slowly, looking about carefully. She moved to the back half of the house, the kitchen, the family room and the back sun porch where she and her sisters used to hang out. There were no initial signs that the house had been disturbed in months; no mess on the kitchen floors from looters clearing the cupboards. No broken window glass. The door to the garage was closed. Rochelle looked back into the formal dining room. Her mother's Wedgwood china was intact, in the cabinet.

She'd been holding her breath for more than a minute and was forced to let it out with a whoosh. She inhaled gently, carefully, sampling. The air was musty and, yes, there was that slight tang of rot. But it was faint, not overwhelming, not choking. She glanced up the stairs and then at Kevin. He nodded that he understood what that meant.

Confluence

In a low tone, he asked, "Do you know where you'd like bury her? If there's a shovel around, I can start digging."

Rochelle led him through the kitchen to the garage, past her Mom's and Nerissa's cars, to the back shed, where the garden tools had been kept. They were coated with dust and a few cobwebs. In the backyard, she scanned about. It was a fairly ordinary yard. The tulips and daffodils had bloomed and faded, leaving stalky leaves. Those were at the edge of the border around the yard, an undulating strip of bark mulch dotted with bushes, small trees and a couple of very large old trees that had been on the property even before the house had been built. The center of the yard was grass, with an expansive brick patio protruding into it. The grass was inches tall, dotted with dandelions and other weeds. Patches were still yellow from winter, while other areas were verdant green.

Rochelle strode to a far corner of the yard. A huge lilac bush had been planted there years ago. It was almost done blooming and only a trace of the distinctive floral odor remained. "Here," she said and started edging a rough rectangle into the grass in front of the bush. All the girls had loved the plant for it's blooms and heavenly scent. It would be a fitting place to lay Nerissa to rest.

Once she had the shape of the grave roughed out, Kevin gently took the shovel from her and started into the hard chore of cutting up the soil into chunks and heaving them into a tidy pile to the side.

While he worked, Rochelle faced the house. She took another deep breath and clenched her teeth. She knew it wouldn't be pleasant but it wasn't going to kill her. Her plan was to wrap Nerissa in whatever bed sheets she was on and tie up the bundle. She'd seen that done in movies. It seemed like something other cultures did, ones that didn't use caskets. And of course, she didn't have a casket so a bundle would be best.

Inside the house, she retrieved her bag of gear, smeared a little ointment under her nose and seated the respirator on her face. She had deliberately not eaten any breakfast, so she wasn't terribly worried about throwing up.

Solemnly, she turned and climbed the stairs. There was slightly more light filtering through the gauzy liner curtains of the upstairs bedrooms. The room at the end of the short hallway was Nerissa's. The door was half open. She approached it slowly and pushed it all the way open.

Exactly has she had expected, had feared, her sister's body was on the bed. She'd died lying on her side, slightly curled up, facing the the empty space beside her on the queen sized mattress. Her cell phone lay beside her, also dead. The top sheet and comforter were rumpled over her. Rochelle studied her for a moment. The body had darkened and shriveled, losing mass as fluids had seeped and evaporated. Her eyes were closed and sunken. Rochelle considered the mechanics of how she would flip the sheet over and under her. Should she remove the top sheet and just wrap her in the fitted mattress sheet? Or use both? She twitched the heavy comforter aside and then cringed when she realized it was slightly glued to the sheet under it, which had been soaked in fluids and then had dried. With a slightly firmer tug, the comforter came off and piled on the floor. Examining the top sheet, Rochelle concluded there was no saving it. It was so completely and permanently stained, there was no further use for it but to be a burial shroud.

Rochelle started to un-tuck the fitted sheet from under her sister. She glanced up at Nerissa's face and abruptly lost it. As her physical eyes landed on her sister's formerly pretty hair, now dry and stiff, her mind's eye saw Nerissa as child, as a young woman. Images rolled up: Nerissa trying to balance on roller skates, squealing in laughter and then squealing in pain from a skinned knee. Nerissa playing soccer on the high school team. Nerissa sneaking french fries off her plate in some restaurant somewhere. Nerissa dressed in a beautiful white mermaid gown, glittering with sequins.

Rochelle felt the bile rising in her throat. She may not have had breakfast, but she had drunk water and it was coming back up. She ripped the respirator off her face, running for the bathroom. She barely made it in time, to heave up the acidified water in her stomach into the dry bowl. Incongruously, she noticed the faint stains left behind on the porcelain as the toilet water had slowly evaporated.

When she finished retching, she automatically tried turning the faucet on the sink, wanting to rinse her mouth. But nothing came out. Groaning, she closed the tap again. Carefully focusing her vision on the carpet, she made the diagonal path from the private bathroom to the bedroom door and then back downstairs. She had several bottles of water in the car. Retrieving one, she swished water about in her mouth, spit and then swallowed several more mouthfuls. She wondered if that was going to come back up, too, so she did not drink any more.

From the inside of the house, she looked out the back porch windows to check on Kevin. He was still methodically shoveling dirt in the backyard. He was about knee deep now.

Once more, she clutched up her resolve and climbed the stairs again. She found that by intensely focusing her concentration on the mundane tasks at hand, she could keep control. She pulled the corners of the sheets free. She tied them in knots, sandwiching the body in between the top sheet and the fitted sheet. It still seemed loose, so she looked about. She spotted a knitted winter scarf hanging on the closet door knob. It was too thick, too woolly, too colorfully cheerful, but it gave her an idea. She rummaged about in the dresser drawers, looking for other scarves she could knot about the body. Nerissa had rarely worn scarves, so Rochelle dashed to her mother's room and rummaged in her drawers, too. Catherine had plenty of scarves, in both bright and subdued tones. Rochelle took several of them and returned to Nerissa's room.

She tied the scarves about the body's waist and knees, cinching up the loose sheets. In the process, she realized the body weighed less than what Nerissa had before she'd gotten sick. Experimentally, she tried lifting the body, planning to cradle it to her chest, her arms under the neck and knees. While it was much lighter now, it was still too heavy and awkward for Rochelle to carry in that position. She'd risk losing her balance and dropping it, which would be horribly undignified. She contemplated the "fireman's carry" position, of heaving it up over one shoulder. Would that be dignified enough? Did it matter?

She quickly decided that contemplating the dignity of body transport would only lead to another session of heaving up. Refocusing on the minutia, she pulled the legs to the side of the bed and prepared to lift the torso up and over her shoulder. Rigor mortis had long disappeared, but so had most of the lubricating fluid in the joints, so the body was still somewhat stiff and inflexible. She heard small pops as the joints were involuntarily flexed. She heaved the body up, trying very hard not examine the stained mattress underneath. It was heavy, but not so heavy that she couldn't walk or get down the stairs. She paid very close attention to every step, thinking about where the body's head and feet were, so that they didn't accidentally bang into walls and railings.

She pushed her way through the kitchen door onto the patio. Kevin looked up at the noise. Seeing her struggling under the load, he quickly climbed out of the low pit and came to take the bundle.

"Whoa there, hey, easy now... You didn't have to carry her down. I could have done that..." He gently pulled the bundle from her shoulder and laid it beside the grave. Rochelle looked down. The floor of the pit was uneven and not very deep yet. Kevin jumped back into the hole, saying, "I think it needs to go a little deeper than this yet. No way we're going to make six feet, but I'm aiming for three." He resumed his shoveling.

Rochelle looked about, heaving deep breaths of fresh outdoor air. She wondered where she had left her mask. Right, in the bathroom, after she had thrown up. She returned to the tool shed and found a second shovel. She wondered why they even had two. Her mother didn't do her own gardening. She had hired that service out. Rochelle returned to the grave and jumped into the pit. Kevin made room for her and they each worked to shovel up spoonfuls of dirt. At this layer, the ground was softer, nearly permanently damp and easy to cut up into chunks. The work went faster than she expected.

When they reached a depth she felt seemed right, they climbed out. She looked about the yard, up at the tree canopy above, at the house. Anywhere but at the body. She wondered if she should say some words. Or maybe she should move the body into the hole and then say some words. *What should she say?*

Kevin was watching her carefully. He must have realized how confused she was. "If you're ready to lower her in, I'll jump back down and guide her?" he asked. Rochelle nodded, so he hopped back down and gestured. Rochelle half lifted, half dragged the body to the edge of the hole, where Kevin grasped Nerissa to his chest, exactly as she had wanted to, upstairs in the bedroom, but didn't have the strength. Cradling Nerissa carefully, he squatted down and gently laid the bundle on the ground at his feet. He didn't jump back up immediately, though. He paused for a long moment, a hand to his mouth, looking down.

After a moment, he slowly stood straight. The body at his feet was between him and Rochelle. He stepped to the end and climbed out, taking care not to step on Nerissa. He joined Rochelle, standing at her side, looking down.

Rochelle said, "I don't know what to say now. I should say something but I don't know what."

Kevin opened his mouth, but then closed it again. He did that a couple more times, before shrugging. He didn't know, either. Finally he said, "Do you want to tell me about her? What she was like?"

Rochelle thought about that. "I can do that any time. I don't want to stop talking about them, stop thinking about them, just because they're buried and gone. We should be able to talk about our people, whenever we want."

Kevin nodded in agreement. "Sure," he said.

Rochelle considered what she wanted to say to Nerissa. She should pray? Wish her well in the afterlife? Did she even believe in an afterlife? If there was a heaven, Nerissa was certainly there already.

"Okay. This is what I have to say. Goodbye, Nerissa. Only, not goodbye, because I might still talk to you, if I need a sister to listen. This is just goodbye to your body. This is just goodbye to the past. Goodbye to the crap that we can't change. Goodbye to the stupid Superflu. It's time for me to move on."

Rochelle picked up her shovel again, stepped around to the back side of the shallow grave and started scooping up the dirt piled to the side. She gently let it fall from the shovel onto the bundle. As she turned scoop after scoop, her eyes only blurred a little bit.

Kevin helped her fill in the hole. When the last of the loose dirt has been packed back into place, he tried to carefully arrange the sections of sod on top. Rochelle feared that without a good watering to help the roots reattach, the patch might not take well. But she appreciated the thoughtfulness of the gesture. When he finished patting down the last section, he looked up and faced her.

Once again, the grief erupted out of her with virtually no warning. Kevin immediately stepped over to her and closed his arms about her, gripping her tight, keeping her standing, but letting her sob as hard as she needed to. She mashed her face into his t-shirt, soaking it with tears. Her shoulders shook. A sensation of deja vu washed over her, only the other scene was of a much wider, taller man, than Kevin. But that man had held her just the same, letting her cry herself out, months ago last autumn.

She wept for her sisters. She wept for her friends. She wept for the kindness of strange men. When she was finished crying, she stepped back. She smiled tremulously and nodded. She was going to be okay for now.

They put the shovels away and prepared to lock up the house again. Kevin asked her if she wanted to take anything? Did she have any clothes or belongings she wanted to keep?

She looked about, thinking. She had fully moved out of the house when she went to Chicago, five years ago. But there were a few family photos scattered about. She selected a few, but decided the majority of them could stay in place here. She could come back at any time and get more if she wanted. So they locked the doors firmly behind them and drove back to D.C.

Chapter 22

For the next several days after the burial, Rochelle and Kevin went for bike rides in the morning. She showed him the tony suburbs to the north of the city. On breaks during their rides, they talked. They discovered they had some things in common. Naturally, there were plenty of movies, TV shows and video games they had both liked. Neither of them was much for reading books. Their tastes in music differed though. Rochelle tended to like pop music, rhythm and blues and other softer music. Kevin called it "brunch music." Instead, he preferred hard rock, especially heavy metal.

They also discovered that they had experienced similar parenting patterns, having been raised by one, while the other was effectively absent from their lives.

There were many more things they did not share in common. Like, Kevin was a natural morning person. He liked to watch sunrises. Rochelle groaned and said she couldn't even remember the last time she'd seen a sunrise. School and bar meant she kept late nights. Her idea of "early" in the morning was about 9 a.m. Maybe 8:30, if absolutely necessary.

Rochelle was puzzled by Kevin. Aside from the hug and crying jag, he did not try to touch her during their many talks. His attempts to flirt were awkward and strained. There had been moments when he could have leaned in for a kiss or taken her hand. Rochelle was pretty sure he was attracted to her, so she was a little baffled at what was holding him back. She had decided she liked him well enough, but without some kind of signal from him, she wasn't sure what was going on. Was he waiting for her to be over the loss of her family? Or worse, over Gavin? She didn't need any time for that. She had ejected the woefully misconceived fantasy of what she had wanted Gavin to be. Now that she saw what the mistake she had made was, she felt like she was ready to try something different. Very different.

Rochelle checked herself, to see if she was trying to fit Kevin into any new templates. After discarding her mother's mold of the perfect boyfriend, she wanted to avoid the same pattern. Of course, Catherine would never have approved of Kevin, so there was that. Instead, Rochelle had a mental conversation with her sisters. They would have asked the hard questions. Who was the guy? What were his good qualities? What were his not so good qualities? How did he approach problems? How did he respond to adversity? What were his goals in life?

Rochelle considered the hypothetical questions. She knew the surface details: his age, his education, his hometown. She was well aware that he came from a deeply different background than she did. But at a deeper level, she understood that he was reasonably kind and considerate. He'd brought her chocolate. He helped out with whatever was asked of him, by her or by anyone else that she'd seen. He'd helped her bury her sister, even after admitting that he hated dealing with dead bodies as much as she did.

On the negative side, he still had a bit of a chip on his shoulder about how the whole Superflu thing had been handled in the beginning. But he recognized the chip was there and was whittling it down. Any time the resentment rose up in him and some negative comment erupted from him, a look from her or the guys, or even his own conscience talked him back down. Of course, sometimes that inner monologue could become an outer one. He did tend to talk a lot. Rochelle didn't really mind that, though. It usually only happened when she didn't feel like doing any talking herself. Sometimes it was nice to have the silence filled with a human voice. Sometimes he had a different perspective on things that she had never thought of.

He seemed pretty good at coping with adversity too. She knew he carried a pistol, but as far as she knew, he had never pulled it and pointed at another person. If something frustrated him, he didn't seem prone to lashing out in violence. He might yell a bit at times. He said he liked to yell *about* situations, not *at* situations. He said it was scream therapy. And besides, girls who smashed dozens of mugs were not really in any position to be critical, were they?

Rochelle considered the last hypothetical question: goals. He definitely had one. He had to get back to Arizona. She got the sense he was stalling on leaving, but that his time was coming to an end soon. And the thought of him leaving town left her feeling a tiny bit of panic. Why would that be? Did she want him to stay? And do what? She agreed with his friends' assessment: he had a serious case of wanderlust. He was always interested in seeing what was around the next bend in the road, what lay beyond the next hill. Clearly, sitting still on a bar stool for weeks or months was not going to work for him.

Rochelle's fear about him leaving materialized far too soon.

After the crane incident, Gary and Marty had encouraged Kevin to go to the other high rise construction sites about town and secure the cranes on those building as well. There had been about half a dozen of them. He had finished the last one that afternoon, after bike riding twenty five miles with Rochelle that morning, no less.

Gary was teasing Kevin about needing to find him a new project, now that the cranes were done.

Marty interrupted Gary, "Hey, I thought this guy already had a job. Wasn't he supposed to scout about, gathering information? Kev, didn't you say you had to report back home soon?"

Kevin nodded, lifting his bottle of Bud Light to his face, but not yet sipping. "Yeah, I really do have to get back there, in person. They're having an election and I want to vote in it. I want to take a northern route back, through Indiana, Iowa, Colorado. I've got about a month to make that. Before, I could have done it in four days in my big rig. But now, I don't know the road conditions or where I'll find supplies. I need to make sure I have plenty of time. So I really need to get started soon."

Kevin had been looking down at the bar or at the guys, anywhere but at Rochelle. But as he spoke the last part, he looked up, staring hard into her eyes.

Rochelle's heart sank. Even though she knew it had been coming, she'd hoped maybe he'd stall some more.

Gary and Marty looked back and forth between themselves. Frankie, on the end, watched them all. It was still a little bit early for the other evening regulars to have arrived yet.

Marty spoke up. "You know, Rochelle, you should consider going with him. It'd be safer out there on the road for him, than going alone."

And there it was. Right out there in the open.

Rochelle's throat threatened to close up on her. Her palms went sweaty. She glanced down, not looking any of them in the eyes. She heard Kevin's beer bottle thunk down onto the counter with a little more force than strictly necessary.

Gary spoke for her. "She can't go with him! Who'd run this place?"

"Frankie," said Marty promptly.

Gary's mouth hung open, wobbling a little bit, looking for another objection.

Rochelle was trying to figure out for herself if she could or couldn't. Yeah, technically there was no physical reason why she couldn't set off on a long car trip half way across the continent. Except, of course, the Apocalypse and everything.

But the more important question, she realized, was: Did she want to go? And did Kevin want her to go with him?

She glanced back up at Kevin. He was still staring hard at her, no expression. Or rather, she didn't know how to interpret the expression on his face.

After more glances about, Gary stood up off his stool abruptly and said, "Come on, Marty, let's go play pool upstairs."

He casually bumped Marty's shoulder to get him moving. They were halfway up the stairs, when they realized Frankie had not followed them. He was still sitting on his stool, studying Rochelle and Kevin. Gary stopped, bending down to peer under the first floor ceiling. He whistled and called, "Hey, Frankie! You too! Come on!"

Frankie looked up at his name and then levered himself off his stool. He smiled at them knowingly but followed the bar flies up the stairs. A few moments later, they heard the clacking of pool balls.

Rochelle didn't know what to do or say. She nervously wiped at the counter. She straightened bottles. Every time she glanced at Kevin out of the corner of her eye, he was staring intently at her. She thought maybe there was a tiny little flutter of a pulse at his throat, but she was too scared to look closely enough to be sure.

Then she realized she was acting like a silly little school girl. She took a deep breath, squared up to him across the bar counter from herself and looked him in the eye. "So?" she asked evenly.

"So," he said, equally calmly. After another moment, he asked, "Would you like to come to Arizona with me?"

She stared intently at him. She read the steely seriousness in his face. He meant it. He really did want her to come. But could she? Could she unlever herself from this one safe place in her life? Could she put herself into a vehicle, sitting next to this man, who she barely knew, for weeks at time, driving across the country? What if they discovered they couldn't stand each other? What would she do then? Worse, what if it was good?

Slowly she asked, "And then what?"

Kevin squinted, his face puckering briefly. "What? After we get to Arizona? Whatever you want. Take another trip. And then another. We could go wherever we want. Help out wherever we're needed."

Rochelle still considered. Slowly, she asked, "Could we go through... Colorado, on the way there?"

A small smile played on Kevin's lips. "Sure."

"Could we visit... the Grand Canyon?"

His smile widened a little. "Sure."

Rochelle felt her own smile starting to grow on her face. She considered for just a moment longer. In the same slow tone, she conceded. "Okay. I'm in. Let's go to Arizona."

Kevin grinned, but before he could say anything further, they heard a whoop from the stair well. The three guys were clustered on the stairs, trying to simultaneously hide from and spy on them. They reminded Rochelle of little kids watching mommy and daddy throw a house party.

The guys stood up and clattered the rest of the way down the stairs.

Gary practically shouted, "Come on, girl, get out here! This calls for a celebration!" He whooped again and raised his arms. "Where's the music? Get the champagne!"

Marty was laughing and clapping Kevin on the back. Frankie was beaming at everyone.

Not really sure why Gary was so excited, Rochelle walked around the bar to the middle of the room to accept Gary's hug. "Geez, Gary, calm down. It's not like he proposed, or anything. We're just going to be traveling companions," she said, flustered at all the fuss he was making.

Gary gripped her in a bear hug, tilted back and twirled her around once. "Oh, it's a big deal and you know it. It's about time you got some movement. It'll be good for you! Get out, see the country."

Other people in the bar, the irregular regular pair of women, a few others, clustered around them, wondering what all the commotion was about. And, just to add to the general merriment, Henry and Wenrick also appeared in the doorway, clearly confused. Explanations were made and general partying commenced, before Rochelle even had a moment to fully process what she had just consented to. Someone turned on a CD player and springy dance music started blaring. She saw Henry shaking hands with Kevin. And then Wenrick gripped Kevin's shoulder, pointed his free hand in Kevin's face and said, "Don't forget what I told you about the satellites and heat seeking missiles!" He widened his eyes at Kevin, nodded once, firmly and released him. Rochelle was confused, but didn't have a chance to ask what that meant.

A moment later, Gary pulled her aside and pointed out, "You know, Frankie really needs this, too."

"Needs what?" she frowned.

"The bar. Frankie needs something worthwhile to do too. He'd never try to take this away from you, but he needs it too. So it's good that he has this now."

Rochelle nodded, but a fresh stab of doubt gripped her. "Yeah, but what if it doesn't work out? Can I still come back here?"

Gary answered, "Of course you can! You're always welcome here. But it's going to be fine. Look, I know you said we're not your Dads. But if you were my daughter, I'd tell you this: you know that hotness scale I've heard you kids talk about? Well, Kevin, right now he's about a four. With a little work, a little grooming, some coaching to rein in that run-away mouth, he could be a seven. But you? Sweetie, you're a ten. No matter how much Kevin comes up on that scale, you will always be *way* out of his league. And on an instinctive level, he knows that. So if the odds line up in his favor, if the heavens decide to smile down on him and gift him with a miracle, you can bet your last dollar that he will treasure you. He will do his utmost best to protect you, shelter you and treat you like a princess, because he knows he will never ever have anything better than you in his life."

Rochelle recoiled. "I don't want to be a princess. I just wanted to be treated like a regular person. I'm not perfect. I have flaws, too."

"Yes and you'll balance each other out, in time. But Kevin knows that he's getting something special. He won't dare to touch you, until you make it crystal clear that you want it. And besides, Wenrick put the fear of God in him. He wouldn't dare do anything to hurt you. Not like that prick, Sadler."

Rochelle rolled her eyes. That did explain why Kevin had been so hands-off, so far. Clearly, she'd have to make the first move, if she wanted anything to happen.

Rochelle watched the swirl of motion. The bar was actually crowded now. And noisy. It was staring to feel like it used to, months ago. She looked about, wondering if she should bus a table or get a fresh round of drinks out. Frankie had taken her station behind the bar and was uncapping a bottle for someone. Across the room, Kevin was trying keep an eye on her, but was distracted by other people asking him questions about the upcoming trip.

She sidled through the crowd and gripped his arm. "We've got some planning to do!" she said, to excuse him from his conversation with the others. She steered him out the bar's front door.

Outside, it was quieter and cooler. Rochelle grasped Kevin's hand and led him across the street to the narrow park lining the river bank. She sat down on the park bench, Kevin beside her. The overgrown weeds and grass brushed against her legs. In front of them, the river was dark, smooth and glassy, flowing past on its way out to the sea.

"So, I don't have the slightest idea what to do to get ready for this," Rochelle announced. "In fact, I can't remember the last time I took a driving trip across the country. Or anywhere. Well, that's not true, I drove to Chicago and back. But you know, any longer trips I did before, we flew everywhere. Or took the train, if it was on the East Coast."

Kevin seemed to still be in shock from the sudden change in his plans. "Uh…" he said.

"So, what do I need to bring?"

"Uh, Clothes? And… your girly stuff?"

"Girly stuff?" she asked, a little surprised.

"You know, soap, shampoo, whatever you use…"

Indignant, she said, "I meant, do I need a weapon? What are we going to do for gas? Should we pick a route now, or do you just make it up as you go?"

"Oh! Nah, don't worry about that yet. Tell you what, let's take tomorrow to prepare. We'll get some stuff together, go get my Jeep Rubicon. I left it at a house out in the 'burbs. Then we leave first thing in the morning the day after. How's that sound?"

Rochelle studied him. Was she really going to do this? Kevin smiled at her again, a little uncertainly. He was seated a few inches away from her, carefully keeping visible space between them.

Rochelle realized she had nothing to lose and everything to gain. This trip was an opportunity to be someone she had never been before. She smiled back. Yes, she really was going to do this.

She turned to face him. She raised both hands and placed them gently on his face. His expression grew startled. But his arm moved behind her to enclose her. She drew his face forward and kissed him gently. He kissed her back. Tentatively, at first, and then more eagerly. It was sweet and warm and full of potential. She leaned back, dropped her hands to his chest and looked him in the eye again. The grin bloomed on his face.

"That sounds perfect," she replied.

Epilogue: Five months later

Outside the bar, the November night was dark and rainy. But the street lights were on and warm light poured out the windows of Paulbicki's. Rochelle pulled the borrowed hotel van into one of the parking spaces across the street and parked. Then she led the group of Chandler people through the front door of the bar. Gary and Marty were seated on their usual stools and Frankie was behind the bar. They looked up at the large group walking in. Their faces beamed in happy surprise when they recognized Rochelle at the head of the group and Kevin at the back.

"Hey, guys!" Rochelle greeted them shyly. "Bet you didn't think you'd see me back so soon!"

Gary levered himself off his seat, to give her a hug. "Rochelle! What are you doing here?"

Marty followed suit and then Frankie, each giving her a hug. They told her they were glad to see her and looked curiously at the group of strangers behind her.

Rochelle explained, "We're in town for the Congressional Congress. Kevin and I drove this group here all the way from Arizona!" She waved at the group of six or seven people milling around behind her, looking about curiously.

Gary exclaimed, "You've been in town all week and you're just now getting over here to see us? You should have let us know you were here!"

"Yeah, well, this group kept us hopping. Hey, let me introduce you…" Rochelle started naming off names, pointing. Everyone waved and smiled at each other. When she finished, she faced the newcomers she had led in and suggested, "Let's go grab those tables over there. I'll bring some beer over." The group nodded and started taking off coats to hang on nearby hooks. While they settled in, Rochelle turned to the bar flies and said, "I'll come back and visit with you guys in a few. Just let me see if they want to get any food or whatever."

The guys nodded and watched the newcomers over their shoulders. After a few minutes of looking at a short menu, Kevin volunteered to go out and get food from Whigs. The gang of Zonies settled down with their beer and chattered away amongst themselves.

Rochelle rejoined her old friends at the bar, taking a seat next to Marty. She was not surprised that Wenrick and Henry weren't there. They were probably still busy wrapping up things at the Congressional Conference.

Gary pounced first. "So, you were in the middle of all those meetings over there on the Hill?"

"Nah, I was doing chauffeur duty and other stuff around and about. I'm sorry I couldn't get over here sooner but it just seemed like I had so much stuff to do to help these guys out. I did get over to my condo a few days ago, to pick up a couple of things, but it was so early, this place wasn't open yet," she patted the bar counter with her palm. Frankie just shrugged. Rochelle smiled back, to let him know she wasn't upset.

"So, all those people were in the meetings, then?" Frankie asked her.

Rochelle turned sideways, discretely pointing and explaining her flock. "Yeah, they're all part of the management team in Chandler. Well, not that guy - that's Jerry. He's from the utility company, which technically is for the whole metro region. He's trying to keep the power on all over the Phoenix area. And so is that big guy, Gordon, next to him. He's an electrical engineer. He's working with Jerry to figure out what to disconnect and what to keep on. They move a lot of solar panels around, mess with transformers and stuff and I don't know what. The next guy over, that's Robert. He's the water engineering guy. He was last man standing in the official city management staff. Well, him and this other woman, but she's still back home, keeping things running back there. And then the next guy, that's Richard. He's the finance guy on the new City Council they just elected…"

Gary interrupted her, "So you and Kevin made it back in time to vote in that election, like he wanted?"

Rochelle nodded, "Yep. Well, he voted. I didn't. I wasn't a resident then and didn't know any of the people who were running. So that woman, the one with the dark hair, that's Kevin's friend, Maggie Shearin. She's the new City Mayor. And the last one, the blond next to her, that's Sharon. She's the telecommunications and technology expert. So, yeah, they were all in the various conferences this week. I guess it was all about how to restore stuff, going forward."

The guys smiled at her. They explained they were familiar with the meeting formats, and had contributed to the preparations in their own small ways. However, they had not actually sat in on any of the really boring sessions.

Marty added, "You seem to really like Kevin's people a lot. I take it things are going well out there?"

Rochelled nodded some more. "Sure. They're all super nice. Maggie, she's an artist too. They designed and built this huge memorial for all the Superflu victims. It'll probably be done by the time we get back."

Gary beamed at her. "So, how do you like Arizona?"

"Oh, my gawd. The heat is unbelievable! Kevin warned me, over and over, but you don't understand what its really like until you actually experience it for yourself. We got there around the beginning of July and I thought I landed in an oven!" Rochelle rolled her eyes. Gary and Marty chuckled at her.

Gary said, "And you've been there the whole time since then?"

"Oh, heck no! We've been all over the country and then all over Arizona and then drove to Nebraska and then back to Arizona and then drove a bus back here! Oh, did I tell you? Kev taught me how to drive a real truck. An 18-wheeler!" She raised her arms in a mock muscle pose, flexing her biceps, while the guys grinned and clapped her on the back in appreciation of her accomplishment.

Rochelle shared several more stories of her recent experiences. Kevin returned with the food, which he passed out to the people around the tables. Then he joined Rochelle at the bar. He sat back and let her do all the talking, only adding a clarifying detail now and then. Her surrogate Dads beamed, thrilled that she had finally launched out into the world and was experiencing life.

When she wrapped up her narrative, she sat back considering the sensitive topic she wanted to bring up. Finally she prompted them, "So, can you believe that Sadler actually won that farce of an election?"

The guys pursed their lips, shook their heads and grunted their disapproval. Kevin arched his eyebrows at her. He knew what she was planning on telling them.

"So, guys, you need to pass word back to Henry. We heard some stuff about Gavin, some things he may be tied to, out in Texas and California. Henry needs to know to keep a very close eye on him. If they can get a Justice Department put back together, they need to maybe run an investigation or something. Because it could be real bad."

Gary and Marty frowned at her. "Could be?"

Rochelle nodded. "That's the thing. We don't have any solid proof. Just hearsay, innuendo and stories. And he's denied everything so far."

Over the next few minutes, Rochelle spun one more story for them. When she finished, she pulled a white envelope out of her purse. "Look, I wrote all this down for Henry. I know he's heard the military's version of this story. And I think they talked about some of it during the meetings in the Capital. But they only know part of it. Henry needs to know a few other details that may not have gone through the official channels. Can you give this to him? Discretely?"

Gary accepted the envelope, "Of course we will, Chelle. You know you can trust us. Of course, you also know that we never thought much of Sadler in the first place."

"Yeah, I know. I realize now what a jerk he was. I'm still pretty pissed at myself for not realizing it right from the very first minute he walked in here." She shook her head in disbelief at her own stupidity.

Marty's face broke into a broad grin. "Hey, remember that stupid limo he pulled up in here, that one night?"

"Yeah?"

"It's still parked over in the garage at the Watergate! You should go take it! He'd probably never even know it's gone. He's got that bullet proof Presidential one from the White House now!"

Rochelle was taken aback at the idea. "Ya know, that's actually not a half bad idea… They all need to get to the Inaugural Ball tomorrow night…" She hooked a thumb over her shoulder at the loud table of people behind them. She thought a moment more. If she could get into Gavin's apartment, she could find the limo keys. And she was pretty sure her key to Gavin's apartment might still be sitting on the counter of her condo, just a block away. The wheels started spinning in her head. She gazed at Kevin. He was following her line of thinking. She could tell by the gleam in his eye. He grinned back at her.

They were interrupted at that moment, when one of Rochelle's new Chandler people approached them, returning an empty beer pitcher.

Frankie smiled and offered, "Can I refill that for you?"

He grinned back, but demurred, "Uh, thanks, but no. This has been great, but I think we're almost done for the night. Everyone is pretty exhausted and just about to collapse. Rochelle?"

Rochelle smiled at the newcomer, but spoke to the bar flies. "Everyone, this is Gordon Barriston, the electrical engineer I told you about before. Gordon, this is everyone. Gary, Marty and Frankie." She pointed at each of them in turn. Then she realized what Gordon was really asking her. "Oh, you want to go back to the hotel, don't you? Duh! I should have realized!" She hopped off her bar stool, heading for the front door, intending to bring the hotel van she had borrowed to the front door.

Kevin stopped her, "I'll go get it. You should stay here, visit a little bit longer."

Kevin took the van keys from her with a smile.

Gordon exchanged pleasantries with the bar flies. "You know, we really appreciate everything Rochelle has done for us this week. She's been ferrying my foster son around town all week. Without her help, he might not have seen nearly as much stuff. It's been an incredibly valuable experience for him. So I'm super grateful to her."

Gary raised an eyebrow at her. "Rochelle? Babysitting? How very… maternal… of you," he drawled out.

Rochelle rolled her eyes. "Stop! It's not like that. The boy is thirteen years old. He's perfectly capable of taking care of himself."

Gordon shrugged, "Still, I appreciate the assist." He grinned at everyone.

Gary smiled back. "And we appreciate you welcoming Rochelle into your town. She's pretty special to us too."

Gordon studied him a moment. "Yes, I can see that. She's always welcome in Chandler. She's been a good influence on Kevin, too. It seems like she got him to rein in that mouth of his." The guys guffawed out loud at that.

Gordon grinned back and then added, "You know, it's really nice in Arizona, at this time of year. You could come out for a visit. We have this nickname for winter visitors. We call them snow birds." He winked at everyone.

A horn honked outside. The gabby group in the corner gathered up their coats and shuffled to the door. Rochelle gave Gary, Marty and Frankie one last hug. They reminded her that there was this new-fangled old thing called the Internet and that she could use it to keep in touch with people who were far away now. They even gave her newly printed business cards with email addresses on them. Rochelle laughed and agreed to do a better job of staying in touch in the future.

She gave Gary one last extra hug and whispered in his ear, "You guys will always be my Dads from now on!"

Then she herded her flock out into the night.

More from the Author

If you enjoyed Rochelle and Kevin's story, check out the *Consolidation* series, available in eBook format on Amazon and Kindle Unlimited. Paperback editions are also available in Barnes & Noble, Kobo and other major book e-retailers.

Consolidation: Book One

Consolidation: Book Two

Consolidation: Book Three

About the Author

Lisa Harnish is a potter, writer and desk jockey. She has lived in Chandler, Arizona, since 1995. As a full time telecommuter since 2016, Lisa has been practicing social distancing techniques for several years. When not pushing keys on a keyboard or playing in the mud, she can usually be found hanging out on the living room couch with her dogs. Visit her website at www.lisaharnish.com for more information.

Confluence